Nocturnal Premonitions

Val watched until his taillights disappeared at the end of the street. She turned her face to the wind and braced herself. Then she inhaled deeply.

Blood and rot and crawling things. Skittering, slithering. Writhing. The thickness filled her nose and went straight to her brain, to the place where pure animal fear ruled. She realized that the soft whimpering she heard was coming from her own throat.

Then, just as suddenly as the scent had appeared, it was gone. All the breeze carried now was the dry earthy smell of dying leaves. Her heart slammed; her hands were shaking. Every muscle screamed at her to run as fast and as far as she could.

No. Even as she thought it, the fear had begun leaching away. Val willed her fists to unclench. Deep breaths, as much to make sure no traces of that horrible scent remained as to calm herself down. For years, she'd been the scariest thing in Edgewood, aside from finals and dissertations.

Now it seemed something new had rolled into town. She hoped it hadn't come here looking for her.

She'd thought she'd left that all behind.

Night Owls

Lauren M. Roy

ACE BOOKS, NEW YORK

THE BERKLEY PUBLISHING GROUP
Published by the Penguin Group
Penguin Group (USA) LLC
375 Hudson Street, New York, New York 10014

USA • Canada • UK • Ireland • Australia • New Zealand • India • South Africa • China

penguin.com

A Penguin Random House Company

NIGHT OWLS

An Ace Book / published by arrangement with the author

Ace Books are published by The Berkley Publishing Group.
ACE and the "A" design are trademarks of Penguin Group (USA) LLC.

For information, address: The Berkley Publishing Group,
a division of Penguin Group (USA) LLC,
375 Hudson Street, New York, New York 10014.

ISBN: 978-0-425-27248-0

PUBLISHING HISTORY
Ace mass-market edition / March 2014

PRINTED IN THE UNITED STATES OF AMERICA

10   9   8   7   6   5   4   3   2   1

Cover art by Don Sipley.
Cover design by Erica Neumann.
Interior text design by Tiffany Estreicher.

For Mom, Dad, and Greg, who have always believed

ACKNOWLEDGMENTS

I don't believe a book can be written in a vacuum. Mine certainly wasn't, and this is a brief (and likely incomplete) list of the people who've kept both my oxygen and my ink flowing. A thousand thank-yous, all of you.

Thank you to my editor, Rebecca Brewer, who not only let me keep some of my darlings but also laughed in the right places.

To Miriam Kriss, my rock-star agent, who dug my ensemble cast, saw something neat in the Creeps, and found these guys an amazing home.

To my family at Hachette Book Group, especially the sales force, and *especially* especially the telephone sales team: Erica Hohos, John Lefler, and Lily Goldman. Your support and well-wishes mean so much to me.

To my new family at Penguin Random House and Ace Books. I hope to do you proud.

To my instructors, staff, and classmates from Viable Paradise XVI. This book is stronger because of you.

To Deb Wedding, Becky Kroll, Vonnie Frazier, and

Shannon Glass, who were among the first readers to meet the Night Owls crew.

To Marty Gleason, who gets excited on my behalf when I'm trying to be all dignified and restrained.

To David and Matt Finn and Eric Tribou, who've been so understanding when game night occasionally gets sacrificed on the altar of deadlines.

Thank you to my crit partner, coconspirator, and friend Hillary Monahan, who said, "What about that thing with the vampire in the bookstore? You should finish that," when I was flailing for something to write.

To my husband, Greg Roy, for keeping me caffeinated and respecting my writing time even before this transitioned from hobby to career. Thank you for always taking it seriously.

And to my parents, Barbara and Arthur Digan, for indulging my love of Story as far back as I can remember. All those bedtime stories, all those trips to bookstores, led to this. Thank you, thank you, thank you.

1

FATHER VALUE HAD taught Elly everything she knew about living to see another day. His number one lesson, drilled into her over and over since childhood, was: *Never get cornered by a Creep.* Advice she was trying desperately to heed as she pelted down the kind of alleyway that tended to host muggings or murders. She figured if someone popped out of the shadows demanding her wallet, she'd toss it to him and keep running. Maybe the Creep would let her go and gnaw on the thief counting her money instead.

Not likely. Her knapsack slammed into the small of her back with every jolting step. The item within pretty well guaranteed an extended chase.

Father Value had taught her other things, just as important: *Always carry something silver and pointy.* And, *If one happens to be nearby, virgins make excellent fodder.* Creeps found the flesh of the chaste particularly tasty. It might not be the nicest tactic, but when it was a choice between your own hide and someone else's, well, she'd been raised as a survivor, not a savior.

Elly had lost her own virginity when she was sixteen. She was never quite sure which desire had been stronger— wanting to get in Billy Chambers' pants, or wanting to make herself less delectable to the Creeps. It came in handy a few weeks later, though, when Billy became one of them himself right before her eyes. The fact that she'd been deflowered kept him from leaping upon her immediately, and it bought her those few heartbeats she'd needed to reach for her Silver and Pointy and drive it into his chest.

They said you never forgot your first. Every time she thought of Billy, it was his blood on her hands that she remembered, not his come on her thighs. Not so warm and fuzzy, as memories went.

For the most part, she stuck to Father Value's teachings. After all, they'd kept her alive so far, even if some were steeped more in superstition than in survival. Would the universe really notice if, just once, she didn't leave three strands of hair on the windowsill during a full moon? Would the Creeps win by default if she just wiped up the salt she spilled and didn't fling some over her shoulder?

Those were things she probably should've asked Father Value to clarify, but she'd never gotten around to it, and now he was dead. The police had declared it an accident, but Elly knew exactly what had killed him. The old man had broken one of his own cardinal rules when it came to the Creeps: *If you have something they want, sometimes it's best to hand it over.*

That way, you had a chance to live another day.

So what could be so important about this damned book that Father Value had died trying to keep it out of the Creeps' hands?

And how stupid was she, that she'd gone and stolen it back to find out?

Her feet slapped along the pavement, the other end of the alley getting closer with every ragged breath. She felt like she'd been running for hours; her lungs burned, her muscles screamed in protest. But Creeps didn't get tired like humans did, and if she slowed down now, the one behind her wouldn't even have to break his stride to scoop her up.

She burst out of the alley, casting about frantically for somewhere to go. During the summer, this strip of the beach road would be filled with tourists until all hours. But Labor Day had come and gone and the clam shacks and clubs closed up early. She didn't even bother looking both ways as she streaked across the street.

Two choices: the bus stop or the pier, both of them deserted. The bus stop was well lit, but that wouldn't deter the Creep. The water, though . . .

Elly's footsteps thumped hollowly along the wooden planks. For a moment, she fostered the impossible hope that the Creep wouldn't venture out with her at all, that he'd stand at the place where sand met dock and be unable to follow— did the ocean count as running water? Then she'd just have to wait until morning, until the sunrise drove him back to his hidey-hole.

Thump. Thump. Thump.

So much for hope.

Thirty feet on, Elly ran out of pier. She spun around, shrugging the backpack off so it slipped from her shoulders. She held it in one hand, dangling it over the water as the Creep closed the distance.

"That's close enough." Too close, in fact. She could smell him—wood shavings and rancid meat, making her want to gag. He wore the hood up on his sweatshirt, so most of his face was in shadow. But the tip of his snout protruded out from it: thin, angular. Sharp-tipped teeth glinting in the dim light. The better to eat her with.

Or tear out her throat, *then* eat her with.

The Creep stopped. He held out his hands and spoke in a dusty, raspy voice: "Give it to me and I'll let you live."

"No." She took another half step back, feeling the edge of the dock beneath her heels. "Leave me alone, or I'll drop it."

"Do that and you'll die."

She let the bag dip lower, until the tails of the adjustable straps touched the water. "Maybe. But you still won't have your book. Something that old, it's not going to survive half a minute in salt water. And you can't go in after it, can you?" Her heart slammed. She should give it to him. She should give it to him and live another day, just like Father Value had always taught her.

But she remembered Father Value's broken body, how small he'd looked beneath that sheet. The accident report said the fall had killed him, that all those shattered bones were consistent with a dive from several stories up. Bullshit. The Creeps had worked him over before they'd pitched him over the side. Elly only hoped he'd taken a couple out first. For the thousandth time since it happened, she wondered if things might have been different if they hadn't decided to split up.

The plan was solid. Even now, she knew she'd have made the same calls as Father Value had. *Plans can go bad, Eleanor.* That was one of his lessons, too.

Was the Creep standing in front of her one of the ones that did it? If he hadn't pushed the old man to his death, had he been there to witness it? Had he laughed in that dry voice while Father Value's life bled out on the pavement?

Headlights flashed along the road, their beams reflecting out over the water: the bus, on its late-night circuit. It trundled down the hill toward the stop.

Elly edged to her left, keeping the backpack out over the water. "You stay right here. Take one goddamned step and I'll drop it."

The Creep glared. His eyes caught the moonlight, two spots of amber glinting beneath his hood. But he didn't move to snatch at her as she inched past him and back toward the beach. "We'll find you," he said, turning to watch her retreat. "And it will go as well for you as it did for the old man." Those leathery lips peeled back into a grin. He sounded eager for that day to come. "Always remember you had a choice."

"Screw you." She backed up as quickly as she dared, feeling her way along so she wouldn't have to take her eyes off him. At last, her sneakers sank into the coarse sand. Only then did she put her back to the Creep, as she took off toward the bus.

"Wait! Wait! Oh please, wait." Father Value had always said she had a hell of a set of lungs. Her voice echoed off the closed-up clam shacks and the shops across the way. With every step, she expected the Creep's hands on her shoulders, yanking her back. She put on one last burst of speed as she reached the sidewalk, hollering for all she was worth at the idling bus.

The driver heard her. He waited, one hand on the lever that opened and closed the doors, a grin splitting his face. She imagined what she must look like to him, winded and windblown, her mouse brown hair in wild disarray from her run. Her clothes were old and oft repaired, but clean. No one would have called her intimidating at a glance; usually they saw her petite frame and dismissed the possibility of danger altogether. That was usually their mistake. With the bus driver now, it worked to her advantage.

"Didn't want to say good-bye to your boyfriend until the absolute last minute, eh?"

Fumbling for her wallet, Elly followed his gaze. Out at the end of the dock, the Creep's silhouette was visible against the moonlit waves. He could have caught her. It wasn't even a matter of him worrying that the bus driver might see and interfere. *He let me go because they like to hunt.* This was a head start to him, nothing more. She shuddered and fed a fistful of quarters into the collection box.

That had been another of Father Value's lessons: *Always carry bus fare.*

THE BUS ROLLED into Edgewood a little after two a.m. It had picked up a few more passengers after Elly's frantic boarding, mostly college kids coming off closing shifts at restaurants and coffeehouses. Elly watched them as they pulled out their cell phones and texted their friends or dragged huge textbooks into their laps for some after-hours studying.

She wasn't much older than they were, and yet their world

was so alien to her. She'd tried hanging out with normal kids once, a couple of years before. It had been easy enough to slip into the party, which had overflowed from the house into the street. All Elly'd had to do was walk in the door. Whenever anyone asked, she'd said she was "Mark's friend." No one had challenged her, which meant either there really was a Mark, or the other partygoers were also only loosely acquainted with the house owners.

She'd lasted maybe ten minutes.

She'd walked into the kitchen and plucked a beer out of a basin filled with ice. She'd stood at the edge of a gaggle of people and listened to the guy in the center holding court. She'd even laughed with the rest of them when he got to the punch line of his story.

But soon enough she found herself eyeing the doors and windows, planning exit routes and scoping out the décor for likely weapons. Silver and Pointy was a reassuring weight along her forearm. Her long sleeves hid the sheathed spike— she couldn't help but wonder what people would say if they saw it.

She couldn't help but wonder if she'd need it.

The walls had started closing in then, and from the side-long glances the others were giving her, she knew she'd gotten twitchy. In the end, she'd deposited her half-drunk beer on an end table and fled out into the night before anyone could question her.

Father Value hadn't known how to comfort her when she came home with red-rimmed eyes, hiccuping out her story between sobs. Not that she'd expected him to understand. That sort of life hadn't ever been his.

That was what you gave up, being one of Father Value's kids: being like everyone else.

Elly managed to hold it together on the bus ride, at least. She'd chosen a seat near the emergency window, the one you could pop out if the bus rolled over or plunged into a lake. If the Creeps decided to descend upon them, she had the instructions to get out of there memorized.

But that wasn't the Creeps' MO.

She made sure she was in the middle of the weary pack of late-shift workers when they disembarked in Edgewood. Anything looking to pounce on her would have to go through the coeds first, and while that wouldn't buy her her life, it'd give her the opportunity for a good running start.

The streets were quiet, for the most part. Light spilled onto the sidewalk halfway down the main drag from a smattering of still-open shops. A coffeehouse, maybe, and probably a copy shop. The college kids shuffled along in that direction, headed for the campus on the other side of town. Elly had to fight the urge to shadow them—there was safety in numbers, and odds were at least one of them was a virgin.

But her destination was the other way, toward the huge white house on the outskirts of Edgewood. With a sigh, she turned away from the cluster of bodies and toward the one place Father Value had said might take her in.

Might.

She practiced speeches as she waited for someone to answer: *I'm sorry it's so late, sir,* and *I'm sorry to be leading monsters to your door.* But when the silver-haired woman answered, all Elly could manage was, "Um, hi."

Even though it was almost two thirty in the morning, the woman was dressed in jeans and a sweater, her hair pulled back in a bun. She might have been about to go out for a late dinner or a PTA meeting, to look at her. She regarded Elly with impatience. "Office hours don't begin until eight, young lady."

"Um," Elly said again. "I'm not a student." She shrugged off her backpack and held it to her chest as she opened the zipper. "I'm sorry to bother you so late, ma'am, but I need to speak to Professor Clearwater right away." She let only the corner of the book show, enough so the woman could see that it was old. "A . . . a friend of his sent me."

The woman's eyes narrowed. For a moment, Elly was sure she was about to have the door slammed shut in her face. She choked down despair—she had nowhere else to go.

Then the woman's shoulders sagged and the harshness left her eyes. "You're one of *his*, aren't you." It wasn't a question.

"My name's Elly Garrett. Father Value said that if I needed help, I could come to Professor Clearwater. Please, is he home?"

The woman shook her head. "Not at the moment, no. But if you're here, alone . . . You'd best come inside."

"Thank you, Mrs. Clearwater."

The woman chuckled, a low, rueful sound. "Call me Helen. If things are as bad as I think they are, we may as well dispense with the formalities."

"What do you mean, as bad as they are?"

Helen pursed her lips, as though searching for a delicate way to put it. "He kept Henry at a distance these last few years. For his ward to show up at our door in the middle of the night, I'd imagine the situation has to be particularly dire." She stepped back so Elly could get past her, then shut the door and turned the lock. Her hand fell gently on Elly's shoulder. "Otherwise . . . Tell me, Elly. Is Father Value . . . ?"

"Dead," she said, and the weight of the last two nights crashed down on her at last. She tried taking a deep breath, but it turned into a sob. Another followed, then another. All she could see were Father Value's eyes, cold and staring—the only part of his face she could even recognize under the blood and bruises.

Then Mrs. Clearwater—Helen—was there, pulling her into an embrace and murmuring nonsense words as she stroked Elly's hair.

That set off another spate of tears. She couldn't remember the last time someone had held her like that, not even Father Value. No, that wasn't true. She *could* remember, but it only dredged up a deeper hurt.

"I'm sorry," she said after a while. She wrangled hold of the sadness and fear coursing through her and gave Helen a watery smile.

"Don't be. Let's get you some tea, and you can give me the short version before Henry gets home."

Elly lifted her pack from where she'd dropped it and followed Helen further into the house. The pack felt heavier than it had before. *I thought burdens were supposed to get lighter when you shared them.*

Only, she wasn't feeling any relief. Elly looked out a window into the night. Somewhere out there, the Creeps were coming. A day, maybe two, and they'd find her here. They wouldn't be kind to anyone aiding her.

Burdens might get lighter, but guilt? Guilt bears down harder.

First thing in the morning, I'll go.

2

THE KID HAD been stalking the aisles for the better part of ten minutes, drifting from the self-help books to the horror shelves and back again. He'd browsed through psychology and human sexuality; he'd run his fingers over the spines of every book in the science section twice. When he finally gave up and headed to the front to ask for help, he walked with that cringing don't-judge-me posture Chaz usually saw on grown men looking for books written by "Anonymous."

Chaz paused in Travel, pretending to set the U.S. guides in alphabetical order by state. Really, it was just the best place to stand and listen in on the conversation at the register without appearing like you were eavesdropping.

Which, of course, he was.

Val had taken over an expanse of the counter, intent on using the late evening lull to match packing lists to invoices and get some bills paid. The way she was bent over them, you couldn't tell how damned tall she was; she actually had an inch or two on Chaz, putting her close to six feet. She tucked an errant lock of dark red hair behind her ear, unaware of the hilarity rapidly approaching.

The kid didn't even wait for Val to look up from her paperwork before he blurted out his question: "Where do you keep your books on vampires?"

Chaz couldn't help the snicker.

Val shot a frown in his direction, but he could see her fighting to keep a straight face, too. "Fiction, or nonfiction?"

"Non, please. Do you . . . Do you have any that say how you can tell if someone is one?"

Chaz faked a coughing fit to hide his laughter.

"Up that aisle," said Val, "past the astrology books on the left. We have a ton on vampires."

"Thanks." The kid took off at a run in the direction Val pointed, nearly crashing into Chaz on his way by. "Sorry," he muttered before heading deeper into the store.

Chaz got a decent look at him: pressed khakis, collared shirt, hair definitely not styled at the local Supercuts. He headed up to the register. Val stood with her arms folded, waiting for it. "Roommate?" he asked softly. He set his armload of books down on the counter and pretended to look them up.

"Girlfriend," said Val.

"Five bucks?"

"Yep."

Chaz swept a lock of pale blond hair out of his eyes and turned around to peer at the kid, who was now running his fingers along the spines of books in the proper section, lips moving as he read each title. "What makes you say girlfriend?"

"Eyeliner. You wear it to impress a girl, not your new roommate."

"No way. I didn't see any." The kid hadn't looked the eyeliner type; not with those clothes, at least.

"Trust me, it's there."

Chaz shrugged and returned to punching numbers on the keyboard, occasionally making the computer go *ping*, like he'd done something useful. He leaned against the counter, waiting for the kid to make a selection. Val said when you added in the ponytail, Chaz' picture ought to be in the dictionary next to "slacker." On his third run through the stack, the kid returned, clutching a book close to his chest. Sure enough, an unsteady line of kohl ringed the kid's eyes. Chaz swore under his breath.

Val grinned triumphantly before she turned to ring up the sale.

"This one, please," said the kid. He glanced at his watch—a fancy chunk of silver from Tag Heuer that also didn't jive with the eyeliner—and smiled. "I'm glad you guys were still open."

Chaz pushed himself up to sit on the counter and pointed at the hours painted beneath the owl on their picture window. "It's early yet. We're here until three."

Night Owls Books sat just off the campus of Edgewood College, making it the perfect place for an almost-all-night bookstore. Since it was only eleven o'clock, a few clusters of students sat on the couches up front, laptops out, textbooks open. More would arrive after the library closed half an hour from now.

Chaz took a look around to be sure the three of them were the only people in earshot. The studying kids didn't look likely to get up anytime soon, and Justin, tonight's other late-night employee, had exiled himself to the children's section sometime around nine-thirty, determined to undo the damage from the whirlwind that was Activity Night. He had yet to resurface. Leaning around Val, Chaz snagged the kid's book and peered at the title. "So, you think the girl you like might be a vampire, huh?"

The kid turned crimson. "Um," he said.

"Tell you what. I'll save you ten bucks. She wear a lot of black?"

". . . yes."

"Burns incense and smokes clove cigarettes?"

"Um, yes. To the cloves." The kid rolled his eyes toward Val pleadingly, but she knew better than to try to stop Chaz mid-defanging.

"Listens to Bauhaus and the Cure, and other bands who probably broke up before you two were born?"

". . . yeah."

Chaz hopped off his perch and ambled closer, so he could lean in and drop his voice. "Son, does your dream girl write really, really bad poetry? Especially stuff with angels and blood and graves?"

The kid blinked, torn between acknowledging this last and his loyalty toward the girl. He went for a noncommittal shrug.

"Yep. Not a vampire," said Chaz with a firm nod. "She starts drinking blood, you tell her that shit'll make her sick. The human stomach can't digest more than a few drops."

"Uh. Oh." The kid managed to look both defeated and relieved at the same time. It was like Chaz had stuck a pin in him and let him deflate. "Yeah, I guess it is kind of silly, isn't it?" He backed away from the register, not making eye contact. "Thanks anyway," he said toward Val, and sped out the door. *Dating the Paranormal* remained on the counter like an accusation.

"Huh. Girlfriend. You were right." Chaz dug into his pockets. "Five bucks, we said?"

"Fifteen."

"What?"

"Your little speech just lost us a sale. Oh, and add that book to your shelving pile, while you're at it."

"Yes, ma'am," he said, and forked over the cash. "But I was right, wasn't I? The lady friend's not a bloodsucker."

He fled down the aisle when she brandished the stapler.

Chaz had been through this a few times in the five years he'd been working for Val: a student coming in, convinced their roommate or love interest was some kind of otherworldly creature—vampire, werewolf, demon. Most of them were just normal kids who'd fallen for a very good angsty act. Only once in all that time had one of the kids been right.

That was why, after the kids left with their purchases (or in this case, empty-handed), Chaz would turn to Val and ask the question: were they right? He asked because he knew her secret: she could smell the supernatural on these kids the same way you might smell the traces of a girl's perfume on her boyfriend's jacket.

Valerie McTeague was a vampire, and Chaz was her Renfield.

It wasn't a bad gig, all things considered. Chaz' daylight duties mostly consisted of the mundane: keep the bookstore up and running, deal with bank deposits and customer service departments whose hours ended before nightfall, sign for the shipments that showed up while Val was home hiding from the sun. Only rarely did the paranormal requirements of his job kick in—less now than in his early days. Val hadn't dragged him to a meeting with the colonies out of Boston for almost three years. She hadn't been to one herself in nearly that long.

They didn't really talk about it.

When the eleven-thirty munchies hit, Val lifted the petty cash box from its spot beneath the register and gave it a good rattle. It was Chaz' official duty as a Night Owls minion to go to the cafe next door, charm the elderly twins behind the counter, and bring back coffee and pastries for the late crew.

"You know," he said, making his way up front from the back of the store, "you could always just buy a dog whistle. It might be less humiliating."

"Yeah, but you wouldn't hear it." She grinned and passed him the same ten dollar bill he'd handed over earlier. "New flavor tonight. I'm tired of cinnamon."

"Gotcha." He pocketed the bill and shuffled out the door, whistling as he went.

He didn't notice the figure in the beige trench coat lurking outside.

VAL WATCHED CHAZ swing around to the left, heading in the direction of the cafe. The other man's posture suggested he was watching Chaz go, too.

She went back to her invoices; she could feel the figure staring through the window. If she looked up, she knew she'd catch his eye beneath one of the owl's painted wings. Chaz had only been gone two minutes. He'd be back within fifteen, he always was. *Come on, you old bastard. You planning on waiting all night?*

After a moment, the bell jingled merrily. Val glanced up, looking bored. The man had only taken two steps inside. He removed the crumpled fedora from his head and craned his neck, summoning a defiant glare, but none of the other customers had noticed his entrance. Satisfied, he bustled up to the counter. His sharp blue eyes stared up at Val from a wrinkled face.

One hand reached into the inside pocket of his jacket and withdrew a slim white box. It thumped heavily on the counter as he set it down.

"Helen made fudge," he said, and smiled at her. "I thought I'd bring some for you."

"That's . . . that's so sweet of you two, Professor. You'll have to thank her for us."

"Us," sniffed the old man. He stole a glance toward the door, as though he'd find Chaz glaring in at him. When he turned back to Val, his gaze was hopeful. "Is the room open?"

She smiled and reached beneath the register, where a silver key hung from its chain. Most of the time, customers who wanted to look in the rare books room had to leave their licenses up at the front while Val or Chaz escorted them to the door and unlocked it for them. The professor, however, received special treatment. He'd been coming to the store for five years now, and had brought as many precious titles to Val as he had bought from her. She was thinking of having a key made for him, so he could come and go as he pleased.

Now, though, she dangled the key above his outstretched palm and let it drop, the chain pooling atop the key. He closed his fingers over it, his expression beatific. "It's all right if I browse?" His voice was a reverent whisper.

"Yeah," she said. "Go on back. There's a pile of unsorted stuff on the stool. Maybe you'll find a gem." He bustled up the aisle with determination, a treasure hunter nearing the *X* on the map.

"WHAT I DON'T get," Chaz said ten minutes later, dropping his voice as Val sniffed at her cup, "is why he's so totally convinced I'm a werewolf, yet he doesn't come around here with crosses and garlic for you."

Val snorted. "I guess you're just more sinister looking."

"No, but think about it. Have I ever, I dunno, not come into work when the moon's been full? Bitten a customer? Peed on the rug? No. But you, shit, he at least has to have noticed that you're nocturnal." A couple came up to the register, and Chaz turned around to ring up their sale, shaking his head.

When they were gone, Val set her cup down and peered up at Chaz. "He has noticed. He thinks I have a skin condition. Don't you remember Helen sending along all those homemade salves last Christmas?"

As Chaz opened his mouth to argue, the rare books room door squealed, announcing Professor Clearwater's exit. He turned the key and gave a satisfied nod as the tumblers slid home with a click, then headed to the front of the store with an armload of books.

He and Chaz spent a long moment exchanging chilly stares as he set his pile down. "Will you set these aside for me? I've some books at home from Helen's mother's estate that you might be interested in trading." He spoke to Val, but his gaze never left Chaz.

"Of course. I'd be happy to take a look."

"Thank you." Professor Clearwater held out the key for Chaz to take, a sudden gleam in his eyes.

Chaz returned the look with a feral grin and closed his hand around it, making a show of transferring the key slowly from one hand to the other before returning it to its hook.

The professor looked almost disappointed. He shook his head and tipped his hat. "I'll be on my way," he said, and tottered to the door.

When his silhouette disappeared around the corner of the building, Chaz let out a growl. "Did you see that? He was watching to see if I could hold silver. Crazy old fuck." He drained the last of his coffee and tossed the cup into the wastebasket with extra force, then eyed Val's. "You done sniffing?"

She slid it across to him as he opened the fudge.

IT WAS EARLY enough in the semester that the store was dead by closing time. Outside, the street was quiet except for the occasional scatter of leaves drifting across the pavement. The other storefronts were dark, proprietors and customers long since gone home for the night. Night Owls was on Edgewood's main drag. Were it not for the influx of students every September, the sleepy college town might otherwise be called a hamlet.

Val walked Chaz to his car, an ancient, '84 Mustang that looked like it would just barely be able to make it out of the parking lot. But, in the way of well-built older vehicles, it ran like a dream on regular oil changes and tune-ups. Chaz swore it would outlast pretty much everything on the planet in the event of a nuclear war—with the exceptions of maybe the cockroaches, Twinkies, and Val.

Chaz slid behind the wheel and waved the envelope containing the morning's bank deposit at her. "You know, usually it's the man who's supposed to escort the woman to her car."

"I'm bucking the trends. Look at me go."

"You're protecting the profits. Let's not be coy."

Val grinned. "Gotta keep my investments safe."

Chaz glanced around. Even the crickets had gone to bed. "Yeah, from all these thugs hanging out in Edgewood. I think someone ran a stop sign the other day. Or rolled through it."

Val opened her mouth to retort, but before she could speak, her nostrils filled with the scent of blood. Not a bright, fresh-from-the-vein smell. This was old, congealing, like blood left to pool in a dark place and forgotten. She wanted to retch as her taste buds kicked in and helpfully supplied the rancid companion to the smell.

"Val?" Chaz started getting out of the car. He squawked as she shoved him back down into the driver's seat. "The fuck?"

"Go home, Chaz. Get the hell out of here."

"Val, what—" He just barely swung his legs back inside before Val slammed the door shut.

"GO. I'll see you tomorrow night."

He looked ready to argue, but something in her glare made him reconsider. Although she couldn't hear his muttered curses, his lips were easy enough to read as he jammed the keys in the ignition and started the car.

Val watched until his taillights disappeared at the end of the street. She turned her face to the wind and braced herself. Then she inhaled deeply.

Blood and rot and crawling things. Skittering, slithering. Writhing. The thickness filled her nose and went straight to her brain, to the place where pure animal fear ruled. She realized that the soft whimpering she heard was coming from her own throat.

Then, just as suddenly as the scent had appeared, it was gone. All the breeze carried now was the dry earthy smell of dying leaves. Her heart slammed; her hands were shaking. Every muscle screamed at her to run as fast and as far as she could.

No. Even as she thought it, the fear had begun leaching away. Val willed her fists to unclench. Deep breaths, as much to make sure no traces of that horrible scent remained as to calm herself down. For years, she'd been the scariest thing in Edgewood, aside from finals and dissertations.

Now it seemed something new had rolled into town. She hoped it hadn't come here looking for her.

She'd thought she'd left that all behind.

3

The tea was something herbal, probably one of those ones with bogus aromatherapy claims on the box: *mood-lifting*, or *sweet dreams*, or *energy booster*. It was all horseshit, but Elly wasn't about to explain that to Helen. She had a feeling Helen knew it already, anyway.

The older woman sat in an enormous wingback chair; Elly was snuggled in its twin. The chairs themselves were far too big for the room, which Helen had referred to as "Henry's second library." Floor-to-ceiling bookshelves covered the walls, and not an inch of any single shelf was empty. Elly had wandered around while her hostess was off making the tea. She'd touched the various volumes, mouthing the titles as she went along. Most of them were scholarly works, studies on the lives of long-dead poets, or treatises on how historical and socioeconomic factors had informed one classical artist or another. They were boring enough to make her feel sleepy despite the adrenaline still coursing through her from the encounter with the Creep.

Helen had mentioned that this room served as the professor's at-home office. Crammed into the corner by the window was a small mahogany desk. Elly'd peeked at the papers in the brushed-brass inbox and confirmed as much: students' essays, waiting for their grades. So this was the place where he received regular visitors—kids from the college who went through their days oblivious to the nasty things waiting in the dark.

I could write a paper that'd make their heads explode. And I wouldn't even need footnotes.

If this was the second library, Elly wondered where the first one was. Probably upstairs. That would be the one with information that might help her. Help all of them, now that she'd been invited into their house. She itched to ask about it, and about what kinds of books Professor Clearwater had stashed away, but Father Value's voice was in the back of her mind, reminding her not to be rude. Even though he was dead, she could still hear him chiding her.

So she sipped her tea and tried to remember her manners. When she was little, Father Value had made her practice polite conversation. She hunted around in her memory for something that normal people might ask one another in this situation. *Do you have any crossbows?* didn't strike her as a good opening foray.

Helen came to her rescue. "How long were you with Father Value, Elly?"

Familiar ground, if painful. "All my life, really. If I had any family before him, I don't remember them." She'd thought about it, now and then, wondered who her parents were and what they'd been like. Father Value had some old pictures of the man and woman he'd said were her mom and dad, but she'd never felt a connection to the people in them. They were just faces on photo paper. In the made-for-TV movies, the long-lost child always felt some jolt of recognition. Elly hadn't, no matter how hard she tried.

"Then you must have spent a lot of time moving around. Henry said members of the Brotherhood never stayed in one place for very long."

Elly frowned. Father Value hadn't spoken about his

former organization very often, but he'd been quite clear on one rule: don't talk about it to outsiders. "The Brotherhood?"

Helen studied Elly for a moment, then sipped her tea. It was a knowing gesture, one that clearly read, *I see you playing dumb.* "Henry had been gone from it nearly ten years when we met. Plenty of time for certain old . . . taboos to lose their imperative. He told me some of what he was before. Not everything, but enough. Your Father Value came up often."

Damn it. Busted. This woman had invited her in in the middle of the night, and Elly was already lying. "I never met anyone else from it. There was only ever Father Value." *At least that part's true.*

"I never met anyone else from it, either. But this man Value came sniffing around every once in a while, when he needed something. The phone would ring in the dead of night, and it was always him, asking for Henry's help."

Elly opened her mouth to argue—Father Value *hated* asking for help—but then she remembered being ten years old and waking to Father Value's voice drifting in through an open window. When she'd peered out, she'd seen him on the street below, his broad shoulders hunched over the pay phone. Now that she remembered that first time, she realized, there had been a few of those calls scattered over the years, often followed a few days later by a delivery or a drop of something they'd needed—clothes, supplies, books.

If I thought back, would we have been near Edgewood when they happened? She thought maybe they were.

From down the hallway came a rattling that nearly sent Elly out of her skin. Tea sloshed over the rim of the cup, scalding her hand, but she ignored the pain. She was out of the chair in a flash, settling herself in a crouch in front of Helen and digging the knife out of her boot. "Stay behind me," she said. Her eyes flicked from the doorway to the window. She wondered how heavy the desk was, if she had time to barricade the door. *Stupid of me. Should've checked its weight when I was walking around.*

Then Helen's hand was on her shoulder, her voice soft and soothing in Elly's ear. "Elly. It's only Henry. He's home."

"Oh. Oh, I . . ." *So much for manners.* "I'm sorry." Sheepishly, she slid her knife back into her boot and stood.

Helen Clearwater took it with grace; you'd think she had students go all combat-ninja on her on a nightly basis. She patted Elly's hand, set the teacup aright, and glided out into the hallway. "Come with me. I think Henry will like you."

THE OTHER LIBRARY—the *real* one—spanned nearly half of the second floor. The books here were much more to Elly's taste—texts on monsters, survival, rituals from hundreds of years ago. One whole bookcase was dedicated to Bibles in all different languages and editions—King James, American Standard, New International—she had a feeling Professor Clearwater had leafed through most of them over the years. The chairs up here were twins of the ones downstairs, but they looked more lived-in, the leather far more supple. Elly sank into one and breathed in the smell of pipe smoke and old books.

When Helen brought a fresh pot of tea, Professor Clearwater produced a flask and poured a healthy dollop of whiskey into Elly's cup.

He waited until Helen had closed the door behind her and Elly had taken a scalding sip before he spoke. "My wife tells me I've kept you waiting. My apologies."

"It's all right," Elly said. "I'm the one who showed up at two in the morning. I didn't know where else to go."

He patted her hand, a grandfatherly gesture unlike anything she'd ever received from Father Value. It made her feel awkward and comforted at the same time. "You came to the right place, my dear. You'll be safe here."

She smiled, but couldn't keep it up. "I wish that were true, Professor."

"Henry, please."

Just like his wife. "Henry, then. You know I wouldn't be here if it wasn't bad. The Creeps killed Father Value, and they're coming after me. If they're not here by morning, then they'll come tomorrow night. Nowhere's really safe."

"You're safe enough for the moment, that I promise." He sat back in the chair, the leather creaking as he settled in. He even *looked* grandfatherly, his white hair neatly trimmed, his wrinkled features kindly and nonjudgmental. "Elly, why don't you tell me exactly what happened?"

She took a deep breath. He wouldn't turn her out, that much she knew. He'd have done it as soon as Helen announced who she was, if he was going to. Still, the urge to snatch up her backpack and run out of this room, out of this house, nearly overwhelmed her. Her hands gripped the smooth wooden arms of her chair as if they were all that anchored her.

The professor pulled out his flask again. It hovered over her teacup for a second before he passed it to her directly. "Go on," he said.

Elly accepted it and took a long swig. It burned as it went down, but she kept from coughing. Father Value had let her have the occasional sip, too. She couldn't be sure, but Elly thought the men drank the same brand. She returned the flask and went back to her tea. "A few weeks ago, Father Value found out they were looking for something. A book. He didn't say what was in it, only that they were after it."

She remembered those first fevered days. Father Value always tried keeping the Creeps from getting whatever they were after, but she'd never seen him seek anything out with such urgency before. He'd eaten only when she forced a plate in front of him; he'd slept on bus trips or in the backs of cabs as he dragged her from city to city. She'd been sure he'd collapse from exhaustion sooner or later, and there was no way they could afford hospital bills.

But he hadn't collapsed. Two days ago, they'd found the book.

ELLY WASN'T BIG on churches in general, but she really wasn't keen on being in them after dark, when the doors were locked and the lights were off. She didn't worry about

being struck by lightning or burning in hell—churches were
by and large some of the safest places to be when it came
to the Creeps. Her fears were more practical.

She was pretty sure breaking and entering in a church
could get you arrested.

Father Value insisted it would be all right. He knew the
clergy there, he said. Or he had a decade ago. Or two. Either
way, they'd be in and out. The book was right under . . . right
under . . .

"Right under here." He was on his hands and knees
behind the altar, prying at a slate. "Come help me with this,
Elly, it's heavy."

She gave up her spot by the door reluctantly. If someone
came in while they were yanking up the stones, there'd be
no warning. But if she didn't help, he'd give himself a stroke
trying to do it on his own. She crowded in beside him and
got her fingers under a loose part of the slate. *Dear God,
please don't let this slip and crush my fingers. I kind of need
them. Amen.*

Father Value counted to three and they lifted. The scraping filled the church, echoing off the stone walls and stained
glass windows. Elly half expected a clap of thunder to sound
at the desecration, but none came.

She had just enough time to wedge her shoulder beneath
the slab and bear its weight. Father Value let his edge go
and stuck his arm into the hollow beneath the floor. He
leaned over so far she was sure he'd fall in, and they could
add a broken neck or dislocated shoulder to the hospital bill
racking up in her mind. He rooted around, muttering to
himself. Elly's muscles began to quiver from the strain.

"Father, I can't hold this up much longer."

"Patience, Eleanor. It's here."

"What if someone else found it first? What if they already
have it?"

"Hush. It's here, I'm sure of it."

Elly gritted her teeth and held on. She counted seconds,
ignoring the tremors coursing through her arms and legs. A
minute passed by. Two. Father Value was halfway in the

hole now, the scrabbling sound of his questing hands sending odd echoes around the vestibule. Elly's knees bent further and further as the slab's weight bore down. "Father, I—"

"I have it!" He scuttled backward, crablike, a dusty tome clutched in one gnarled hand.

Just in time, too. Elly's strength gave out a second after the old man was clear. She stumbled forward; the slate fell back into place with a crash that rattled off the walls. If anyone had been asleep in the rectory, surely that would have woken them. "We have to get out of here. Someone'll be coming."

At first, she didn't think he'd heard. He looked almost like a friar of old, standing in the darkened church in his plain black robes, clutching the book to his chest. All he needed to complete the outfit was a belt made of rope. Of course, the running shoes peeking out from beneath the hem killed the illusion. Beneath the monkish garb, Father Value wore jeans and a sweater.

"Father?" She'd drag him out if she had to. Even if the priests in residence hadn't called the cops, the Creeps might be on their way.

Father Value opened his eyes. They glinted with triumph, but there was an urgency there, too. "The side door, Elly. We'll want to be as far from here as we can get." He'd left his knapsack on a pew on the way in. Now he tucked the book inside it and headed for the door. He paused with his hand on the knob, head tilted. He leaned his ear against the wood. After a moment, he looked back at her, his mouth set in a grim line. "We'll have to look at it together in the morning. Tonight, I think we'll be rather busy."

"THAT WAS FRIDAY night. Well, Saturday morning, I suppose. They were outside, waiting. We ran. I don't know how we got away, but we did. He spent Saturday making preparations, making sure the place we were holed up was defensible." Elly's tea had gone cold while she talked. "He never got to look at the book. They came that night, and we had to run again. They broke through his wards inside of an hour."

Professor Clearwater grunted at that. "If they're determined enough, they'll barrel through anything. Even if it hurts them."

"That's what they did. The first ones who came through were bleeding something fierce."

"Why did you two make a stand? You could've put half the country between yourselves and them."

Elly shrugged. She'd argued the same: *Let's get on a bus and go to California. There's a train to Chicago leaving in an hour. Let's be on it. I'll steal a wallet and we'll charge flights to London on the credit cards inside, put the whole damned ocean between us and the Creeps.* But he'd vetoed every suggestion, and his reasons for *why* were flimsy at best. *No time, Eleanor,* he'd said, as if that were enough explanation. *No time.*

Still, Elly had survived as long as she had doing as Father Value told her. She hadn't fought him too hard on it.

Maybe if I'd fought him more, he'd still be alive. She shook that off. "He wanted to stay close, said there wasn't much time. He said you'd know what to do with it, but he wanted to shake them off first."

Henry got up and began to pace. "He should have come straight to me and let me *help*. But to stay just out of reach? It's foolish in the extreme." He paused by the window, looking out over their expansive backyard.

"He said . . . He said he didn't want to bring trouble to your door. Or as little of it as possible." She shifted in the chair. Dancing around a delicate topic wasn't something Father Value had taught her how to do. She felt like the conversation called for tact, but she'd never been good at employing it. All she'd ever really learned was, *If you don't want to tell the whole truth, hedge.*

Of course, she'd learned that from Father Value, and that meant Professor Clearwater was probably familiar with the tactic, too.

He turned back to her, the set of his jaw somewhere between amused and annoyed. "What you're saying, then, is he thought I'd gone soft since leaving the Brotherhood."

Damn. "He thought you might be out of practice, a little."

"I suppose I might be. I've not had to fight for my life in a very long time." He must have seen her tense up, because he held his hands out, palms up. A calming gesture. "That doesn't mean I'm unprepared for it. Come here." He beckoned her closer.

Elly set aside her tea and stood with him at the window. She squinted into the darkness, but nothing struck her as obvious. The dark shapes of a patio set and charcoal grill were all that broke up the neatly mowed lawn. "I don't know what I'm looking for, sir."

"Not out. *Down.*"

Frowning, she glanced down. And grinned. Lining the inside of the windowsill, in the groove between the glass and the screen, was a thick line of salt. It wouldn't stop the Creeps outright—she'd learned that the other evening—but it would slow them down. And if the Clearwaters had salt wards, they'd have others, ones that weren't so easy to spot.

"If they want to come in here, they're going to hurt for it. But they won't try tonight." Outside, the first tinges of dawn lightened the sky. "There's not enough time." He guided her back to the chairs and peered into their empty teacups. Out came the flask. He poured a generous splash into each. "I'd suggest we get some sleep, but if you'll pardon my saying, you still look wide awake."

"Part of the lifestyle. We keep late hours."

"Nearly nocturnal ones, I'd imagine."

"Yes sir. But you don't have to stay up with me. I can entertain myself." Her fingers itched to flip through some of the books in this room, but, at the same time . . . She found herself hoping he'd insist on staying, found herself wanting the company.

He smiled. "Surely you must have questions for me. I've always found that getting answers helps me sleep."

4

A SMART VAMPIRE would have gone home and gone
to bed.

*No, a smart vampire would have built up her wealth over
the years, amassed a small army of devoted minions, and
built an impenetrable fortress-mansion somewhere exotic.
I went with the "sink all your money into a bookstore and
barely scrape by in a quaint college town."*

And she'd sent her one minion home.

That had been the right decision, though. Chaz might be
good at getting rid of the frat kids when they got bombed
and came in to titter at the books of nudes in the art section,
but no way in hell was he prepared to face what she was
sure had loped its way into town. Hell, she wasn't sure *she*
was prepared to handle it, either.

More than ten years had passed since she'd last been
face-to-face with a Jackal. It was another life, on another
coast, and she'd been with five others. Back then, they'd
been armed with stakes of rowan wood and vials of ash
when they'd headed into the nest. Tonight, all Val had were
fangs and claws. She wished she'd gone back to the store

and grabbed a roll of quarters. Not that they'd help all that much.

She scuttled along Edgewood's silent streets, heading toward campus. The scent hadn't returned, though every now and then she'd stop and turn in a circle, sniffing the air just in case. They could have gone anywhere, might not even still be in town, but Val had to be sure. If they were on the hunt they'd find easy pickings at the dorms.

And plenty of virgin flesh.

It wasn't often she wished she could turn into a bat or a shadow or a column of mist and speed through the night, but right then it would have come in awfully handy. Those things would come with age and training, not to mention a whole lot of ass-kissing. For now, the best she could do was will her legs to push harder, dig her heels in deeper, and launch herself headlong up the road to the student housing buildings.

Edgewood College had four dormitories in addition to the houses on Greek Row. Val dismissed the fraternity and sorority houses right away—lights still burned in the windows of Phi Lambda Lambda and Delta Mu, and from the looks of it the Gamma Rho Epsilon girls were having an all-night lawn party with the boys from Beta Epsilon. It was possible that a Jackal would hang around and watch from the shadows, waiting for an unsuspecting sister to totter away from the main festivities—it was how they'd earned the other name she'd heard them called: Creeps. But crowds made them nervous. If there was easier prey, they'd take it.

That also ruled out the two coed dorms. It was closing in on five thirty, but even with most of their inhabitants asleep, there were too many windows glowing softly from students' monitors or lamps clipped to their headboards. The single-sex dorms, though, were a different story. The Jackals wouldn't know it, but Ward and Bryant Halls were the places you lived if you wanted peace and quiet and early lights-out. Kids who lived in them did their partying elsewhere and tiptoed if they came home in the wee hours. It was where the campus geniuses lived.

Both were also—conveniently for a Jackal—nestled in at the far end of the street, and their back halves looked out at the woods. Now the trick was figuring out which kind of virgin flesh the Jackal was in the mood for tonight. *Sugar, spice, and everything nice, or snails, pails, and puppy dog tails?* Val stood halfway between the two buildings and sniffed again. *Maybe it was a false alarm. Maybe it was just passing thr—*

There.

Val hurried around to the back of the boys' dorm, following the smell of rot and blood. The streetlights' glow didn't carry back here, but her eyes adjusted almost instantly. On the second floor, a window was open. She got up close to the building and ran her hands over the old brick. Just above her head, she felt the gouges from where the Jackal's claws had dug in as it scaled.

What's good for the goose, as they say.

Val held her hands out in front of her. This was the part she hated, the reason she suspected she'd never go for the whole bat-form thing even if she *could*. Bones cracked as she willed her hands into claws. They grew gnarled and twisted, the fingers becoming hooked and knobby, the nails lengthening, thickening, sharpening. She bit down on her lip to bear the pain of it, which was a mistake. Her fangs unsheathed and stabbed down, slicing into the tender skin of her lower lip.

The wounds sealed as soon as she opened her mouth to pull the fangs free, but it still hurt like hell. At least the surprise of it had distracted her from the last seconds of transformation as the fine bones in her hands finished adjusting themselves.

Of course, there was one last problem.

She hadn't been invited in.

If she entered without a come-on-in, she wouldn't be repelled; no unseen force would throw her back to the ground. Nor would entering unasked mean agony with every step she took. But her abilities would be weaker, the reserves

she could call on nearly nonexistent. Ten years since she'd
faced a Jackal. Long enough since she'd even needed her
claws that she made the fledgling mistake of tearing her lips.
Val *needed* that invite. Fast.

There hadn't been any screams yet, which meant the Jackal
inside was either being extremely cautious or savoring its next
meal. Val fumbled her cell phone from her jacket pocket,
cursing the clumsiness of her freshly warped hands and
thanking the gods for voice dial at the same time. She only
hoped the fangs didn't garble the preprogrammed names.

"Call Justin." The call went through with no trouble, and
somewhere deep in Bryant Hall, a cell phone rang.

He picked up on the third ring, his voice muzzy with
sleep. "'Lo?"

I knew there was a reason I hired him. "Justin, it's Val.
Can I come in?"

"Time izzit?"

"Just say yes, Justin. Can I come in?"

"Uh. Yeah, 'kay."

"Good. You're dreaming. Hang up and go back to sleep."
She put a bit of Command into her voice. It didn't always work
through phone lines, but it helped if the person was inclined
to do whatever you were asking them to, anyway. Justin
already trusted her, which made him more susceptible.

The call ended and she shoved down a pang of guilt.
She'd feel bad about manipulating him tomorrow, when the
Jackal was gone and a freshman remained uneaten. She
snapped the phone shut and shoved it back in her pocket.

Then she began to climb.

VAL TUMBLED THROUGH the window onto the cold, hard
bathroom tiles. Whether the window had been opened to
let out smoke, steam, or stink, she didn't know and didn't
much care—laid over all of it was the gag-inducing psychic
stench of the Jackal. Now that her fangs were out, the reek
was even stronger. She stalked down the length of the

bathroom, past shower stalls and urinals. If luck had been with her, the Jackal would've been lurking in here, waiting for a victim to stumble in for a late-night piss.

Luck seemed to be taking the night off.

She cracked the door inch by inch, sniffing as the darkened hallway was revealed. She stuck her head out and peered in both directions. No light spilled from beneath any of the doors. This floor's inhabitants were all asleep. Good for her and the Jackal, bad for its prey.

The scent was sharper out here in the hall, as though it had paused awhile before moving on to find a victim. It likely had; human scents tended to muddle together for Val until she was up close, but in that regard Jackals' noses were far more refined. It had probably stood in this same spot, taking in the residents' scents the way a mall-goer might look at the options in the food court before deciding what was for lunch.

In this case, lunch—*or breakfast,* Val supposed—was off to the right. She followed, pressing herself as close to the wall as she could. Bryant Hall was one of the oldest buildings on campus, built in the early nineteen hundreds. The floors were hardwood, prone to creaking if you tromped down the middle of the hallway. The boards were tighter at the edges, quieter. Val was good at moving silently, but she wasn't taking any chances. As it was, she had to hope the Jackal was too involved in its prey to have caught a whiff of its own predator.

One door down, two doors, three. *Here.* The trail led to a door with a whiteboard hanging from a nail. *Jarrod's Room: Beware of shark!!!* it read, with a picture of a shark about to devour a stick-man to illustrate the point. Someone had drawn a T-Rex eating the shark, and captioned it, "FLEE, PUNY HUMAN!"

The knob turned easily. *Don't these kids ever listen to the "keep your doors locked" speeches they get at orientation?* At the start of every semester, she allowed kids from the student union to hang campus safety posters in the store. That one was always on there, right beneath reminders about the buddy system and sticking to well-lit areas. Maybe Jarrod wasn't worried about someone stealing his stuff, but leaving his door unlocked had let in something far worse than a thief.

She opened the door just enough to squeeze through. The rotten stink assaulted her as soon as she entered, making her skin crawl and her gorge rise. *Meat gone bad and old, dead blood. Midden, filth, and milk turned sour. A feast for vultures and flies and—*

The boy. Help the boy.

She shook her head to clear it and crouched down low, creeping off to the left so she could see both the kid and the Jackal. The room was small, maybe ten by twelve. Jarrod had pushed his bed beneath the window against the far wall.

The boy was kneeling up in bed, clad in a pair of cutoff sweatpants. His skin was pale, nearly paper white, and he was so scrawny his ribs stood out in the dim light. His open eyes were blank, already under his intruder's spell. The Jackal stood over him, a thin figure in a long grey coat. A hood rose up from beneath the coat to cover its head—most of them wore hats or hoods to hide their faces. Val peered at it; it seemed small for its kind.

The thing tilted its head back, taking a long, deep, ecstatic sniff. The hood fell back as it did. Val caught a glimpse of the thin, pointed muzzle, the mouth open slightly to drink in more of Jarrod's scent. A cascade of greasy black hair, freed from the confines of the hood, tumbled down the Jackal's back. The tips of two long ears poked up from the tangle.

It's a woman. As the revelation slammed home, Val's prey went rigid. *And she's realized she's not alone.* Val sprang forward as the Jackal started its turn. She meant to get an arm around it, catch it around the throat, but the damned thing was fast. It sidestepped. All Val got was a handful of air.

She caught herself on the desk, her claws gouging the pine surface. She felt a whoosh of air and jerked to the left. Something heavy and hard-cornered flashed past her face and smashed into the desk, sending splinters flying. When Val looked up, she saw the Jackal holding a trophy by its gold-painted plastic man, the corner of its marble base lodged in the wood.

Before it could yank its weapon back for another strike, Val's hand snaked out and grabbed it by the wrist. She dug her claws in, piercing through layers of trench coat and sweatshirt, into its skin. The Jackal hissed its pain as warm blood leaked over Val's fingers. It pressed itself against her, its other arm coming up to scrabble at her throat.

Damn it, that was my move. Val let it get a grip. She even let out a few convincing gags. The crushing of her windpipe hurt like hell, but the Jackal had either forgotten something very important or had never fought a vampire before: Val didn't actually *need* to breathe. She bent her knees and let her free hand get purchase on the edge of the desk, keeping the claws on the other hand in the Jackal's wrist. Then she launched herself backward, like a swimmer pushing off from the edge of a pool.

They sailed across the room, the Jackal along for an unwilling ride before they crashed into the far wall. A thud and the sound of shattering glass came from the room next door as their impact dislodged whatever Jarrod's neighbor had hanging on the other side. *Time to get the hell out of here.* The maneuver had also knocked the Jackal's hand away from Val's throat. "Jarrod," she rasped. *Yep. Crushed windpipe.*

The kid's head turned toward them slowly. The Jackal's lull still held him in its sway. *Well, good.* Val could use that.

She filled her voice with Command. "Open your window. Screen and all."

He turned without a word and did as she asked. Then stayed there, swaying slightly. In her way.

"Jarrod, lie back down." The Jackal struggled behind her. Val jabbed her left arm back, hearing the Jackal's grunt as her elbow connected with its stomach. "This was a dream. You were sleepwalking, even."

He nodded, his head bobbing comically.

"And from here on out"—she caught the Jackal's other hand and pulled its arm around her waist tight, like a lover's embrace—"*lock your goddamned door.*" Val threw herself forward, dragging the Jackal along with her up onto Jarrod's bed, through the wide-open window, and out into the night.

They didn't stay suspended in midair like Wile E. Coyote in the cartoons. The arc of descent started immediately, cold wind rushing up past Val as the ground surged up to meet them. She had just enough time and momentum to twist them around; she got a good gander at the stars, even, or what few were still left in the sky.

Dawn's coming. Have to end this fast.

The Jackal hit first, taking the brunt of the impact. Val heard the air *whump* out of its lungs.

She rolled off it, skin and fabric tearing further as she pulled her claws out of its wrist. Then she was back on top, straddling the former woman and pinning its arms beneath her knees. The Jackal bucked weakly, but it couldn't shake her off. Val leaned on its shoulders and bent until they were nose-to-snout. The rot was worse this close up, coming from the Jackal itself and exhaled with every shuddering breath. Val could see the vestiges of humanity in its face, and knew that when it wasn't hunting, it could pass for human. The snout would push back in, the eyes lose their glow. Just like she'd lose her fangs and claws later on.

"This town's off-limits to you." Command didn't work on them, but intimidation might. Val bore her fangs and saw the Jackal's tawny eyes roll down to see them.

It wheezed beneath her, trying to suck air back into its chest.

"You understand me? Nod if you do."

Instead, it grinned, revealing its own row of sharp teeth. "Can't . . . kill me . . . can you?" It bucked again, a little stronger now.

"Right this second? No, I can't. But you'd better damned well believe I'll be carrying rowan and silver next time we meet." She glanced up again. No more stars, and the sky had gone from black to indigo.

The Jackal snorted. "Have to get . . . to ground? *Leech?*"

Val brought one gnarled, taloned hand up and let it rest on the Jackal's cheek for a second, before she raked it downward. Four parallel grooves opened up, oozing black blood down into the thing's hair. Half an hour ago, they'd have closed up almost as soon as they'd been opened. With dawn coming, they continued to bleed. "We both do, and you know it. But I'd wager I can stand it longer than you can. You want to take that bet?" She sat back, settling down on the Jackal's stomach. "I can get nice and comfortable, if you want to test it out."

Panic crept into the thing's eyes. "No . . . *No.*" It writhed, whining and mewling when it realized Val wasn't going to budge. *"Please."*

"I'll let you up. But you'd better *run*. Clear? And tonight, when you drag your ass out of whatever hole you've crawled into, you keep running, until you're out of this town."

It nodded again, eager. "Anything. Please."

Val let it squirm a second or two longer, then climbed off it and gained her feet. The Jackal scrambled up, too, backing away from her toward the woods. They regarded each other for a moment, as Val felt the fatigue creep into her bones. She suspected she *could* hold off longer than the Jackal, but it wasn't something she truly wanted to test. Then the thing flashed its yellow teeth at her one last time, and loped off into the trees.

Val didn't watch it leave. She turned and fled herself, as fast as she could go. With each step, she felt her speed draining away, her muscles protesting against the abuse. She felt the burn in her bones as the sun came ever closer to the horizon. The sight of her street filled her with relief and dread at the same time. She'd never seen the Maple Road sign in light this bright, ever. It stung her eyes.

She didn't bother with her keys, or even her front door. Val rounded the back of the house and scrambled up the drainpipe, not caring if any of her neighbors saw. The sun was coming. *The sun was coming.* She tore out the screen and flung it to the ground. She set her palm flat against the window frame and pushed upward. The old wood groaned, then the locks gave way and the window was open.

For the third time in as many hours, Val found herself diving through a window. This time, into her own bedroom, where—when she regained her feet—she drew her velvet blackout curtains behind her and panted with relief. She was safe. She'd beaten the sun, chased off a Jackal, and saved a kid's life—a full night's work if ever there was one.

Val shuffled toward the bed. *I'm going to sleep like the dead, har har.* She collapsed onto the mattress, not even bothering to get under the blankets. As she drifted off, a breeze made its way through the still-open window and around the edge of the curtain. She could smell the rot of the Jackal on it. *Probably went to ground not far from here.*

Except, there was something else tangled in with the decay, acrid and sharp, like a dog had marked its territory. *Her* Jackal hadn't smelled like that. This scent had a distinctly male tang, which meant—

Which means there are more of them. She fought against the fatigue, managing to sit up and even getting one leg over the side of the bed. But it was too late. Outside, to the east, the sun peeked above the horizon.

Darkness descended.

5

E LLY SETTLED BACK into the chair. She tapped at the rim
of the teacup, trying to organize the flood of questions
that had sprung to mind. Father Value had never been forth-
coming with The Big Answers, preferring to tell her what
she needed to know when she needed to know it. Most often,
that came in the form of a crash course while they fled from
terrible things.

So to sit here, calm and relaxed, with the whole day in
front of her to pick Henry Clearwater's brain, was a bit
overwhelming. She sipped at the whiskey. Father Value had
taught her to ask the most important questions first, usually
because the Creep was dying and you needed information
before he could gasp out his last breath.

Outside, the sky had gone from dusky blue to robin's egg,
and she relaxed a little more. Professor Clearwater was right;
they wouldn't come until nightfall now. Maybe there was
time for the interesting questions, too.

"Why did you leave the Brotherhood?"

Henry smiled, but it wasn't one of amusement or mirth.
His eyes went somewhere far away, and his fingers made

hollow thumps as he drummed them on the arm of the chair. "Because it was time to, Elly. Our job was done."

"Done? I've helped kill fifty Creeps in the last three years, and there are still more out there. How can it be done?" It probably wasn't too polite to yell at him, but she couldn't help the anger that crept into her voice. How could he *say* that? How, after hearing her story, after she'd told him that a nest of at least six or seven had come after them the other night?

At the rise in her voice, he came back to the present. "Fifty in three years. That's, what, thirteen or fourteen a year? There was a time when we'd kill thirteen or fourteen in a *week*. And that would only be enough to keep their population under control. Don't get me wrong. What you two have done is admirable. However, they're dying out, and soon enough they won't be a worry any longer."

"Shouldn't you have stayed long enough to see it through, then? To finish them off for good?"

"I thought it best to let their natural predators do the job. It was quite a point of contention between Father Value and myself."

Elly blinked. As far as she knew, the only ones hunting the Creeps in the first place had been Father Value and herself. He'd mentioned a few other scattered branches of the Brotherhood now and then, but there weren't any formal reports, no tally board boasting the numbers of dead Creeps across the world from week to week. "What natural predators?"

Professor Clearwater sat forward, peering at her like she'd said something outrageous—*I've never seen the color blue*, or *Electricity? Never heard of it.*

"He never told you?"

"Obviously not." She bit back her frustration. It wasn't this man's fault that Father Value had been secretive and paranoid. He'd withheld information. She'd always suspected it, but no amount of wheedling or coming at questions sideways had ever worked. Once Father Value decided she didn't need to know something, that was the end of it. "I don't suppose you'd care to fill me in?"

"Of course." He cleared his throat, took a sip of whiskey, and cleared it again. "We're not quite certain what the Creeps *are*, at heart. They take the bodies of their victims, usually after death, but not always. They've been able to turn the living as well. Whether the original personality remains seems to depend on the circumstances of their turning. Some retain pieces of themselves, some don't."

"I know. I've seen it happen." She thought of poor Billy Chambers, the sweetest kid ever to have Silver and Pointy rammed into his belly. He'd recognized her, but he'd also been a colossal jerk in his last moments: Billy, but not Billy.

Professor Clearwater stood up and began pacing, hands folded behind his back. All he needed was a chalkboard and a podium, and he might as well have been teaching a class. "We don't know precisely what it is that enters the bodies. Some kind of wraith, perhaps, or lesser demons too weak to have forms of their own. But once it's done, the change is permanent. They'll go around, killing indiscriminately, feasting on flesh and causing a panic." He paused and looked at her. "They give others of similar ilk a rather bad name."

He wants me to make some kind of connection here. Her palms started to sweat. Ask her to figure out why a crossbow was jamming, and she'd have it apart and fixed in seconds. Hunting the Creeps had always been ninety percent instinctual for her—she knew the things she needed to know, and acted on them. But delving deeper, putting disparate things together . . . that had been Father Value's job. *His and one other. But they're both gone now. It's just me, from here on out. Think, Elly. Similar ilk.* Something else that took over bodies and ate people for a hobby. She groaned. "Vampires."

Henry snapped his fingers. "Correct. Some werewolf packs, too, but primarily the vampires."

Elly couldn't help the proud flush that rose to her cheeks, but this was no time to bask in success. "So, what, the vampires pick off the Creeps over food?" *If by food, we mean people.*

"In some places, it *is* as simple as that. But those kinds of conflicts are mostly in . . . less civilized places. Places where the human inhabitants don't have the same means of hunting as we do. I see you're nodding. I assume Father Value educated you at least somewhat about the vampires, then?"

"Mostly that we leave them be. That they tend to police themselves, and only drink from willing donors. But that any of them we found preying on *un*willing humans were fair game." In all her time hunting, she and Father Value had only come across one rogue vampire. The kill had been clean and easy, but Father Value had been summoned away the next night by somber-looking, pale-skinned men. All he'd said, once he'd returned, was that he'd spent several hours "playing politics," yet he'd walked like a man who'd been badly beaten. There had been no bruises to speak of, but he'd gone through nearly a whole bottle of aspirin over the next few days.

"Indeed." Henry's voice tugged Elly back from her recollection. "But where vampires can subsist on blood alone, the Creeps need more. They'll eat flesh, and if their victims are afraid first, all the better. You can see how that might negatively impact the vampires' food source. So they police the Creeps, too. They know where their local nests are and keep an eye on them. Now and then, they'll simply send out a party to eradicate them."

"But they can make more. You said it yourself—you were only killing enough to keep them from creating a whole swarm. We've been nowhere near those numbers."

He shook his head and returned to the chair. "Elly, before I left, we learned something, Father Value and I. We caught one just before daybreak and interrogated it. Sunlight works on them like bamboo shoots under the fingernails. So we—" He licked his lips and bunched his hands into fists, dredging up a memory he'd rather leave buried. "We tortured it. We sat it in a chair beside a black-curtained window, and whenever it stopped talking or resisted, we pulled the drape aside. It was in agony. Probably half the things it said were lies to get us to stop. But it told us something we'd already suspected: they were losing the ability to procreate."

He shuddered and turned a haunted gaze on her. "Without that, the vampires will take care of them all, over time. The vampires are immortal; the Creeps, less so. Especially if they're not feeding as much as they'd like. It slows their aging, but it doesn't halt it altogether. The vampires don't have to rush."

He was quiet for a few minutes. When he spoke again, his voice was hushed. "You asked why I left the Brotherhood. It was that knowledge, and the knowledge—that I could spend ten hours willingly *torturing* another living being—that made me say 'enough.' "

"It wasn't a human, though. It was a Creep. It would've done worse to you if it could."

He regarded her sadly. "So I should stoop to its level? No, Elly. Not that. Never that, ever again."

Part of her wanted to comfort him, to tell him he'd done something important, as painful as it was. It wasn't what he wanted to hear, though, and she suspected he'd pick up on the hollowness of the sentiment: she'd torture one of them without reservations. It was the least they deserved. Something else itched at her, though, something Professor Clearwater was missing.

She thought of Billy Chambers' face, his eyes wide with surprise as his skin turned to ash and flaked away around her spike. "Professor, you're wrong. They *can* make more. I watched them do it to a friend of mine."

He held up his hands. "They still can, certainly, but only in rare cases. It's taxing on the creators and what comes through is often too weak to survive the first night. When did your friend turn?"

"Three years ago."

"Have you seen it happen since?"

"No, but . . ." She scuffed her feet against the floor. Her right foot met resistance: her backpack. "Oh no. Professor, do you think . . . What if that's what's in here?" What else would Father Value have given his life to keep out of the Creeps' hands? What else could be more important?

"In where?"

"The book Father Value and I stole. What if the secret to . . . to being able to make more is what they were after?" She leaned down and unzipped the backpack. The book she withdrew was sealed in a huge Ziploc bag—even if she'd dropped it in the water back at the beach, it would have been all right, though the Creep hadn't known that. Now she yanked the bag open and set the book on her lap.

It was plain, bound in old brown leather. The corners were bent and dented, as though it had been taken off shelves and replaced many a time. Most of the gold leaf had flaked off the cover, but the writing was still there, stamped deep into the leather. Only, the language . . . "Aw, crap." She held it up for Professor Clearwater to see. She'd been hoping for English, but would have settled for Latin or German or anything that could be easily translated.

No such luck.

Scrawled across the cover were a dozen or so letters she'd never seen. Elly had a decent eye for runes, but these were unlike anything she'd ever come across. "Maybe it's different inside," she said, lowering it again.

Before she could open the cover, Professor Clearwater was out of his chair. He sprinted over and snatched the book away from her. "Don't!"

Elly scrabbled up herself, putting distance between herself and the professor. If he was going to go batshit *now* . . . But he'd retreated to the other side of the room, the book clutched against his chest. He wasn't going to attack her. "Professor, what the hell?" Then she thought of his collection, and understanding dawned. "I know how to handle old books."

He gulped in a few breaths. "I don't doubt that, Elly. But this. It's not fit for human eyes." He turned to glance outside. The sun was well above the horizon now. Further in the house, a clock chimed seven. "I have somewhere I can take it. Somewhere safe, until we can figure out what to do with it. Will you let me do that?"

She stared at him. *It's mine, though. It's what Father Value died for. If I give it away, I'm giving away the last thing he fought for.* But wasn't this where he'd always intended to bring it? Wasn't this man the one person he'd trusted with the book? Maybe she wasn't abandoning their last mission by letting Henry Clearwater take it away; maybe she was *completing* it. She cleared away the sudden lump in her throat. "Okay. Okay, yeah. But I want to be part of any decisions about it."

"Of course." He relaxed and set the book down on his desk. "My coat's in the front closet. Would you fetch it for me? I'd like to check this for wards before I go."

Trust was leaving an old man you'd known for all of four hours alone with the one thing you'd sworn to protect. Especially after the one *person* you'd sworn to protect was dead. *If Father Value had been a little more trusting and come straight here rather than running, he might still be alive.* Elly would have to do better than he had.

She'd start with fetching Professor Clearwater's coat.

6

CHAZ WAS OUT back, counting up the day shift's register when Justin came in. Four p.m. had come and gone, and four thirty wasn't far away. Tardiness and Justin simply didn't go together—it was probably even a picture in some beginner science textbook, *Things That Don't Mix*: oil and water, toothpaste and orange juice, Justin and *not-on-time*. "You're late," Chaz said, looking up as Justin shrugged off his backpack.

"I know. I'm sorry." Justin bent over the keyboard to punch in, and Chaz caught the shadows under his eyes. He decided to let the kid off the hook; after all, it was Val that had him annoyed, not Justin.

"You look like shit. Late night?"

Justin's shift had ended at one, but Chaz had never known him to head out after work in search of a bar to close down, especially not when he had classes in the morning. His short, dark hair corkscrewed in the back like he'd just woken from a nap, and his face split into a yawn as he straightened up. "No," he said, when his jaw finally returned to normal size. "Early morning." Justin knelt and unzipped his backpack, removing the item within as though he'd carried the Holy Grail across campus and down the hill to work.

The book was stuffed in a gallon-sized Ziploc bag. It looked old, but Chaz couldn't make out a title or anything else that identified it. "What's that?" He motioned for it, but instead of handing it over, Justin drew it close to his chest. *World's nerdiest teddy bear.*

"Professor Clearwater called me this morning and asked me to meet him before office hours started. He said he doesn't want anyone opening it up unless he's here. Not even Val."

Chaz frowned. "The professor was just here last night. Why didn't he bring it then? Or swing by after classes?"

"I don't know. He said he had things to do today. As soon as he gave me this, he canceled all his classes and his office hours."

"He sick?"

"Didn't seem it. Tired, maybe. He probably stayed up grading papers. He does that sometimes." Henry Clearwater was Justin's favorite professor, and the respect went both ways. Some students wrote extra research papers to boost a flagging grade; Justin wrote them for *fun*, and Professor Clearwater encouraged it. They were two nerds in a pod. It was kind of endearing. He spent as much time talking Shakespeare and Milton in the professor's office as he spent working or sleeping.

"Okay. Well, do you want me to put it in the rare books room until Val gets here?"

Justin bit his lip.

"Let me guess. He told you I'm not to be trusted with it."

The wince said it all, but Justin went for the diplomatic answer anyway. "He just really doesn't want anyone else handling it, is all."

"Uh-huh." Chaz had no idea what he'd ever done to piss the old man off, or to make him so oddly suspicious, but he wasn't going to drag Justin into it. *Yeah, your mentor thinks I'm some sort of werewolf. Isn't that crazy? What a kidder.* Easy enough to laugh off unless Justin started believing it, too. Then it wasn't Chaz' cover that was in danger of being blown, it was Val's. "Go ahead and stick it on the desk in there. We'll let Val know about it when she gets in."

Justin headed out front, the book cradled in his arms. Chaz glanced up at the clock. Val would be here within the hour, and she had some explaining to do of her own.

In five years as her companion, he'd never been dismissed the way Val had dismissed him last night. It had managed to both piss him off and terrify him.

On one hand, he was her right-hand man, wasn't he? Shouldn't she trust him with whatever she'd smelled on the air last night? Shouldn't she have told him to grab a crowbar and try to keep up, rather than bundle him in the car and send him away? He was supposed to be useful for more than making sure the bookstore's electric bill was paid, and yet when something was going down, she'd sent him home.

Then again, he'd only seen her scared like that once, and even that memory was hazy and half-formed; sometimes he thought he'd only dreamed it until he rolled up his sleeve and looked at the souvenir twisted into his flesh. Which was a good argument for her maybe thinking he *couldn't* handle the heavy shit, and that pissed him off all over again.

After Val had sent him packing, he'd gone home and fretted, staring at infomercials and resisting the urge to call her cell to make sure she was okay. If she was off sneaking around—which was what he figured she'd headed out to do from the way she sniffed the air—a ringing cell would be bad. He'd dozed fitfully for an hour or so, waking up anytime the infomercial audiences clapped on cue. Finally, with dawn lightening the sky, he'd grabbed his keys and headed to Val's.

The window screen he found on the ground in the back-yard had nearly given him a heart attack. He'd gone tearing into the house—a spare key was one of the first things Val had given him when he became her Renfield—and took the stairs three at a time. He didn't breathe until he turned on the bedside light and saw Val's red hair spilling over the pillow. She was sprawled awkwardly atop the comforter, one leg thrown over the side of the mattress. Chaz had lifted her gently, resettling her the rest of the way onto the bed so she wouldn't wake up with a crick in her neck.

That was when he'd noticed the fangs and claws, and the dark blood caking her fingers. She was covered in dirt like she'd been rolling in it. Leaves clung to her hair. *What the hell has she been up to?*

He'd stood over her awhile, wondering what to do—was whoever she'd gone after truly gone? Should he stay and stand guard in case someone sent a minion to stake her?

But, no. If she'd made it home, it meant she was safe. Otherwise she'd have called him. Val was proud, not dumb. Chaz wouldn't get any answers until she woke up, though, and the combination of knowing she was safe for the time being and seeing her fast asleep had made his own weariness kick in.

Now he sat in the bookstore's back room, stewing and eyeing the clock and the sunrise/sunset chart he kept tacked to the corkboard. She wasn't due in for five hours yet. *When she comes in, she's getting an earful.*

IT WAS JUST after nine thirty when Val slipped into Night Owls' back room and closed the door behind her. She was grateful to have the space to herself for a moment, the haven of controlled chaos promising her everything was normal, everything was fine, despite this morning's brawl. Once or twice a year, she'd get it into her head to give it a thorough cleaning and organizing, but even her best efforts were reversed within a week or two as shipments came in and returns went out. Val embodied the concept of knowing where everything and anything was in the piles of clutter. It was *her* clutter, damn it, and after what she'd smelled on the air this morning, the scent of dust and books and someone's tuna fish sandwich was a comfort.

Her peace and quiet didn't last long.

Chaz must have been lying in wait out front, waiting for the telltale creak of the hinges, judging from the way he burst through the back room door and swooped down on her. "The hell was that about last night?"

Val glanced up at him and winced. Under the best of circumstances, she'd never have called Chaz intimidating. His build was too scrawny, the muscles cording in his folded arms more like stereo wire than steel cable. He did, however, do a high fury extremely well. She could hear his pulse pounding away in his throat. The smell of anger rolled off him in waves.

"It was nothing. I handled it." The lie came smoothly. Like the invite she'd commanded out of Justin last night, Val tucked the guilt away for later. Telling Chaz what had happened would send him into panic mode, and right now she wanted stability and calm. Or at least a semblance of it. *I need to make a phone call first. Get some advice, or directions, or even some help. Then I'll fill him in.*

Chaz stared at her. "Really, now. So much nothing you practically took my legs off shutting me into the car?" He ran a hand through his straw-colored hair. "Val. Whatever it was had you scared out of your wits."

She sighed, the guilt not completely vanquished. "All right. Fine. I don't know what it was, not exactly. But it smelled wrong, and it smelled close, so I wanted you out of there while I took care of it." The last part was true enough, at least. She stood and retrieved a hair elastic from beneath a sheaf of invoices. "Good Renfields are hard to find, you know."

"Goddamn it, Val, I'm not kidding." Usually the reminder that he was—technically—her servant got a smirk out of him. Now his scowl just deepened.

"I know you're not. I'm sorry. Look, whatever it was, it's gone now, okay?" Val flexed her hands. They still ached from the previous night's abuse. She was thankful she'd been passed out for the day while they reset themselves: it meant she hadn't had to feel the bones cracking and warping all over again. She caught Chaz eyeing them and clasped them behind her back. "It probably just wanted a snack. If it *was* looking for someone, it wasn't me."

"Because there are so many other supernatural creatures in Edgewood."

He had a point. Other vamps passed through occasionally, and a pair of succubi were shacking up a few streets over, but she was pretty much the town's only permanent paranormal resident. Still, she kept her nose clean—mostly by keeping it *out* of bloodsucker politics in the first place—so there was truly no reason for something big and nasty and foul smelling to come after her at all. "Maybe they were passing through on their way to Boston."

It was a weak explanation; the look on Chaz' face reflected that. But for some reason, he let it go. "Fine. But next time, remember I keep a crowbar in the backseat. I can help."

I'm not letting you anywhere near a Jackal if I can help it. "Deal." She finished twisting her hair back into a messy, half-assed bun, and stuck out her hand to shake. Chaz took it, and just like that, they were okay again.

"Listen," he said, back to business. "Justin brought in a book from the professor for us. He asked if we could keep it in with the rare stuff for now. I put it on top of the other books you keep meaning to get around to pricing." He held the door open for her as they passed into the front of the store.

Justin was up at the front register, flipping through the latest issue of *Rolling Stone*. He tried slapping it closed and shoving it to the side when he heard Val and Chaz approaching, but Val had been through close to thirty employees from Edgewood College in the decade she'd owned the store. She knew the sound of cast-aside magazines by now. Combine that with the hangdog look and the fervor with which Justin was straightening a stack of bookmarks, and the kid was busted.

"Chaz says you have something from Professor Clearwater," Val announced. She looked pointedly at the magazine, but didn't comment on its presence.

Color crept into Justin's cheeks. He was one of those kids who never got in trouble in class, so reprimands from authority figures—even the gentlest rebukes—got the guilt flowing. "Oh. Uh, yeah." He stopped fiddling with the bookmarks and looked at her sheepishly. This was the other reason Val didn't call him out on reading at the register: a verbal warning would've given him fits.

"Did he say anything about it?"

"Just that he'd be in for it later, and that we should leave it sealed up. I guess maybe it's superfragile."

"That's unlike him. He always brings his finds in himself."

Justin had been halfway through a flinch at her frown. Realizing it wasn't directed at him, he relaxed. "Maybe he just wanted to get it here. He looked like he'd been up all night, and said something about going back home to sleep. He canceled his classes today, too. Even my directed study."

That *was* unusual. Even when classes were canceled, Professor Clearwater made time for Justin. In many ways, the two were as close as a grandfather and his favorite grandson. It was the professor who had suggested they hire Justin, when work-study proved not nearly enough to cover the expenses of living on campus. And boy, had the kid ever worked out. He'd been at Night Owls for a year and a half now, and Val dreaded his eventual graduation. Finding an employee whose worst infraction was to peek through the occasional magazine during slow times was rare indeed.

As rare as the books in the reading room. As rare as someone like Chaz.

Val patted Justin's hand. "There's a cold going around. Tell you what—if he doesn't swing in by ten o'clock, we'll call and see if he or Helen need anything. All right?"

That brightened him up. "Okay, yeah. Thanks, Val."

Val held the reassuring smile another few seconds, until she was well away from Justin. By the time she reached the reading room and sorted through her key ring (rare books room, bookstore, delivery door, her house, spare key to Chaz' Mustang, several more whose locks were on the other side of the country . . .), it was gone, replaced with a scowl. *Up all night and canceled his classes. Don't tell me you went Jackal hunting, old man.*

But if he had, he'd survived. Justin had seen him in the daylight. The silver key turned in the lock, and Val pushed into the rare books room. She stood in the dark for a moment, breathing in the musty scent of dust and paper, old leather bindings and furniture polish. "Let's see what you've brought us, Professor," she said, and switched on the light.

Val liked to call the room cozy; Chaz called it the veal box. She had to concede the aptness of that description— even Jarrod's closet of a dorm room had had a few square feet on it. Still, it was neat and well lit, and filled floor to ceiling with books that had been around since before most of the Edgewood students' grandparents had been born. Some of the tomes in here were older than the college itself. A few even dated back to colonial times.

Everything was in its place—the books on their appointed shelves, the older ones in glass cases. The box of cotton gloves sat on a ledge to Val's right, set there for visitors to use while browsing so the oils on their fingers wouldn't damage the delicate pages. Val probably didn't need to use them; she doubted her skin secreted much of anything since she'd been turned. But she tugged a pair on anyway, partly keeping up appearances in case Chaz let a customer in, partly because you never could be too careful.

Justin had set the book down in the middle of the rolltop writing desk that served as the room's reading area. It sat, thick and squat, wrapped in one of those Ziploc bags that could hold enough cereal to feed a small army. Just because the professor had said they shouldn't *open* the bag didn't mean Val couldn't pick it up and *look* at it.

Sitting down in the creaky old chair she'd picked up at an estate sale was usually a comfort. Tonight, she sank into it with dread. Books weren't supposed to be scary; in fact, they should be the very opposite. Books made sense of the unknown. They were physical manifestations of order and sanity.

Why, then, did the book on the desk make her want to slink into the corner and hide?

I'm being ridiculous. He probably found an old Haw-

thorne or Dickinson and didn't want to leave it in his office all day. It has nothing to do with last night. Nothing.

But if he *had* found something like that, wouldn't it have come up when he brought the fudge by last night? *Maybe it was one of the books from his mother-in-law's estate that he'd mentioned.* No, that didn't make sense, either. He'd have brought it up right then, and even if he'd forgotten, he'd simply have waited and brought the book by during a normal visit.

Giving it to Justin leant an urgency to it.

Val pulled the book closer, feeling its heft as it slid across the desk's polished surface. She could see plain, mud brown leather beneath the plastic, but no title. The binding and the stitching were hard to assess through the bag. She pressed her fingers to the cover, questing for indents. *There.* The gold leaf might have worn off, but the title had been stamped into the leather. Val stretched the plastic tight and brought the book closer to the lamp to reveal its name.

"Oh no. No, no, no." The book fell back to the desk with a thud. Wood creaked as Val shoved violently back in her chair.

The last time she'd seen this writing was in the nest outside of Sacramento. Letters like these had been smeared on the walls and carved into the bodies that were strewn about like discarded fast-food containers. She hadn't asked anyone to translate. Hadn't really needed them to.

How had the professor come to possess such a thing? Had the Jackals she'd smelled last night left it behind somewhere, or had he taken it from them? She pulled the seal apart on the bag, just an inch, and sniffed. She could smell the Clearwaters' house and, beneath that, human smells—the professor's for certain, and someone else's. Helen? And there, beneath the fresher scents, she could smell the Jackals' rot.

Val resealed the bag and shoved it into the top drawer of the desk. She strode from the rare books room, willing herself not to run. The silver key turned in the lock; as she pocketed her key ring, she wished she'd had a dead bolt installed, too. And a moat.

Chaz was already hurrying down the aisle toward her as she spun around. She didn't give him a chance to talk. "There you are. Good. I need to go out for a little while. *No one is to go in that room*, are we clear? In fact, I'm taking the register key—" His pale face and too-wide eyes finally registered. "Chaz? What's going on?"

He spoke in a whisper, but the words seemed to echo through the store. The whole place had gone dead quiet. "We just got some terrible news." He laid his hand on her shoulder, like he thought he'd have to steady her. Somewhere near the front of the store, a girl hitched a sob. Chaz winced at the sound and took a deep breath.

"What is it?" But she knew. Even before he said it, she knew.

"Henry and Helen Clearwater are dead."

7

VAL WAS MOVING before the words were out of Chaz'
mouth. He caught her by the elbow and tugged her back
to him. Shaking him off would have been easy—Val was
far, far stronger. But there were eyes on her here. She spoke
through gritted teeth. "I have to go there. See what happened."

He shook his head, the grip on her arm tightening. "You
can't. It's a crime scene. There are going to be cops everywhere, and you can't just go barging in."

"I won't let them see me. I'll make them forget if they
do." She had to *go*. She had to *see*. If the Jackals had killed
the Clearwaters, Val could track them. She could catch up
to them and . . .

And what? Take down a pack on her own? She had three
small stakes of rowan with her, buried deep at the bottom
of her messenger bag—hardly enough to face down multiple
Jackals. There couldn't be a whole nest in town, but without
going to the house, she had no way to tell how many there
really were. One or two she could destroy on her own, but
not without difficulty. Probably not without serious damage

to herself. Val closed her eyes and sighed. "You're right. I have to wait."

Chaz let go. "If you want to go look around later, I'll go with you. But he loved it here, and everyone knew it. If more information's going to come in, it'll make its way here pretty fast."

Now that Val looked around, she saw that he was right. More people had trickled in, mostly shell-shocked students who stood in clusters, talking in hushed voices. One stood alone, up at the register. Justin. Val strode straight down the aisle to him. He looked frozen in place, ashen and confused. As she got closer, his dark eyes flicked to her.

"Val, they said . . . They said—"

She caught him as he crumpled and pulled him into a hug. Justin didn't sob or moan, but Val felt hot tears wetting her blouse. Every now and then he'd tremble, or his thin shoulders would hitch, but he hardly made a sound. He straightened after a while, not meeting her gaze as he went for the tissues and wiped his eyes. It had to be slightly awkward to be held by your boss. "Thank you," he said at last, pulling away from her.

She nodded and stepped back. "Do you want to go home for the night? Back to campus?"

"No. I think I'll be better staying, if that's okay."

"Of course." He had to be thinking the same as Chaz: people would come here to share news as it was discovered. "Well, you don't have to stay up here. Go talk to whoever you need to."

Justin took another few seconds to compose himself, then stepped down and headed for a group of students. They made a space for him as he approached. A girl Val didn't know slung her arm around Justin's waist and they leaned into one another, offering comfort.

NIGHT OWLS FOUND itself hosting its own wake for the professor and Helen. Val sent Chaz to the bakery for a platter of pastries, and had Justin help her wrangle the monster-sized coffee urn they set up for author signings and book club nights. People stopped in and told stories about classes they'd had with Henry or Helen's unflagging energy on various campus committees. No one knew much about the killing itself, only that the motive appeared to be robbery. Word had it the house had been ransacked.

After midnight, the crowd began to thin. By one o'clock, they were back down to the regulars, only more subdued. Val only saw Justin a few times after she'd relieved him of duty, always standing in a small knot of people, though usually on the outside of the group. The last glimpse she'd had of him had been around eleven thirty, when he'd restocked the supply of Styrofoam coffee cups. As she looked around now, Val realized she hadn't seen Justin at all for the last hour.

Maybe he slipped out and went home after all. But it wasn't like him to leave without letting her know. Her gaze fell on the door to the rare books room, and her stomach dropped. She groped for the hook beneath the register, hoping to hear the rattle of the chain, the clatter of the silver key hanging from it hitting the wall. With the news of the Clearwaters' murder, she'd completely forgotten to take it away. *Shit, shit, shit.*

She grabbed at empty air.

Justin was in the back. Alone with the Jackals' book. She couldn't explain why—aside from *that thing creeps me out*—but she found herself sprinting toward the back of the store, determined to yank the damned thing out of Justin's hands if she had to.

As she passed the end of the shelves and fumbled for her own key, the door opened. Justin backed out, placing his palm flat against the edge of the door and turning the handle all the way to shut it as quietly as possible.

He turned around and yelped when he found himself nose to nose with Val, the momentary fright on his face collapsing into guilt.

"I thought I said that room was off-limits." She'd said it to Chaz, but Justin had been right there. He'd damned well heard.

His cringe intensified. "I just . . . I just wanted to sit in there for a few minutes. It's one of his favorite places. Was." He took the key from around his neck and held it out for Val. "I'm sorry."

The chiding she'd had ready died on her lips. What harm had been done, really? Justin couldn't understand the language the book was written in, and he'd carried it around all day before he brought it here. *It could have been warded.* She could smell it on him, the faint tang of rot on his hands. He'd opened the bag, probably flipped through the damned thing. If there'd been any spells set to go off when the cover was opened, they'd have triggered by now. Since the back room hadn't exploded, she had to assume it was unprotected. Val sighed and took the key. "It's all right. We've all had a long night. Why don't you head on home and get some sleep?"

Justin hesitated and looked around the store.

Val understood. Here, at least, he was among people. The rooms in Bryant Hall were all singles and most of his floormates would be asleep at this hour. She knew what it was like to lie in the dark, alone and grieving. "You can stay if you want."

"No. I'll be okay." He mustered a smile and gave her an awkward squeeze on the arm. "Thanks, Val."

She watched him go, his hands in his pockets, shoulders hunched. In a way, Val envied him: when he got back to his room, he'd be able to cry.

It was one of the few things vampirism had stolen from her that she actually missed, now and then. She could look at as many pictures of sunrises as she wanted to online, or watch thousands of videos shot by amateurs on beaches at dawn. Chaz had gotten used to her telling him what to order a couple times a week, and let her sniff to her heart's content before he dug in.

But being dead seemed to have closed up her tear ducts, and while maybe others could weep *near* her, no one could weep *for* her.

THE JACKALS CAME at closing time.

The store was empty except for Val and Chaz. She was

at the register when the bell above the door jingled. Chaz was somewhere near the back; she could hear the rhythmic sweep of the push broom against the tiles. *Stay back there,* Val thought, even though it was useless: she wasn't strong enough to Command with her will alone, and calling out would let them know he meant something to her.

So she kept her mouth shut as three of them filed in, all trench coats and hidden faces, and hoped the floor in the children's section was covered in dirt and tiny candy pieces. "Can I help you find something?" Her voice was steadier than she'd expected it to be. The rowan stakes were still in the office. Even if she made a run for it, Val knew she couldn't take them all at once. Best just to stand her ground and see what they wanted.

If they so much as look at Chaz askance, I'll make him run.

They wended their way past the display tables, the smell of decay roiling along ahead of them. Two of them were taller than Val, one bulky, one thin. The third was small and slight, and when she stopped on the other side of the counter, she pushed her hood back so Val could see the four long scars running down her cheek. They marred an otherwise pretty face, now that the snout was gone. She'd probably been popular, back when she was human: high cheekbones, pixie-ish nose, full lips. If she gave her hair a wash, she might even turn some heads now.

"Hello, Leech." She grinned up at Val. In the light, her teeth were jagged and yellow.

Well, almost pretty. "Didn't I tell you to get the hell out of town?"

"We're on our way out. Just needed to pick up one last thing before we go." The two behind her lifted their noses and sniffed.

"It's here." The one on the left closed his eyes, panting a little. He looked Justin's age, maybe younger. His cheeks were a minefield of acne scars; apparently becoming a Jackal didn't fix your skin problems like vampirism did.

The other one nodded, turning until his nose pointed toward the rare books room. He was, as Chaz might say, built like a brick shithouse. Val wondered if a blow from the fire extinguisher she kept behind the register would even have any effect on him, or if he'd only grin and shake his head at her like the bulldog did in the cartoons, when the cat finally got in a solid hit. "In there."

The woman's grin widened. "Did the old man bring you a present today, Leech? Something that wasn't his?" She leaned across the counter, dropping her voice. "We went looking for it, and it wasn't at his house. He didn't want to tell us where he'd hidden it, but he talked in the end."

"Screamed, really," said the one on the left, the skinny one.

Val gripped the counter so hard the wood groaned. Blood thundered in her ears; she wanted to lunge at them, tear at their throats and make them howl for what they'd done. Their rancid blood would make her gag, but it would be worth it, so worth it to make the Jackals pay. Her gums prickled as her fangs unsheathed.

"All swept up, Val, just need to—" Chaz froze beside the rack full of maps as four heads swiveled toward him. The dustpan he carried dipped and spilled its sandy contents all over his shoes. "Val?" In his other hand, he held the push broom. He switched his grip on it, getting ready to bring it up like a baseball bat, but before he could, the right-hand Jackal moved.

Its motion was a blur even to Val's preternatural senses; to Chaz, it must have seemed to reach him in an eyeblink. She couldn't Command him to run now: the Jackal's hand slipped around his throat, its grimy black claws making indents in his skin.

For his part, Chaz took it well. After his initial start, he stood calmly, still wielding the broom even though he didn't have the range of motion to swing it. He glanced down at the wrist holding him and saw the fine, dark fur. "Oh. Uh. Fuck," was the extent of his commentary.

"How about you show me that book," said the woman, pulling Val's attention back, "and he doesn't have to get hurt tonight."

"Val, no. Fuck these guys. Don't—"

Right Hand lifted his other arm almost casually and

extended his index finger, the claw hovering less than an inch from Chaz' eye. The unspoken threat shut Chaz up.

"All right." Val reached under the register and retrieved the key from its hook. "All right, you can have it." She let it dangle before the woman, but pulled it back before the Jackal bitch could take it. "I'm going to have to let you in."

The woman growled. "You don't want to piss me off, Leech. Whatever you're trying to pull here—"

"I'm not trying to pull anything." Val set the key down on the counter. "If you pick up that key, it's going to hurt like hell. It's silver. Go ahead and touch it if you don't believe me."

The woman jerked her head, and Left Hand reached past her to prod the key with the tip of his finger. As soon as his skin made contact, the flesh turned black. Tendrils of smoke curled up like a cigarette left to burn in an ashtray. The Jackal yanked his arm away and danced backward. He whimpered as he stuffed the injured finger into his mouth.

Val had expected the woman to react at least a little. Instead, she watched her companion's pain with clinical observation. *She's not an alpha.* She didn't smell like one, and an alpha never would have let Val get the drop on it the way she had last night. *But she might be fucking the alpha, or could be an alpha's pup.* Val tucked that away to mull over later. Provided there was a later.

The woman didn't wait for the whimpering to stop. She shrugged and faced Val. "Fine. Lead the way."

As much as she loathed turning her back on a Jackal, Val stepped away from the register and headed toward the back. She took the aisle that Chaz and Right Hand were in, pausing before them to bare her fangs at the creature holding her friend. Up close, she could see beneath his hood. A network of scars covered his face, souvenirs from years of fights. She wondered how many times he'd challenged an alpha and lost.

Right Hand flashed long canines at her. One of the front ones was chipped. She imagined the ragged bite marks he would leave on Chaz' flesh if she screwed this up.

She dipped her head in acknowledgment—*you win this*

round—and turned to Chaz. "Will you be all right while I . . ." She gestured at the rare books room, but what she meant was, "while I leave you with these things that wouldn't mind having your spleen for a snack."

He grinned at her despite the smell of fear-sweat rolling off him. "Peachy keen."

Then the Jackal woman gave her a shove and got her moving again.

VAL OPENED THE door for the Jackal bitch but didn't follow her inside. She wanted to be able to keep an eye on the two up front. "The book's on the desk. Take it and get the hell out of here."

But of course that wasn't good enough. The woman seemed content to leave Val in the doorway. As soon as she set eyes on the book, it was as if she'd forgotten about the vampire behind her altogether. She stood staring down at the top of the desk for a long moment, the set of her shoulders rigid, breath coming in a pant as she sniffed the air. New mothers weren't half as careful with their firstborns as the Jackal woman was as she lifted the book.

The Ziploc bag fell to the ground like a discarded candy bar wrapper. The woman's eyes shone as she leafed through the onionskin-thin pages. She turned toward the door as she flipped, enough for Val to see the rapture on her face turn to rage. "Where is it?" she snarled, flipping faster.

"Where is what?"

The Jackal woman looked up at her, tawny eyes flashing. "You changed it. You *stole* it." She turned the book around and showed Val the pages.

Blank.

Not the whole book, but a page here, a page there. Val couldn't make sense of the text that remained. A mere glimpse of the writing made her stomach roil. But there were definitely whole chunks of it missing. "I didn't do anything to it. I don't even know what it *is*."

"You did it. Or *he* did it. But since he's dead, *you* get to fix it. But first." She strode past Val and shouted to Right Hand. "Kill him."

"No!" The Jackals could move fast, but so could Val. She grabbed the bitch and shoved her back against the wall. The book thudded to the floor in a flurry of pages. After a moment, the Jackal woman stopped fighting, laying her throat bare for Val—a dog submitting to its master. Val shifted the key in her palm so it protruded out from between her middle and index fingers. She held it against the woman's throat. The flesh sizzled and burned like a piece of plastic held over a flame.

Despite the pain, the woman didn't scream.

Right Hand paused, poised on the edge of carrying out his order. Left Hand wavered up by the register. Val could see him weighing his options—would a sudden move help or hurt? *He's still a pup. Too indecisive.*

"Here's how this is going to work: you do it and I'll kill her," Val called. "Then since my hands will be free, I'll come for you two." The key made a pretty terrible knife, but Val wasn't afraid of a bit of a mess. Using it to cut the woman's jugular would be like cutting twine with a dull blade. *But if they hurt Chaz? Worth it.*

The woman had the balls to smile. "You think you can take them both?"

Val kept her hand at the bitch's throat, but glanced back at Right Hand. She thought about the scars on his face again. *He might just be old enough.* The other two seemed oddly young, as Jackals went, but this one struck her as more wary, more weathered. "Has your alpha ever mentioned Sacramento?"

"What's that have to do with—" The bitch hushed as the silver pressed in harder.

Right Hand nodded, wary.

"I was there. So you know that means I can kill the both of you, easy. Don't you?"

Left Hand whined low in his throat, still sucking on his burnt fingertip. Beneath Val, the Jackal bitch had gone very still, her eyes darting from Val to Right Hand and back. "Let him go," the bitch said. The panicked, wheedling tone from this morning was back.

Right Hand did as he was told, pushing Chaz away from him with a bit too much force. Chaz stumbled forward. He caught his balance with the broom and held it out in front of him as he put distance between himself and the Jackals.

Val dragged the bitch down the aisle and past Right Hand. They swept past Left Hand, too, straight to the door. She shoved the abomination out onto the sidewalk and held the door open for the other two. They got the hint and squeezed past, trying not to touch her as they slunk out into the night.

The bitch crouched down, one hand to her throat, gulping in the chilly air. "Two days," she rasped.

"For what?" Val twirled the key around on its chain. *Wish I'd thought to use it as a garrote. Then she wouldn't still be talking.*

"To find what's missing. To make it whole again."

"You three really want to come back and try my patience?"

"Not just us." Right and Left helped the bitch to her feet. She lifted her glittering eyes to meet Val's. "If you don't get those pages back, we'll bring friends." They backed away, until the shadows covered them. The bitch's voice hung on the air: "We'll bring a whole nest."

8

CHAZ HEARD THE woman's threat float through the door. It should have chilled him, he supposed, but he had something slightly more pressing to address first. "I take it you two are acquainted?" Now that the three were gone, his pants-shitting fear was rapidly melting into anger. He figured that nearly getting his eye poked out—*oh, and then nearly getting killed on command, let's not forget*—gave him the right to kick up a bit of a fuss.

Val locked the door and leaned back against it. "Chaz, I'm sorry. I—"

He didn't bother tamping down the fury in his voice. *She fucked up, she gets to hear it.* "No. Not good enough. I asked you earlier tonight if you knew anything, and you said *no*. Then these three whatever-the-fucks walk in here and it's clear you and the woman have met before. I'm guessing shortly after we parted ways last night." His knuckles had gone white on the broom handle. "You lied to me. Which, you know, whatever, I expect you to now and then. I'm sure there's obscure vampire shit I'm not allowed to know. But not when it's important. Not when one or both of us could get *killed*."

"I know. I was wrong." She spread her hands wide, but stayed where she was. "I thought it was taken care of, and I screwed up, and I'm sorry."

He realized he was shaking. Chaz wasn't the kind of person you crowded when he was angry. He didn't take well to being placated, either. He'd never swung on her—never *would*—but Val was giving him his space all the same. He throttled the broom a little longer, then let it clatter to the floor. *Better than a stress ball.* "What now, then?"

"Now . . ." She hesitated, but seemed to think better of something—probably a suggestion that he go home, which wouldn't go over well. "I'm locking up and going to the Clearwaters'. You coming?"

The words were barely out of her mouth before he answered. "Hell yes."

CHAZ WAS QUIET as he drove to the professor's. The ride wasn't long enough for her to tell him very much, aside from that the creatures were called Jackals and she'd chased the woman out of Bryant Hall the night before. He gripped the steering wheel and kept quiet. Sure, not asking questions was borderline petulant, but he hadn't had a chance to properly seethe yet. Five years as her Renfield—five years under the impression she told him the important shit—made this omission hard to simply shrug off.

Chaz killed the engine in front of a sprawling old Colonial a block down the street from the Clearwater house. He would have thought that every house in the neighborhood would be lit up, but only a few seemed to have anyone left awake. They hopped over a low fence, sneaking past a two-car garage and into the backyard. When he squinted, Chaz could make out the faint spindly shadows of a swing set just before the tree line, but even those melted away as heavy clouds covered the moon. Val led them across the yard and into the woods.

The darkness didn't hinder her, but Chaz didn't have the luxury of night vision. He moved quietly enough, drawing on what little knowledge he'd retained from his Boy Scout troop back in the day, but as far as he knew there wasn't a badge for skulking around in the pitch blackness with a vampire. Or trespassing on a murder scene to see if the crazy dog-people had left any clues behind. Without the moonlight, he was blind out here. Chaz waved his arms in front of himself so he didn't get a branch to the face.

Everything was so quiet. He could hear the shuffle of leaves beneath his feet and his own harsh breathing, but other than that, the night was silent. No night birds called to one another, no crickets chirped. Nothing went scurrying through the underbrush at his approach. Was it the kind of silence that descended when animals caught the scent of a predator?

Val's the predator here. Nothing else. She'd have called it off if there were Jackals lurking.

But if Val was nearby, he couldn't hear her anymore. *Did we get separated?* Chaz stopped walking and peered around, straining to make sense of the darkness. His eyes were as wide as they could go, but all around him was seamless black. He felt his breath grow ragged and raspy edged with panic. His chest tightened even as he gulped down a lungful of air. Shame mingled with the fear; he didn't think *chicken-shit* went with the whole Renfield persona. He didn't know if it was more embarrassing for the Jackals to know he was afraid, or for Val to see the fear on his face.

Cold fingers closed over his. Somehow, he managed not to yelp. Or piss his pants. *It's only Val.*

"Come on," she said, and gave his hand a squeeze. "I'll lead you."

Relief flooded through him, stronger than the shame. He could feel like a pansy in the morning. In the daylight. "Yeah. Okay." He closed his eyes and let her tug him forward through the woods.

CHAZ COULD FEEL the wrongness as soon as they crossed onto the Clearwaters' land. He couldn't have said quite *what* felt so wrong, but the knot of fear that had settled in his stomach twisted into something new. Where before he'd been afraid of Jackals jumping out of the shadows and killing them, or cops tramping through the trees and arresting them, now the panic was on a purely animal level. His lizard brain wanted him to run, and his logical brain couldn't think of a good reason not to. Except for Val. Her presence kept him from letting the flight instinct take over.

By the time they reached the flagstone steps of the patio that had been Helen's last home improvement, Val was breathing through her mouth. *She's smelling them.* It must have been overpowering.

Once Val had started leading him along, he'd kept the freaking-the-fuck-out down to a minimum by wondering how they'd get inside. Turned out it wasn't an issue: the back door had been torn off its hinges. The only things keeping anyone out were a few strips of police tape strapped across the doorway to deter the law-abiding. Now that they were out of the woods and in semifamiliar territory, Chaz let go of Val and reached into the pocket of his Windbreaker. "Here," he said, and pressed a soft bundle into her hands.

"Are these from the rare books room?" Val stared at the cotton gloves, then at Chaz.

"Yeah. I thought . . . fingerprints. I don't know if you'd leave them, but I figured it couldn't hurt to have them. Plus, you know. *I'd* be smearing them all over the place." Talking made the fear recede a bit, enough that he could tamp down the urge to snatch up Val's hand again. *I have to be the world's worst minion.*

She tugged on the gloves while Chaz fumbled out a pair of his own. "Can't have my employees getting arrested. It's bad publicity."

They exchanged tense smiles; Val lifted the yellow tape enough so she could duck through it, but she seemed reluctant to pass through the doorway.

"Val, what's— Oh." It dawned on him: she'd been in the house before—the professor often had her come by to appraise his newly acquired rarities—but now that her former hosts were dead, had their invitation been rescinded?

Chaz stepped around her. His boots crunched on broken glass as he walked into the kitchen and turned around. "Come on in."

Val gave him a nod of thanks and joined him across the threshold.

The kitchen was a shambles: scratches covered the hardwood floor, as if several dogs had come scrabbling through and dug deep gouges with their claws. The table had been overturned, the contents of the cabinets strewn about the room. Val sniffed. "No one's inside. Hasn't been anyone here for a few hours."

"What about the cops? Is there a car out front?"

"Wait here. I'll check." She headed off into the dining room, then along the hallway that led to the front of the house.

While he waited, Chaz dug his penlight out of his pocket. Outside, it might have given them away, but in here, unless anyone was patrolling the backyard, he figured it was worth the risk. He thought he could re-create the Jackals' movements by the marks on the floor. They seemed to have gone straight through the kitchen and deeper into the house. The ransacking must have happened afterward; he found human footprints in the rubble.

When Val came back into the kitchen a few minutes later, Chaz had just about forgotten his earlier terror. As hard as it was to be rooting through a dead friend's cupboards— and now that the professor was gone, Chaz couldn't help but think of him as a friend despite the whole I-think-you're-a-werewolf bit—he was *doing* something, and that steadied him.

"Nothing unusual here," he said, straightening up from looking under the sink. "Unless you count an industrial-sized bag of salt."

Val raised a brow. "If the professor knew what was coming . . ."

"It becomes ordinary, yeah." Salt was for rituals and protection. Chaz hadn't *totally* dozed through Val's Vampire's Minion 101 lessons. But what was Professor Clearwater doing performing rituals?

"All right." She glanced at the stove clock: four thirty. They had an hour before sunrise, an hour and a half if they wanted to push it. "Let's start in the library, then. The real one."

VAL LED THE way upstairs, following the trail of debris. At the top of the landing, a bloody handprint smeared down the wallpaper. Ragged claw marks marred it further. One of the Jackals had taken some damage. The air was heavy with the smell of burnt fabric, singed fur, and something oddly sweet. Across the top step, rune marks were melted into the rug. Val smiled. "You clever old son of a bitch. They tripped your wards."

Chaz leaned down and touched the rune, which was brown and shiny in the beam of his penlight. "Do you think he killed any of them? The ones at the store didn't seem all that hurt."

"God, I hope so." Not that a dead Jackal balanced out the Clearwaters' deaths. A whole *nest* of dead Jackals couldn't do that. But it helped to know they'd gone down fighting nonetheless.

A few steps down the hall, a long, greasy streak of ash on the floor answered the question. Laid atop it was a snapped-off rowan stake, its bottom half covered in ichor. "They got one, at least." She didn't want to look at it too long. She'd seen plenty like it on the West Coast, and heard the screams that went with the burning.

The library door hung crooked; the top hinge was all that held it up. The lower was still fastened to the frame. Runes drawn in blue chalk covered the door. Val could make out some of them—spells of protection, spells set to ward off evil—but others were completely unfamiliar. She traced one with a gloved finger, smudging the chalk. Even out here, with the room closed off, she could smell the blood: Jackal and human, making her want to gag.

Making her want to drink.

She clenched her fists and fought against the fangs and

claws that were clamoring to come out. Her dead heart thumped to life, her already-sharp senses kicking even higher, amplifying the coppery tang on the air. She spoke through gritted teeth. "You should stay out here." Without waiting to see if Chaz obeyed, she shoved through the door and into the library.

The furniture had been smashed to splinters. Not a book remained on the shelves. All around the room were piles of ruined covers and torn pages. And everywhere, the blood. The scents mingled in her nose—the heady smell of human blood with the rot and sulphur of the Jackals. She struggled with the urge to drag her finger through a puddle of the human kind and lick it off like frosting. *No. This is the professor's and Helen's. They're your FRIENDS.*

But maybe just a taste . . . Wouldn't it be like honoring them, in a way? She'd never drunk from them in life, wasn't that respectful? Wasn't it all just going to waste, there on the floor, soaking into the Oriental rug, dripping down the walls? Wouldn't it be cleaned up tomorrow and discarded like trash? Blood was meant to sustain life, and if the original owners were dead, well, wouldn't they have wanted it to go to a good cause? Feeding a friend was a good cause. In fact, it was an *excellent* cause.

"Val? Are you all right?" Footsteps shuffled behind her, and Val groaned.

She could hear his heartbeat, the rush of blood through the veins at his throat, at his wrists. Living blood would be *so* much nicer. Drinking blood that had cooled was like drinking coffee gone cold. Chaz would let her do it. He was her friend. He'd understand if she—

"No. I *won't*!" She slapped her hand down on an empty shelf and was alarmed to see her claws out. *I didn't feel them.* Her tongue snaked out and prodded the tip of a fang. She wrapped her arms around herself and counted to three. Then five. Then ten. When she felt more in control, more *herself*, she hissed, "I told you to stay out there."

"You went quiet. I thought . . . I thought maybe something happened. They'd left one behind, or you'd set off a ward, I don't know." He sounded sheepish; Val half expected to see him scowling at the ground with his hands shoved in his pockets when she turned. Instead, he shone his penlight on her face, and looked relieved to see she wasn't hurt. "Fangs, huh? That bad?" His eyes never wavered from her own.

"Look around. It's as bad as it can get." *Breathe. Stay calm.*

"Yeeeeah. I don't think I'm going to. I've seen enough out of the corners of my eyes to know I don't want to look at it full on." He rubbed the back of his neck with his free hand. "I came in to see if you were okay, is all."

"I am now." She gave him a sharp-toothed smile. "Why don't you go downstairs and check the other library? Never know. Maybe he hid something there." It was a weak out and they both knew it. But it saved Chaz some face, and she didn't want him too close just now. He had no idea how close he'd come to being a snack, and she still felt shaky. If the bloodlust rose again, it was better if he was in another part of the house. *Better if he were in another part of town, but he's not going to leave me here alone.*

He edged backward, sliding his feet along so he wouldn't trip over the debris. His gaze stayed on her until he was in the hall. "If you need me, yell." Then he was out of her sight, and she let out a ragged sigh.

She'd been way too close to the edge. Chaz had seen the fangs and claws plenty of times before; she'd shown him both years ago, so he knew what he was getting into by being her Renfield. He'd seen her feed and he'd seen her fight, but she'd always been in control, even when she was all scratchy and bitey.

Over the years, he'd witnessed things that would have turned other men's hair white. There wasn't much Val could do that would faze him, which was good, but it also meant he hadn't been afraid of her just now, when he should have been. *I could have killed him. I could have been on him before he could draw breath to scream, and God knows if I could have stopped myself once the blood started flowing.*

Val pushed the thought away. Dawn was creeping ever closer, and if she wanted to find anything useful, she was going to have to get used to the gore. She found an over-turned chair that still had three legs intact and set it upright. She grasped the backrest to help steel herself and inhaled deeply. This time, it wasn't as bad. She tuned the bee-swarm gabbling of the Jackals' blood to a distant drone in her head, and made herself concentrate on the human scents.

They didn't rouse the hunger. Instead, the lump of dead flesh that was her heart twinged with sorrow. The two people who'd always been so kind to her were gone. No, that made it sound like they'd died peacefully. They'd been ravaged, their home desecrated. Sorrow gave way to anger, and that was enough to focus her thoughts. Val opened her eyes.

Once more, to be sure I've got this. She breathed in, letting the scent wash over her again . . .

. . . and froze.

"Someone else was here." Whoever it was hadn't bled much. That was why she'd missed it the first time around. It was about as noticeable as a drop of water in a glass of wine compared to Helen's and the professor's blood. Val let go of the chair back and started hunting around the room, playing hot-and-cold with the new scent. It wasn't anyone she knew, though if a student had been visiting when the Jackals attacked, that would explain it. But no one had come into Night Owls with rumors of a friend fleeing from the murderer, and no one had mentioned anyone else being missing.

She crashed about, digging through the wreckage. She was probably destroying all kinds of forensic evidence, but it didn't matter—they'd never be able to arrest the killers, anyway. Finally, she found the place where the scent was strongest. From beneath a heap of ruined books by the door, Val unearthed a backpack. It had seen better days—its zip-pers were held on with paper clips; the bottom was patched and frayed and patched again. The two strips of canvas that had passed for straps had torn away. Had a Jackal grabbed the third person by this, and they broke free because it was so damned old it fell apart?

She tugged open the zippers and dumped the contents out on the ground: a half-empty bottle of spring water, with crosses drawn in Sharpie on the label; a well-worn Bible with "Motel 6, Tulsa, Oklahoma" stamped on the cover; several silver coins, and a piece of notebook paper filled margin to margin with Latin text.

Anger turned to outrage as she recognized the last. She snarled as she crumpled the page, throttling it like she'd do to the backpack owner's neck if they ever met.

A member of the Brotherhood had been here. And they'd left the Clearwaters to die.

9

ELLY DIDN'T KNOW how long she'd been running. The sun had come up, so she *could* have stopped, but by then she wasn't running from the Creeps anymore. Instead, she was running from the awful things she'd seen.

She should have been inured to it by now. She and Father Value had done gruesome things in the name of eradicating evil, and she'd approached it almost clinically, every time. But this . . . this was beyond anything she'd imagined. They'd come howling through the woods, black shapes writhing against the night. It had seemed like hundreds of them; she'd heard their claws scrabbling at every window. But Henry had said there were only a few. He said one of them must have been something *else* before the turning, and he'd brought tricks with him through the veil.

He'd been so calm, telling her these things as he chalked the last runes on the doors and checked the salt wards lining the windows. Helen had sat on the floor in the middle of the upstairs library, weapons laid out around her like a deadly corona. She'd checked the stakes for sharpness and made sure the guns were loaded with silver bullets as if she'd been handling them all her life.

Then the Creeps had come, breaking the downstairs windows, tearing the doors off their hinges. They paid for it; Elly's ears still rang with their pained yelps from forcing their way past the wards. Two or three pups had made way for the others, whimpering as they rubbed out salt lines so their superiors could cross. The smell of charred fur had preceded them up the stairs. When the first one died due to the sigils at the top, Elly'd let herself think she and the Clearwaters might have a chance.

But the elder three weren't nearly as reckless. They'd roamed throughout the house, smashing and breaking things, taking their time. It sounded like an army of dogs down there, snarling and slavering. Helen's eyes had been wide as she clutched a baseball bat to her chest. The Creeps thrived on fear. Elly knew that. Henry knew that. But their own calm hadn't been enough to soothe Helen.

Maybe you had to be born to the Brotherhood. Maybe you simply couldn't learn to suppress terror in an hour.

It didn't matter. Helen broke first, fleeing the safety of the library and destroying God knew how many carefully laid wards. And what else could Henry have done? He followed his wife into the darkness, shouting her name.

It had been blood from there until the end.

Now, with a crisp autumn morning beaming sunlight down upon her, Elly's legs finally gave out. She wobbled over to a patch of recently raked lawn, wondering where she was but not really caring. As she sprawled beside a pile of leaves, she realized she needed to take stock. But she was so damned *tired*. It was shock, she knew, and she ought to fight it.

But what does it even matter now? Father Value's dead. The Clearwaters are dead. The Creeps will sniff out where the book went before long, and it was all for nothing.

She put her head between her knees and dragged in lungfuls of air. Father Value would never have allowed such a defeatist attitude. She could imagine him now: the disappointment in his eyes, the tilt of his head as he said, *You're stronger than that, Eleanor.*

She hated it when he called her Eleanor.

Okay. Okay. I have the clothes on my back. I have my wallet. She patted the lump in her back pocket to confirm. *I have ten dollars and a handful of quarters. I have Silver and Pointy.* The weapon in question was strapped along her forearm beneath her sweater. Its weight was a comfort.

That's where the list ran out. She had nothing left and nowhere to go.

That's not true.

Elly blinked. No. She couldn't. Not ever. *He said he never wanted to see either of us, ever again.* It was more than two years now since he'd left them, and she and Father Value had let him go. They'd hardly spoken his name in that time; she'd pretended the empty seat at the table was just another chair, and Father Value had thrown away the extra plate.

But they both knew where he'd ended up. It was just how they worked. Father Value knew someone who knew someone who knew this medium, and word got back to him. Not a lot, mostly that he was okay, that nothing had killed him yet, but Elly'd eaten those reports up like Halloween candy on All Saints' Day.

One night. I'll knock on his door, and if he even answers, I'll only stay one night. Maybe borrow a few dollars so I can get a change of clothes and a new backpack. Then he can forget all about me again.

Having a plan—no matter how shaky it was—made her feel better. Elly pushed herself to her feet and dug out her wallet. Her legs still felt like they'd been stuffed with jelly, but she could walk a little longer, then stick her thumb out if she had to. She slipped a piece of paper out of one of the credit card pockets and read the address for what must have been the millionth time since she'd sought it out last spring.

He'd walked away from them, but he hadn't gone far. Maybe because, as mismatched and screwed up as they all were, they were family.

Or maybe that's just where he was when he ran out of money.

It didn't matter; she'd find out either way soon enough. Elly set off down the road, composing apologies to her brother with every step.

SHE HAD TO hitch with three different people to get there. Cavale lived about twenty minutes from Edgewood, in Crow's Neck. In the early nineteen hundreds it had been a booming industrial town, but the Great Depression saw most of the textile mills closed, and Crow's Neck had never recovered. Eighty years had taken their toll: the abandoned factories had been overtaken by grass and trees, the glass long gone from their windows. Whole neighborhoods were nothing but boarded-up houses and lawns gone to seed.

It wasn't so much that Cavale lived in a bad part of town, as it was simply a place no one really wanted to go if they didn't have to. The last driver, though, *did* seem to think local thugs were going to steal his hubcaps while Elly got out of the car if he brought her all the way to Cavale's door. He'd insisted on looking up directions on his phone to ease his conscience. It had taken him longer to describe how she could walk to that address than it would have taken him to drive her the last couple of miles.

That was all right, though. Walking gave her time to prepare herself for the possibility that he might slam the door in her face. *Always have a contingency.* It was another of Father Value's lessons. In this case her contingency consisted of two steps:

1. Do not cry on Cavale's doorstep.
2. Practice her best panhandling face.

Hitching rides was fine, but rare were the drivers who'd offer to buy you lunch, too. She'd never stolen—well, never money or food; artifacts buried in churches were a different matter—and she wasn't sure she could get away with it if

she tried. Something about her made shop owners suspicious
even if she walked in waving cash around.

There were signs of life in most of the houses: children's
toys left out on this one's lawn, a few early Halloween dec-
orations in that one's windows, even a television blaring the
twelve o'clock news—but there was an air of abandonment
here, like the people who lived in these houses weren't really
there. This was the kind of place you went when you couldn't
afford better. She wondered how many families said, "When
money's not so tight, we'll get out of here," as their substitute
for grace at dinner.

Forty-five Greenwood Street loomed like something out
of a Lovecraftian dream: its chocolate brown paint was
peeling, half the posts were missing from the porch railing,
and the whole structure canted slightly off true. Cavale's
house was the last in the row of inhabited fixer-uppers.
Beyond his residence, the street was all collapsing houses
and broken pavement.

Where the other residents at least made token attempts
at keeping their lawns neat, Cavale had let his grow wild.
Dry, dead summer grass came up to Elly's knees as she cut
across the expanse, leaving a swath of beaten-down straw
in her wake. She might have thought Cavale had moved on
and abandoned the place if it weren't for the mail in the box
beside the door. The mailbox itself was holding on by one
last nail, its body at a crooked angle. She wondered if she
should take the letters out and have them ready to hand to
him when he answered. Then she wondered if that was
creepy. *"Hi, we haven't seen each other in over two years.
Now here I am with your gas bill in my hand. Look how
helpful I am!"*

Not to mention she'd have to follow that up with *"And
by the way, Father Value's dead. How's your year been?"*

Right. No mail.

It took three tries before she got up the courage to knock.
Then, her first rap on the door was more a pathetic tapping
than anything. Cavale would have to have been standing on
the other side, his ear to the wood, to even hear it. Her second

was better, louder. She thought it was the way a neighbor might knock, even: light and airy and oh-just-dropping-by.

She waited, fighting the urge to peek in the windows. Was he in there, keeping himself out of line of sight in case she looked in, hoping she'd go away?

She knocked again, putting more force behind the blows than she'd intended. From cheery neighbor to angry bill collector. *I wouldn't answer, if it were my house. Someone knocks like that, they're not here for anything nice.*

Well, she *wasn't* there for anything nice, now, was she? The man who'd raised them was dead and she'd landed herself in a world of trouble.

The silence stretched. She started feeling awfully exposed, out there on the porch. It was broad daylight, so it wasn't like there were any Creeps around, but her shoulders started itching all the same, like someone was watching her. *Probably just a neighbor, wondering who the strange girl is, hanging around the run-down shack.* She whipped around, looking for the telltale twitch of a curtain or a shadow ducking behind a corner, but she was alone.

Still not a peep from inside. *Maybe it's Cavale watching me. I should take the hint and go.*

She meant to leave, to head back to her swath of trampled grass and plow through it to the street. She toyed with the idea of writing "HI" in it like a crop circle gone wrong, for him to see. But as she turned to go down the steps, she felt the sob break.

No. No. Rule number one is DON'T CRY. She'd planned for this. It was more likely than any other outcome, really, so why did it hurt? He'd been the one to walk away from them, after all. He'd said he didn't want to see them again, and here she was ignoring that one simple request. Could she blame him for not answering? Or maybe he wasn't even home to ignore her, and here she was taking it personally. She stayed on the porch and leaned against the railing. A few gulping breaths didn't stop the fat tears rolling down her cheeks or the awful squeezing feeling in her chest. Everything pressed in on her, the world closing to a pinpoint.

Her knees buckled. Splinters dug into her palms as her grip on the railing twisted.

Then someone was speaking behind her: "Are you all right, miss?"

She squawked in surprise as she turned, flopping over onto her butt instead of rising smoothly to her feet like she'd meant to.

The man before her in the doorway was sleep bedraggled. His hair was mussed and he was blinking against the brightness. *He's let his hair grow out since he left.* Then his eyes went wide. "*Elly?* Jesus fuck, is it you?"

He was there, then, on his knees next to her on the porch, pulling her into his arms. She couldn't answer, only nod miserably as she lost the struggle with a fresh spate of tears.

"Shhh, it's all right. It's all right." He stroked her hair and murmured to her, the way he'd done when they were little and she'd woken in the dark from a nightmare. Father Value had never been good with comforting either of them, but Cavale had always made her feel better, made her feel safe.

She clung to him now, smelling soap and shampoo and laundry detergent, and was horrified at how she must seem to him. The Clearwaters had let her shower, but that was sometime yesterday, before the Creeps had come. She hadn't changed her clothes in two days, and now that she was smearing tears and snot across Cavale's clean white tee shirt, she realized there were still flecks of dried blood beneath her fingernails.

"Sorry. I'm sorry, I'm kind of a mess." She pulled back, swiping at her nose and eyes with the cuffs of her sweater like a little kid.

Cavale let her have her space, but kept one hand on her shoulder. "You look like hell." He gave her half a grin, but his sky blue eyes were filled with concern. And . . . were those tears he was blinking back? "Why don't you come in and we'll talk?"

"Are . . . are you sure? I know you said you didn't want to see us again, but—"

He cut her off, waving away the thought. "I'm sure." He stood up and held out a hand to pull her to her feet. Now that she wasn't snivelling anymore, or at least, not *as much*, they stood together awkwardly.

The physical affection had stopped sometime after puberty hit, when Father Value had made them start sleeping in separate rooms and had held separate stumbling, embarrassing talks with each of them. There'd never been anything untoward between them, and she and Cavale had never spoken about it—even when they'd still snuck into one another's rooms late at night to talk—but sometime ten years ago, they'd stopped touching each other at all. It was more for Father Value's peace of mind than anything—hell, Elly'd been disturbed by the incestuous twins in *Flowers in the Attic* when she was *twelve*.

But even with Father Value gone, it felt somehow wrong for them to touch any more than they already had.

Cavale stepped back. He ran a hand along his jaw; his palm on the stubble sounded like he was rubbing sandpaper over his skin. "Christ, Elly, I've missed you so much."

"I've missed you, too," she said, her voice tiny. *Oh God, no more crying.* Then her belly growled, saving her.

This time Cavale's grin reached his eyes. "What would you say to burgers and tater tots?" He stepped into the front hall and turned to wink at her. "I'll give you a hint: you should probably say yes, since it's all I have right now."

"Then I'll say *hell* yes." She made one more pass at her eyes with her sleeve and followed him inside.

🐎 10 🐎

THE REST OF their search had yielded nothing. Val had, for the second day running, pushed until it was nearly dawn. She might still have been there, tucked away in the back of a closet somewhere to hide from the sun, if Chaz hadn't pointed out that the police would be back and she'd be yet another corpse on the pile. Unless, that was, they didn't zip up the body bag all the way before they took her out of the house.

Then she'd just be fucked.

She'd taken the backpack with her, to get good and familiar with its owner's scent. A round of sniffing outside the Clearwaters' house as the dawn loomed hadn't told her which way the Brotherhood's coward had gone—the Jackals' reek still covered up any human scents. Chaz, by that time, had been tugging on her arm as he cast anxious glances at the nearby houses. People would be getting up for work soon, if they weren't already, and they'd have another world of trouble on their hands if they were spotted outside by a rubbernecking neighbor.

At home, Val had curled around the backpack before

dropping into her dreamless sleep. She woke that night to the smell of myrrh. It took her a few minutes to place it—she hadn't set foot in a church in decades—but every breath brought to mind memories of a hard wooden pew and the clanking of the thurible as the priest passed by. She remembered Father Pelham swinging it like a pendulum as the smoke curled out of the holes. When she was six, she'd been at the edge of the pew and sucked in a lungful of the incense. She'd had such a coughing fit as the bitter, sharp smoke made its way down her throat that her mother had ushered her out of the service.

As consciousness flooded in, the smell of it filled her nostrils. It wasn't as acrid as that long-ago incense had been, but it was close. Val sat up, still holding the backpack. Sometime during the day, she'd dug her hand into the front pocket, and now she realized she was clutching at something inside. When she rubbed her fingers together, they felt oily. She switched on the bedside lamp as she pulled her other hand out. Nestled in her palm was a lump of burnt umber resin. *There it is.*

It wasn't much to go on, but it was *something.* Different branches of the Brotherhood had different rituals. One lump of myrrh didn't mean much—it might simply be something the backpack's owner used as a salve—but when she had no other leads, she'd take it. In Sacramento, they'd anointed themselves with rosewater before a Hunt and cleansed their hands with lavender after. Myrrh meant an older sect, more orthodox. Those, she knew, were a dying breed.

She set the resin down on her nightstand and relinquished her hold on the backpack. There was work to be done, but first she wanted to wash the stink of myrrh and Jackal out of her skin.

Chaz was behind the register when Val got to Night Owls at eight. Pale purple smudges lurked beneath his eyes. The titan-sized cup of coffee beside him was nearly empty, and when Val peeked into the wastebasket, she saw two others that he'd already demolished.

"How are you not vibrating and twitching from all that?"

The sisters next door made their coffee strong enough to walk on its own most days, but Chaz' heartbeat wasn't even elevated.

"I seem to have built up an immunity."

"Or you're just that exhausted. Did Justin come in? He and I can handle it here. You should go home and sleep."

"He's in the back, taking his break. And I caught a nap this morning. I'm fine." He took another swig of coffee and offered her a toothy grin. "I left the newspapers on your desk. Nothing in there that we didn't know already, but I figured you might want a look. I tried getting a copy of the police report, but no luck."

"Well, you're not quite as charming when you're all rumpled." She took the key to the rare books room from its hook. Her own had flakes of skin and ichor stuck to it from where it had touched the Jackal-woman's neck. Val didn't want to touch it any more than she had to. "I'm going to go spend some time with that damned thing, see if anything jumps out at me. Try not to drink so much of that your heart explodes, okay?"

"You got it."

She headed to the rare books room, smiling a little at the sign tacked to the door in Chaz' scrawl: *Room reserved for private research. Please pardon the inconvenience.* He'd known she wouldn't want anyone going in there today. The smile faded as she entered and was hit with a waft of stale Jackal scent. The book sat on the desk, where she'd placed it last night after the three had left. Why hadn't they taken it with them? Surely the other few hundred pages were useful to them, even if a few were missing. Val slid into the chair and stared at the book.

It seemed . . . *less* somehow. The air of malevolence that had emanated from it last night was, if not entirely gone, then certainly diminished. Tonight, it was just an old book on an old desk. She could have tucked it into any empty space on the shelves in that room and searching eyes would have skipped right over it. So what had changed?

The cover was cool beneath her fingers. She looked at

the box of cotton gloves, but decided against wearing any. Magic was often tactile to some degree, especially when an object had been imbued with it. Val was no sorcerer—if this thing was warded, or if spells were nestled between the lines of text, she wouldn't know what they were by touch. Still, she might be able to tell if something had been broken. She'd heard stories of casters hexing their spell books so that if the wrong person opened it, all the letters jumbled up and became so much gibberish. She'd even seen someone perform the trick once, changing a pocket volume of Shakespeare's sonnets into two hundred pages of *lorem ipsum dolor sit amet*. Had this happened here?

She steeled herself and opened the cover. Just because the Jackal bitch had opened it without repercussion didn't mean there wasn't something nasty waiting to give her a jolt. And yet . . . nothing. The parchment felt brittle, like dried onionskin, but it was simply parchment. The ink had faded to brown, but it was definitely ink, not blood. The book felt, well, *dead*.

Val peered at the Jackals' runes, trying to make sense of them. Some, she almost knew; others she recognized from seeing them in the nests. But her ability to actually read this book was about as strong as someone who'd learned Spanish from *Sesame Street* trying to read *Don Quixote* in its original form.

She set about looking for patterns instead, seeking out runes that appeared in the same order across several pages. She found a few, but all she got for her troubles was a full sheet of notebook paper and the start of a headache.

A soft knock came on the door. Chaz poked his head in and shook a small coffee at her. The liquid sloshed inside. Hazelnut tonight. "Want a sniff?"

Val pointed at him. "Heart. Exploding. Didn't we talk about this half an hour ago?"

"I didn't say I'd listen. And you've been in here three hours. It's almost eleven." He stepped inside and closed the door. Setting the coffee down in front of her was a poorly disguised cover for a peek at her notes. "Anything we can use?"

She shook her head. "Not unless there's a Jackal-to-English translator on the Internet." The warmth of the coffee cup felt good on her palms. "There's got to be *something*, at least the reason she left it behind. But hell if I can see it."

Chaz reached a tentative hand for the book "May I?"

She hesitated a moment, then smiled. The professor would have opened it up before he sent it along with Justin, and she'd suspected Justin of opening it up last night. If it was warded against humans, those had been broken already. Plus, Chaz was scary good at word puzzles, snagging new books of them as they came in and completing them on his break. Maybe he'd see something she hadn't: a repetition, a symbol, some sort of Rosetta stone buried in the text. Val pulled a pair of gloves from the box and passed them to Chaz before she handed over the book. Her dead skin might not leave oils on the pages, but Chaz' would.

Plus it never hurt to have an extra layer of precaution between him and the page in case there *was* any lingering magic.

There weren't any other chairs in the room, so Chaz plunked himself down on the floor, the book in his lap. He donned the gloves and began turning pages. After a few minutes, he glanced up. "You can start breathing again anytime now. I'm not getting turned into a pillar of salt. And it's really starting to freak me out."

Val hadn't even realized she'd stopped, but he was right—her lungs itched and her chest felt heavy. Breathing was still a necessity if she wanted to talk, but her kind didn't need to do it to carry oxygen around their bodies anymore. She inhaled and exhaled a few times for Chaz' benefit. He shook his head and went back to scrutinizing the book.

It grew so quiet in the room, Val could hear the murmur of conversations in the store. The register hummed steadily along every few minutes—not the busiest night, though she knew she should go out and relieve Justin soon. Her hovering wasn't going to grant Chaz any sudden insights.

As if thinking about him had summoned him, Justin's steps came padding up the aisle. He had a timid gait, like he was afraid walking past someone might disturb them. His knock was equally soft. Val opened the door and winced. Chaz might look like shit from his lack of sleep, but Justin looked ten times worse. His eyes were red rimmed, his nose rubbed raw.

"I'm sorry, Justin. I'm coming out now. Chaz can—"

He spoke over her. "It's okay, I just need help with a special order. Will you come take it? Please?"

The tremor in his voice gave her pause. It wasn't sorrow. She peered at him, searching beyond the grief and exhaustion. His eyes were wide, nostrils flaring. His fingers twisted together, apart, together. A jolt went through her—this was *fear.*

Val's head snapped up. *Are they back? It hasn't been two days. Did they come to check up on us?* But no, if the Jackals were here, she'd have smelled them. The only person up at the front of the store right now was a forty-ish woman in an expensive-looking tracksuit—the kind made more for fashion than working out—jangling her keys and glaring daggers of irritation at Val and Justin.

Val squeezed Justin's shoulder as she passed by him. "I've got this. You go take five, splash some water on your face." She plastered on a smile and went to help the woman.

"Honestly," said the woman, raising her voice for the other customers' benefit. "I don't know what your employee is playing at, but wasting my time isn't funny. I have kids I need to get home to, and he's sitting there doodling rather than taking down my information. I was very tempted to just walk out of here and order my book online."

Doodling? That wasn't like Justin at all. "I'm very sorry, ma'am, I'll speak with him. And I'm happy to offer you a twenty percent discount for the inconvenience."

The woman grunted. "That will do, I suppose."

Val smiled. "If I could just take your name and phone number?" She pulled a blank special order card from the stack. They took orders by hand and entered them into the computer at the end of the night. It was probably less efficient than entering them directly into the computer, but Val believed it made them focus on the customer, not the screen.

The woman recited her information, and Val jotted down the book's title and ISBN. Justin had at least gone as far as looking it up and confirming its availability. "We should have it in two days. We'll call when it comes in and you can pick it up next time you're nearby."

"Well. Thank you. And I do hope you'll talk to that boy. Maybe if he didn't spend so much time partying, he'd be focused on his job."

Val blinked. "Partying?"

"Surely you saw his eyes. They're bloodshot. He's either hungover or strung out, miss, and that's only going to cost *you* in the end."

You bitch. Maybe she didn't need to breathe, but Val took a deep breath anyway before she answered. Yelling at customers wasn't good business. "Ma'am, you might not be from Edgewood, so maybe you haven't heard, but we had a murder in town last night. That young man who was helping you was close to one of the victims. He hasn't been drinking; he's been grieving. I think, if it's all right with you, I'll cut him some slack."

Spots of color rose in the woman's cheeks. "Oh. Oh my. I'd heard, about . . . a professor, wasn't it? From the college?"

"And his wife. They were good friends of ours."

She looked down at her shoes. "I'm . . . I'm terribly sorry, miss. I should have thought."

"It's all right. Why don't you head on home to your kids. We'll take care of this order for you."

The woman scurried out, her shoulders hunched. Val wondered if she'd show up when the book came in.

As she tucked the card in with the evening's other orders, she glanced around the register. The woman had said Justin was doodling, but the scratch pads were all blank. Justin knew better than to do homework up here, and even if he'd decided to break that rule, she didn't see any textbooks stashed away. She looked in the trash can, to see if he'd tossed anything out.

In the bin were three special order cards, two torn in half, one crumpled, all of them covered not in doodles, but in runes.

Just like the ones in the Jackals' book.

CHAZ PUT THE book aside reluctantly when Val asked him to watch the front of the store, but one look at the tattered special order card she held up stopped his grumbling. "*Justin* knows how to read it?"

"That's what I'm going to find out."

"You don't think he's, like, in league with them, do you?" Even as he said it, he was shaking his head. "No, that makes no sense. He's a good kid."

"And he would've just brought the damned thing straight to them." She'd already run through the possibility in her head and dismissed it. Unless he was an amazing actor, Justin's reaction to the Clearwaters' deaths was real. Something like that, if you knew who did it—especially if they'd screwed you over—you got angry. Justin was just plain heartbroken. "I'll tell you what I find out."

Chaz grabbed an armload of books that needed shelving. "Here if you need me."

Val stepped over to the break room and punched the code to unlock the door. She opened it slowly, not wanting to startle Justin. *Or, if on the off chance he's had us totally snowed and is waiting on the other side with a stake, I want to be able to get away.*

But he wasn't waiting with an implement of doom. He sat at the supervisor's desk, his head in his hands. When the door creaked open, he flinched.

Val dragged a chair over next to him and lowered herself into it. "You want to talk about it?"

"I don't even know what it *is*." He raised his head at last and looked at her pleadingly. "I can't make it *stop*."

"Tell me what's happening. When it started." She kept

her tone low and neutral, putting a tiny bit of Command into the words—more to calm him than drag words out of him. She took his paper cup and refilled it from the watercooler next to the desk.

He took a sip and sighed. "It started this morning. I tried taking notes in my Milton class and it all came out . . . weird. Every time I've gone to write something down, it's just these scribbles. I thought." His tongue snaked out to wet his lips. "I thought maybe I'd hit my head, or, I don't know." Another sip. This time when he looked up, he seemed embarrassed. "I spent the afternoon googling brain tumors and psychotic breaks."

"I think we can rule those things out, don't you?" She set the card in front of him. "You've seen that writing before."

Justin's cheeks went as red as his eyes, but he powered on through the guilt. "That's what I mean. I saw the weird writing in the last thing Professor Clearwater gave me, and the next day I'm copying it. Isn't that . . . Wouldn't that signal that I'm having some sort of episode?"

"I don't think so."

He blinked at her. "What, then?"

"You're not going to like this very much. I don't even know if you're going to believe it."

"Hey, if it means I don't have a tumor . . ." A tiny laugh escaped him, born more of anxiety than mirth.

"I think when you opened that book, or when you read certain pages, you triggered something. A spell, a ward, I don't know what, exactly. But whatever it is, it's hanging out in your head now." The dubious look on his face made her words tumble out faster. "I know how it sounds. And if you want to go and get your head x-rayed, I'll drive you right now. But they're not going to find anything."

"Magic, Val? That's . . ." He spread his hands, not quite ready to tell his boss what he thought of that sort of thing.

"I know. But tell me, did you have any other symptoms of what you researched?"

"Nnnnooo." There was something else keeping him from getting up and walking out on this conversation. She could see it in his hesitation, in the way his eyes darted around, but always came back to hers. How they held a little steadier each time.

"What aren't you telling me?" No Command, not now. She could make him see things her way, but it was better if Justin came around to it on his own.

"I heard things about their house. The crime scene. There are all kinds of rumors on campus, about a cult or a ritual killing." His voice broke. Val reached out to comfort him, but he waved her off. "You know what he said to me when he gave me the book? The very last thing he'd ever tell me?" He rubbed at the back of his neck. "He said, 'Trust Valerie.' And he quoted Shakespeare at me."

"Shakespeare?"

"From *The Tempest*: 'The hour's now come. The very minute bids thee ope thine ear. Obey and be attentive.' I think maybe he meant . . . Maybe he meant we'd be having a conversation like this. Or maybe I'm in denial and you're an asshole for indulging it, but . . ." He shrugged at her. "But let's go with the former for now, huh?"

"We'll figure it out, Justin. I promise."

They sat quietly for a few minutes, staring at the runes scrawled on the card. Finally, Justin cleared his throat. "So do you, y'know . . . have any ideas how to make it stop?"

"I have a friend who might." *Chaz is going to hate this.* But it was for Justin, and as much as he'd balk at her plan, he liked the kid. It would work out. It would have to.

⤟ 11 ⤠

CHAZ *REALLY* DIDN'T like it. The three of them stood in the back room, the last customers gone, the lights in the front of the store switched off. Justin had caught a nap on the tattered old couch that served as the break area, but it didn't look like the rest had done him much good. He sat, his forearms on his knees and hands dangling, as he watched Val and Chaz argue. From the resigned look on his face, Chaz got the sense he'd seen his parents argue like this on a regular basis.

"Aw, c'mon Val. *Him?*" It was the third time Chaz had asked that question. He stood leaning against the wall with his arms folded, scowling at her.

"What's wrong with Cavale?"

"That dude's a bell tower and a sniper rifle waiting to happen."

Val pressed her fingers to her temples. "That's not fair. He's . . . eccentric, but—"

" 'Eccentric' is what the neighbors call serial killers after the bodies are found. He's a barrel of crazy."

Chaz and Cavale had a mutual dislike for one another. The first time they'd met—the first *second*—each had decided the other was fundamentally flawed. Cavale thought Chaz was a shiftless prick; Chaz had several variations on "batshit crazy" he liked to drag out whenever Cavale's name was mentioned.

Most of the time, Val tried not to bring one up in front of the other. Chaz could count on one hand how many times they'd been face-to-face over the last couple of years. It worked out better that way.

"Look, you don't have to come with," she said. "Justin and I will be fine."

Chaz' scowl deepened. "No. I'm coming. I'm not letting him poke about in Justin's head unsupervised."

Justin straightened up, eyes wide. "Poke about in my . . . ? Val?"

The glare she gave Chaz could have melted stone. "He's not going to do anything to you unless you give him permission, and it's certainly not going to involve actual poking."

Chaz snorted. "Remind her she said that when he starts looking for blood to put on his altar."

"Chaz? A moment?" Holding the door open, Val jerked her head toward the darkened, empty store.

Oops. Too far. He heaved a theatrical sigh as he unfolded himself and trudged past her. When they got out of Justin's earshot, halfway down the romance section, he jumped in before Val could speak. "Look. I know you're trying to help him. But this is just asking for trouble. There has to be another way to do this that doesn't involve"—he opened his mouth to call Cavale another name, but stopped himself when Val raised a brow—"him."

"I'm open to suggestions. How many warlocks do you have on speed dial?" Val waited, watching Chaz' face in the dim light as his argument fell apart. "That's about what I thought. We have less than two days now, and Cavale's our best hope. Are you going to fight me on this, or can we move along?"

He almost dropped it. His shoulders slumped; his gaze hit the floor. Then he spoke, his voice just barely audible: "You could still put in a call to Boston."

The palm of her hand made a flat crack as it hit the shelf beside her. Down the row, several paperbacks tumbled to the ground. "You want to repeat that?"

Chaz flinched, but he lifted his eyes to hers. "They could send help. Or protect him."

She took several slow breaths, the way she did when she was trying to keep herself from yelling. "I can't even believe you'd suggest that after the last time."

A few years back, Val had sought the help of one of the colonies in Boston when an overzealous monster hunter had come passing through Edgewood and twigged onto her true nature. One of the women the *Stregoi* had sent down had taken a liking to Chaz and tried claiming him as part of the fee. Stealing another vampire's thrall by offering them a sweeter offer was considered rude. *Commanding* someone else's and mucking about with their free will was expressly forbidden.

A shudder coursed its way through Chaz as he remembered, but sometimes, you had to sack up. This was one of those times, even if Val didn't want to see it. *It's my job to make her see it.* "Two people are dead, Val. And if Cavale can't get this thing out of Justin, who knows what the Jackals will do if they find out it's in his head. That's a little more important than your pride."

He'd left out the part about his own freedom. Provoking her anger would work better if he didn't drag guilt into the mix.

Unfortunately for Chaz' argument, those three awful days were inextricably linked to her feelings on the Boston colonies. "I've got this under control." She laid a hand on his right arm. "Give me another day. If it's not fixed by the time we close tomorrow night, I'll call them. Okay?"

"Promise me."

"I promise."

He looked at her hand for a long moment. Beneath her palm, covered by his sleeve, were the fading twin scars from the *Stregoi* woman's fangs. It was no accident Val had touched him there, and they both knew it. "All right. Fine. One day." He pulled away from her and moved toward the back room. "Let's go pay the nutjob a visit and get this over with."

CHAZ SOMETIMES JOKED about Cavale living in the creepy old house on a hill, but the truth was, it was the best Cavale could afford. He was barely twenty-five, but he'd raised enough cash for a down payment in less than six months, acting as a sort of supernatural odd jobs man. *Gotta hand it to him,* Chaz thought as they turned onto Cavale's street, *he owns his own place. I still live in the same shitty apartment I got after college.*

During the day, Cavale's official, taxpaying job was as a tarot reader at a shop that sold everything from healing crystals to ritual robes. At night, though . . . If you needed it done, Cavale could take care of it: evicting poltergeists, cleansing psychically tainted houses, finding out why Uncle George had been slamming that door in the dead of night ever since he died. Or whether it was really Uncle George doing it at all.

Chaz and Val had met him a couple of years back, when the succubi had hired him to come ward their house. They'd brought him in to Night Owls, and Val had liked him from the start. He was often somber and, Chaz suspected, lonely, but Chaz had to admit he was a bright kid, too. Bright enough, in fact, that if she hadn't had one already, Chaz had a sneaking feeling Val might have tried enticing Cavale to be her Renfield.

It was likely part of the reason he disliked Cavale so vehemently, but he'd never say that aloud.

As Chaz pulled into the driveway, Justin—who had been curled up in the backseat trying to catch another nap on the short ride to Crow's Neck—sucked in a nervous breath. "If no one's home, maybe we should come back tomorrow."

"He's home." Val turned around and offered her best reassuring smile. "I called before we left."

Justin smiled back. It just made him look like he was

about to vomit. Chaz couldn't really begrudge him his apprehension—first he'd contracted an unexplained mental malady on the heels of his mentor's brutal murder, and now he was being whisked off in the dead of night to a decrepit house in a bad neighborhood so someone he'd never met could attempt a cure. Chaz' remarks from earlier probably weren't helping. *I'll apologize later.*

Chaz killed the engine and they all got out. Justin stuck close behind them, nearly climbing into Chaz' jacket. As they ascended the porch steps, a sliver of light sliced down the edge of the window closest to the door. *Peeking out through the curtains.*

The rattle of locks being undone followed—doorknob, dead bolt, chain—and the front door swung open, bathing them all in warm golden light. A long, trim figure stood in the doorway, silhouetted by the glow from inside. Chaz muttered something about theatrics, earning an elbow to the side from Val.

Cavale held his pose as they stepped onto the porch, probably to annoy Chaz even further. He folded his arms as he eyed Justin. "So I hear you have something hitching a ride in your head, huh?"

Justin looked to Val before he shrugged. "I, um. I guess?"

Cavale nodded, a sheaf of pale brown hair falling into his eyes. He must have been growing it out recently; the last time Chaz had seen him it had looked almost scruffy. Now it fell more naturally, just shy of ponytail length. "Well, we'll get you sorted." He smiled at Val and Chaz. "Why don't you guys come on in? I've got a pot of coffee on."

Chaz didn't respond. He walked in past Cavale and waited for Justin to join him. The two of them peered around, Chaz with mild disdain, Justin goggling at the bunches of herbs hung up to dry along the walls and the runes painted around every entryway. He reached up to touch one of the symbols but stopped at a shake of the head from Chaz.

Val smiled as she stepped inside. "Justin was worried we'd woken you up."

"Do these look like my pjs?" He wore a pair of faded

blue jeans and a black button-down shirt. About the only concession to an evening at home were his sock-clad feet.

Chaz couldn't resist. "They do look a little slept in."

A lazy smile quirked at his lips as he gave Chaz a once-over. "At least they're from this decade."

"Enough." Val stepped between them. "Can you two please zip up so we can get back to the problem at hand?"

They both had the grace to look embarrassed. Cavale swept an arm toward the back of the house. "You're right. I've got some things set up in the kitchen, if you want to get started." He glanced at Chaz. "Truce?"

He was tempted to drag the moment out, make Cavale work for it a bit. The near-instant acquiescing was nothing more than ass-kissing. Val had to know that. *Still, if that's how he wants to play this . . .* Chaz stuck out his hand, glancing sideways to be sure Val was watching how *utterly reasonable* he was being.

But she wasn't watching him. She stood, sniffing the air, nostrils flaring. When she'd smelled the Jackals last night, she'd looked terrified. It wasn't terror contorting her features now, though.

It was rage.

Cavale cocked his head at her as she sniffed the air. "Val? What's wr— VAL!"

But Val had already taken off down the hallway.

SHE BARRELED THROUGH the sitting room and the empty kitchen, ignoring the confused shouts of the men behind her. The scent led her to the back stairway, where she went up the creaky steps three at a time. Her fangs and claws were out before she gained the top. The pain of their emergence barely registered: the whole of her awareness was focused on her prey.

Why would Cavale be harboring him? Did he come here looking for protection but didn't say why? She shoved the questions aside. They could get sorted later. After she'd had words with the son of a bitch. After she'd inflicted some pain.

Whoever Cavale's guest was, he had to know she was coming from the racket she was making as she pounded down the upstairs hall. That was okay; Val wanted a fight.

No light came from beneath the guest bedroom door, but that was where the scent of myrrh was strongest. *If he thinks he'll have the advantage, he's going to be surprised.* She stood outside a heartbeat longer, letting the thrill of the hunt wash over her. Whoever was in there wasn't afraid; Val couldn't hear any ragged breathing or frantic crashing about.

Three sets of footsteps thundered up the stairs. Chaz and Cavale were calling for her to *hold on, slow down, wait.*

Val was done waiting. She strode forward and planted her foot halfway up the door. Splinters flew as the old wood shattered. As Val stepped inside, she caught sight of the room's inhabitant diving off to the right. The figure stayed low, balancing on the balls of his—no, *her*—feet, ready to move. In this small space, Val could smell the faint odor of girl-sweat.

The Brotherhood's woman rolled to the right, coming up on her knees. Knowing it was a female drove Val's anger to new heights. If she was a Sister—a full-fledged, been-through-the-rites *Sister . . . It would explain the myrrh.* The older sects of the Brotherhood used myrrh for anointing before attacking a Jackals' nest, but the Sisters used it during the battle itself, laying healing hands on the injured so they could keep fighting.

She could have saved them. Val bared her teeth.

"Come on, then!" the woman shouted as she lurched to her feet.

The words worked like a starter pistol: Val charged forward, a snarl ripping the air as she closed the distance between them. The woman had set her feet apart to brace herself for the collision, but Val caught her by the forearms and drove her backward easily. The woman's feet left the ground as Val let momentum carry them both along. She'd been hoping for some gibbering—or at least a sputtered, too-late apology—but the woman remained stubbornly silent.

A framed poem hung on the wall, a gift to Cavale from

one of the succubi; distantly, Val recognized the spiky handwriting. There was a flat, dull crack as the Sister's head smacked into it, spiderwebbing the glass. The woman grunted—*sound at last!* The smell of her blood filled Val's nostrils.

Good. Let her bleed like she should have last night. Images of the destroyed library and the dark smears of the Clearwaters' blood flashed in Val's mind. "You let them die!" she shouted. "You *let* them, you—" She took her right hand off the Sister's arm and closed her clawed fingers around her throat.

Even lifted up and pinned against the wall, Val was taller than the Sister. She leaned down before she started to squeeze, wanting to look in the woman's eyes, wanting to see remorse in them, or guilt, sorrow, *anything.* They were all there—fear, too, even though Val still couldn't smell it on her. But there was something missing. It took Val a moment to place it: the Sisters she'd met had had a wisdom to their gaze, a serenity gained through their training.

This woman was simply afraid. Val pulled back an inch or two, her grip already loosening. *No crow's-feet, no laugh lines, hardly even a crease to her brow.* The woman's skin was smooth except for a smattering of acne on her chin.

She's just a kid.

Bright pain bloomed in her stomach.

Before she could drop the girl, light flooded the room. Two sets of hands took hold of Val, hauling her back: Cavale on her right, Chaz on her left. She was too stunned to resist when Chaz snaked his left arm up under her own; she felt pressure on the back of her neck as he locked his grip into some sort of quarter nelson.

Everyone was shouting except Chaz, who whispered in her ear: "I'm asking you nicely not to yank my arms out of their sockets while we sort this out. Deal?"

Val looked at the mousy girl leaning against the wall. *Not nearly old enough to be a full Sister, not by at least a decade.* "Just a kid," she murmured, slumping against Chaz. "Just a fucking kid."

In her peripheral vision Cavale nodded at Chaz, then crossed the room to fuss over the girl. She had dark hair that fell to about her chin. The ends were ragged, like she'd cut them herself with a dull pair of scissors. She kept darting glances at Val while Cavale's fingers fluttered over the back of her head and came back bloody.

"Elly? You okay?" He sounded shaken, and with good cause. Val could have torn out her throat and had time to lick her fingers clean before they'd arrived in the room.

The girl crooked a smile. "I'm fine. Just a cut." She swatted him away. "Cavale, get *off*. I'm okay. *She's* not." In the hand she gestured with was a wicked metal spike. Streaks of Val's blood still were dripping from it.

That was when Justin, apparently realizing the violence was over, came around in front of Val. His eyes widened as he stared at her middle. Val glanced down, remembering the flare of pain before they'd yanked her off the girl. The spike had left a silver-dollar-sized hole in her white cotton shirt; the fabric was slowly turning red as blood seeped from the wound. Val marveled at it for a moment. It should have closed by now.

Unless . . .

That spike must be silver. This thing's going to take forever to close.

She thought I was a Jackal.

"Jesus Christ!" Justin whipped his cell phone out of his pocket. "What's the address here? She needs an ambulance. Chaz, let her go. It can't be good to stretch the wound."

Cavale, Chaz, and Val shouted *"No!"* together, their voices echoing off the walls in the tiny room.

Cavale crossed over to Justin—who stood gaping at them all like they'd lost their minds—and snatched the phone from him before he could finish dialing. "Val's going to be okay."

Justin blinked. "Your friend *stabbed* her. In the *stomach*. If she punctured anything, it'll go septic or something." He held out his hand. "Give me my phone."

"Justin." Val offered him a tight-lipped smile despite the

dull throbbing in her gut. Now that the fight was over, her body was letting her know that, *By the way, this fucking hurts.* She shrugged in Chaz' grasp, testing his hold. He got the message and let her go so she could spread her arms—*ta-da.* "I'm okay. No need for nine-one-one."

Justin's mouth opened and closed, fishlike, as his glance darted around the room. When at last it came back to Val, he did a double take. "Val? Your, uh. Teeth. And, um." His gaze drifted down, first to her still-seeping wound, then to her hands. Her gnarled, claw-tipped fingers. "Your . . . You have . . . What . . . ?" He looked like he might pass out.

Val sighed. This wasn't how she'd wanted confession time to go. "It's fine, Justin. Really. We'll explain." He nodded dimly, his lips trying to form questions. He'd gone paler than Val imagined she must be right now.

Chaz stepped around so he could get a look at the wound. He grunted in annoyance. Cavale held the phone out of Justin's reach, not that he was trying for it anymore.

The girl—*Elly*—stopped watching Justin and followed Chaz' gaze. Her mouth twisted and her brow furrowed, like she was doing a crossword puzzle and trying to remember a word. After a moment, understanding dawned. "What are you?" she asked, though the way her eyes focused on Val's lips—or, more specifically, the tips of her fangs peeking out from under them—said she'd figured it out.

Val looked at Justin for a long moment before she addressed Elly. *I was hoping we wouldn't have to have this talk just yet.* The professor would have had something to say about that, involving barn doors and escaped horses. "You used the wrong kind of stake, kid. Silver hurts like a bitch, but it won't kill me."

"You're a vampire, then." She might as well have said, "You're a mailman, then," for the lack of surprise in her tone.

"Guilty as charged." They exchanged cautious smiles. *I might like this girl, after all.*

There was a thud as Justin tried sitting on the bed and missed.

12

CAVALE HERDED THEM all down to the kitchen to talk. He poured generous cups of coffee into mismatched mugs, and set a bottle of whiskey down in the middle of the round table for anyone who felt they needed some reinforcement.

Elly couldn't help but marvel at how *normal* Cavale seemed. He owned a house. He did laundry in a washer-dryer unit in the basement rather than skulking into an all-night Laundromat at three a.m. and keeping watch while the clothes tumbled around. He had honest-to-god dishes, not a glorified mess kit. Sure, the place was warded all to hell, and there were some signs of his old life with her and Father Valuc in his mannerisms, but still. After he'd left them, he'd gone on to have as close to a normal life as their kind could. He'd even made *friends*. Granted, the woman was a vampire, but they sat beside one another without clutching at hidden weapons under the table. Cavale even turned his back on Val now and then.

Elly had squeezed herself into the corner, so *her* back was to the wall.

Justin had taken the revelation pretty well, for someone

who'd lived his life blissfully unaware of their dark little niche. Since they'd picked him up off the guest room floor, he seemed to be taking a *This is fucked-up, but I'll just go with it* approach. Now and then he'd look around, startled by something he saw—a gris-gris bag on the windowsill, jars and bottles of ingredients for spell work, an actual book of spells left open on a table—mutter "*weird*" under his breath, and return to the spooked-but-cheerful demeanor he'd apparently decided was most appropriate for the situation. He sat next to her now, cradling his coffee cup and eyeing the whiskey bottle. So far no one had added anything but cream and sugar to their mugs.

The blond man, Chaz, sat on Val's other side, scowling through her at Cavale. He'd insisted on Cavale breaking out the first aid kit and had dressed the puncture wound Silver and Pointy had left in Val. It wasn't going to make it close any faster, but at least it stopped the slow leak.

Val herself was looking pretty pale. Well, she'd been pale to start, but now her skin had taken on an ashen tone. Elly had been surprised when Cavale had set a cup of coffee down in front of her; vampires couldn't digest food and drink. Father Value hadn't taught them as much about vampires as he did about Creeps, but that much, Elly knew. Val didn't take a single sip, though. She just curled her fingers around the mug and sniffed at it while they talked.

Vampires were weird.

They sat in awkward silence for a while, the only sounds the clinking of spoons against mugs and the rattling motor of Cavale's ancient fridge. Elly wondered if she ought to say anything to kick off the conversation, but "I'm sorry your friend died" seemed inadequate, and she was already on the vampire's bad side. Some hornets' nests were best left unpoked.

Finally, Val set her mug down and cleared her throat. "I don't have a lot of time left tonight, so here's what I need to know. First, why was a member of the Brotherhood—no matter how green—at the Clearwaters'? I'm guessing it had something to do with the book Henry had Justin bring to me, but why bring it to *him*?"

Elly tried not to bristle at being called green. She'd spent her *life* with Father Value. She'd hunted Creeps with him. She could do spells and wards and runework better than most people her age could do math homework. A slew of rebuttals rose to her lips, but Val wasn't done.

"Second, why are you *here*, with Cavale? Third"—here, she turned to Cavale—"how do we get this thing out of Justin's head?" She settled back into her chair and picked up the mug once more. She looked at Elly. "You start."

Elly wasn't used to being hit with such a barrage of questions from anyone other than Father Value. The questions were straightforward enough, but still she froze. Father Value's prohibition about talking about the Brotherhood to the uninitiated echoed in her head again, like it had with Helen Clearwater. Val might not count, being part of the supernatural set herself, but Justin was definitely new to all of this, and judging from Chaz' scowl, his mistress hadn't shared much of her knowledge, either.

Yet, Father Value was dead, and the only contact within the Brotherhood he'd left her was Professor Clearwater. With both of them gone, who was going to punish her if she talked? She opened her mouth to speak, but Cavale cut in first.

"Elly's here because we're *both* Brotherhood. Or were. Sort of. We were raised by one of its members."

Elly caught Chaz squinting between them, scanning their faces for similarities. "Siblings?"

Cavale shook his head. "We're not related by blood, no, but we might as well be." He reached over and took her hand, though whether it was to reassure her or himself, Elly wasn't sure. "I walked away from that life a couple of months before I ended up in Crow's Neck. There's enough supernatural activity happening in the area to make a living off of, but it wasn't so hopping that I'd have to get caught up in vampire politics or anything. Gave me room to figure things out, I guess."

"And Val"—now he took Val's hand in his free one—"Elly was at the Clearwaters' because the professor was one of us, too. Retired, you might say, but one of us all the same."

The vampire went still. Her face might as well have been

chiseled from marble, for all the expression she showed at first. Only the crystal blue of her eyes gave anything away as the twin revelations sank in. Shock turned to disbelief turned to grim acceptance. When the rest of her face caught up, or maybe when she *let* it catch up, Val simply looked hurt. "You never told me," she said. "Either of you."

"Why do you think something always came up for me when you tried getting me to meet him? I was afraid he'd take one look at me and *know*, and I'd left that life behind." His grip on Elly tightened. "I severed every tie I had."

"And the professor? Why wouldn't he . . . ?" She shook her head. "No, I guess that should be obvious. It's not the sort of thing you reminisce over." The hurt remained, though.

Elly cleared her throat, compelled to help ease the sting. Part of it was compassion, but mostly it was a good tactical move: if Cavale cared about this woman, it would be smart to have her as an ally. "I don't think it was because Professor Clearwater distrusted you. He talked a little about why he left them. He'd done things that he couldn't justify or make peace with, and the only way for him to come to terms with it at all was to get out. Those things still haunted him. So if he hid what he'd been, it wasn't about you. It was about . . . about trying to forget. Or move on. Or something." As she finished speaking she noticed every eye at the table was on her. She shrank back, wishing her chair would swallow her up.

"I have a question." Justin raised his hand like he was in a classroom. He waited for Val's nod before asking, "Um. What *is* this 'Brotherhood'? You guys make it sound like some sort of secret society." He looked from Val to Cavale to Elly, hopefully.

Elly shrugged. "Close enough. One that hunts monsters."

Val had recovered a bit. She reclaimed her hand from beneath Cavale's and sniffed her coffee again. "They're an old organization. Different sects can trace themselves back hundreds of years, if not thousands."

"What, like the ancient Egyptians had a branch?" Justin gave Chaz a help-me-out-here look, but didn't get the support he was looking for.

"Why not?" said Chaz, nodding thoughtfully. "Shit's probably gone bump in the night since people started wearing loincloths and cooking their meat instead of eating it raw."

"A slightly inelegant way to put it, but yes." Val pointed at the window above the sink. Carved into the peeling paint were several wedge-shaped runes. "That's a cuneiform ward against evil, right there. This stuff gets passed down because it *works*."

Now Justin *really* goggled at Val. "You're not . . . um. I mean, are you—"

"Do I *look* Sumerian?" She held out her pale, freckled arms and pointed at her spill of red curls. "My great-grandparents were off the boat from Ireland."

"Oh," said Justin, clearly biting his tongue against a follow-up.

"At the turn of the century." Exasperation crept into her tone.

"Um." His fingers twitched on the tabletop, like they wanted to lead the charge and shoot his hand back into the air. His mouth lost the battle first. "Which—?"

"*The last one.* Can we get back on track, please?" Val pressed her fingers to her temples. "I'll answer more questions for you tomorrow night. For now, we need to focus on what we came here for." She turned away from Justin to face Cavale. "What do you need to do?"

Cavale got up and went to one of the wide drawers next to the sink. It took him a few good tugs before it opened with the telltale rattle of a junk drawer. The times Father Value had let them settle down for a while, he too had found a space for the flotsam of day-to-day life to collect: pencils and pens, matchbooks, half-used bottles of glue, lengths of twine and bottle caps. She'd never given it much thought before, but now she wondered if it meant that, before the

Brotherhood, Father Value had had a house like this, if he'd been like Justin once, even—someone from a normal home, a normal life.

Cavale returned with a green-paged steno pad and a handful of pens. He plopped the pad down in front of Justin and laid the pens alongside it. "Go ahead and start writing."

Justin picked up a blue pen, considered it, then switched it for a black one. He flipped the cover of the notepad over and stared at the blank page for a long moment before he began to write. The pen's point scratched across the paper. What little hope there was on Justin's face died quickly as the Creeps' runes flowed forth across the top three lines. Justin tossed the pen down in frustration. "So, yeah. That's *not* a John Donne poem."

"We'll figure it out. Did you guys bring the book?"

"Yeah." Justin's backpack hung from the back of his chair. He pulled it onto his lap and unzipped it. Elly felt the dread rising as he peeled the canvas down and revealed the book she'd hoped never to see again. The urge to get up and check the windows and doors was so strong, she found herself gripping the seat of the chair to keep from standing up. *This is Cavale's house. I can see the wards, and he knows what he's doing.*

But wards hadn't stopped the Creeps at the Clearwaters'.

She tamped the thoughts down as fiercely as she could, and discovered something even weirder underneath. As awful as it was to see the book again, she felt *relief* at its reappearance, too. Much as she knew she should want to be rid of it, its sight was a comfort. Father Value had died for it, and so had Henry and Helen. Elly had nearly died for it, too—*twice over, even*—and since she was still kicking, she felt like maybe it was her responsibility from here on out. Seeing it here meant the Creeps hadn't gotten it, not yet. It had come back to her, sort of. Father Value would've called that a sign.

Across the table, Cavale had broken out the salt and drawn a circle around the book. He poured two lines across and over the book, dividing the circle into quarters. From his back pocket, he produced a piece of chalk and filled in the sections with sigils. When the last one was placed, Cavale stepped back. Everyone was holding their breath.

Justin leaned forward, his voice barely above a whisper. "What are we looking for?" He jumped when Cavale answered at regular volume.

"A flash, maybe, or a shifting of the symbols. But it would have happened by now." He picked the book up, the salt hissing off it as it tilted. "Good news is, there aren't any traps waiting between the covers. Looks like you triggered the only one. Nothing in there to help them track it magically, either."

"That's . . . good? I guess?" Justin toyed with the edges of the paper. "So what about me? How do we get this out of my head?"

"For now, get back to writing. Keep going until it repeats, okay?" He clasped Val's and Chaz' shoulders. "Meanwhile, can I talk to you two alone for a few?"

They got up, the legs of their chairs scraping along the linoleum. Elly wanted to tag along, but she hadn't been invited. Once they'd left, the kitchen seemed cavernous. Except for the table, where Elly and Justin still sat with their elbows almost touching. Their close proximity must've dawned on Justin at the same time; he shifted a couple of inches to his right while Elly scooted her butt a little to the left.

They shared an embarrassed laugh. "I'll, uh." Elly glanced around, looking for something useful to say. "Do you want more coffee while you write?"

"Oh God, yes please. I've been up since six o'clock this morning. Er. Yesterday morning now, I guess."

Elly smiled and stood, glad for an excuse not to have to make conversation. After a moment, she heard the pen scratching away again. Once the coffeemaker was burbling, she dared a glance at the table. Justin had his head down, his arm curled around the pad of paper like a kid afraid someone the next row over might try copying his answers.

It wasn't his writing she craned her neck to see; she already knew what Creepscrawl looked like. Instead, Elly squinted at the things Cavale had chalked onto the tabletop. He'd told Justin the truth about there being no wards or tracers on the book. The checks for those were in the first three quadrants of his circle. But he'd neglected to mention the last bit.

The fourth quadrant should have flared bright purple if any *power* was left in the book. Father Value had drawn the same sigils the day after they'd stolen the book from the church, and they'd stayed lit up for the better part of an hour. If the book was dead, logic said the power had to have gone into Justin. Writing the words out on a crappy dime store notepad wouldn't draw out the energy behind the spell, and the energy mattered as much as—or more than—the words. Cavale had to know that.

So why hadn't he said it?

13

VAL FLOPPED ONTO Cavale's tattered couch. The blood loss had made her woozy, and it had been several days since she'd last fed. The wound would close over time—a day's sleep would do wonders—but in the meantime, blood kept seeping out of the hole in her torso, and the skin around it itched from contact with the silver spike.

Chaz and Cavale took one look at her sprawling form and ashen face and, without a word, sat on either side of her and rolled up their sleeves.

"Oh no. *No.* You two stop that." Val struggled to sit up straight, digging her elbows into the back of the couch and heaving her upper body forward. "I'm not drinking from either of you. Or *anyone* in this house," she said, as Cavale's eyes flicked toward the kitchen.

"Val, you have to." Chaz sounded like he was speaking to a child reluctant to take her medicine. "We need you sharp for this."

"No you don't. Sun's up in an hour or so. You won't need me until tomorrow night, and by then this will have closed."

Cavale piped up from her other side. "But you'll still be weak."

"So I'll feed when I wake up. I'm not drinking from either of you. Now put your sleeves back down." The gesture was noble and even sweet, but much like some people had a policy never to sleep with friends, Val refused to drink from them. Especially these two. *Especially Chaz.*

Some vampires did drink from their servants. Matter of fact, a lot of Renfields considered it a point of pride to provide a meal for their masters. They didn't get any special benefit from it. Being fed from worked a lot like giving blood: you sometimes ended up dizzy and dehydrated. You weren't supposed to lift heavy objects for twenty-four hours in case you reopened the bites. Some of the more well-to-do vampires kept several Renfields, and watched them jockey for favorite status. They'd drink from whoever had pleased them best as a kind of reward.

If the minions lived long enough and didn't fall out of their master's good graces, the most loyal were first in line to be turned. What better way to prove your worth—and your future subservience—than exposing your throat to your superiors and granting them sustenance?

While the endless maneuvering made Val vaguely uncomfortable, it outright disgusted Chaz. To him, the human servants were not only being treated like pets, they were *enjoying* it. He'd told Val that he suspected some serious mind-fuckery there as well—he didn't talk about his three-day nightmare with the *Stregoi*, but Val thought whatever had happened, he'd gotten all the proof he needed.

Maybe it was different in some of the newer communities; she certainly hadn't seen debauchery to that extreme in California, though it still existed. But here in the Northeast the old blood ran strong. Which meant the old ways were kept— if occasionally bastardized—and used to claim superiority over the New World vampires. In New England, every colony had at least one person claiming that a sire's sire had come over on the *Mayflower.* Val only knew of two who actually *had*, neither of whom were on the passenger manifests you could look at up in Plimoth Plantation. Others came later, after the Revolutionary War, and brought with them the bloodsucking traditions of Eastern Europe, the British Isles, and any number of ancient rules and practices.

Val herself was relatively young, as vampires went. Born in the late nineteen forties, she'd come of age at a time when the country's youth was busy questioning authority and demanding change. So, too, did the newer brood of vampires start chafing against the draconian practices of their elders. Some of them even insisted on existing without any thralls.

Val wasn't *that* good, or at least, not for the kind of life she wanted. If you owned a business, you needed someone who could be there during the day. She and Chaz worked well together, and though he *was* her Renfield, he was first and foremost her friend. He'd had a taste of how others like him lived when the *Stregoi* woman had taken him. Val had sat with him through weeks of nightmares after she'd brought him home. Sometimes, even three years later, the paranoia still crept in. And yet, here he was, offering her his wrist because he trusted her not to go that far.

She pushed both of their arms away and plucked at their cuffs, trying to smooth them down. "Guys, please. Don't make me *make* you."

They exchanged one last, hesitant glance, then Chaz shook his head and rolled his sleeve back down. "Fine. But if you're not a thousand percent better tomorrow . . ."

"I will be." She waited until he dipped his head in acquiescence, then turned to Cavale. "Is this why you wanted us out here, or did you have something about Justin for me?"

"I have something. But it's not good." Cavale finished buttoning his sleeve before he continued. "We can hand over whatever he writes to them."

"But?"

"But all it's going to do is buy some time, and that's assuming they don't test it for themselves before they leave, or worse, know just by looking at it that it's useless."

Chaz leaned forward, hands on his knees. "How can it be useless? He's writing out the stuff that went missing, isn't that what they wanted?"

"Not quite. I—mmph. Watch." Cavale dragged the coffee table closer and produced his chalk again. He drew a simple rune on it. Then he pulled out a pin, pricked his thumb, and squeezed a few drops into the middle of the rune. It lit up for a few seconds, then subsided. "Most magic needs a source. I can draw runes all day, but if nothing powers them, they're just pictures."

"But there were things all over the Clearwaters' house. There's no way they ran around jabbing themselves to power them all." Chaz jerked his thumb toward the back of the house. "If that were the case, shouldn't your friend look like a pincushion?"

"Not when you can go buy a tub of animal blood at your local butcher shop."

"You can *do* that?" Chaz' jaw dropped. His idea of going food shopping was browsing the aisles at the gas station quickie mart when he filled his tank.

"Sure. People cook with it."

"Fuck this. I'm going vegan."

"*Anyway.* Those runes I drew over the book should've lit up like a Christmas tree if there was any magic left in it. But they stayed dormant." He wiped the chalk lines from the tabletop with his hand, avoiding Val's eyes. "I think if I'd drawn them on Justin, they'd have activated. That spell and its source are in him now. And it's not the sort of thing where you can substitute, I don't know, chicken blood and call it good. Something like that, in a book that old, it was imbued with a specific kind of energy. They'll need that, too. Not just the words."

"So how do we get it out of him?"

He looked up at her. Worry drew down the corners of his mouth. "I don't know yet. You're going to have to buy me some time. I have some ideas on how, if you want them."

Justin wrote for ten minutes or so, pausing only to sip at his refilled coffee. At last, he put his pen down and massaged his hand. "Do you think this looks like it's repeating?"

Elly pushed herself off the counter and took the seat formerly occupied by Chaz. Creepscrawl filled six pages' worth of notepaper, the letters jagged and rough. A shudder ran through her as she looked at it. Memories from the previous night threatened, but she forced herself to stay calm. She flipped back and forth, from the first line to the last and back again. "Yeah. That looks the same to me."

He stared at the page. "You'd think since I'm writing it, I'd be able to read it, too."

"That's not how these things work."

"No, I know. Okay, well, I *don't* know, but . . ." The silence stretched as he scrutinized the marks.

Elly shifted in her seat, more aware with each passing minute how close they were sitting. They were separated by a good foot or two, but her perception of the kitchen had done another dimensional flop. Gone was the cavernous feel of twenty minutes ago. Now that she was within arm's length of Justin, with no idea what kind of small talk was even appropriate, the walls had started closing in on her again. The low murmur of conversation drifted through the door to the living room. Elly inwardly cursed Cavale for not feeling her distress.

Stop it. He's not psychic.

Maybe he thought she'd developed social skills in the two plus years since he'd seen her. She hadn't. If anything, her only companion being fifty years her senior might have made the few skills she'd had deteriorate. Badly.

Father Value had sent them to school, sometimes, when they were somewhere he thought they could settle down for a while. He'd have his contacts draw up fake transcripts and send Elly and Cavale off to whatever grade was appropriate. They never stayed more than a few months at a time, though, usually just long enough for the other kids to move from *pick on the new kids* to *hey the new kids are kind of weird*. The days they came home to find their stuff boxed up and ready to go to the next place felt like how she imagined most children felt the day school let out for the summer.

That wasn't to say either of them were uneducated,

though. When they weren't enrolled anywhere, Father Value insisted they learn on their own. Sometimes they had textbooks as guidelines; sometimes he'd even know someone who could come tutor them. Most of their schooling, though, came from Father Value himself and each other. "We're book smart," Cavale used to say to her, in those days when they were watching each other's backs against new classmates, "but I wouldn't say we're people-smart."

What she wouldn't give for some people-smarts right now.

The salt from Cavale's runework was still on the table. Elly gathered it up in front of her, smoothing it out into a thin layer along the tabletop. With one finger, she drew patterns in it: spirals and squares, tic-tac-toe grids, whatever came to mind and helped her pretend she could *totally handle* sitting next to someone.

When Justin looked up from the notepad and spoke, Elly bit back a yelp.

Justin didn't seem to notice. "Do those, um. Do something?" He pointed at the salt symbols, careful not to actually make contact with them.

"No. They're just, y'know, doodles." A blush crawled up her neck; the tips of her ears felt like they were burning.

"The thing is, I *don't* know." He tapped the notepad, then, tentatively, the edge of the salt pile. "Before today, I'd've thought these were just about the same thing."

The edge of the circle she was tracing wobbled. "How could you think *Creepscrawl* was a doodle?"

"You ever sat through a lecture on the metaphysical poets?"

Elly blinked. She had no idea what he was getting at. And she'd never even sat through a lecture, unless you counted Father Value's. She was pretty sure Justin's version of a lecture was vastly different. "No. But it sounds interesting. Metaphysics?"

He chuckled. "Not that kind of metaphysics."

"Oh." *Great. Now I sound like an idiot.* She wanted to crawl under the table and die.

"Hey, no." He reached over and touched her wrist; she

jerked it away. To his credit, he didn't make a big deal of it. He placed both hands on the table in front of him, right where she could see them. "I just meant, your kind would probably be kind of neat to hear about. But unless you're a huge nerd"—he dipped his head to indicate that yes, he was one—"those classes can sort of drag. I watch people who are just taking them for filler credits, and they've zoned out five minutes in. The girl who sat beside me last semester doodled the whole time. Never took a single note as far as I could tell. It looked a lot like that."

Elly stared. "But . . . but Creeps can't go out during the day."

"Believe me, there are plenty of creeps at Edgewood. They're out at all hours."

"Not that kind of Creep."

"Oh."

Now it was Elly's turn to reassure him. She couldn't bring herself to touch him, though, so instead she refilled his coffee cup.

He murmured his thanks and loaded more sugar into the mug. "So, okay. Are your Creeps the same as Val's Jackals? She gave me a rundown, but I don't remember her calling them Creeps."

"Yeah, they're the same." They were back in familiar territory. She didn't even know how to talk about college life, let alone poetry courses.

"So are they . . . ?" He struggled with the words. Started again. "Val said they're what killed Professor Clearwater. And Helen."

Shit.

Elly looked at Justin. His eyes were shiny with unshed tears. *What the hell am I supposed to tell him? "Yes, your mentor died a horrible death?"* She opened her mouth, casting about for a good way to hedge, hoping for a platitude to fill the silence. Or for lightning to strike her dead so she wouldn't have to speak.

"Please don't," said Justin, softly.

"Don't what?"

"Don't soften it. Don't . . . Look. You don't know me. You don't have any reason to protect my feelings." He scrubbed his hand beneath his eyes and drew a steadying breath. "I want to know what happened to them."

"I don't know if I . . ."

"Please."

It wasn't going to help him. It never did. She'd watched from below as they pitched Father Value off that roof. She'd heard them kill Helen Clearwater. And Henry . . . There were things burned into her brain from the last week that'd give her nightmares the rest of her life.

But if I hadn't been there when Father Value died, I'd want someone to tell me what had happened. It would have driven her crazy not to know. Things like that had a way of eating at a person; their imaginations tended to step in and make it even worse. She should tell him. It was his right to know.

She took a deep breath and plunged ahead. "Okay. Yes, the Creeps killed them both. But we got a few of them, too."

"How?" He pulled the paper and pen close like he was going to take notes. A small sound of frustration escaped his lips as he realized the futility of it.

"Hey. We'll get them. I promise."

" 'We'?" He looked dubious.

"Cavale and me. Your friend Val. They're not going to hurt anyone else. Not on our watch." It sounded more confident in her head. Hunting without Father Value's guidance seemed wrong, like this was some sort of test to see if she *could* do it without fucking it up. But he wouldn't be there at the end to praise or criticize, and she had to start accepting that.

Empty as she thought her speech had sounded, Justin nodded along. "How did it happen, though? I mean, did they swarm, or break in, or . . . ?"

So Elly found herself starting at the beginning, trying to show him how brave the Clearwaters had been, how calmly they'd both set about barricading doors and readying the small arsenal of stakes and knives Henry had kept locked away in the cellar. "Helen asked if we could draw some of the runes with sugar instead of salt," she said, "so when a Creep crossed them it'd explode and the boiling sugar would stick to it. She said molten sugar hurts like a bitch. We didn't know if it'd work, but . . . it did."

Justin got that look people had when they were remembering something good about someone who'd died. She and Father Value had crashed more than a few wakes in the past, and she'd seen the same look on the faces of the bereaved. "Helen made candy," he said. "She loved it, but it was just the two of them, and Henry wasn't supposed to have too much sugar. So she'd bake things and send them to campus with him. There's a joke that if you're in one of his classes you don't gain the freshman fifteen, you gain the freshman fifty." He ducked his head. "If you were in one of his classes."

Elly was hoping maybe the prelude had satisfied him: *Your friends died well. They faced it bravely. Let's stop talking and wait for Cavale to bring Val and Chaz back.* But no such luck.

After a few deep breaths, he lifted his head. "What happened when they came? What did they want?"

"They wanted—" She stopped. How much had Val left out? Had she really not told Justin they were after the book, or was he testing her? Paranoia, never truly suppressed, reared its head. *No, stop it. He has no reason to do that.* She tried thinking like a vampire, to suss out Val's motive for leaving Justin in the dark, but Father Value had only ever taught her to think like a Creep.

Think about it like you're his friend. Great, another thing she had no idea about. But it made sense: Val was his boss, and she seemed to like him. Every step she'd taken so far— bringing Justin here, trying to find a cure for him—had been about protecting him. Hell, even keeping her own nature from him was probably as much about sparing Justin a ride on the freak train as it was about keeping herself safe.

Then it hit her: that hungry look wasn't only a need to know the specifics of their deaths; it was fear that he'd played a part somehow. *He'll blame himself. That's why she didn't tell him. He finds out they're after the thing in his head, he'll think it was his fault.* Just like she thought it was her own, for bringing the book to them in the first place. *He's going to blame me, too.*

Difference is, I actually deserve it. She'd brought the Creeps to the Clearwaters' door. Henry had chosen to send the book away. Nothing Justin could've done to prevent that. Elly, on the other hand, could have just stayed the hell out of town.

"Elly?" He leaned forward. "What did they want?"

Tell him. It's only fair. "They wanted—"

She was saved by the kitchen door banging open, making them both jump. Cavale entered first, followed by Val, then Chaz. Elly caught Cavale's eye and glanced pointedly at the clock: *How could you leave me alone for so long?*

He seemed to catch her meaning, wincing and shrugging an apology.

Val reclaimed her seat at the table. More blood had seeped from beneath her bandage, staining the cloth a rusty red. Earlier, Elly had thought her thin. Now Val's skin had tightened, the hollows beneath her eyes deepening until she looked almost skeletal. Her collarbone jutted out, sharp and unsightly.

Justin was halfway out of his chair. "Val? Are you okay?" He shot a glance at Chaz, who'd gone to stand in front of the coffeemaker, arms folded, the scowl back on his face.

"Don't look at me, kid. She says she's fine."

"I *am* fine." Val picked up a mug and sniffed. Its contents had to be cold by now. "Change of plans, though. It's too close to dawn for me to go home for the night, so I'm going to stay here. Chaz is going to take you somewhere safe for the day, and probably through tomorrow night."

"But I have classes. And I'm scheduled four to nine thirty tomorrow at the store."

"You're playing hooky and Chaz will get someone to cover your shift."

"And you're staying here?"

"Cavale has graciously offered me lodging in his basement." She threw Elly a tired grin. "As long as you're not going to drag me out into the sunlight once I'm asleep, that is."

Elly shook her head. "No, ma'am."

"Good. Justin, are you going to argue with me, or can we agree that missing one day of classes won't kill your GPA?"

He'd looked ready to argue, but after a moment he relented. "I'll e-mail my professors. I'll . . . I'll tell them I need a day to myself."

"Good. Because I think you *do* need one." She clapped her hands together and got shakily to her feet. "If anyone needs me, I'll be dead to the world." The cellar door was adjacent to the sink. The thumb bolt looked like it was probably the original, which meant it had been painted over every time the door got a new coat. Layer after layer had worked like glue, fusing the parts together. Elly'd toyed with it earlier while she'd toured the house and been unable to make it budge.

Val flicked it up and slid the bolt back like it was newly installed and well oiled. Flakes of paint drifted to the floor. The hinges screamed as the door opened and the smell of dank earth rushed up from below, the musty scent of an old New England basement wafting through the kitchen.

They were all quiet for a moment once Val's footsteps disappeared down the wooden stairs. Finally, Justin cleared his throat. "Um, Chaz? Where is this safe place we're going?"

Chaz grinned. "I'm dropping you off with the succubi."

14

CHAZ COULDN'T REMEMBER the last time he'd seen the interior of Hill O' Beans lit by early morning sunlight. His brain kept trying to fill in nighttime shadows, with ancient, white-haired Margaret behind the register and her twin Adele working the coffeemakers. He certainly didn't know the two young women manning the counter this morning. They were probably students at Edgewood, like the majority of the small crew at Night Owls, but to him they looked *wrong* there.

Everything on the drive from Crow's Neck back to Edgewood had been that way; landmarks that were usually draped in shadows looked alien in the pinkish glow of sunrise. It went with the territory of being a Renfield—you traded some of your own daylight so you could be available during your master's waking hours. Chaz preferred sleeping through the mornings and starting his day around noon. He supposed others did the opposite, waking at sunset like their masters and staying up to watch *Good Morning America* and take care of daytime business, but he'd never really had a chance to swap notes with any others.

He didn't care to, either. His brief glimpse into how the other half lived a few years back was quite enough, thankyou-verymuch. Chaz' impression of other Renfields—what little he could remember through the three-day haze of pain and mind-fuckery—was that most of them were obnoxious fucking sycophants. Most of them would have thought it an honor if their masters drained them to a husk and dumped their bodies into Boston Harbor. *You don't get a trophy for being a tasty snack. Christ.* Now that he thought of it, getting rid of bodies was probably about as close as vampires got to defecating. He grinned. Val would appreciate that one, when she woke up.

The girl at the register must have thought the smile was for her. She returned it as she arranged the four coffee cups in a carry-out tray for him. Silver braces with hot pink bands covered her teeth. "You manage Night Owls next door, don't you?"

"Yeah, but I'm usually on the night shift." He peered at her, trying to dredge up some recognition, but nothing came. A good bookseller knew the regulars, and Chaz was usually pretty good with faces, even if they didn't shop at Night Owls often. Still, nothing, not even a hit on the braces. "I'm having trouble recalling your name—I blame this ungodly hour."

"Nah, I don't think we've met. I usually go there during my morning break. I just noticed Justin out there in your car. He sits next to me in Western Civ, and he usually goes straight from class to his shift." She tilted her chin toward the front window. "He looks beat. I'm not sure even a shot or six of espresso would wake him up."

Chaz half turned. Justin was asleep in the front seat, head tilted against the backrest, with his eyes closed and mouth hanging open. "He's had a long night."

"I'd bet he's had a couple of them. With Professor Clear-water and all." She rang up the coffees and stuck a couple of chocolate croissants in a bag. "Here, on the house. Tell him Nadine from Dr. Forrester's class says hi."

"Will do." Chaz dropped a healthy tip in the jar and headed out to the car.

At the creaking of the driver's side door, Justin jerked

awake. He accepted the tray and the bag of pastries blearily as Chaz passed them over. "How long was I asleep?"

"Maybe ten minutes. Nadine says hi."

"Nadine?"

"From one of your classes. She saw you all conked out and drooling and sent me away with free food for you. Either she thought you looked like a kitten in need of rescuing, or she's crushing on you." The Mustang roared its way to life, and Chaz backed out of their spot. He saw Nadine watching them leave, and gave her a wave. "She's cute. You should ask her out."

Justin looked up from contemplating the croissants and waved in the same general direction as Chaz had.

"You didn't even make eye contact."

"I'm still half-asleep!" It showed, too. He stared down at the coffee cups and touched the lid of each, counting. "Four cups? Are Cavale and Elly meeting us?"

"No, they're staying put. These are for Sunny and Lia."

Watching Justin trying to make the connection was like watching the Mustang trying to start on bitterly cold mornings. He could almost see the check engine lights coming on in the kid's eyes before the memory of where they were headed kicked in. "Wait, the succubi?"

"Yep."

"Their names are Sunny and Lia. *Succubi*."

"Yep. Well, no, but close enough. They said their real names for me once. I don't really remember the next hour or two." They'd told him he'd just sat there, entranced by a pattern on the wallpaper in their parlor, but whenever it came up, Lia and Val dissolved into snickers and Sunny succumbed to outright *cackling*. Chaz was just fine not knowing the specifics.

"Should I be, um. Worried, or anything?"

Chaz glanced sideways at Justin. The kid had turned bright red. *Oh shit, he thinks he's going to be babysat by porn demons. Don't laugh, don't laugh . . .* To buy some time, he reached over and retrieved his coffee, settling it between his thighs to pry open the lid—the way you weren't supposed to unless you wanted to risk burning your junk. But the Mustang was older than cup holders, and Chaz had yet to spill a drop in the ten years he'd had the car. Still, he figured showing amusement at Justin's sudden embarrassment would be a great way to invoke karma, so he made sure his voice was steady and the hot coffee wasn't hovering over his bits before he answered. "No. You shouldn't be. Listen, I'm going to let you in on something about these girls, okay?"

"Okay?"

"Sunny and Lia are more interested in each other than they are in either of us."

Justin's brow creased as he puzzled that one out. "You mean . . . ?"

"Yep."

"But I thought . . . I mean, aren't succubi supposed to, um. Like men?"

"Technically, yes. And they do, I guess, but that's none of my business so I've never asked for details. But you can stop worrying that they'll spend the day trying to jump your bones."

He let out a huge sigh of relief. "Okay, good."

"You going to break out those croissants, or no?" It had been hours since either of them had eaten, and Margaret and Adele's pastries were beyond amazing. Chaz' disappeared in under two minutes. Justin ate more slowly, picking his apart in slow strips. He was at least being careful to keep the flakes falling into the bag rather than all over the seat, which Chaz appreciated. "Here's what I don't get. A guy your age, I'd think you'd be *disappointed* that you're not in for a day of something straight out of *Letters to Penthouse*."

So much for keeping the seat clean. Or the windshield for that matter. Justin spluttered, spraying crumbs all over the passenger side. *"What?"*

"Just saying."

"I'm . . . I'm not like that. That's not, it's not my, I mean . . ." He cracked open his coffee and took a scalding sip. They'd come to a four-way stop, and Chaz took the opportunity to get a good look at Justin. The red, which had been subsiding, returned in force. Now he was full-on crimson from forehead to chin as he mumbled, "I wouldn't even know what to do."

A car behind them honked. Chaz waved an apology in

the rearview and got going again. You didn't flip off your fellow drivers in Edgewood; chances were they were also your patrons. "Are you telling me you're a virgin?"

"I, um. Yeah."

"Weren't you with Annie for like a year?" Chaz had liked the tall blond girl who, up until a few months ago, used to come around for Justin's dinner break. Something had happened over the summer, though, and she'd stopped swinging by. Justin had never said much about it, though he'd filled the poetry section with a slew of really depressing collections after the breakup.

"Yeah, but we never. You know." From the look of things, he was about to spontaneously combust, and boy would *that* ruin the interior.

"Hey, that's fine. Nothing wrong with it. And? It's not any of my business either." He waited a beat, then winced as he added, "Listen. Sunny and Lia will just *know*, okay? And they're going to find it endearing."

" 'Endearing'? *Toddlers* are endearing."

"They'll probably give you some shit about it, but I'll tell them to lay off. I just figured, forewarned is forearmed, yeah?"

Justin groaned and took another sip of coffee. "Anything else I ought to know?"

"One other thing. Do you still think of Annie a lot?"

"Sometimes, I guess. I mean, I know we're not getting back together, but I miss her, you know?" He paused and eyed Chaz suspiciously. "Why?"

"Just . . . Try not to be too freaked out if one of them starts looking like her. It's a succubus thing. They pick up on who it is you're wanting and sometimes they react to it. It happens subconsciously for them. Especially if you still have feelings for her. It's not a big deal. If you ask them to turn it off, they will."

Justin gaped at him for a good thirty seconds before he found his words again. "Are you sure I can't just go back to the dorm?"

"Yes, I'm sure. Seriously, don't sweat it. They'll probably stick you in their spare room, tell you how the TV remote works and where the bathroom is and leave you alone." He pulled into the driveway of a neat little Victorian and killed the engine. They had arrived.

Sunny and Lia's house was their pride and joy. They'd spent most of the summer up on ladders, touching up the paint. Lia kept a vegetable garden out back, and she'd lined their brick walkway with pots of red and orange chrysanthemums. It was cozy and welcoming, the picture of domestic contentment. None of the neighbors would ever have suspected they lived next door to a pair of demons.

"You ready?" Chaz leaned over to take the coffee tray from Justin.

The kid took a deep breath and plastered on an exhausted smile. "My boss is a vampire and I have some kind of evil spell stuck in my head. How could spending the day with a pair of succubi be any weirder, right?"

"That's the spirit."

The front door opened when they were halfway up the walk. Sunny came out onto the steps in a blue and white tee shirt that read "Edgewood College Athletics Dept." that was three sizes too big for her. Her bare feet peeked out from the bottom of her blue plaid pajama pants. She was short today; Chaz guessed she was only a hair over five feet. Her skin was nut-brown, her hair thick, black, and bobbed. Huge chocolate brown eyes peered up at him from an otherwise plain face.

Chaz could feel the confusion emanating from Justin. Sunny's appearance didn't exactly scream "sex demon." Chaz knew this face of hers, though. It was Lia's favorite, and thus the one Sunny usually wore.

"Sunny, this is Justin. Justin, Sunny." Chaz gestured with the tray of coffee as they climbed the steps. "Val wanted me to tell you how much she appreciates this."

"Oh, please. Anything for you guys." She stepped back, beckoning them inside. "Lia's out for a run. She should be back any minute now."

They followed her into the living room and sat down on the black marshmallow leather couch. Chaz deposited the tray on the glass coffee table and sat back with his cup.

Sunny plunked down on the matching love seat across from them and took in their rumpled clothes and tired eyes. "No run-ins on the way?"

Chaz shook his head. He'd told Sunny the Jackals might be after Justin, and she'd insisted he floor it to get there. "None. Val says they go to ground during the day, and they don't know that what they're looking for is cozying up next to *The Complete Works of Christopher Marlowe* in Justin's head."

"Yet," muttered Justin. He got that sluggish-engine look again, then startled. "It *is* what they're after. That piece of Professor Clearwater's book."

Shit. Chaz had told Val the kid wasn't stupid, that it wasn't a hard leap to make. She'd been hoping that exhaustion combined with the whole "my boss is a vampire and my handwriting's been hijacked by some fucked-up spell" thing might distract him from drawing the obvious conclusion. With your average kid, that might've worked. But Justin was almost frighteningly smart, and, well, when a kid spends that much time thinking, sooner or later the brain was going to rejoin the party.

I was just hoping it wouldn't be on my goddamned shift.

He felt guilty for even thinking that, but Chaz had never been very good at reassuring and comforting. *I'll probably just make it worse.* Damage was already done though; he had to at least try. "Listen, Justin . . ."

"Sweetie, it's not your fault." Thank God for Sunny. She reached across the table and took Justin's hands in hers. "If I understand it right, Professor Clearwater gave you the book, not the other way around, yes?"

"Yeah, I guess."

"Because he trusted you with it. He knew you could get it where it needed to go, and that he wouldn't have to worry about it. You eased a burden for him by taking it. Do you see?" While Sunny spoke, she stroked her thumb slowly back and forth across his knuckles. Her voice was low and smooth, and her eyes . . . It shouldn't be possible for that brown to get deeper, but it had. They seemed almost liquid now, and even bigger than when Chaz and Justin had first arrived.

The smell of sandalwood filled the room, earthy and deep. Had she lit a candle? Or a stick of incense? Chaz found he couldn't remember, and *that* was what brought him out of the stupor. Sunny never broke her eye contact with Justin, but Chaz was fairly certain the amused quirk of her lips was aimed at him.

She kept murmuring, too low for Chaz to make out the words. Justin nodded now and then, deep in her thrall. *Probably should've told him she's a therapist for her day job.*

Chaz let his mind wander as Sunny eased Justin's worry. He had very little to do until tonight. Night Owls' daytime crew could take care of itself, and the plans for the Jackals' return depended largely on Val, Elly, and Cavale. Which meant he could close his eyes, let his mind slip into neutral for a few minutes, and quietly freak the fuck out.

It had been bad enough having a Jackal come within millimeters of stabbing out his eye the other night. It had been worse when he and Val had gone into the Clearwaters' and he'd seen what those creepy bastards could actually *do*. But what he kept coming back to, now that Cavale had utterly failed to fix Justin like Val had hoped (and wasn't Chaz just sitting on a huge *I told you so* for that), was the Jackal woman's parting threat. *I'll bring back a whole nest.*

They didn't have the pages for her and they weren't going to by tonight. How long would it take for them to rally their troops? Was it just a matter of sticking their snouts in the air and howling, or was there some sort of Jackal message board on the Internet: *Meet up in Edgewood, Friday at midnight. BYOB. Snacks will be provided.*

Maybe they could handle a few of them, between the four of them. Val could fight. Cavale, too, as loath as Chaz was to compliment him. And if miss small, dark, and twitchy had learned her shit alongside Cavale, well, that probably meant Chaz was the weak link in the group.

That girl can hold her own. She stabbed Val, didn't she? He grimaced, remembering the feel of Val's blood on his hands as he bandaged the wound, how warm it felt against her cold, cold skin. She'd looked like hell by the time she'd gone down into Cavale's cellar. If they'd been alone, he would have insisted she let him help her down the stairs, at least let her lean on him instead of Cavale's rickety god-damned railing. But while she might have conceded if Cavale had been the only other person present, she'd never show that much vulnerability in front of an employee and the girl who'd inflicted the wound in the first place.

So he'd watched her descend the stairs, his knuckles turning white on the edge of the chair as he waited for her weakened state to cause her to stumble and fall. It was like watching her descend into the crypt, stink of old earth and all, and he'd *hated* it.

He'd see her tonight. He knew that, logically. She'd prob-ably insist on feeding first, too, so she really would look a thousand times better by the time she got back to Night Owls. But until then, every second would be tinged with worry for her.

The front door rattled open, pulling Chaz from his doom-filled thoughts. He was about to turn to say hello to Lia when Sunny's expression stopped him. She was no longer hypno-tizing Justin. Instead, she was staring over the top of his head, the color draining from her face. A tiny strangled noise escaped her throat as she shook her head "no."

Justin twisted to follow her gaze and gasped. "But . . . It's *daylight*."

Chaz felt his mouth go dry. He turned slowly, already knowing what he'd see.

Val stood in the archway, dressed in a pink tracksuit, an Edgewood Panthers water bottle in her hand. Her red hair was pulled back into a ponytail, the strands around her hair-line dark with sweat. Only, it wasn't Val.

"Fuck," said Lia, in Val's voice. "I'm sorry, Chaz. I saw the car but I didn't even think— Sec." She disappeared into the hall bathroom, slamming the door behind her. When she emerged a minute later, she'd lost a few inches and gained a few pounds. Her ponytail still cascaded down her back, but now it was honey blond instead of dark red. Her skin was tanned, which made the cotton-candy pink polish on her fingernails stand out. This was the face Lia usually wore: Sunny's favorite. "I'm so sorry about that. I. Um."

"It's okay," Chaz said. "I've just been *worried* about her." He overemphasized the word, hoping the women would back him up. She and Sunny knew how he felt about Val—it wasn't the kind of thing you could hide from two extremely savvy succubi—but he certainly didn't need Justin to twig on to it. "Sunny can fill you in on why later. Or Justin can. Justin, this is Lia."

Justin smiled politely, but kept his eyes on Chaz. He was back to the puzzling-shit-out face.

"Not a word to Val about, uh. That. Okay? She gets snarly when I worry about her too much."

Another nod, this one with a little less suspicion. It probably helped that Justin had actually seen Val get snarly now and then at Night Owls. Usually it was when she'd put off feeding a day or two too long, but he didn't know that. Yet.

"Is Val okay? That was awfully strong." Lia crossed over to sit next to Sunny.

"She's all right. There's some shit going down, but it's being taken care of." Chaz stood and pulled his keys out of his pocket. *I need to get out of here.* "Listen, I hate to run off like this, but I have a few things I need to get done before she wakes up. Sunny said it'd be okay for Justin to sack out here for the day. Is that cool?"

"Of course." Lia bit her lip. She looked like she wanted to cry. "Chaz—"

He smiled at her, doing his best to reassure her without having magical succubus soothing powers at his beck and call. It wasn't Lia's fault his guard had slipped.

"It's okay, really. Take care of Justin for us, yeah?" He clapped Justin on the shoulder and leaned down to stage-whisper in his ear: "No shoes on the furniture, no blaring the radio, and for God's sake, *put the lid down*. Got it? Good. We'll be back tonight to take you off the ladies' hands."

Chaz didn't wait for any of them to answer. He showed himself out, willing his gait to remain steady and calm until the door closed behind him.

15

*T*HE WEIGHT OF *darkness. Of daylight outside the walls, driving her inside. Cold, damp earth against her cheek, the musty smell of the space, mixed with old rags left forgotten in a corner, rotting away into nothing. Rumble of the furnace as it shuddered to life, rustle of mice as they scurried about in the walls.*

Another mouse up above, at the door. Breathing, listening. Hand on the doorknob, hesitant. Come down, little mouse. Come see the monster in the basement. *The creaking of the floor above as the mouse decided to be elsewhere. Just as well. The mouse had a sharp tooth.*

Pain, too. Flesh knitting slowly together, the itch almost enough to pull her to consciousness.

Val turned uneasily in her sleep, a corpse rolling in its grave. Other things moved in the basement—beetles and crawly things, a family of moles—but once she'd subsided, she was as still and silent as stone.

Off and on during the day, there was a shuffling by the door upstairs and a pause as Elly listened for signs of life. At those times, Val's nostrils would flare and her fingers would twitch. But the girl didn't come down, and Val slept on.

SHE AWOKE AT sunset, cold, hungry, and with something stuck in her teeth. She worked it loose with her tongue while she got her bearings. Memory came back bit by bit, full recall dawning at about the same moment the thing in her teeth came free. The Jackals, the book, Justin. Elly and her silver weapon. Val spat the thing out into her palm. It was small and thin, spiky in places. *Oh dear God, is that an antenna?*

She sat up and looked around the dirt near where her head had been. Sure enough, the carcasses of several beetles were scattered about like the shells from discarded pumpkin seeds. *Damn it.* It had been years since something like that had happened. It was a testament to how badly she'd been hurt. Most nights, she didn't make a habit of luring insects to their doom while she slept. There was nourishment to be had in those tiniest of doses, but the last time she'd done it had been back in Sacramento, in the aftermath of those final, dark days.

Rumor had it that it was how some of the Old World vampires had survived the crossing to America. Buried in the ships' holds, nestled in their wooden crates filled with dirt from their homelands, they'd called the rats and vermin to them and feasted while above decks the poorest human passengers starved.

It was, of course, largely bullshit. Most of those Old World bloodsuckers had amassed enough wealth to hire their own ships and crews and make the crossing in style. Perhaps a handful of fledglings had gone the cargo-and-bugs way, but Val couldn't imagine the ones who still clung to their titles—Count this, Baroness that—eating so much as a flea. Still, the legends were steeped in truth, and apparently Val had snacked on beetles like they were peanuts at a bar.

The blood on her shirt had dried during the day; the fabric was stiff as cardboard when she tugged at it. The bandages weren't much better, and now they had grime from the cellar floor on them to boot. She unwound them carefully, dropping them into the rag pile in the corner.

Free of Chaz' field dressing, she poked gingerly at the place where Elly's spike had pierced her gut. It was tender, still, but the wound had closed. She didn't think it would reopen on her if she had to run later. *Or fight, let's be honest.*

She needed to be *certain* it wouldn't, though, and that meant feeding.

A thin strip of yellow light peeked from beneath the door. Val climbed the rickety stairs, holding tight to the railing in case her weight was too much for them after years of disuse and they fell away beneath her. They didn't, though, and as she cracked the door open, Val knew she was alone in the house. She stepped into a kitchen lit by the last remnants of twilight. A night-light plugged in above the stove was losing a battle with the encroaching gloom.

Cavale had left a note on the table: *Gone to prepare. Towels beside the bathroom sink. See you tonight.* Val smiled. She'd noticed over the years how meticulous Cavale was when it came to grooming. Most of the twentysomethings she knew tended to let things like shaving slide, or would wear a pair of jeans a day or two past when they ought to be washed. Granted, most of the twentysomethings she knew still brought their laundry home to Mom on the weekends, or spent the quarters intended for the washing machine on beer instead.

Now that she'd met Elly and understood a little bit of how they'd lived, it made more sense. The girl had been clean, to be certain, but her hair looked like it had been hacked at with a knife. Probably because it had. She'd been wearing one of Cavale's sweatshirts, but her faded jeans had been patched and patched again, just like the backpack. If you left a life where things like new clothes, haircuts, and maybe even reliable showers were a distant dream, why not indulge in those things when they became available?

Val made her way into the bathroom to clean up. She scrubbed the dirt from her face and brushed most of it out of her hair. One of Cavale's shirts hung from the shower curtain rod. Val shrugged it on and stuffed her ruined blouse into the trash. She squeezed a dollop of toothpaste onto her fingertip and swabbed it around inside her mouth. Nowhere near as good as a real brushing, but she wanted the taste of beetle—pine nuts mixed with pennies—gone.

One last glance in the mirror showed her looking almost human again. Pale, sure, and more gaunt than she cared to be, but passable enough to draw in her prey. She smelled a little musty, but by the time anyone noticed, it'd be too late.

Outside, the street was quiet. Val could see lights on in several of the houses as she slipped past. She could smell the people within, beneath the aromas of cooking meat and macaroni and cheese: their blood, calling to her. Her own stomach growled, the hunger gnawing and buzzing at the back of her brain. *Not here. Not in Cavale's neighborhood.*

She sped on, sticking to the shadows until she got out to the main drag. Rush hour had come and gone, but traffic was steady enough that Val didn't have her thumb out for too long before someone pulled over. The car was a late-nineties Hyundai that had seen better days.

So, for that matter, had its driver. The woman was in her early forties, but there were twists of grey in her hair that made her look a decade older. Her maroon lipstick stained the filter of the cigarette clenched between her teeth. As Val pulled open the door and slid in, the woman said hello. "Hell of a road to be hitchhiking on. No one watches their speed."

"I've noticed. Nearly been clipped a few times. Thank you for stopping."

"Well, it's not something I normally do, but you looked harmless enough."

Val winced. Was the calling still in effect? Did it matter? Her intent was to feed; if latent abilities were helping her out, so much the better. She forced a smile. "Are you going anywhere near Edgewood?"

"I can get you most of the way there, sure." She offered up the pack of Marlboros. "Smoke?"

"No, thank you."

"Hope you don't mind if I do."

Val shook her head. "Not at all." Normally, she didn't like smokers' blood. Afterward she felt like she'd licked an ashtray. Once in a while though, it wasn't so bad. Especially now, when she didn't have time to be picky.

The woman chatted amicably as she drove, gesturing with her cigarette to punctuate her points. Her name was Jane. She'd just come off the day shift at a plant where she "screwed this into that, and passed it on down the line." Now she was headed home to scarf down dinner with her daughter before she headed off to her part-time data entry job. Val warmed to her quickly, but the hunger grew with every passing mile. Soon enough she was concentrating more on the rhythm of Jane's pulse than the rise and fall of her patter.

There was a weigh station off the highway just outside of Edgewood. In the years she'd lived in town, Val had never seen anyone actually pulled off into it. It seemed as good a place as any. "You can let me off here," she said.

Jane glanced at her. "I figured I'd take the exit, let you off at the Dunkin' Donuts that's there."

"It's not necessary." Val pushed the Command into her voice. "Pull into the weigh station."

Jane's face went slack, her eyes blank. Her head swivelled forward again as she obeyed. All the animation was gone—everything that had lit her up as she'd spoken of her daughter, the sardonic smirk that had made the cigarette bob when she talked about her cubicle mate on the second shift—it was as if it had all leaked out of her and all that was left was this Jane-like husk.

It'll come back. Five minutes after I'm gone, she'll be herself again. Still, it was the worst part of what she was, the part she'd never been able to shut off the way the others did. The concept of humans-as-cattle repulsed her. She delayed that moment where their eyes went dead and their personalities took a walk as long as she could, every time.

The car rolled to a stop. Jane put it in park, then her hands returned to the steering wheel at ten and two. The cigarette smoldered between her lips as she stared straight ahead.

"Put that out, then give me your right wrist."

There was no hesitation. Jane stubbed out the butt then held her right arm straight to the side, her wrist tantalizingly close to Val's nose. The rest of her body hadn't moved. It was like watching one of those robot demonstrations, where the programmers gave orders and the machine carried them out with perfect efficiency.

Val encircled Jane's wrist and squeezed gently a few inches below the heel of her palm. With her other thumb, she massaged the veins until they stood out against the woman's pale skin. "I'm sorry," she said, but her fangs unsheathed as she said it, giving voice to the part of her that was not sorry at all. As they pierced the skin, the hunger surged.

Jane's blood coursed hot and thick over Val's tongue. Val felt her own pulse quicken as her body opened up to the sudden rush. She imagined it was how a man would feel diving into a lake after wandering through the desert for several days. The wound in her middle throbbed as it healed the rest of the way. In the dim amber of the streetlights, Val watched her skin smooth out, the wrinkles and rivulets that had sunk in over the last day disappearing. She could feel it in her muscles, too, the strength flooding back with every swallow.

Enough. Enough. STOP.

Jane groaned as Val tore herself away, but she still hadn't moved. Her arm bobbed a bit, but it stayed stuck straight out. Val glanced down at Jane's mangled wrist. The neat twin puncture wounds they showed in the movies were laughable. Teeth *tore*, especially in places where the flesh was thin. Maybe the vampires who drank from the femoral artery could leave a perfect pair of bite marks, but taking from the wrist . . . not so much. Blood pulsed out from Jane's wound, inviting. Heady.

No more.

Val pressed her fingers to the broken flesh. She scooted closer to Jane so she could bend her elbow and hold her wrist up as high as it would go to slow the blood flow. Then she steeled herself and bit her tongue, hissing at the flare of pain. This time, the blood that filled her mouth was her own. She worked it around a moment, mixing it with her own saliva like some kind of gruesome mouthwash.

When the blood seeping from Jane's wound had slowed to a trickle, Val lifted the injured wrist to her mouth once more. She smeared the blood-and-spit mixture over the worst parts of the wound, pushing the ragged skin together to help it knit back together. It took a few minutes to heal, but when she was done, the only evidence she'd fed was the leftover blood. Val lapped that up, too, then hunted around in Jane's glove box hoping to find some napkins to wipe up the last vestiges of red. She found something even better: a stash of wet naps.

She returned Jane's hand to the steering wheel, then cleaned it all, every drop she could find. Jane sat there totally checked out until Val spoke again. "When the car door closes, get back on the road and go home. If you're late it's because, uh, you hit some traffic. No smoking for three hours or so." She patted Jane's shoulder. "And you never saw me."

Then she got out of the car and slammed the door, hard. She watched from a few steps away as, inside, Jane jerked awake. The woman didn't turn to look out the passenger window as she got her bearings. Val knew that the fog of Command was lifting, but it wouldn't dissipate fully until Jane had put some distance between them. The Hyundai's taillights flashed as it pulled away, heading for the on-ramp. Val watched them grow smaller and smaller, until they were two red pinpricks in the distance. Then the road curved, and they were gone.

Val struck off toward the woods that crept right up to the edge of the weigh station. Edgewood was only a few miles' run from where she was now. She could have hitched the rest of the way, or even called Chaz to come get her, but Jane's blood was singing in her veins. She felt like she could run a million miles. She wanted to feel the autumn wind against her face and the ground churning beneath her feet. Everything was so much sharper after a feeding, every sense almost painfully keen.

The euphoria could last for hours, if she went slow and savored it. But it was distracting, too—altogether too easy to get caught up in the sensory overload. She needed to be alert when they faced the Jackals, but this was *too* much. The edge had to come off.

Val stood at the tree line and inhaled. Small animals rustled around in the leaves, but the night birds had gone silent, sensing the predator in their midst. To her eyes, the trees were lit up like noon. She picked out a likely-looking path and set off toward Edgewood in a blur.

16

CHAZ HAD HOLED himself up in the office most of the shift, only coming out when a customer threw a curve the register monkeys couldn't handle. Then it was right back to the office, where he claimed to be poring over the Macmillan catalogs for an upcoming sales appointment. In reality, he was mostly sitting with his head in his hands wondering where the hell Val was.

She hadn't answered her cell phone, though he supposed if she were feeding it'd be kind of hard to: *Sorry, I have to take this. Can you stop bleeding for a sec?* It had bothered him at first, the thought of her out stalking the streets of Edgewood, looking at its residents like they were walking dinner menus.

But it wasn't how she operated. There was a club in Providence with willing donors. Every few weeks she'd make a trip up there to feed and come home smelling like cloves and pretension. She'd never taken him with her, but he had their card. *If she's not here by one thirty, I'm calling them.* He didn't really think she'd be there, though. Not tonight, when there was so much to do before the Jackals came.

One twenty-five.

Fuck it. Close enough. He snatched the card from where he'd set it on the keyboard and pulled out his cell phone. He was halfway through dialing when the back room door creaked open and Val peeked in.

"Anybody home?"

He gaped at her. Last night she'd looked like a walking corpse. Now she stood before him, cheeks flushed and filled out again. It had been a long time since he'd seen this much color in her complexion. "Holy shit."

She executed a little twirl. "Ta-da!"

"How's the belly?"

Val grinned and lifted the bottom of her shirt. When last he'd seen her, he could have stuck a finger in there and had some wiggle room left over; now the skin was smooth and unblemished. There was no evidence she'd ever been stabbed at all, not even the tiniest scar.

Chaz reached out like a strange sort of Doubting Thomas and poked at the place the spike had pierced. Val's skin was warm to the touch; usually she was slightly cooler than room temperature. And the wound . . . *Perfectly healed. Must have been a hell of a feeding.* He grinned at her. "I think you should tell everyone this closed because I'm an ace at vampire first aid."

"Done." She tucked her shirt back in and leaned against the desk. "You ready for this?"

He wasn't, not really. They'd given him a crash course in the Jackals' weaknesses, and he'd spent a good chunk of the afternoon finding silver and rowan, but if he actually had to do any hand-to-hand fighting he was fucked. Last time he'd taken a swing at someone was high school. Still, if he told her he was nervous, Val would send him right home. "Much as I can be."

"You could still back out, you know. Go home and sleep, head to Sunny and Lia's and play cards with Justin . . ."

"Uh-uh. No. This isn't up for debate. I'm going." His part was simple enough: just drive. He didn't plan on fucking that up. And this way, he'd know the outcome right away.

No sitting around waiting for Cavale to call and tell him how it had gone.

For a long moment, she just looked at him. Out in the store, the register spat out a receipt. There was a series of thuds from the other side of the wall as one of the kids set to some late-night reorganizing. Chaz held Val's gaze steadily. He knew that if she wanted to, she could order him to stay home. He wouldn't even have the wits to question it until hours later, when the meeting with the Jackals had come and gone. The idea of it made his heart pound. Val could probably sense his agitation, but there wasn't much he could do about that.

Don't make me stay behind.

She crooked a smile. "Okay. Fine. We stick to the plan. What else have I missed?"

He let out a sigh of relief, ignoring the twitch of her lips. "It's been quiet. I checked in with Justin earlier. He's damned near jumping out of his skin over there, but he's fine. The Clearwaters' funeral is tomorrow. I told him I'd take him."

"We need to send flowers."

"Already taken care of. What do you think you pay me for?"

Val straightened up. She was moving fast, faster than normal people. She was in front of Chaz before he could blink, squeezing his shoulder. "You do good work. I probably ought to say that more."

"Does this mean I'm getting a raise?"

"Nope."

It was an old joke between them. The patter felt good, something normal on the heels of a weird fucking day and a moment of mundanity before the night went right back to fubar.

By two thirty, the store was dead enough for Val to send the last of the register monkeys home. At two forty-five, the last late-night browser left. Chaz flipped the sign on the door to the closed side, with its picture of an owl with its head tucked beneath its wing. They went through the motions of closing the store for the night: cash register emptied, money counted and put in the safe, one final pass made with the push broom. It wasn't until Chaz was killing the lights that Val snapped her head up and sniffed the air.

"They're outside."

The Jackals were waiting on the sidewalk, the same three from the other night as far as Chaz could tell: the woman, who he'd decided was named Bitch, stood in front with her arms folded; the smaller one, whom Chaz had dubbed Twitch, flanked her on the left; the bigger one with the scars, aka The Guy Who Was Going to Put Out My Fucking Eye—Asshole for short—flanked her on the right. They all wore hoods or hats, pulled far enough forward that their faces were hidden in shadow. Still, every now and then he could see flashes of their yellow eyes glowing within the deep recesses.

Bitch watched as Val locked the door and gave the handle an experimental tug. Her eyes flicked to the keys when Val turned, like she was looking for the silver one that went to the rare books room. Apparently the fear of her face being seen didn't extend to the rest of her body. Her sweatshirt was unzipped, giving Chaz a glimpse of the burn marks on her neck; they hadn't healed the way Val's wound had. *Does that mean they haven't fed? Or does it work differently for Jackals?*

"Did you find the pages?" Her voice was raspy, too. Had Val taken her by the throat the other night? He couldn't remember. Asshole's claw had blocked his field of view.

"We did." Val shook her head ruefully. "But you're not going to like where they are."

When Bitch growled, Twitch took it up, too. Asshole settled for some extra looming. "Where are they?"

"The professor had some property in Weston, the next town over. He hid them there."

The empty hood turned toward Chaz. "Why didn't you bring them back? Or have your lackey fetch them?"

He didn't have to put on an act when he scowled. "Lackey" was one of those words that set his teeth on edge and made him want to punch someone in the dick. "There were complications." He left the *you bitch* unspoken and prided himself on his diplomacy.

Bitch looked between them for a few moments. Twitch and Asshole shifted, watching her for cues. If she was considering violence as an option, she dismissed it fairly quickly. "Show us."

Val glanced back at Chaz. "You mind them stinking up your car?"

"You're paying for me to get it cleaned after." In truth, he minded plenty—carting around a trio of creatures who had threatened your friends and killed your acquaintances never would have made his *unreal shit I'll have to do as a Renfield* list, but it was part of the plan they'd worked out with Cavale last night. Having the car there wasn't utterly vital, but if they had to switch to Plan B, it'd help.

"I'll buy you a vat of Febreze."

"Done." He pulled the keys out of his jacket pocket and jangled them. "You three are in the back. I'd appreciate it if no one tried putting my eyes out while I'm driving." He looked up at Asshole, but the larger Jackal didn't react. As he led the way toward where the Mustang was parked, he caught Val's eye. "This is going to be the most fucked-up clown car ever."

ELLY WAS FEELING fidgety. They'd slept through the morning, though she'd woken up a few times to go check the cellar door. It wasn't that she'd thought Val would come upstairs while the sun was up and tear out their throats—if the woman hadn't killed her poststabbing, she probably wasn't going to. Still, there was a predator in the basement, a blood drinker, and damned if Elly could wander off into dreamland knowing that.

Around one o'clock that afternoon, they'd headed out for supplies. It wasn't easy finding rowan wood here, but Cavale knew of a few copses that contained trees they could take cuttings from. They'd gone to a freshwater spring after that, filling up soda bottles with the clear, cold water and mixing in a few drops of silver nitrate before screwing on the caps. Cavale had spread his hands over the shopping cart full of bottles and said a prayer. You didn't need to be ordained to bless the waters, Father Value had said. If regular people could baptize a baby in an emergency, then it had to follow that hunters like themselves could make some holy water to hunt the Creeps.

From there they'd hiked to the site he and Val had hashed out the night before and got the lay of the land. The cemetery had been abandoned before the Civil War. There'd been a church here once, but its walls had crumbled long ago, the congregation subsumed into other parishes. The land was privately owned now, Val had said, and no longer consecrated.

One lone, decrepit mausoleum still stood, a solitary sentry in the midst of gravestones that leaned precariously or had just plain fallen over. Elly had played her flashlight over some of them, just barely able to make out some of the names etched into the thin slate. Faint impressions of winged skulls survived at the tops of a few. She'd read somewhere that they'd signified angels to the colonists. *Either angels are awfully ugly or the Pilgrims were awfully morbid.* She guessed this one was probably on the Pilgrims.

They'd finished their preparations by twilight, the last rays of the setting sun throwing their shadows along the ground. When they were done, Cavale had checked her wards and she'd checked his, then they'd gone over all of them twice more.

After that, there wasn't much else to do besides hunker down in the woods and wait. The ground was cold and damp. Wetness seeped through the knees of her jeans in no time, but she refused to spread out the jacket she'd borrowed from Cavale and kneel on it. Her stuff could get dirty; his, she ought to take care of. She checked the straps on Silver and Pointy and glanced at Cavale. He was leaning against a tree, whittling the rowan sticks into points.

She waited until he sensed the weight of her stare and

looked up. "I still think we should kill them while we have the chance," she said. "We brought more than we need for just-in-case supplies." The holy water alone was enough to melt off their flesh a few times over.

Cavale tested the point of his stick, then went back to whittling. "Val said the woman's not the alpha." He sounded weary; they'd gone around in circles about this several times already. "Which means she's probably reported to whoever is the alpha, and if they don't come back, he'll send the nest in tomorrow night."

"But it'll be the nest minus three. Father Value always said it was better to cull when you can."

He didn't answer her at first. For a second, she thought maybe she'd gotten through, that invoking Father Value's name had swayed him. After all, Father Value had taught them both how to hunt the Creeps. It only made sense to do the things that had worked, didn't it? It was how they'd survived as long as they had.

Then Cavale sighed and set down the stick. "Elly." His voice was soft, hesitant. "This isn't Father Value's mission."

"N-no. I know. But—"

"I need the extra day, El. We need to get that shit out of Justin's head, and if the Creeps are busy chasing their tails, that gives us more time to prepare."

She swallowed down a protest. The plan had too many holes in it: they were counting on the Creeps to follow Val, counting on Chaz to play his part convincingly, counting on the wards to do what they were supposed to.

Stop it. It's not a bad plan at all. And it wasn't, either. It was close to what Father Value would have done, back when he'd had all three of them together. The bit about culling when you could, well. That was what you did when times were desperate. Two people could handle a small amount of Creeps if they were clever and quick, but it would never be pretty.

Adding a third tipped the scales. Some of it was purely tactical—an extra set of eyes on your targets, an extra set of legs in a chase. But there was power in threes, too. Father

Value had often spoken about the legs of a tripod when she and Cavale were growing up, how sturdy they were, how each supported the others. He'd told them how chords had three notes, each blending with the other two and transforming them into something bigger. Into something whole. So much of it had gone over her head, back then. She'd been too small to comprehend the full extent of Father Value's meaning, but whenever he'd talked that way Elly had felt like she was part of something special.

Maybe there were rites they would have gone through, some mystical Brotherhood ceremony to tie them all together, had things gone differently.

But when Cavale left, they were only two again. Easier to knock down. Diminished.

Now that Father Value was gone, they were still only two. Or worse, one and one. That depended on whether she stuck around after this. *If Cavale even wants me to.* For now, there was a job to do, and Cavale was watching her, waiting to see if she was going to argue the point any further. She shook her head. "No, you're right. It's a good plan. It's . . . it's what *he* would have done, if he could have."

His nod was slow in coming. It took a minute before she understood why. *Oh God, I'm an idiot.*

"You disgust me," he'd said, standing there with his fists clenched and his breath coming in ragged hitches. *"If I stay here, I'm afraid I'll end up becoming like you, and I don't ever want that. I'd let a Creep turn me before I'd go that way."*

"Cavale, I didn't mean—"

He hunkered down beside her and put a hand on her shoulder, shutting her up. "It's okay, El. I know. I'll take it in the spirit it was meant, all right?" He leaned back and retrieved the sticks and his knife, then pressed them into her hands. "How about you finish these for me? I want to give the wards another once-over."

She accepted them mutely, but both wood and blade hung from her limp hands as she watched him walk away. From the rigid set of his shoulders, she could tell he was upset. She wanted to get up and run after him, hound him with apologies until he forgave her like she'd done when she was ten. But they were a long way from childhood now, and there was work to be done. Elly tore her eyes away from Cavale's retreating form and snuck a glance at the moon. It had to be nearly two o'clock. Val and Chaz would be here soon, if everything went the way it was supposed to.

One and one, and another two. She wondered if that meant anything. Father Value had never talked about the meaning of four. *It has to be stronger. If three's good, four must be better.*

17

THE DRIVE FROM Night Owls to the abandoned cemetery plot in Weston was tense and silent. Val sat beside Chaz, watching his knuckles go white and whiter on the steering wheel. He was going to leave finger-sized indentations on the leather by the time he was done, but she couldn't blame him. The big, scarred Jackal sat directly behind him, sneering into the rearview anytime Chaz glanced into it.

The skinny one was in the middle. The Bitch had pushed his hood back so she could stroke the back of his neck. Seemed he didn't like cars very much, from the occasional low whine he let out. Val got a good look at him in the flashes from oncoming headlights—he hadn't transformed all the way. The top half of his face looked perfectly human. The only thing that betrayed him there was the amber tint of his eyes. But below that his nose and mouth had pushed out, his nostrils lengthening until they almost touched his top lip. His chin jutted forward, giving him an underbite. It didn't look comfortable, this in-between state.

It also meant he hadn't learned full control yet. *We can use it to our advantage.* She just had to figure out how.

Ten minutes later, Chaz pulled over on the edge of an overgrown field and killed the engine. "Last stop," he said, a little too loudly. "Everyone out of the pool."

The lackeys got out on his side. Without Bitch next to him to calm him, the skinny kid whined and panted while he waited for his companion to exit. The other Jackal took his time, ignoring the sounds of distress coming from his right. For a moment, as the bigger one used the door frame to steady himself, Val was certain Chaz would slam the door closed on his hands. She tried catching his eye across the Mustang's roof, giving her head a tiny shake, but he was too busy staring down the emerging Jackal.

Chaz had muttered his nicknames for them to her on the way to the car. Now, the one he'd dubbed Asshole finished unfolding himself from the backseat. He towered over Chaz, standing close enough to kiss. It was a dare. The Jackal's breathing stayed even, his heartbeat steady. Beneath the stench of rotten meat, Val thought he smelled . . . amused.

Chaz' heart, on the other hand, was thudding along fast and loud. Bitch heaved a sigh—they could sense it just as well as Val could. But if she wasn't calling her lackeys off, neither would Val. Throwing down now would ruin the plans, but making Chaz back down would show weakness. That was just as bad.

There were vampires who didn't have to speak to Command. Val wasn't one of them. The best she could do was think *don't do it* at him as hard as she could and hope he'd come to the conclusion that the timing wasn't right on his own. After a moment in which Val was pretty certain he'd counted to ten, Chaz stepped away and swept an arm out to the side to let Asshole by.

Of course, that meant when Twitch got out Chaz feinted toward him, making him flinch. *Can't win 'em all.*

"Let's go," said Bitch. Her tone suggested boredom, but they were racing the sun, too. Wherever they went to ground during the day, they'd have to allow for time to get there, or at least to find somewhere they could hole up. This part of Weston was all fields and farmland. The roads didn't even warrant streetlights out this far, and the last house they'd passed was back near the Edgewood town line.

Val took point, picking her way over the low wooden fence that ran along the property. Its rails were old and soft with rot. God only knew the last time it had been repaired. They struck out across the field, cutting a swath through the overgrown grass. Soon enough Chaz' car was only a boxy lump of shadow in the distance.

Eventually they joined up with the dirt path that came in from another angle and continued on through a line of trees up ahead. In colonial times, the path had probably been well trod by churchgoer feet. Now it was little more than an overgrown rut, but it let Val know they were getting close.

The ruins were on the other side. The moonlight picked out three crumbling, blackened stone walls, about thirty feet to a side. Two of them still had arched windows, though the glass was long gone. The wall closest to them was probably ten feet high, with a gaping maw that used to be the front door.

Chiseled into the stone above the lintel was a cross.

Bitch snarled and threw out an arm to stop Twitch and Asshole in their tracks. She turned to Val, yellow eyes flashing. "Holy ground? You think we're stupid enough to walk on *holy ground*?"

"Of course I don't. And my guess is, neither did the professor." Val nodded toward the structure. "Chaz spent the day researching. Henry Clearwater bought the property not long after he came to Edgewood. This church was active in the colonial days, but it burnt down in the early eighteen hundreds. The people who worshiped here joined up with a bigger parish nearby and let this place go to ruin, but the higher-ups never officially decommissioned it. Which means it's still consecrated."

"Shit," said Bitch.

"Yep. And if Chaz found all that on Wikipedia, I'm guessing Henry Clearwater knew a hell of a lot more. Pretty convenient place to stash things you don't want the local demon-souled rabble getting their hands on, wouldn't you say?"

The Jackals' heads all swung toward Chaz. Twitch

stepped up behind him, considering. "But *he's* not demon souled."

Chaz held up his hands. "Uh-uh. Oh, fuck no. You think the professor would've left a loophole like that open? Look at the door frame. Shit, look at the grass." He pointed his penlight a little ways ahead of them, then a bit to the right, then a bit further. Every ten feet or so, sigils were burnt into the dry grass. Several other, smaller rings were visible closer in. "Those things ring the whole clearing. And there are more on the building itself." He sidestepped away from Twitch, but bumped into Asshole. He pretended not to notice the big man, addressing Bitch instead. "I can't read runes for shit, but it's a safe bet those are wards to keep out everything that's not, y'know. You guys."

Val watched the other woman, trying to gauge her reaction. This was the part where Cavale's plan branched off into any number of possible outcomes. So far, it had gone smoothly—the Jackals had come to this place; Chaz' lines had been pitch-perfect. Best case, Bitch and her lackeys would dismiss Val and Chaz and puzzle out their own way across the grounds. When they called it a night, Elly and Cavale would follow them home. Val glanced around at the line of trees ringing the meadow. Whatever Cavale had done to hide the two of them had worked: if Val hadn't known they were dug in somewhere nearby, she'd have thought her own little group was all alone.

But the Jackals hadn't stopped staring at Chaz. He seemed to notice the thoughtful expressions Bitch and Twitch had adopted, and when Asshole shrank the distance between them from inches to centimeters, he swore and tensed.

"Leave him alone," Val said. "He's not your guinea pig." She didn't have to fake the nervousness that crept into her voice. Cavale had drawn the wards, but if Chaz stepped past them and they didn't do anything, the game was up. "There has to be a better way. Get someone down here to dismantle them and send in your own servants. Leave mine out of this."

Bitch folded her arms and eyed Chaz. "Why should we waste our own?"

At her nod, Asshole grabbed Chaz' shoulders and started forcing him forward.

"Hey, what the fuck? *Hey.*" Chaz thrashed in the bigger man's grip, but it did him no good.

Even if Asshole hadn't had the size advantage, a Jackal's strength would rival Val's own. "Come on, no!" Chaz whipped his head back, his skull smashing into Asshole's chin. Asshole barely even grunted. He didn't slow down.

As they approached the outer ring, several of the closest sigils started to glow a deep cobalt blue. Chaz threw a panicked look back at Val.

"You don't have to do this," she said. Still no movement from the woods. Cavale and Elly had to be able to see what was happening, but they hadn't broken cover. What did the glow mean? Cavale hadn't said anything about real, working wards. So what the hell were these? "No one has to get hurt."

Bitch shrugged. "Maybe not. But this is so much more efficient. We can tell our people what to expect." She turned back to Asshole. "Go ahead."

At first, as Asshole's shove sent Chaz staggering across the runes, Val thought the glow was the extent of the effect. Then *all* the sigils lit up, so bright that they all had to shade their eyes. The air around Chaz sizzled as the glow coalesced around him.

Chaz wheeled back around to face them. His mouth opened in a silent scream as brilliant blue flame licked up over his face. Val screamed aloud *for* him, shoving her way past Bitch. A few feet away, she stopped. Cavale's runes started in the same place as the consecrated ground, and even though Chaz was just out of arm's reach, he might as well have been a mile away. She could see his eyes, bright with pain, but moving through this was like swimming through molasses—if a swarm of angry bees were mixed into the molasses, that was.

Every inch of her skin stung as she forced herself closer.

If I can get to him . . . If I can just get a hand around his wrist . . . The Jackals had gone silent behind her. She almost had him. She was *so damned close.* Then his eyes rolled up in his head and he crumpled to the ground.

No breath. No heartbeat. The body on the ground before her was lifeless and unmoving.

She fell to her knees as she broke through the other side of the barrier. The sluggishness was gone, but the stinging intensified. Val shoved it aside and crawled the last few feet to Chaz. "No," she muttered, pulling him into her lap. The last of the cobalt fire guttered out. It didn't burn, but then, maybe it wouldn't. She had no idea what Cavale had *done.* "Oh God, Chaz, I'm sorry, I'm—" She broke off when she saw the smirk on his lips.

His eyes were open and tight with pain and confusion. Beneath her hands, she felt his heart give a few stuttery thumps as his chest rose and fell with shallow breaths. Her supernatural senses insisted that the man in her lap was dead, but plain old touch and sight told her differently.

Then, infuriating as ever, he winked.

Relief coursed through her, drowning out the sting of holy ground for the moment. She could hear the Jackals moving away, twigs and branches snapping as they tromped off in the direction of the road. A glance back confirmed it. The three of them were visible for a few more seconds until the trees and the dark swallowed them up. *They must have seen enough.* The chase was up to Cavale and Elly now.

Val peered down at Chaz. His grin had grown to shit-eating proportions. "I'm going to kill you," she mouthed.

"VAL'S GOING TO *kill* you," said Elly. "Both of you." She watched the runes trigger and squinted as the fire flared around Chaz. "And there she goes." The vampire's scream rent the air. The night-creatures, who had restarted their chirping and scurrying once they realized Elly and Cavale weren't there to eat them, went silent again. She turned to Cavale. "How long can she stay there?"

His eyes were fixed on the Creeps at the edge of the woods. "She'll be fine for a few minutes. She knows to get out before it gets too bad."

Chaz collapsed. Elly saw Val reach him, but then the fire went out and she couldn't make out more than a hunched shape in the middle. In theory, Val was finding out that Chaz was just fine right about now. The wards had been pretty ingenious on Cavale's part. He'd spent most of the day trying to figure out something that'd keep the charade going if the Creeps decided to call their bluff and make Chaz go into the husk of the church. At first, he'd wanted to go with a simple illusion, something that would *look* like the wards had tripped. Chaz could have run inside the ruin and hidden there until the Jackals left.

It had seemed solid enough until Elly mentioned the attack at the Clearwaters, and the impression of hundreds of Creeps attacking. One of them—she guessed it was the female—could make illusions of her own, which meant it was possible she'd see right through Cavale's. But a smaller one, confined to Chaz himself, might work. Cavale had run it by Chaz and they'd both agreed to leave Val out of the loop on it. It was better if her reaction was real. Elly wondered if Cavale had told Chaz the part he'd asked her to add in, where his heart really *would* stop for a few seconds.

Probably not. It was a tactic they'd used once before, while hunting with Father Value. That time, Cavale had been the bait. Even though Elly'd known he'd come out of it—that his heart would start beating again and he'd get up and stake the Creeps as soon as the trap was sprung—she'd been haunted by the image of his waxy skin and dead eyes for weeks after. She knew the fear and relief that had to be coursing through Val right about then.

Cavale was tugging on her arm. "The Creeps are leaving. Let's go." They hefted their backpacks, holy water sloshing away inside. Elly hated having to leave some of the supplies behind, but they could come back for them. They had enough to take these three on if it came to it, even though the mission was to follow, not to fight. Still, she couldn't help hoping for *some* kind of fisticuffs.

It was easy enough to follow the Creeps' trail through the woods. They weren't concerned about subtlety, so they left a swath of broken branches in their wake. Every so often their voices echoed back to Elly and Cavale, usually one of them laughing at something the others had said. They sounded like hyenas, then, only throatier. Once they got to the road, though, they picked up speed.

Elly and Cavale could run, but for nowhere near as long as the Creeps could. "We're going to lose them. Should I go back and see if Chaz will give us the car keys?"

"No. Hang on."

Hanging on wasn't easy. Every second they delayed, the trail got colder. Father Value had taught them both how to track, but doing it on pavement was unreliable at best. Unless . . . "What are you doing?"

"Check this out." Cavale pulled a small, round mirror out of his pocket. Glued to the back of it was a safety pin. He opened the pin and pricked his finger, then squeezed a few drops onto the mirror. He smeared them into the shape of an arrow-headed rune. It lit up, then began to spin. Seconds later, the arrow pointed along the road toward the center of Weston. "Chaz let me draw another one in black chalk on the backseat. One of them leaned against it enough for it to transfer. As long as they don't decide to go swimming or something, we're set."

They grinned at each other. Creeps hated water.

The rune-compass led them through Weston proper, past all four of its streetlights, and right up to the Edgewood town line. From there, they turned onto the road Elly recognized as the one from her bus trip. They were on a stretch that was neither Edgewood nor Weston now, made up of clusters of small businesses separated by long stretches of empty plots. Elly counted two car repair shops, a landscaper's headquarters, and a place whose sign announced *Snowblowers are now in stock!!!*

Just as they passed the sign, Cavale stopped short. "They're up ahead."

Past the next set of streetlights, a corrugated metal

building sat in the center of a dirt lot. It was maybe thirty feet by fifty, with no windows aside from the ones on the garage door at the front. Those were painted over with black. Elly craned her neck and saw another, regular door on the side. "We should go get a better look, see how many are inside."

"The sun'll be up soon. We can do it then."

"But if we go *now*, maybe we can hear who it is they're reporting to. Whether it's someone inside, or if they're making a phone call."

He was winding up with an argument, but before he could make it, he went very still. "Elly," he said, staring at a point over her shoulder. He didn't need to finish. She ducked and whirled, Silver and Pointy falling into her palm. She couldn't help the smile that broke out on her face—after spending most of the day either preparing or watching Cavale do *his* thing, it felt damned good to finally be able to do *hers*.

The Creep hadn't expected her to drop. As his momentum carried him past her, she reached out and snagged his ankle. Gravel skittered across the road as he went sprawling. Something clanged against the asphalt. *Tire iron?* Elly scuttled over to him, keeping out of range in case he sat up and swung. She could see the L-shaped rod clutched in his hand. *Yup. Tire iron.*

To her side, Cavale had set down his backpack and retrieved a soda bottle filled with holy water. He loosened the cap and tossed it to her. She caught it with her free hand as the Creep pushed up onto his elbows. Now she had a dilemma: give him a good dousing, or go straight to her old standby?

Use every advantage, Eleanor. Father Value hadn't survived as long as he had by ignoring that rule. It wasn't time for her to start. She gave the cap a twirl and heard it spin away along the shoulder of the road. She advanced on the Creep, the bottle in her left hand, Silver and Pointy ready in her right. The Creep was on one knee, his right leg behind him. He looked like a runner waiting for the starting pistol.

Elly wasn't much for waiting. She squeezed the bottle,

sending an arc of water out in front of her as she charged forward. The Creep sprang, too, face-first into the water. His howl of pain choked off as his skin started to smoke. This close, Elly could see the fur on his muzzle and the sharp points of his teeth as his lips pulled back. He swiped at where she'd been standing, but she'd gotten him right between the eyes. He was fighting blind.

She dodged beneath the first swipe and danced back a step as he swung the tire iron in a wide arc. It whooshed through the air less than a foot from her head. She glanced to see where Cavale was and realized they had more company. He and another Creep were circling one another like boxers. A third was jogging toward them from the corner of the building.

None were the Creeps from earlier. *Which means these ones are buying them time. For what, though?* Elly dodged another swing. She needed him to get rid of that tire iron so she could get close enough for a staking. She let her instincts guide her through the motions of fighting while she turned plausible explanations over in her head.

Dawn was coming. It made no sense (duck, sidestep, try to flank) for the Creeps to finish their briefing if there were people who could come in during the daylight and (hop back, feint, pitch the empty bottle in the other direction) kill off the rest of their nest while they slept. Creeps weren't known for bravery and sacrifice—they wouldn't (leap while he sniffs in the direction of the noise, raise the spike high) trap themselves in a warehouse just to get information to their betters.

So either they think these three will take us out easily—

Elly drove Silver and Pointy home right between the blinded Creep's shoulder blades. He shrieked as the tip pierced his heart from behind. Beneath his clothes, greasy ash spread outward from the wound, leaking out from his sleeves and cuffs. The clothing held his shape a moment longer, until Elly yanked out the spike and stepped away. Everything fell in a heap.

—or these ones have been abandoned and the rest of them are busy fleeing.

She turned to see Cavale shove his Creep up against the snowblower sign. They were captured in silhouette for a second, the Creep's neck stretching as he snapped his teeth at Cavale's face. Then Cavale pulled a rowan stake from his belt and plunged it into the Creep's eye. It went down yelping, cradling its head. Rowan didn't work as fast as silver, but this one wasn't getting up again anytime soon.

Cavale straightened and pointed across the lot. The third Creep seemed to have changed its mind about joining the fight. It loped away past the building, a man-shape running on all fours.

Elly moved over to stand with Cavale. The Creep writhed in pain at their feet. "I don't think anything's going to be inside that place."

"They ought to have swarmed us, if they were defending their territory."

"Do you think we tipped the other three off? Did they know we were following?" She looked down at the Creep. "Wait, we can just ask."

Its good eye rolled in fear when she hunkered down beside it. The stake still protruded from its other one.

"Is anyone left in that building?" She pointed with her silver spike, making sure the light from the sign caught the metal.

The Creep moaned. "Please . . ."

"Answer me and I'll help you. Who's in there?"

"No one. No one! Everyone ran." He bucked beneath her as a spasm hit. The rowan was making its way to his brain. *Not yet.* "Why did they run?"

"Alpha. Alpha said . . ." He trailed off and barked a harsh laugh.

Elly shook him, resisting the urge to twist the stake. It might wake him up, but it might do more damage and render him incapable of answering. "What did your alpha say?"

"Said. Said the leech wasn't alone. Said . . . *Value.*"

So they know we're here, too. She'd never thought of herself as particularly egotistic, but she couldn't deny the swell of pride that came with knowing she and Cavale had factored into the Creeps' retreat.

Its speech degenerated into moans and babbling, then. Its other eye filmed over and sunk in.

Elly took Silver and Pointy and finished the job. She wiped the spike off on the bottom of her shirt, then picked up a handful of dirt from the side of the road and dry washed her hands with it. She didn't think she'd been hit by any blood, but the ash was a pain in the ass to get off.

Cavale held up one of the bottles of holy water. "You know, you could have used this."

"Meh. We might need that later." She waved it away. Picking up her backpack, she headed across the lot.

The side door of the Creeps' former nest was unlocked. She opened it carefully, in case they'd left one unlucky pack-mate behind for an ambush. Cavale stood directly behind her, ready with a bottle and the tire iron he'd retrieved from beside Elly's Creep's remains. Nothing. The place wasn't empty, but it had clearly been abandoned. Rags were strewn everywhere. Flies buzzed atop piles of garbage. Creepscrawl covered most of the walls.

They picked through the refuse, looking for anything that might be useful. The best they found, though, were three discarded sweatshirts. Cavale held up the mirror and the rune pointed at them. He picked one of them up and ran a finger down its back. He held up a chalk-smudged digit for Elly to see. "So much for tracing them further with this."

Dawn had lightened the sky by the time they trudged out of the nest. Elly was dead tired. They still had the trek back to Crow's Nest ahead of them. She looked hopefully along the road, willing a car to come along so she could stick out her thumb. But the ones that did pass by kept on going. No one wanted to stop and pick up two grimy-looking kids in the wee hours. Okay, *one* grimy-looking kid. Cavale was rumpled but nowhere near as filthy. Though it probably didn't help that he'd held on to the tire iron.

Then there came the rumbling of an engine. It had to be an older car; nothing new made that much noise. Cavale squinted uphill as the car crested it. "Son of a bitch," he said, but he was smiling. He waved wearily at the Mustang as it approached and pulled over on the opposite side of the street.

Chaz unrolled his window. "You kids want a ride?"

They clambered in, Cavale in front, Elly in the back. It felt good to sit down and close her eyes.

"I've been driving around for an hour trying to find you guys. You two okay? And where the hell did you get that?" Elly cracked one eye open to see him gesturing at Cavale's prize.

"Oh. Yeah." Cavale held the tire iron up so Chaz could see it. "Thought maybe you could use this. As long as you're not going to hit me with it for what the wards did."

"Nah," he said. "But you probably don't want to hand it to Val. She might use it."

Elly lifted her head up off the seat rest. "Where *is* Val? Did she have time to get home before sunrise?"

In the mirror, Chaz winced. "No, she's, uh. She insisted I come find you and make sure you were all right."

"So did she go to ground or something?"

The wince deepened. "She's in the trunk, asleep."

❦ 18 ❦

Chaz had time to catch a nap and a shower after he dropped Elly and Cavale off in Crow's Neck. They'd stopped in Edgewood first, to maneuver Val inside. Good thing she had a garage that connected to the house and had given Chaz the automatic door opener. It would've been awkward explaining the body-shaped bundle they'd carried inside otherwise. Plus, he'd have had to find a tarp to wrap her in, first.

As it was, they'd left her on the living room floor, covered in blankets. Val was a hundred and fifty-something pounds of dead weight, and Chaz and Cavale had taken one look at the stairs and said forget it. The floor wasn't as comfortable as her bed, but it was carpeted, and Chaz had tucked a throw pillow beneath her head. He was pretty sure it'd beat spending the day stuffed in his trunk.

Three hours later, tired as hell but at least clean shaven and presentable, he knocked on Sunny and Lia's door. When it opened, he was greeted not by either of the women he'd left Justin with yesterday, but instead peered down into the eyes of a young Katharine Hepburn. She could have been straight out of *Philadelphia Story* if it weren't for the flannel pajamas and the bunny slippers.

"Chaz! Hi!" she said, in Hepburn's smoky voice. "Come on in. Lia's trying out Rita Hayworth."

"Trying . . . out?" He followed the succubus inside, confused.

"Mm-hmm. Did you know Justin likes old movies? He spent most of yesterday watching one of those black-and-white-film channels. We thought we'd put on a show."

Chaz glanced at the bunny slippers again. Whatever they were up to, it clearly wasn't the kind of show *most* men would expect a pair of succubi to put on. When he entered the living room, Lia was in a huge fluffy bathrobe, dancing a barefoot samba across the floor. Tendrils of red hair spilled down her back, and now and then the robe would flare open, revealing a pair of perfect legs that went all the way up to . . . the hem of Lia's running shorts.

Justin looked like he wanted to dive behind the couch. When he noticed Chaz, he sprang to his feet, relieved. "Hey, uh, you ready to go?" He dodged around Lia, who was trying to snag him for a dance. Sunny stepped into her arms instead, and the two waltzed a few steps before collapsing onto the love seat, giggling.

"You know," said Chaz, "someone out there on the Internet would *kill* to see this." He elbowed Justin. "You're turning your nose up at the opportunity of a lifetime, dude." It was amusing as hell watching the kid go from pink to tomato red. "Not like *that*. I mean, think about it. Right now, there are like a thousand fans who are feeling a sudden, overwhelming disappointment and they don't even know why. But *I* do. And Sunny and Lia do. It's because you were sitting there trying to meld with the furniture when you could've been reenacting scenes from *The Lion in Winter*. Talk about missed opportunities."

"Oh, oh! Like this!" Sunny sat up and yanked a doily off an end table. As she tied it around her head, those sharp cheekbones softened a bit. A few strands of grey wound through her auburn hair and crow's-feet appeared around her eyes: Hepburn at sixty. She held an imaginary necklace to her chest and intoned, "I'd hang you from the nipples, but you'd shock the children."

Justin threw Chaz a pleading look.

"Aww, cut him some slack." Lia dragged her fingers through her hair. With every stroke, the red faded and her usual blond streaked its way in. "He's been a complete gentleman since you left. Even when we were being utter shits."

"We must've tried to get a favorite face out of him for two hours. *Nothing.*"

"Well." Chaz clapped a hand on Justin's shoulder. "You might get another chance. Shit's still getting resolved, and if Cavale can't get the weirdness out of our boy here this afternoon, we might need him to stay another night."

There was a gasp from his side. Justin ducked away from him. "Don't I get a say?"

He grimaced. "Right now? No, you don't. And I'm sorry for that, but these things don't fuck around and we don't know what they're up to right now."

"I thought you had a plan. I thought you guys were fixing things. Like, you know. Me."

"We are."

"But?"

"But we need more time."

Lia padded over to them. While Chaz and Justin were arguing, she'd reverted the rest of the way back to her regular face. It was probably why Justin allowed her to straighten his tie. All of her previous flirtation was gone as she smoothed out his collar and brushed a piece of lint—or maybe cat hair from their evil fucking cat that was lurking around somewhere—from his shoulder. "You're welcome here anytime."

"Yeah." Sunny unwrapped the doily from around her head. She ducked behind the lace for a second, and when she emerged, Katharine Hepburn had made her exit. "You did the dishes last night. Dishes *suck.*"

As hard as Justin tried to look miserable, he couldn't resist a little grin. "I'm your guest. It's just polite."

"Yeah, well, if you can't figure out what to do with your

English degree after you graduate, we'd be happy to hire you on. You can recite Shakespeare while you dust."

"Well, um. I'll keep it in mind. Thank you."

Lia beamed at Justin. When she turned the smile on Chaz, it seemed to say, *See? This is how it's done.*

That settled, Justin and Chaz set out for the Clearwaters' funeral Mass. They were partway down the street when Justin started twisting around in his seat to peer into the back.

"I promise you," said Chaz, "there aren't any succubi hiding in the back waiting to jump out and torture you."

"It's not that," he said, his nose crinkling. "What the hell did you have in here? It smells like wet dog."

Chaz sniffed. All he got was a noseful of his and Justin's aftershaves and the mineral oil he used to protect the Mustang's seats. "I don't smell anything."

"How can you not? It's, like, everywhere." Justin was leaning halfway into the backseat now, his seat belt off so he could get a better angle.

"If I have to slam on the brakes, you're going right through the windshield. You know how much that'd cost to replace?"

"You really can't smell it? It's even worse back here." He squirmed around to the front again, though, and dutifully buckled up. "It's really nasty."

That was when Chaz got a better look at Justin. His nose was high in the air and he turned his head this way and that, trying to catch the scent. It might've seemed funny, if he hadn't been witnessing Val doing the same damned thing for the last five years. "Oh, shit, dude."

That brought Justin's nose back to normal-people level. "What?"

"I, uh. I think you might be smelling the Jackals. They were in here last night."

Justin blinked. "But that . . . Why would I be able to smell them when you can't?"

Chaz didn't have to answer that one. Dismay spread across Justin's features as it came to him.

"Oh."

"It'll probably go away when Cavale gets that shit out of you. It's just some sort of, I don't know. Psychic side effect." This was one of the disadvantages to being a minion whose vampire avoided others of her kind. The Boston Renfields were better versed in magical dealings because they were surrounded by it twenty-four-fucking-seven. Nine times out of ten, it just made them even more pretentious. But right now, this one time, it would've been nice to be able to put more authority behind his assertion.

Justin peered at him. He seemed to be on the brink of more questions, but he let it go. "Sunny and Lia are nice," he said, blessedly changing the subject.

Chaz grinned. "Yeah? They didn't fuck with you too much?"

"Nah. I mean, they teased me a lot at dinner but not in a mean way."

"Good."

"Well, except when in the middle of trying to pick my crushes out of my head, Sunny turned into my mom."

Chaz snorted. "They got you with the Oedipus trick, huh?"

"They did it to you, too?"

"Oh God yeah. They think it's hilarious." It had been Lia, not Sunny, but they'd played the same game with him when they'd first met. High school girlfriends, college flings, a couple of hot professors he'd had, then, smack in the middle of the cute customers list, bam. Chaz' mother. "Don't worry," he told Justin, "they really were just fucking with you. You don't actually want to bone your mom, subconsciously or otherwise. At least, probably not."

One thing he'd been grateful for, and hadn't even realized until after the giggling had stopped and they'd moved on to a game of Scrabble: they'd never once turned into Val.

THE CHURCH WAS packed when they arrived. Every pew was filled, students and faculty crammed together like sardines. Chaz and Justin were prepared to stand in the back, but before they could find a spot, the head of the English department found them and ushered Justin (and thus Chaz) to a pew closer to the front. They'd set aside a section for Professor Clearwater's grad students.

Chaz hated to think it, but it was nice to sit down, after being up all night and catching an inadequate nap. Especially since the day wasn't likely to get much easier. And tonight . . .

He'd think about that later.

The Mass went smoothly and, to Chaz' tired brain, quickly. A lot of the crowd thinned out afterward, most of the students opting to go back to campus rather than attending the graveside service. But Justin wanted to go, and Chaz wasn't going to deny the kid. He looked rough, as if *he'd* been the one running around all last night.

Justin was quiet as they pulled into the line of cars that comprised the procession, staring out the window and watching his classmates go about their days. At the first stoplight, Chaz was concentrating on making sure an asshole in an SUV didn't cut off the rest of the line. It took him a minute to realize Justin's shoulders were shaking. He caught a glimpse of Justin's reflection, and the tears flowing down his cheeks. "Hey, man, you okay?"

Justin swallowed hard a couple of times before answering. "Yeah, I just. I'm sorry. It just hits me now and then."

Chaz reached over and gave him an awkward sort of bro-pat. He wished Val were there. She was so much better at this shit. "It's okay. That's gonna happen. There's, uh, well. I don't think I have any tissues, but there ought to be some napkins in the glove box, if you want them."

"Thanks." He popped it open and pulled out a handful of bright yellow fast-food napkins to dab at his eyes and blow his nose with. By the time they reached the cemetery, he was mostly composed again, though he'd shoved a couple of dry ones into the pocket of his dress pants, just in case.

Edgewood Cemetery was a pretty place, with rolling hills and well-kept plots. The trees scattered about blazed with color, but hardly any leaves carpeted the ground. In another section of the cemetery, Chaz could hear the rhythmic whisper of groundskeepers' rakes as they tried keeping ahead of autumn's organic litter. But here, near the Clearwaters' side-by-side graves, all was quiet except for the shuffling of feet and the soft sound of mourners sniffling. The priest, a round-faced, greying man with a full, neatly trimmed beard uttered the benedictions somberly, then invited the Clearwaters' family and friends to come and take flowers from the many arrangements that had been sent in remembrance.

Chaz hung back, letting the immediate family pay their final respects. He wanted to take a couple of iris buds back to Val; she would have been here, if it weren't for the whole sun-killing-her thing. He nudged Justin, who was still standing beside him. "You can go on up, if you want. You were close to him."

But Justin wasn't paying attention. He wasn't even facing the caskets.

He'd turned away, sniffing the air again. He was up on his toes, like he was trying to get higher for a better shot at the scent.

"Justin? What's going on?"

After half a minute or so, at the point where Chaz was about to give him as subtle a shake as he could to get a response, Justin lowered himself back onto his heels and looked up at Chaz, troubled. "I smelled it again. Wet dog."

Chaz turned in a slow circle, as if he were admiring the view the Clearwaters would have from their eternal resting places. Really, he was looking for anyone that seemed out of place, even a mourner in a too-big hat. But there was nothing to be seen. He put on his best *everything's cool* smile and mustered what little certainty he could find. "Probably a real one, kid. People bring their dogs here all the time. Maybe Spot got a bath before walkies."

"You sure?"

"Think about this," he said, and bent his head closer to Justin, so no one could hear the crazy coming from his mouth. "Two things I know for sure about Jackals: they can't step on holy ground, which depending on your religion, this technically is."

"Okay," he said, but his eyes darted to the roads that wound their way through the cemetery.

Chaz could guess what he was thinking, since it was on his mind, too: Did the roads count as consecrated, too, or just the plots that had, like the Clearwaters' five minutes ago, been officially blessed? Was the whole cemetery off-limits, or were the graves some kind of macabre hopscotch board? *Doesn't matter. There's still Thing Two.* "Thing two: it's daytime. They can't come out and play right now."

That seemed to make him relax again. "Yeah. Okay, yeah." Only a handful of people were still by the graves now, family members talking quietly. "I'm . . . I'm going to go say good-bye." From the way Justin's eyes lingered on the caskets, Chaz didn't think he was talking about the living.

"Go ahead. I'm going to grab some flowers for Val. You want to meet me at the car when you're ready?"

"Yeah. I won't be long."

"Take your time." Chaz stepped forward and plucked a pair of irises from their basket. Their stems were inter-twined, the buds still closed. As he headed back to the Mus-tang, he found himself peering around, looking for anything that seemed off. He couldn't shake the feeling he was being watched.

When he slid into the front seat, he made sure he had a line of sight on Justin. The tire iron that Cavale had given him earlier was in the backseat. Chaz retrieved it without taking his eyes off the knot of people at the Clearwaters' grave, and held it across his knees until Justin returned to the car.

Just in case.

❧ 19 ❧

ELLY WOKE TO Cavale moving furniture around.

She understood why, of course. Some rituals needed plenty of space, and if he was trying to yank the Creepscrawl out of Justin, well. It was a good idea to have a lot of room. There might be thrashing.

Still, she'd been fast asleep, and it had been . . . Elly frowned. She wasn't a deep sleeper, as a rule. Living with Father Value pretty much killed that possibility—too much likelihood of having to get up and go if Creeps or cops came sniffing around. But here she was, in a cocoon made of down comforters and feather pillows, feeling positively languid. Sunlight streamed in through the window, warming her even further. She felt like a cat, curled up in the toastiest spot and not wanting to move.

If she'd ever been this comfortable in her life, she didn't remember it. She lay there awhile longer, marveling at how strange it was to feel so . . . so . . .

What?

Safe.

Sure, she'd felt safe with Father Value, but that came from

knowing they could get away from almost any dangers. She'd never felt this way about a *place* before, aside from churches. That was a short-lived kind of safety, though. Eventually a priest would come along and kick you out. Sanctuary was kind of a bullshit concept, she'd learned.

She'd only been at Cavale's house a couple of days. She'd made sure to learn the best escape routes the first morning she'd crashed here. If she had to go out the window, she was fairly certain she could get to the ground without breaking her legs, provided she could make the jump across to the garage roof. Cavale's presence was a comfort, but the awkwardness of separation still hung between them. It wasn't that she thought he wouldn't have her back in a fight. After the confrontation with the Creeps last night, she knew he was just as good as he'd been two years ago. Better, even. But he still wasn't Father Value, and Cavale had left her once. Father Value never had.

Yet she couldn't shake the feeling that things were okay here. Solid. Sturdy. The frightening thought that maybe she could cobble together some semblance of a *life* if she stayed niggled at her. They could patch things up the rest of the way, conversation closing the wounds better than myrrh.

If she stayed.

Which, she wasn't going to, was she? She'd promised Cavale she only wanted a day or two, and she was only breaking that to finish what she'd started with the Creeps. Then she'd go. No more bothering him, no more forcing him to remember what he'd left behind. "Take all the time you need," he'd said, but she'd been sobbing when he said it.

A particularly loud *thud* and an even louder curse from downstairs propelled her out of bed. She told herself it was guilt at letting Cavale do all the work, but getting away from the tangle of her thoughts was a nice bonus.

She found Cavale in the kitchen putting iodine on a cut. "I should probably save this." He was referring to the blood, not the ointment.

"You think we'll need a lot?"

"Hopefully not, but Chaz called. He said he thinks Justin

can smell the Creeps now. Which means whatever's in his head is making itself at home. We'll see how the watered-down stuff works first." He jerked his head toward the sink. A half-gallon plastic tub sat within, a layer of frost on the outside from the warmth of the room. "You want breakfast? There's, uh. Coffee, and we could toast some hamburger buns."

Elly grinned. He'd never been good at shopping. Well, at shopping *lists*. Between the two of them, Cavale had always done far better with actually going into stores and buying the food, but left to his own devices, he'd come out with cans of Chef Boyardee, a box of Pop-Tarts, and some exotic fruit that neither of them knew how to break into, "To prevent scurvy."

"What are you smiling at?"

"Just the time you found the sale on maraschino cherries. You came back with ten jars of them and a loaf of bread, remember? And we made sandwiches out of them."

He snickered. "We pressed the edges together and called them cherry pies."

"And we drank the syrup straight from the jars like it was juice. We got it everywhere, turned everything bright red." Even as she said it, though, her smile faded. The warm feeling shrank and shriveled, like a cherry left out to dry.

"Then *he* came home." Cavale said it quietly, looking away.

Father Value had found them both sprawled out on the floor, clutching their bellies and groaning from fullness. He hadn't interpreted the sounds as happy ones, though, since the first thing he'd seen was all the red. He'd thought it was blood. The first few moments were filled with panic, then relief as they explained their unconventional dinner and offered to make him a pie with the last jar of cherries and the heels of the bread.

That was about when he'd started yelling at Cavale. How he was older, and how he ought to know better. How he had to set a good example for Elly. How he was in charge during the day and had to be more responsible. How that had been the last of their money for the next few days, and now what would they eat.

Cavale had been all of nine; Elly, six.

"I'm sorry," she said. "He was hard on you."

"It was what, sixteen years ago? He never raised a hand to me. To either of us. There's that, at least." He struggled briefly with something else, on the edge of saying more. Emotions flickered across his face: hurt, hesitation, *calculation*. The last reminded her of Father Value, when he was about to say something neither of them would like. Elly tucked that away—it would be entirely the wrong thing to say right now. Then they all disappeared, and whatever he'd been thinking went unsaid.

"Anyway. Toast, if you want it. I'm going to finish up in there. Chaz is bringing Justin by in a half hour." He ducked out of the kitchen. The thumping and scraping started anew. To Elly's ears, it sounded more aggressive than it had when she was lazing about upstairs.

Way to go, Elly. Brilliant.

CHAZ AND JUSTIN arrived a little after two. They were still dressed in their funeral clothes, though if they'd worn ties for the ceremony, they must have taken them off and left them in the car. Justin looked more composed than he had the other night; still sad, his eyes red rimmed, but she had to admit he looked good all dressed up.

The living room had been transformed. The other night it had been cozy enough, with Cavale's mismatched, yard sale furniture making a fairly large room look just shy of cramped. Now, with the couches shoved against one wall, the smaller chairs and end tables relocated to the kitchen, and the rug rolled up and tucked away, the room seemed huge.

Once they'd finished clearing it out and swept the floor, Cavale had truly set to work. The circle was a work of art: six feet in diameter, it had a ring of tiny Norse runes along the inside edge. Coming in from those, Cavale had drawn from several other traditions, tying the symbols together as if their ancient creators had lived a few miles away from one another and shared a language rather than being half a world away. Sumerian cozied up to Pictish, which flowed into Japanese hiragana.

Elly understood most of it, but something like this would have taken her hours. Cavale had done it in twenty minutes, while Elly stood by and handed him new pieces of chalk when he wore his down to a nub. She'd also gone and heated up the pigs' blood for him. It hadn't had time to thaw, so she'd stuck it in the microwave. A bit unorthodox, but it worked. The only drawback was the smell of burnt copper that permeated the house. The kitchen windows were open, but in here, the curtains were drawn, the windows closed.

Justin took it all in, wide-eyed. He pointed at a particular hieroglyph that repeated throughout the circle. Inside a cartouche were a feather, a box beneath a squiggly line, a bird, and a dog. "What does that one do?"

Cavale wiped his hands on his jeans, leaving blue-chalk palm prints on his thighs. "It's the symbol for Anubis."

"Is that . . . is that who they worship? Or who gives them their, um, power?" Another thought dawned and he paled even further. "I'm not possessed by him, am I?"

Chaz snorted. Cavale shot him a glare, his jaw setting in what Elly thought of as his argument face. *Better cut this off before it starts.*

"It's just a symbol, this time. Anubis was jackal-headed, so his name can stand in for the Creeps. The circle's all wrong for actually summoning Anubis himself." She thought back to the colorful jumble of chalks and paints that made up Cavale's junk drawer. "Plus, I didn't see any lapis in with the supplies."

Justin's eyes bulged at her casual mention of summoning a god. He didn't ask any more questions.

Cavale made a few final adjustments to the runes, then stepped back, satisfied. "Okay. Take your shirt off."

"What?"

He retrieved the tub of pigs' blood from the only small piece of furniture left in the room. It was a plain brown stool, the finish on its seat worn pale by countless bottoms. Set beside the tub like an artist had left them behind were several paintbrushes. They varied in length and width, from hair fine to a half-inch thick. Cavale selected a medium one and eyed Justin. "You can leave it on if you want, but that's an awfully nice shirt, and this stuff'll stain."

Justin looked at the blood, then at Elly, Chaz, and back to Cavale. "This is getting *really* weird. You guys all know that, right?"

Considering what he'd been through the last few days, Elly probably shouldn't have blamed Justin for feeling that way. It *was* weird, all of it. Especially to a kid who'd never believed in this kind of thing. But that meant he thought *she* was weird, too. In this room, standing there with herself and Cavale and Chaz, *Justin's* normal life was the abnormality here, and yet she felt like the freak.

And it pissed her off.

"You know what?" she said, advancing on him. "Maybe it is. But when it's done you can go back to your boring little Creep-free life and leave the real work to the rest of us. Until then? Shut up and do what he says."

Regret set in as soon as the words were out of her mouth. Justin went bright red and mumbled an apology. He shrugged out of his suit jacket and handed it off to Chaz without further argument. His fingers drifted up to the top button on his shirt, but paused there. After a moment, Elly realized he was looking at her, the blush deepening. "Um, do you think you could . . . ?"

Oh, for fuck's sake. She turned to Cavale. "Let me know when you're starting. I should be in here for this."

Chaz followed her into the kitchen. Getting to the table meant picking their way through the maze of displaced end tables and plant stands, but they managed it without knocking anything over. He sat down across from her and offered her a friendly grin. "Hey, go easy on him, okay? I know he touched a nerve there, but he means well. He's just . . . new to this."

Another twinge of guilt. She picked at the chipped

Formica. "I know. I'll apologize to him. It's been a long morning."

"You kids fighting? You and Cavale?"

She blinked. "No. I mean, not really." After she'd had her toasted hamburger bun—dry, since Cavale was out of butter, too—she'd ventured in to help him with the re-arranging. The first few minutes were tense and awkward, but then he'd started talking about how the ritual would go, and the mood had cleared. Cavale wasn't much of a grudge holder, but she still felt awful.

Chaz wasn't buying it, either. " 'Not really' implies that there was *something*. My mom used to say my sister and I bickered like magpies. It's just what siblings do." He broke off, his gaze flicking to the open window and back to her, almost too quick to notice.

But Elly had grown up learning that people ought to trust their instincts: if you thought you heard a noise or saw a shadow move, Father Value had said you probably did. She glanced outside, studying the overgrown backyard. After-noon sunlight played on the dead brown grass. A breeze sent leaves skittering. Nothing else moved. "Did you see some-thing out there?"

For a long moment, he didn't answer. He turned his whole head this time, scanning the backyard for a full thirty sec-onds before looking back at her. "No. Sorry." He looked a little longer, then gave up. "I assume Cavale told you Justin can smell them now? Or so we think?"

She nodded.

"He caught a whiff at the cemetery. I've been on edge all damned day." A self-conscious laugh escaped him. "I made him take a few deep sniffs when we got here, just in case. He didn't smell anything."

"It's daytime," she said. "They can't—"

"I know. Maybe they were at the grave last night, or someone there had been at the professor's house before the service and picked up the scent. Whatever it was, it freaked me the hell out." He took a deep breath. "*Anyway*. I'm just saying, hang in there. Cavale can be a colossal shithead when he wants to, but he's a decent enough guy. You two will be fine."

She wasn't used to pep talks, didn't know what you were supposed to say when someone gave you one. "Thanks." It was a start. "We're okay now. I mean, there's a lot of old stuff that sucks, but . . . we'll figure it out." Or she'd be gone when all this was done. That was the easier thing.

Chaz' green eyes bored into her like he was trying to glean more, but he let it go. "Okay. Well, if you need someone to beat some sense into him, I'm your man."

"I'll keep it in mind."

Then Cavale was in the doorway, beckoning them into the living room. The ritual was ready.

THE CURTAINS HAD been thrown wide, letting the sunlight in. Cavale had moved the stool into the center of the circle. Justin sat on it gingerly, his feet on the rungs like he feared touching them to the floor and smearing the chalk. He looked miserable up there, and extremely uncomfortable. Runes covered him from his collarbone to the top of his dress pants and from his shoulders down to his fingertips. He looked as though he'd traded his crisp white button-down shirt for a close-fitting red one, so dense was the runework.

It would have been strange enough for him if a stranger had simply drawn on him with paint, but the frequent crinkling of his nose meant he couldn't quite pretend it was anything other than animal blood.

The Creeps' book sat in his lap, open to the empty pages where their spell had been. Elly hadn't the faintest idea what they'd do if the words went back onto the page—destroy the book? Hide it somewhere? Send her off on the run again? No one had thought to address that yet, even though her whole "steal the book and run away" plan had brought the Creeps here in the first place.

Cavale handed her a bundle of branches wrapped tightly with red yarn. She sniffed it and smelled white sage, yarrow, and lavender. He must have made them from the sprigs of drying herbs that hung throughout the house. In his hands he held a bundle that was a twin to Elly's. He lit the end, getting a good, smoky smolder going, and looked up at Chaz. "You should probably hang back for now. Once this starts, stuff might get . . . hectic."

Chaz didn't scoff or snicker, moving back toward the doorway without argument. The lack of smartassery made Justin shift on the stool. "Um. What do you mean, hectic?"

"Paranormal side effects, basically." Elly tried to keep her tone gentle and unworried. "If there's resistance from what's in your head, stuff might get knocked around a bit. But you'll be okay," she said quickly, as he went even paler. "You're in the middle. It'll radiate *out* from you."

"Will you guys be okay?"

Cavale lit Elly's smudge stick and winked at Justin. "We'll be fine. I'm an old pro at this."

Justin didn't look terribly convinced.

They were ready.

Cavale stepped around the circle, so he was on the opposite side from Elly. They worked counterclockwise, wafting the smoke from the sticks into every corner of the room. Elly's nose itched as she did it; she'd never liked the smell of burning yarrow. It worked almost like a coat of primer on a wall, clearing lingering energy from the air and getting the area ready for new spells. They'd work just fine without it, but they held better this way.

They met at the eastern edge of the circle and Cavale passed his stick to Elly. She stubbed them both out in a small stone bowl and went to stand by Chaz. Cavale pushed up his sleeves, closing his eyes as he took several deep breaths. He began to chant.

The words were in Latin. Father Value had taught them how to conjugate verbs in the ancient tongue even while they were stumbling their way through Little Golden Books. She recognized the rich, round vowels and the rolling *r*'s, broken now and then by the names of some decidedly *non*-Roman deities: Anubis was an obvious choice, but she heard Thoth in there, too. Cavale was an equal-opportunity invoker. He called on Hindu gods and Gaelic ones, their names not nearly as important as what they stood for: gods of language and scribes, protectors, defenders. Gatekeepers and banishers. Mostly, he intoned the words, but sometimes he seemed to sing.

And the runes started to glow.

At first it was faint, especially with the sun streaming in. Then Cavale's voice rose and the glow strengthened in response.

But what *really* made them blaze was the blood. Cavale pulled a penknife from his pocket, pried it open, and sliced into the pad of his left thumb. He reached into the circle, toward Justin, and gestured: *Give me your hand.* Looking queasy, Justin did. Cavale pricked Justin's thumb, too, and without breaking the rhythm of the chant, indicated Justin ought to shake the drops onto the floor while he did the same.

As soon as the blood hit, the symbols flared. Elly watched through slitted eyelids as the light swirled up and around Justin. The daylight seemed dim by comparison. Cavale stopped chanting, letting the spell do its work.

It wasn't much more than a light show, to start. Justin sat in the center, confused and uncertain, but unaffected. Then a breeze lifted Elly's hair off her neck, and she felt goose-flesh break out on her arms.

The tub of pigs' blood flew from its end table, straight at Cavale. He dodged at the last second. It splattered against the wall behind him, leaving a gruesome slash of gore on the wallpaper. The blue glow turned it black. He had to weave again as the now-empty container sailed back toward the center of the room.

Justin flinched on his stool, but the tub didn't reach him. It got caught up in the vortex of light that surrounded him, circling like a miniature tornado. Smaller objects were drawn in—the paintbrushes, the smudge sticks, loose odds and ends Elly and Cavale hadn't bothered relocating to the kitchen. The bigger things were flung around the room, smashing against the walls.

"Get down!" Elly had almost forgotten Chaz was beside

her. He grabbed her and pushed her to the floor, covering her with his own body as an end table shot over their heads and left a dent in the hallway wall.

She peeked out from beneath his arm in time to see Justin go rigid.

The book fell from his lap, its pages fluttering like some invisible reader was trying to find where he'd left off. Justin rose off the stool, his feet six inches above the ground. His whole body bowed, and Elly could see veins popping in his forearms as his fists clenched. His breath came in short barks of pain.

This isn't supposed to happen.

Cavale seemed to be thinking the same thing. He made for the circle, pulling his sleeve up over his fist to help rub out the edge of the chalk line. The stone bowl Elly had put the smudge sticks out in slid across the floor, lifting off when it got near Cavale and missing his nose by inches. Other objects shot out of the swirling around Justin, pelting Cavale and driving him back.

Elly nudged against Chaz, who was still wrapped around her. "The circle," she whispered, though she didn't know if he could hear her over the racket. He eased up, though, giving her room to push off. She dove across the living room. Whatever it was they'd pissed off remained focused on Cavale; nothing came at her until she was right on top of the circle. The couch and the love seat both came toward her like something had shoved them, but it was too late. Elly swept her hands across the chalk lines, wiping out boundaries and inscriptions in one long arc.

The blue light winked out. For a split second, silence reigned. Elly opened one eye to find the tattered corner of the now-motionless couch about a foot from her face.

Then came the rattling and clattering as everything that had been swirling around fell to the floor, and one heavy thud as Justin came down, too.

❧ 20 ❧

ELLY SCRAMBLED INTO the center of the now-dormant circle and knelt beside Justin. Chaz was right behind her, debris crunching and crackling beneath his feet. "Is he all right?"

"He's breathing. It's a good start." Elly peeled back one of his eyelids. His pupils darted back and forth like he was dreaming. "Help me get him on the couch."

Chaz eyed it suspiciously. "You sure it's done attacking us?"

"Yeah. The circle's broken. It's just a couch again." Elly glanced at Cavale, who was surveying the war zone that had been his living room. A normal person would have been overwhelmed by the mess; Cavale's reaction was the opposite. He wasn't looking around and assessing the damage. He was retracing the ritual's steps to figure out where it had gone wrong. Mundane messes you could clean up easily. Magical ones took more effort. She cleared her throat and waited until his gaze settled on her. "Do you have a first aid kit?"

The request pulled him out of his contemplation. "I'll go

get it." Casting one last frown at the circle, he set off toward the back of the house.

Justin didn't stir when Elly and Chaz moved him onto the couch, or when Elly pinched the webbing between his thumb and forefinger. That should have hurt like hell and woken him up. He was down for the count. Whether from physical injury or magical trauma had yet to be seen.

Cavale came back with a mixing bowl filled with water, a dish towel, and a small tackle box that had a red cross drawn on it in permanent marker. The contents of the box rattled and clattered when Cavale set it down beside her.

"It's a little understocked," he said, looking sheepish. "I was never as good with it as you were. But you should have the basics."

She undid the clasp and opened the lid. The bottom half of the box held Ace bandages and gauze, cloth tape, a pair of tweezers, packets of antibiotic, and a box of Band-Aids. The top part, though, the shelf that was intended for fishing hooks and lures, held wax envelopes of dried herbs and a series of small jars whose contents were noted on a strip of masking tape on the lids. Elly's fingers danced over their tops until she found the myrrh. She uncapped it and set it down in easy reach, then dipped the dish towel in the water and began washing the pigs' blood from Justin's chest and arms.

Cavale got up after a minute, returning to his study of the remaining runes. He seemed content to let her do her thing while he paced about, looking for places he might have gone wrong. *He won't find any. Every piece was perfect.* It was a conclusion he'd have to draw on his own; Father Value had ingrained the concept of independent verification into them before they could even pronounce the terms.

Chaz hovered over the back of the couch, watching her work on Justin. "Will he be okay? What the fuck happened?"

Elly didn't look up. "Probably, and I don't know. That's what Cavale's trying to figure out." What *should* have happened was far less dramatic than what they'd witnessed: once Cavale's spell finished, Justin would have written in the book one last time, the ink setting not just Creepscrawl down on the page, but transferring the magic the Creeps were after with it as well. They certainly hadn't figured on spontaneous levitation and pissed-off furniture.

The cushions turned pink beneath Justin as Elly cleaned off the runes. Cavale didn't seem to object to her ruining his couch; she had the sneaking suspicion the pillows had been replaced several times before. They didn't exactly match the rest of the upholstery when you looked closely.

Only a little of the blood was Justin's, abrasions he'd most likely received when he fell. When she came across a nick, she dabbed it with myrrh. Chaz' nose wrinkled at the bitter, smoky smell. "The hell is that?"

"Myrrh. It's a good antiseptic."

"Yeah, but so is hydrogen peroxide. Probably easier to find, too."

Elly eyed him. "This works better."

He opened his mouth to argue, but Cavale spoke up from across the room. "*Elly* makes it work better."

That wasn't entirely true. "I just do what F—" *Best not to bring him up right now.* "I just do it the way I was taught," she amended, lamely. It wasn't even anything arcane. Father Value had taught her how to be efficient in her work, how to quickly staunch bleeding or to sew a neat line of stitches if a cut was too deep. She knew *how* to use drugstore remedies, but she preferred the old methods.

Plus, myrrh didn't sting quite as much as rubbing alcohol did.

She was pulling a splinter from Justin's shoulder—probably received when he hit the stool on his way down—when she noticed his breathing change. Her nose was nearly touching his skin while she dug around with the tweezers. She could smell the last traces of his soap beneath the coppery smell of blood, and was fighting the ridiculous urge to inhale deeply once more. He'd already called her lifestyle weird. If she started sniffing, that'd only prove how weird *she* was, too. His chest still rose and fell evenly, but the pause between *in* and *out* went away.

Above her, Chaz said, "Hey, look who's back."

Elly lifted her head slowly and met Justin's sleep-muddled eyes.

"What smells like church?" he asked.

"That would be you." She got a grip on the splinter and pulled it out, then dabbed on a bit of myrrh. She hoped looking down would cover her sudden, utterly stupid, blush. "The ritual went wonky and you fell. Just taking care of some scrapes, is all."

"But did it work?"

"I, uh." She sat back on her haunches and cast about for her brother. "I don't think we know yet. Cavale?"

He rose from where he'd been crouching at the center of the circle, the Creeps' book in his hands. "The pages are still empty. But whether it's still in your head or not . . ." From his back pocket, he produced a memo pad. Several pens had been caught in the spell's whirlwind. He plucked one from the debris and brought it over to Justin. "You want to give it a try?"

"Why not, right?" Justin pushed himself up to a sitting position and flipped back the memo pad's cover. The pen hovered over the paper for a moment, while Justin closed his eyes and muttered, "Please work."

Everyone held their breath as he wrote. Chaz and Cavale leaned in closer. Justin's hands blocked the lines from Elly's view, but she didn't need to see them: all three men swore at the same time. Chaz turned away, looking like he wanted to punch something. Cavale pinched the bridge of his nose and sighed. Justin sat there stunned, staring at the Creep-scrawl like he'd failed a test.

In a way, Elly supposed, he had. "We'll figure something out," she said, even though she had no idea what else they could try. "Cavale will work on it, right Cavale?" She nudged him with her elbow. She was out of reassurances and needed him to take over.

Unfortunately, he was too busy thinking to be useful to her. "Yeah, we'll get it," was all he said.

Chaz wasn't much more help. "Fuck this. I'm calling Boston. Val can argue with me later."

That got through to Cavale. He blinked at Chaz, incredulous, his mouth agape a moment before he recovered. "You know she hates dealing with them."

"Yeah, well, I told her if this wasn't sorted, I was going to do it. We're about eight hours past my deadline now. I'm done stalling."

Elly frowned. "Who's in Boston?"

Chaz already had his cell phone out. He didn't look up from the screen as he replied. "More vampires. They're a colossal band of assholes, but they're not entirely useless."

"Why doesn't Val like them?"

His jaw tightened, the way people's did when they stumbled across bad memories. "See 'colossal band of assholes.' But if the Jackals are bringing a nest here . . ." He looked from Elly to Cavale. "You two might be good, but are you *that* good?"

They glanced at one another. *Yes,* she thought, *we are.* She heard the Creep from last night: *"Said the leech wasn't alone. Said . . . Value."* She knew Cavale was thinking it, too.

But before either of them could answer, Justin broke in. "Um, guys?" He held up the notepad and pointed at its eye-wrenching lines of Creepscrawl. "I . . . I think I can *read* this."

They stared at him.

Cavale's throat clicked when he swallowed. "What does it say?"

Justin squinted at the words, his finger tracing the Creepscrawl as he read. "The syntax is all weird, but this line is talking about the harvest moon. Uh. I think it's 'The blood runs strongest beneath the harvest moon.'"

"Well, shit. That's this month," said Cavale. "It'd explain some of why they wanted it so quickly." He passed the Creeps' book to Justin and opened it to a page of text. "Can you read any of this, or just what you write down?"

His lips moved as he scanned the page. The book was bigger than a college textbook, its cover heavier. It made Justin look like a kid trying to read from a grown-up's library, especially when he seemed to be sounding out some of the words. "This is disgusting," he said after a minute. "I can read it, but I don't think I *want* to."

Chaz came back and leaned on the back of the couch. "You might have to, kid. Especially the missing pages."

"You can't be thinking of handing them over." Elly stood up so she could glare without craning her neck. "People *died* for this. Even more will if they learn how to kick-start their breeding process again."

Chaz held up his hands, the cell phone still awaiting his command. "Easy there. I didn't say a word about handing anything over, did I?"

She paused. "No, but—"

"But Val's going to want to know, and I'd bet you and Cavale could use some inside information, too. Are you telling me you'd turn down a glimpse at the enemy's playbook?"

"No, of course not." In fact, it was all she could do not to turn the book to the very first page and demand that Justin start reading aloud. He could tell her what Father Value had died for. Maybe she could use what was in there to carry on his work. *And avenge his death.* She itched to sit down on the damp, blood-stained couch and get started, in case this new ability was only temporary. What if it wore off before they could learn everything? Her breath caught.

If Chaz had noticed her sudden anxiety, he was ignoring it. "That's all I meant. So how about this. Sunny and Lia are expecting you guys for dinner. I'm thinking safety in numbers is good, especially now. Let's let Justin wash the rest of that shit off and we'll hit the road; he can translate to his heart's content on the way." He glanced at his cell phone and grimaced. "I'm still calling Boston. This shit just got even bigger. But I'll follow you to Sunny and Lia's, then I'll go get Val and we'll meet you there. Sound good?" He addressed the question to all of them, but his eyes were on Justin.

Justin peered at the mixing bowl beside Elly. The water in it had turned a dark pink from her repeatedly wringing out the dish towel, and she'd only washed off his front. His back was still covered in runes.

"This has probably gone cold," she said. "I can go refill it with warm water, if you want."

He blinked. "I, um. I was going to ask if I could just, you know. Take a shower?"

Cavale saved her from mortification. "Sure thing. Second door on your left upstairs, towels are in the cabinet. El, help me pick up a bit?"

As they swept up the broken things and moved some of the furniture back where it belonged, Elly's eyes kept straying to where Justin had left the book on the couch. *We'll get them, Father,* she thought. *We'll finish what you started.*

ELLY HAD NEVER been *anywhere* as nice as Sunny and Lia's. Sure, Father Value had taken her to meetings in fancy places before, but they'd never lasted long, and she'd always felt people's eyes on her while she waited for him to finish his business. She stuck out, she knew it, and she could practically hear people wondering why she didn't leave so they could stop pretending she wasn't there.

But it was different with the succubi. They'd kissed Chaz' and Cavale's cheeks, hugged Justin long enough to make him squirm, and, when Elly stepped across the threshold and tried to act invisible, they'd taken her hands and welcomed her. Then they'd let go well before the contact made her uncomfortable. She'd never been good with strangers touching her. It was like they knew exactly how long was safe. *Well, duh. Of course they do.* Except, it hadn't seemed calculated.

She didn't have much time to ruminate on it, though. Once the round of introductions were done and Chaz had ducked out to go to Val's, the demons had swept their guests into the brightly lit kitchen. Sunny bustled around getting everyone drinks and fussing with the appetizers they'd laid out—crackers and cheese, little spinach pies, and tiny hot dogs in matching tiny crescent rolls. Their bigger version had been Elly's specialty, once upon a time. She almost opened her mouth to see if Cavale remembered, but after this morning's cherry pie disaster, she didn't quite dare.

While her partner was making sure everyone had a plateful of food, Lia settled them around the table and held court.

She focused mostly on Justin and Cavale, but made sure Elly was part of the conversation. It was so smoothly done, in fact, that Elly forgot to fidget whenever Justin took his eyes off the book to answer Lia's questions. He'd hardly looked up from it at all on the ride over, only pausing to make notes on the legal pad beside him. Elly had spent the trip entranced, wishing he'd write faster.

But now she'd relaxed a bit. The spell hadn't faded at all. If anything, Justin had said the Creepscrawl was getting *easier* to read, not harder. Cavale seemed to think their ritual had made the magic dig in deeper, though whether that was something they'd triggered or whether it was the nature of the Creeps' spell to resist ejection, he didn't know.

She felt slightly guilty about hoping that Justin's affliction would last long enough for him to finish translating, but she couldn't help it. Whatever was written in that book was a potential weapon they could use in fighting the Creeps. Father Value would have been hovering over Justin's shoulder, chivvying him on and scowling whenever Justin traded the pen for his fork to take a bite.

Her semicontent feeling lasted until dinner was nearly over. Then Elly screwed it up. Again.

She had a bellyful of roasted chicken and mashed potatoes. The green beans had actually been *green*, and had a bit of snap left to them, not the sickly snot brown rubbery things she'd eaten out of cans for as long as she could remember. She was so full, every movement felt languid. She knew that she'd need to be alert soon, especially with the sun on its way down, but that safe feeling was back and she let herself ride it a little longer.

Sunny had poured coffee. The cream was near Justin, but his head was bent over the book again. Rather than interrupt him, Elly reached across for the pitcher.

And knocked over the salt shaker.

She pinched a bit of it and tossed it over her shoulder. Father Value had ingrained the habit in them so young, she didn't even think about it. When she looked up, Cavale was watching her with a sad little smile. "For good luck?" he asked.

"Mm-hm." She should have stopped there. He wasn't judging her with the question. If there was anyone in the world she didn't have to explain herself to, it was Cavale. She couldn't even say *why* she went on—Justin was deep into the text; Sunny was cutting monster-sized slices of chocolate cake, and Lia was stealing a dollop of frosting. No one was paying attention to her but Cavale, and yet she kept talking. "The only time I didn't do it, I broke my wrist the next day."

His smile faded. "I remember."

Sunny and Lia's playful banter cut off. Their heads swiveled to Cavale, worry creasing both of their brows. *They sensed his mood change.*

Of course he remembered it. He'd been watching her. It was maybe two years after the cherry pie incident. She was eight, he was eleven, and they'd gone to the park to play. They were practicing moves on the monkey bars, taking their climbing far more seriously than the other children present, and Elly had slipped and fell. It was an accident. A stupid playground accident, but Father Value had blamed Cavale. She remembered the yelling only vaguely, through the haze of painkillers the hospital had prescribed.

"It wasn't your fault," she whispered. "It wasn't."

"I need a minute," he said, and pushed away from the table.

Elly stared at his retreating back, fighting tears. Sunny set down her cake knife and came over to squeeze her shoulder. "He'll be all right, honey," she said, but Elly shook her off.

"I'll go apologize." She held her back straight as she left the kitchen, ignoring the compassionate stares of the succubi boring into her back.

She found him in the sunroom, looking out over the back lawn. The way he stood, hands folded behind his back, head bowed, reminded her achingly of Father Value. Whether Cavale knew it or not, he'd always carried himself the way their guardian had. She crept in behind him and stopped a couple of feet to his side. "He shouldn't have yelled at you for that," she said. "He was worried and scared, you know? The hospital was going to call Child Services on us, and he thought he was going to lose us."

She remembered that much—the concerned faces on first the adults at the playground, then on the EMTs, then on the doctors and nurses in the ER. There had been questions that had nothing to do with her wrist. They'd taken Cavale away to ask her some of them, even though she'd been crying too hard to answer. It wasn't the pain that had her sobbing; it was the fear that she'd never see him again. Father Value had warned them both about the possibility of separation, should something like this happen.

In the end, they'd answered enough of the questions correctly so that when Father Value arrived, the staff let him take his wards home with him. Whatever papers they'd demanded, he'd had. They *were* his wards. That much was true. But their address, the way they lived, that's where the lies came in. There hadn't even been time to get in her pajamas when they got home. Father Value sent Cavale to fetch her teddy bear and they were on the move again.

But didn't it go to show how much he cared? That he'd packed up and moved them around to keep them rather than sending them off to foster care, which would have been worlds easier?

That wasn't how Cavale saw it. He turned to her. The fading sunlight cast long shadows on his face. "You keep making excuses for him. And I get why. I do. You're still mourning him."

"Of course I am. How could I not be? He raised me. He raised *us*."

She might as well have slapped him, the way he rocked back. "Did he, Elly? Because from where I'm standing, it was more like he taught us some shit, left out a whole lot more, and let us raise ourselves when it came to anything *other* than fighting Creeps. And look what a fucking brilliant job we've done there."

Now it was Elly's turn to get angry. The man wasn't a week in his grave—if they'd even buried him yet—and

Cavale couldn't even spare ten seconds of respect for him. "You seem to be doing just fine for yourself. You wanted a normal life and you got it. *By walking away from us.*"

"By walking away from *him*! Elly, I know you loved him. I know he was a hero to you. But he was just a *man*. And a fucked-up one, at that. His name was John Reed, not Father Value, and he was just. A. Man."

She'd heard the name before. It was the one they'd given to the doctors at the hospital, the name he'd gone by before he'd become Father Value, but so what? What was Cavale trying to prove by invoking it? It didn't diminish who he'd been or the things he'd done. It didn't change the biggest, most important thing: "Our parents died fighting the Creeps and he took us in. Shouldn't that be worth something?"

Cavale stared at her. For the second time today, she saw the look that meant he had something to say that she wouldn't like. His eyes tightened, his jaw clenched. But this time, he didn't swallow whatever it was. The anger drained out of him and her name came out like a sigh. "Elly. El."

"What? What is it?" It scared her, how quickly he'd gone from furious to sad. It scared her even more when he reached for her hands.

A long moment passed before he spoke again. "My parents died," he said. "Yours didn't."

"I— I don't understand." Father Value had always said her parents were gone, the few times it had come up. *"Gone," he said. Did he ever say "dead"?* She couldn't remember. They were two very different things.

"It's a cult. The Brotherhood is a big goddamned cult, and your parents gave you to him so they could get right back out there to fight the Creeps." He squeezed her hands and led her over to the love seat. It was nice of him to do that; the room's proportions had gone all strange on her. "I was only three, so I don't remember much. Faces coming and going, but they're hazy. I think they came to see you, at first, and there were babysitters who watched us while . . . While Father Value was out." Even in her shock, Elly could hear how hard it was for him to say his name.

"But it was only ever us. Just the three of us."

"No. Not always. They stopped coming when I was six or seven, I guess, but for a while, there were more people around. Then one day he said I was old enough to watch over you by myself, and that was the end of the babysitters." Cavale leaned in and put an arm around her shoulders. "I think maybe that's when he and the Brotherhood had their falling out."

"Are they still alive, do you think?" Not that she cared. *I don't.*

"I don't know. If you want to look for them, I'll help you."

She turned the thought over in her mind. Growing up, she'd never understood the fairy tales where the heroine learned that the people who raised her weren't her *real* parents. She couldn't imagine any other family. She didn't *want* to imagine one. "No. They gave me up. Why should I care who they are now?"

He opened his mouth, but no answer came. After a minute, he nodded. "Okay. If you change your mind—"

"I won't," she said, and considered the matter closed. She leaned into him, watching the shadows gather as the sun slipped below the horizon. "Are you mad at me?"

"No, and I never have been." He ruffled her hair. "Are you mad at *me*?"

"No."

"Good. You want to go back out there and see if there's any cake left? Sunny's an amazing baker."

Elly grinned and sat up straight. "You go ahead. I'm going to go outside and get some air first."

He looked like he might protest, but then his eyes cut to the darkening sky. They both knew that she wasn't going for a simple evening stroll. She was going to go check the perimeter and set a few wards, and in a few minutes he'd do the same thing inside.

Because they were Father Value's children.

༽ 21 ༄

V AL WOKE UP disoriented and with a crick in her neck. She was also hot, which was unusual considering her normal corpse-like temperature. Something lay atop her, not the heavy, gritty weight of dirt, so she knew she hadn't gone to ground. This was soft and fuzzy. *Blankets?* She wriggled out from under them, dislodging enough throws and quilts to keep an Eskimo family warm in the dead of an arctic winter. She realized she was in her own living room, the fading light of dusk filtering through the drawn blinds. The events of the previous night came back to her, including her undignified climb into Chaz' trunk.

At least he was thorough. He must have stripped her bed and raided the linen closets to find all of these. It was a good call on his part: her bedroom was the only place in which she'd hung blackout curtains. She probably wouldn't have caught fire from what light seeped in, but she might have woken up with some pretty nasty burns.

As it was, she'd just woken up sweaty. Her hair was plastered to her neck. She was just contemplating a shower when her cell phone buzzed, and Chaz' number flashed across the display. She picked up, grinning.

"Thank you for not leaving me in your trunk all day."

"You're welcome," he said, but he sounded harried. "Listen, uh. I'm on the way over. You've got about five minutes to tidy up."

She glanced around the room. It was cluttered, sure, but not a pigsty. "It's not so bad," she said. "You've seen it in far worse condition than this."

He cleared his throat, and when she spoke, she could hear the wince. "I have, but Ivanov hasn't."

Suddenly she wasn't sweaty anymore; she was clammy and cold. "Ivanov?" She hadn't seen the head of the Boston *Stregoi* in three years. At the end of their last conversation, she'd suggested she might stake him if they were in the same room together within the next decade. It hadn't been her finest moment, but she'd also been carrying a dying Chaz in her arms at the time. A bit of theatrics were understandable, even justified.

"I told you I was calling them today if we hadn't resolved the problem."

Val put the phone on speaker so she could dart around picking things up while they talked. "You did, but I figured you'd, you know, set up a meeting."

"It's what I intended to do, but when I called . . . Shit, Val, I got the sense they were going to show up here whether we called them or not."

"You think they know what's going on?" She didn't have time to fold the blankets. Gathering them up in a bundle, she carried them into the kitchen and shoved them through the cellar door. Her house wasn't prepared to receive visitors, not the vampire kind, anyway. As a rule, she didn't keep blood packs on hand to offer as refreshment. Or people, like they did in Boston.

Well, that's their own problem, not giving me any notice.

"They must. Or at least part of it. Whatever lackey answered the phone put me right through to Ivanov's primary

Renfield. I wasn't on hold more than ten seconds. And since they said he'd be here right after sunset, they have to have put him in the car while he was still out cold."

Her stomach roiled. That didn't bode well. "All right, well. Good to know." His sucked-in breath was loud in the quiet room. "What are you leaving out?"

"Don't freak out."

"Time's ticking, Chaz. Spit it out."

"He's bringing Katya."

The stack of magazines she'd collected fell to the carpet in a flutter of pages. "He's *what*?"

"She's his right-hand now. That's what the Renfield said."

"Don't you dare come here," she said. "Turn around and go back to Sunny and Lia's."

"Fuck that."

"Chaz—"

"No. I'm pulling into your driveway now, and I'm staying for this." Headlights splashed across her front window, and the roar of the Mustang's engine cut short. "How about you turn on some lights for the sorry-ass mortal, huh? I'll be in in a sec." He ended the call.

Numbly, Val wandered around turning on the lights. She could Command Chaz to leave as soon as he came through the door, but then she'd lose his input. He'd be able to fill her—and therefore Ivanov and Katya—in on what had happened during the day.

But, Katya . . . She'd threatened to stake Ivanov, but she'd flat-out *promised* to do it to Katya. Of course, not until after she'd garroted the woman with silver wire, poked her full of holes and stuffed said holes full of garlic. The *Stregoi* bitch was the one who'd stolen Chaz away and drained him to the point of death. She was the reason Val had refused to have any dealings with the Boston vampires ever since.

And now she was coming to Val's house.

The key rattled in the lock. Chaz stepped into the living room, holding a paper bag. "Lamb's blood," he said. "Best I could do on short notice. I had to buy a whole fuckton of lamb chops, too. You got any good recipes for mint jelly?" His voice was light, but she could see tightness behind his eyes and smell the fear emanating from him.

"Chaz, you don't have to stay."

"Yeah, I do. I'm not going to hide. My job is to serve you. I'm not letting her chase me away from that."

"You're not my servant. That's not how we work, you and I."

He set the bag down on an end table. "No, but they don't understand that. We need their help, Val, and that means conforming to their shit. So I'll play the part." He grinned wryly. "Plus, she probably *expects* me to make myself scarce, or for you to hide me away. Consider my presence a bit of a 'fuck you.'"

They looked at each other for a moment, Val tried to find another way around it, but he was right. Ivanov and Katya already held most of the cards. She and Chaz needed to slip whichever ones they could up their own sleeves. "Okay. Fine. But that means that if I dismiss you, you go. No arguments."

He didn't like it, but he nodded his agreement. "Go get cleaned up," he said. "I'll finish down here."

Ten minutes later, Val had changed into clean jeans and a tailored shirt. She'd dragged a brush through her hair and twisted it into a bun. By the time she came back downstairs, Chaz had cleared away the rest of the clutter in the living room. He'd broken out her tea service and transferred the lamb's blood into the china pot. Three delicate cups and saucers, pale roses curling around them, were set out in anticipation of their guests.

They didn't have long to wait. Chaz had opened the blinds as part of his tidying, and now they both watched as a sleek black town car pulled up to the curb outside. A liveried driver got out and opened the rear passenger door.

Ivanov got out first, dressed in a suit that had been cut to scream Old World. He looked no older than thirty-five, but his face was all hard angles and shrewd expressions. At first glance you might take him for a young up-and-comer at a law firm, but that impression never lasted for long. He was the kind of man who demanded deference. It had probably been centuries since someone had dared refuse it.

He held out a hand, and a set of slender, ring-laden fingers slipped into his. Katya didn't so much exit the car as she slithered from it. She was tall and reedy; thick chestnut curls cascaded down her back. Her outfit made Val do a double take. Where Ivanov's suit had something antique about it, Katya's was ultramodern. It was so cutting-edge that Val suspected it wouldn't officially hit the runways in Paris until *next* season. *The last time I saw her, she was dressed like a street rat.* Gone were the torn jeans and scuffed leather jacket, though when the breeze lifted the other woman's hair Val caught a glimpse of the line of studs marching their way along Katya's ear. Katya seemed a bit unsteady on the heels of her spiky shoes, too. *That means her getup is Ivanov's doing.*

Which led Val to an odd thought: if Ivanov and Katya had left Boston before the sun went down, not only had their servants bundled their sleeping masters into the town car, they'd very likely *dressed* them as well. She repressed a shudder. Bad enough that Chaz had had to drag her out of his trunk this morning and deposit her in the living room. She couldn't imagine making him dress her like an oversized Barbie doll.

Still, in the face of the two fashion plates out on the sidewalk, her own jeans-and-a-nice-blouse ensemble felt suddenly shabby. At least Chaz looked sharp; he still had on the suit he'd worn to the Clearwaters' funeral.

Katya peered around the neighborhood, a look of disdain on her perfectly made-up face. Edgewood clearly didn't meet her tastes, which, unless she'd had a personality transplant, ran toward the seedy. Edgewood's biggest dive bar was still terribly white-collar. She shook her head and let Ivanov guide her up the walk.

Chaz opened the door as they ascended the front steps, sweeping his arm aside and letting them past. Ivanov walked straight by him, but Katya paused, her eyes lighting up.

Val clenched her fists, fighting the instinct to lunge forward and drag the woman away from him. By the hair.

"Charles!" she exclaimed, drawing out the *A*. "I'd hoped to see you here." She reached out and cupped his cheek. "I see you're handsome as ever."

He used the open door as an excuse to pull away from her touch, moving smoothly to close it. "I've never won any beauty pageants," he said.

"You looked so ill, last I saw you. I'm glad you've recovered."

Chaz stiffened. His scent shifted from terrified to furious, and for good cause: he'd been so ill because *Katya had nearly killed him.* Much as Val wanted to let him give her a piece of his mind—much as she wanted to join in on it herself—she saw the tiny grin playing about Ivanov's lips as he watched the exchange and knew she had to head it off.

"Lord Ivanov. Katya. Why don't we all sit? You've come all this way. Perhaps we should get straight to business."

Ivanov smiled indulgently. Katya scowled for the briefest instant, then turned to greet Val at last. She glided forward, clasping Val's hands and kissing her on each cheek. Her cold hands and lips took Val by surprise—she'd been away from others of her kind for so long, the warmth of human touch had become the norm for her. Katya's grip was cool iron as she looked Val up and down.

"Valerie," she said. "We've missed you in Boston." The lie was obvious in her ice blue eyes.

"Well, maybe it's time I made my grand return." If Katya wanted to play that particular game, Val could join in, too. Especially since she was the better liar. The other woman's plastered-on smile faltered. *Score one for me.*

Ivanov cleared his throat and touched Katya's shoulder. "I do believe Valerie had the right of it. Perhaps we should discuss what we've come for."

"Of course." Katya squeezed Val's fingers once before letting go, a cold marble warning.

They moved the rest of the way into the living room and sat, Ivanov and Katya on the couch, Val in the armchair. Chaz followed silently, pouring three cups of lamb's blood from the teapot then exiling himself to the corner. He placed himself within sight of all three vampires. Blood drinkers were an untrusting lot; standing where they couldn't see you made the more paranoid ones wonder if you were coming up behind them with a stake. He stayed just on the edge of Katya's peripheral vision, to fuck with her. If she wanted a good look, she'd have to twist around.

Ivanov took a sip from his cup. He was far too polite to grimace at the poor vintage, but he set it down on his saucer and didn't touch it again. "I understand you've come into conflict with some Jackals," he said. His mouth twisted as he said the last, like the word tasted worse on his tongue than the blood had.

"You could say that," said Val. "A friend of mine came into possession of something they want. He died for it, but not before he arranged for it to come into my keeping."

"And when they showed up to retrieve it, you refused to hand it over?"

"I *couldn't* have." She left out the part where she'd tried. If Ivanov pushed for details, she'd tell him, but she didn't want to admit they'd taken her by surprise and overpowered her if she didn't have to. "It's a book. We don't know exactly what's in there, but one of my employees had a look at it before they came. Whatever they want so badly, it's not in there anymore."

"Oh? And where did it go?"

"Into him." She shrugged. "We don't know how, and we haven't been able to put it back. When he writes, all he can do is write the words that were in the book, but none of the magic gets written out with it."

Ivanov spread his hands. "Your solution seems simple."

"You know a way to help him?"

Katya snorted. Ivanov smiled like he was speaking to a dim child. "In a manner of speaking, I suppose." His steady gaze locked onto Val's. "Kill him."

Val nearly spat out her mouthful of lamb's blood. "What? No! That's . . . that's not on the table. No." She glanced at Chaz. He hadn't moved, but his eyes were wide and angry.

Ivanov's smile faded. "It's the easiest way. You end his troubles and the spell dies with him, keeping it out of the Jackals' hands. Two birds, one stone." He tilted his head. "I'd have thought that would please you."

"If you don't want to do it," Katya said, "you could give him to us. We can do it for you."

"NO." Chaz advanced on them, fists clenched at his sides. "Fuck that, and fuck *you*. You heard Val. It's off the table."

"Chaz—" Val started, but it was Ivanov who stopped him.

He was a blur as he rose, even to Val's eyes. To Chaz, it must have been a shutterblink. "Kneel," he said, the Command in his voice so strong that Val almost wanted to get to her knees, too.

Chaz dropped like a puppet whose strings had been cut. His eyes were clear, the anger in them flaring, but the sheer psychic weight of Ivanov's influence kept him opening his mouth to argue. It showed how old the vampire was, that he could utter a one-word Command and his subject would obey the *unspoken* orders buried within it. In this case, "Shut up."

Ivanov stared down his thin, aquiline nose at Chaz. "I see your Renfield is still allowed free rein with his tongue," he said.

"You just suggested I kill one of my employees. I think his reaction was pretty justified, considering."

He waved that away. "A good vassal keeps his passions to himself. Unless, of course, you're suggesting he speaks for you?"

"He speaks for himself, and that's how we prefer it." Out of the corner of her eye, she caught Katya's sudden smirk, but dismissed it. *One fight at a time, here.* Ivanov was far more important.

He stood over Chaz, rubbing his chin. "Some of our kind allow the same because they feel their servants can offer wise counsel. I'm not sure I'd believe that of yours, Valerie. He's only ever shown a smart mouth in front of me, not a clever mind."

"He can be coarse," she said, reminding herself to apologize to Chaz for that one later, "but he's the only person I'd trust guarding my tomb when the sun's up." It was an old saying, since most New World vampires didn't sleep in cemeteries anymore, but Ivanov caught the meaning.

"All the same, I think perhaps this would go more

smoothly if he were to recuse himself from the discussion. Of course, that is your decision to make, not mine." The look he gave her quite clearly told her what her decision ought to be. He stepped away from Chaz and said, "You may rise."

Chaz got to his feet slowly, as if Ivanov might order him right back down again. He looked at Val, waiting.

"It's all right," she said. "I'm not going to let anything happen to Justin. Why don't you go wait in the kitchen for now? There should be something in the liquor cabinet if you want to pour yourself a drink." It was the kindest way she could think of to dismiss him without belittling him.

Chaz gathered his dignity and gave her a curt nod. He sketched a bow to Ivanov as he backed toward the kitchen door, but he might as well have shown the vampire his middle finger, for all the contempt there was in the movement.

Ivanov remained standing until Chaz was out of the room, then shook his head and sat beside Katya once more. "Better," he said. "Now. Back to your unfortunate employee. You won't kill him, and the Jackals will keep coming until they get what they want, which, let us be honest, means *they* might kill him instead. Or, if they keep him alive for the thing dwelling within him, it will be an unpleasant existence for him. They won't treat him like an honored guest. You know this as well as anyone." He folded his hands in his lap and eyed her.

Val grimaced. It was true. If the Jackals got hold of Justin, they'd keep him chained until they got what they wanted. Then they'd tear him apart. "I don't intend to let them have him."

"And yet your servant informed mine that attempts at restoring the spell to its rightful place failed." A glint entered his eyes. "We should speak on that, as well."

"The ritual? It happened during the day. I didn't see it, Chaz did. And you've had me exile him to the kitchen." The back door slammed hard enough to make the cups rattle in their saucers. Val sighed. "And now he's gone for a walk to cool off. So there's not much I can tell you."

"No, I don't care about the details of that." He smiled

like a snake about to strike. "Valerie. You didn't tell me you were associating with *Value's children*."

She blinked. "Pardon?"

"The boy you've befriended, the freelance warlock."

"Cavale?"

"Yes. And the girl who I'm given to understand brought the Jackals upon you in the first place. Surely they've told you who they are?" It wasn't really a question. Ivanov always knew more than he let on.

"Only a little. They've mentioned a man named Value, but he's dead."

"And their ties to the Brotherhood?"

"Severed, from what I understand. At least, Cavale's were. I didn't even know that's where he'd learned his trade until two nights ago. The girl . . . I think Value was her only link." She peered at him. "Does it matter? Should I have contacted one of theirs instead?" Not that she had the faintest idea how to get in touch with the Brotherhood out here. She'd remained intentionally ignorant of that for the last ten years, and that suited her just fine.

Ivanov smirked. "Certainly not. It's simply curious to me, Valerie. You renounced that whole life when you came east, showed up on my doorstep proclaiming you were out of the Hunt and wanted to be left alone. Yet, here you are, mired in it once more."

"I told you," she said, trying to keep the snarl out of her voice, "I didn't know they were Brotherhood. This was dropped in my lap, and as soon as Justin's safe and the Jackals are gone, I'm done. Again."

"Perhaps you should reconsider."

Val went still. Katya watched her, smirking. *This is political.* "I thought the Boston covens abstained from the Hunt." It was part of why she'd come here, after the disaster that was Sacramento. Everywhere else, she'd be sure to run into a cluster of Hunters who would expect her to pick up the stake again. The Brotherhood's numbers were thinning, their members leaving the Jackals' extermination to the vampires. But the Boston covens seemed content to let the

Jackals be, provided they didn't wreak too much havoc. When they did—and they always did, eventually—the covens would call in Hunters from the South or the Midwest to take care of it.

Ivanov nodded. "We do, as a rule. But perhaps the game has changed."

"How?"

Katya snorted. "I thought you were supposed to be clever."

Val ignored the barb and looked at Ivanov. "I'm clearly missing something here, but I don't have time to try sussing it out. If there's something I ought to know, or something you want, just say it."

She winced as soon as the words were out, certain the disrespectful outburst would raise Ivanov's ire, but he only chuckled and took another polite sip of blood. Val was fairly certain he'd only lifted the cup to his lips.

"I'm saying these two have forgotten more about magic and ritual than most members of the Brotherhood will ever learn, and they're both young yet. Father Value was a madman and a zealot, even by the Brotherhood's standards. They threw him out, Valerie, but no one ever took those children from him."

"And now you want them."

"Think what an asset they'd be! They make most members of the Brotherhood look like hedge mages. And if there's ever a time when the Brotherhood has something we want . . ." He trailed off, letting Val fill in the rest.

He might not have an immediate use for them, but Ivanov thought in the long term. If the *Stregoi* did need something from the Brotherhood, Elly and Cavale's influence would be useful.

"I can't speak for them," she said. "I can ask if they'd like to meet with you, but that's all."

"And your own return to the Hunt?"

"No."

He looked disappointed, but not upset.

This conversation isn't done.

"Katya, will you be kind enough to get the colony on the phone? I've some business to discuss with them." Katya rose and swanned out of the room, cell phone to her ear. Ivanov waited until the front door clicked shut, then turned the full force of his gaze on Val. "It wasn't a question, Valerie, and I believe you know that."

"You want me to Hunt again."

"Yes."

"May I ask *why*?"

"Because your talent is wasted here. You live like a human and it's a shame. We are so very much more and you *know* this. Don't you think it's time to come out of mourning and do the thing you excel at?"

"I don't. And with all due respect, sir, I have to call bullshit. My talent hasn't mattered to you for years. *I* haven't mattered to you for years. So if you're going to ask me to Hunt again, it's only fair you be honest with me about why." She'd already danced right past disrespect, so it wasn't hard to go for downright rude: "You're making a show of power, aren't you? Did some other colony challenge your authority?"

He didn't respond, but the gleam in his eye told her she'd either guessed correctly or come damned close. While it wasn't unheard of for vampires to fight one another, it was rare enough. Subtlety had a way of going right out the window when territory wars escalated. If Ivanov could say he had Sacramento's champion Hunter allied with him—*plus* Elly and Cavale and whatever reputations they brought with them—no one would dare stand against him. He hadn't *needed* them before now, but Ivanov was both arrogant *and* patient: he'd been keeping tabs on her, and thus probably on Cavale as well.

We'd be pawns.

She opened her mouth, trying to think of a way to buy some time, when her cell phone rang. Decorum stated she should ignore it—should actually have shut it off—but Ivanov gave her a little wave: *Go ahead.*

Cavale didn't wait for her to say hello. His voice was calm and cold, a Hunter's voice: "Val. We need you here. They're coming."

22

A CIRCUIT OF the backyard didn't cool Chaz down, so he'd set off around the block to work off the anger and humiliation. In this state, if Ivanov came within reach, Chaz was likely to coldcock him. That wouldn't help Val, nor would it help Justin, so he made *chilling the fuck out* a priority.

But good Christ, was it hard. He rounded the corner to Val's street at a power-walking clip. The sides of his dress shoes were protesting even that, pinching his feet and chafing his right ankle. He might regret it later, but right now, the discomfort leeched away some of his fury. *One more spin,* he thought as he drew up to Val's house, *and I can make another stab at genteel and complacent.* He snorted at the thought of it, imagining himself with a tea towel draped over his arm and the bemused look Val would give him.

The thought lifted his mood for about half a second, then it came crashing down again as Katya appeared from behind the town car. She was snapping her cell phone shut; she must have been leaning against the trunk or perching on the back bumper, blocked from his view.

It was too late to wheel around and head the other way. She'd seen him. *Probably caught my scent before I turned the corner.* She took a few wobbly steps on those impossibly spiky heels, then stopped, one hand against the town car's roof for balance, letting Chaz come to her.

He slowed down as he approached, finally ambling to a halt about a foot out of her reach. Not that it would help him if she truly wanted to make a grab for him. He'd seen how fast Val could move. Katya was older—not anywhere near Ivanov's age, but she had at least a century under her belt. He couldn't outrun her if she decided to pounce.

"Charles. You pissed off Ivanov before we had a chance to talk." She stuck out her lower lip. A pout just looked *wrong* on that feral face, untrustworthy, the vampire equivalent of alligator tears.

"Well, he suggested we kill a friend. It didn't go over big."

Katya smirked and shrugged out of her suit coat. Beneath it she wore a faded black tank top that couldn't have been part of the original ensemble. In the glow of Val's yard lights, he could see the brands scattered across her right bicep. The mark of the *Stregoi* stood out in the center, a Cyrillic rune Val had taught him to steer clear of when he went into Boston. Around it were notches, some of rank—he could see the newly raised flesh from her promotion to Ivanov's second—others marking her kills.

Those last were faded. Vampires weren't supposed to off each other these days, but when they'd been fighting their turf wars, Katya had racked up the trophies. Literally. Last Chaz had seen her, she was wearing a bracelet made from her victims' fangs. He glanced at her wrist, noting its absence.

"I see you've made some changes."

She followed his gaze and the pout turned into a grin. "Not as many as you'd think." Her right hand dipped into her pocket. The fangs clicked against one another as she pulled out the bracelet and slipped it on. "Neither have you." She tilted her head toward the house. "Still hers, hmm?"

"Of course I am. Why wouldn't I be?"

"It's just so sad. You give everything to her, your best years, and for what? What does she give you in return?"

What was she getting at? "I don't—"

"She doesn't love you, and she never will. Not the way you love her."

The statement hit him like a mallet to the gut. "What?" It came out as a whisper.

"Come on, Charles. You don't have to pretend. You told me everything when you were mine." She reached out as if to stroke his cheek, the pout returning as he recoiled.

"I was never yours." But he *had* been, for those three terrible days. Not of his own choice, but the Command she'd dropped on him had made him *believe* he wanted to be hers. Mix that with the blood loss and . . . *What did I tell her? How much does she know?*

Katya took half a step forward; Chaz was too dumbstruck to retreat. "You were mine. And you could be again. No tricks this time, I swear." Her voice was low, intimate. "Come be mine again, Charles, and *I* will love you."

"You don't love anything."

One pale, perfect shoulder lifted in a shrug. "Then I can make you believe I do. It's almost the same. Come be mine, and I'll give you whatever you want."

"There's nothing I want."

"Nothing but *her*." She spat the last word, but the treacly smile snapped right back. "Then do it for just a little while. Give me ten years, and you can go back to her at the end."

"So you'd take my best years and send me packing when I'm all used up, is that it?" Every muscle was tensed to run, but Chaz couldn't pull his eyes away from hers. *Not again. Not this again.*

Katya chuckled. "Perhaps. Or . . . maybe, if you make me happy, I'll reward you." She moved in close enough to kiss. Her palm came up and cupped his cheek. "Think of it. Give me ten years, and I'll pay you with forever. Then you can chase her until the sun swallows the Earth, if you want."

He stared. "That's . . . that's a pretty shitty reason to

become a vampire. Stalking someone for centuries even after they've said no?" At first, his voice felt like it was coming from far away, but the more Chaz talked, the more in control he felt. He kept going. "Talk about an asshole thing to do."

Another shrug. "It works in the movies."

"In stupid movies, maybe."

"So fine, don't chase her." She waved it off, annoyed. "Take my gift and be her *friend* forever." The word dripped with contempt. "Follow her around like a sad puppy for a thousand years. What you do when you leave me is your business."

"Right, because if I fuck off for a decade—with *you*, of all people—she'll be totally cool with it when I walk back into her life. *As a vampire*." He was on a roll now, his fear replaced by scorn. "What do you even want me for? Is it because I belong to someone else and you want all the toys?"

The smile didn't fade, but a dangerous glint came into her eyes. He'd hit close to the mark. Before she could respond—and before he could dig himself in any deeper—the front door opened. Suddenly, the pressure from her fingers was gone from his cheeks, and she was out of arm's reach again.

Ivanov strode out of the house. Val hurried after him, a duffel bag slung onto her back, its strap crossing her chest like a bandolier. Chaz had seen it a few times before, but never outside of the hall closet where it had been gathering dust in the back corner since before he'd become Val's Renfield.

The driver, who up until now had been minding his own business in the town car's front seat, hurried out to open the door for Ivanov. He shot Chaz a look that might have said, "Sorry, buddy," or maybe, "Vampires. What can you do?" Ivanov didn't get in right away. After a few beats, the driver retreated to the far end of the car, getting out of the way while his masters concluded their business.

Val came straight to Chaz' side, peering between him and Katya. "Are you all right?"

"I'm fine," he said, and even meant it. "We were just having a chat."

Katya beamed, showing far too many teeth.

Val gave him a dubious look, but dropped it. "Ooookay. We have to go. Cavale called. It's time." She turned to Ivanov. "You're really not going to help us?"

He shook his head, the amusement on his face making Chaz' urge to coldcock him surge all over again. "No. You are a Hunter, Valerie, and so are your friends. I suggest you do what you were born to do." He started lowering himself into the car, then paused. "However. If you'll consider my request, perhaps I shall be more inclined to consider yours. Let me know what you decide. Come, Katya."

Katya retrieved her suit jacket from where she'd tossed it on the trunk. "My offer stands, too, Charles. Think about it."

Then they were gone, the town car sliding away into the night.

Val let out a frustrated sigh. "What offer?"

"Nothing I'd even consider. You?"

She shook her head. "Later. We have to get to Sunny and Lia's." Her nostrils twitched as she sniffed the air, her mouth twisting in distaste. "There must be a lot of them. I just caught a scent." Something in the duffel bag clanked as she turned to glance up and down the street. "Nobody out. You want to do this fast, or dignified?"

"What's the difference?"

"I can carry you and get us there in five minutes flat, or you can drive over and meet me there."

Chaz winced at the thought of Val carrying him on her back like a toddler. It was a short enough trip to Sunny and Lia's under his own power. "I think my dignity's taken about as many blows as it can handle for one night. I'll drive."

"Okay." She squeezed his hand. "Be careful, yeah?"

"Always am." Then she was off, a blur half-seen heading toward the woods she'd cut through to get to the succubi's house. *To hell with "as the crow flies." "As the vampire sprints" might be faster.* Chaz tucked that one away for later. The Mustang roared to life when he turned the key. It was a good car, reliable even in its old age. Sort of how he hoped to be for Val, someday. It was enough. It *was*, no matter what Katya thought he wanted.

He found the loudest metal station on the dial and cranked the volume. *Entrance music,* he lied to himself. Nothing at all to do with drowning out his own thoughts. Nothing at all.

THEY'D RETREATED TO the living room after their circuits of the house; Sunny said it had the best lines of sight out of any other rooms, and Elly had to agree. Justin lay sprawled on the floor with the book, flipping between pages. He looked up as Cavale strode past to check the windows for the fifth or sixth time, then noticed Elly digging into the backpack full of Creep-fighting supplies. "What can I do?"

"Nothing yet." She checked the caps on the bottles of holy water and laid the rowan stakes out on the coffee table, the blond wood standing out against the mahogany. Elly touched their tips to check their sharpness, then moved on to palm a piece of chalk. "You sure we can't just draw a couple . . . ?"

Sunny shook her head. "I promise you, we're well-warded."

Elly had never seen demonic wards. She thought she could feel them, at least a little, buzzing away at the corners of her senses whenever she touched the holy water. Of course they'd react to one another. For that matter, Sunny had inched away from the bottles as well.

Lia came back into the room carrying a polished wooden box. She'd disappeared upstairs a few minutes ago, muttering something about "bringing the ladies out of retirement." She made a face when she saw the holy water, and set the box down on the far side of the table. When she undid the latch and lifted the lid, Elly saw the four daggers nestled inside on a bed of dark blue silk. Two were long, maybe fifteen inches from butt to tip. The other two were about half as long but identical in design. All four had wicked-looking serpentine blades.

"Keris knives?" Elly fought the urge to reach out and stroke the metal. Cavale wandered over to appreciate them as well, letting out a low whistle when he peered down into the box.

Lia grinned, her fingers playing over the wrapped leather of the hilt. "Old friends."

Elly wasn't so sure she wanted to touch the daggers after all. Some people believed keris knives had spirits imbued in them, forged into the metal. Could the succubi have . . . ? Before she could try to determine whether or not Lia was fucking with her, Justin spoke up.

"I smell wet dog again."

Cavale was back at the window before Elly could react, twitching the curtains aside and peering out into the night. At that moment, the buzzing Elly'd felt from the succubi's wards swelled. The living room was filled with the sound of a swarm of angry bees. *No, not bees. Locusts.* Sunny waved a hand and the noise dropped down to a dull drone.

"I can't see any of them out there," said Cavale. He checked the locks on the window—not like it'd keep out a determined Creep—and glanced back at Sunny. "How close are they?"

"They're on the property." She closed her eyes, as though there were words in the buzzing. "Those wards can't keep them out all night, but they'll slow them down for a few minutes."

Cavale had his cell phone out already, dialing Val. Elly turned to the other three. "Okay. We'll watch the entrances, get any who make it inside. You two stay close to Justin."

Lia eyed him as he scrambled closer to the couch. "I don't suppose you want to go in the other room and have the best, oh, three minutes of your life, do you?"

He blinked at her. "Wh—"

Oh you've got to be shitting me. Elly grimaced, catching Lia's meaning before Justin did. "You're a virgin?"

The crimson came back. He couldn't seem to decide which of them to gape at. "What does that have to do with anything?"

"Because it means they'll fight all the harder to get to you. You'd better hope they want the thing in your head more than they want a snack."

Lia smiled. "We'll be fine. I just thought I'd offer."

Justin scowled at Elly and the succubus, though the blush kept the look from being all that threatening. "How do they even know I'm the one they're after?"

"You can smell them," said Elly. "You've been doing it all day. I'm guessing they've been following you. Or the book's psychic scent. Something like that, anyway."

"But . . . but Chaz said they can't be out during the day."

"As far as we know, no, but we have to figure they know somehow. You smelled them at the funeral."

"It was *ten thirty*."

Sunny and Lia exchanged a look. "Um," Sunny said. She sighed, setting her keris knife down. "There are rumors. Old ones. About Jackals walking in the daylight."

Elly felt a chill go through her. "How?"

"Depends on the rumor. Some said they possessed actual jackals, and the dogs' fur protected them from the sun." There was a loud crash outside, and a flare of white. Sunny grimaced. "They're trying to pass the first set of wards."

"What were the other rumors?" Elly picked up a set of stakes and shoved them in the mini quiver she'd clipped to her belt loop.

"That they sent the sun's flame elsewhere. I don't know how it worked."

"There's something in the book about deflection," said Justin. "I don't really understand it all, but that's the gist of the word. And something about binding."

He didn't get any further than that, though, because the buzzing ward crescendoed then cut off abruptly. Then the howling started.

They weren't the full-throated, blood-chilling howls of wolves. The Creeps' cries were high and reedy, devolving into barks and yips at the end.

"Uh. Aren't your neighbors going to hear that?" asked

Justin. "And see what those flashes are?" He perked up as a new idea struck. "Won't they call the police?"

"Sorry, sweetie," said Sunny. "The property's not just warded against the Jackals. It's about as sound- and sight-proofed as we can make it."

"Old habits," said Lia, though the women exchanged a glance that told Elly there was more to it than that. Probably a lot more.

"There have to be fifty of them." Cavale peered out the window again, squinting into the night. "I can see them moving."

Lia looked relieved to be off the topic of nosy neighbors. "I don't hear that many."

Elly shook her head. "You probably don't. Professor Clearwater thought one of them might be throwing out illusions. It might only work on humans. Or, um." She didn't know the etiquette here. Was it okay to point out that succubi spent most of their time deceiving people, too?

Sunny's lips quirked. "Or because we deal in them ourselves?"

"Yeah."

She took her knives out of the box once more—a long one and a short one for her, the other set for Lia. "They're getting closer. The ladies are *thrumming*."

"They're hungry," said Lia. "It's been a long time." She glanced down at her hands, then, with a sigh, reached over and took a lock of Sunny's hair between her fingers. "I guess we ought to . . . ?"

Sunny kissed her knuckles, a sad smile on her lips. "We should."

The air shimmered around the women, like heat coming from hot asphalt. Lia's skin darkened to a dusky purple, her blond hair thickening and twisting itself into mud-colored dreadlocks. Her face elongated, her nose thinning to a vicious slash. Sunny gained a foot of height, then two. Her dark hair retracted into a short cap and her eyes took on a tilt that made her normally sweet face look severe.

Justin stood between them, gaping. Even Cavale, who was used to this sort of thing, had to tear his eyes away. Elly could see why. In their previous forms, they'd been pretty. The creatures that stood before them now were downright *glorious*. They shed their jeans and sweatshirts like snakes shedding their skin. Sunny kicked off her bunny slippers, one of them skittering away beneath the couch.

Justin's throat clicked when he swallowed. "Do you . . . I mean, shouldn't you—"

Lia giggled, her voice soft and husky. "This is how we learned to fight. Anything else is a hindrance."

He found an interesting spot on the ceiling to stare at.

They didn't have time to revel in his discomfort, though. Elly caught movement by the window. She grabbed Cavale's sleeve and yanked him toward her just as the glass shattered inward, sending shards exploding across the living room. A Creep thudded to the floor, dead, its singed fur crackling and sparking with the remnants of the magic that had killed it.

"Here they come," said Cavale. Sunny and Lia closed ranks around Justin, their keris knives at the ready.

Outside, shapes seethed in the darkness, the shadows stretching back to the line of hedges that marked the end of the succubi's backyard. Golden eyes caught the light from the living room, one pair, two, ten. *There can't be that many. There aren't.* Elly hefted one of the glass holy water bottles. *What's a little more broken glass?* She pitched it outside, aiming for a spot between a pair of glowing eyes.

There came a yelp as the bottle broke, the sound caught between human and canine. A hole opened in the writhing mass of Creeps, but Elly couldn't tell if the empty space was illusion melting away or the Creeps avoiding the water.

Another one came pelting through the window. For a split second, Elly could see the demonic ward, like a spiderweb with strands plucked loose. As this new Creep came through, the web broke for good, its gossamer threads drifting to the ground and vanishing. It did a number on the Creep before it failed, though. This one made it into the room alive, but only barely. It drew one pained, shuddering breath before Cavale was on it, driving his stake into its back.

Then they were pouring in, jamming themselves through the bay window four, five at a time, crawling over one another to get inside. They were in different states of transformation, some still nearly human except for their claws, others with snouts extended and teeth bared but standing upright. A few had turned all the way: heads completely canine, covered in short black fur, their bodies bulging with muscles and twisted so they loped across the yard on all fours.

Elly loosed more holy water on them, snatching up a plastic bottle this time and squeezing it out in a gush. Two of them clutched at their faces, screaming, and fell back. The other three came on, unaffected. "Those ones are fake!" she shouted, but her heart dropped as two more took the injured ones' places at the sill. She didn't have enough water to test every one that came through.

They clambered into the room and more took their places. Another spray of the water had no effect, but the Creep that advanced on her sure as hell *felt* real. Silver and Pointy dropped into her palm as he advanced, snarling.

Elly swung the spike in a perfect arc and felt the resistance as it sunk into the Creep's chest. The ash spread quickly, radiating outward from the wound. She yanked her spike back as the light went out of the Creep's eyes. *But why didn't the water hurt it?* There were burn marks on his face. She *had* hit him, then. He had either ignored the pain, or never even felt it.

If they can walk in the day, can they shrug off the holy water, too?

It didn't seem to be the case with all of them. Cavale had his own bottle, and was driving a pair of Creeps toward the kitchen with it. One of them yowled with pain, covering its eyes where he'd already scored a direct hit. The other . . . the other mimicked its companion's actions—cowering, backing away, taking agonized-looking peeks through its clawed hands—but it didn't make a single sound. Elly realized she could see through that one's arm, and make out the edge of the end table behind it.

So some were illusion, but others were simply impervious to the water. *Good to know.*

She dodged aside at movement in her peripheral vision. A pair of monstrous claws raked the air where she'd been standing. The Creep snapped at her, its rotted yellow teeth clacking as it lunged. Elly dipped and spun, bringing the spike up so the Creep ran right into it.

Another stood right behind it, half-human, with a knife in one hand and the claws protruding from the other. He swiped with the knife first. Too late, Elly realized it was a feint. The clawed hand came up and caught her by the jaw. She swung the spike, but the Creep was taller, his arms longer. She hit empty air.

The claws dug into her chin, five bright flares of pain. She kicked out at him, but he held her fast. She couldn't see Cavale. Judging from the sounds coming from the kitchen, he was holding up fine. Behind the Creep, she could see Sunny and Lia, whirling about, smoke trailing from their knives. A growing pile of Creep corpses lay at their feet.

She couldn't shout; the Creep was already squeezing her jaw so hard it throbbed. One good thrash only dug the tips in deeper and made her see stars. *Not going down. Not like this.*

Sunny and Lia moved apart, giving her a glimpse of Justin in between them. He had his hands clamped over his ears, like he was trying to block something out. He turned toward her, and for a heartbeat, they made eye contact. She tried shaking her head and got another jolt of pain for her troubles.

Oh, don't. Don't play hero. Don't, don't, don't.

He did.

Justin shoved past Sunny, shouting. He knocked one Creep aside, making it fall on its ass by dint of sheer luck. Then one snagged him by the upper arm, its claws tearing through his sleeve. Elly recognized him as one of the three from last night. The big one with the scarred face. Asshole.

All that effort to keep the pigs' blood off the shirt earlier and it gets ruined anyway. Justin cried out as the gash opened on his arm.

Elly shouldn't have been able to hear him over the snarling and the snapping, but that's when she realized the room had gone silent, the last echoes of Justin's pain hanging on the air. One by one, the Creeps' noses—real and illusionary—turned up and sniffed the air. *They smell virgin blood.* Her Creep let her go, the claws retracting and leaving warm blood to trickle down her chin in their absence. He turned toward Justin, his snout getting longer as he let his transformation complete.

Elly checked her grip on Silver and Pointy. Shaking off the agony at her jaw, she darted forward, spike raised.

Not fast enough.

The Creeps surged toward Justin.

23

THE CREEP IN front of her exploded in a shower of ash as Silver and Pointy found its mark. Elly pushed right through the greasy cloud, bits of dead Creep coating her skin. She kept her lips closed; once, she'd made the unfortunate mistake of sucking in a breath right after staking one. She'd tasted rotten meat for weeks.

Asshole had twisted Justin's arm up behind his back and pulled him in close. Justin kicked at his shins, but every movement wrenched his shoulder. Elly could hear him panting from the pain. The wave of Creeps carried her closer, all other enemies forgotten in their desire to get a taste of Justin's sweet, untainted blood. She uncapped another bottle of holy water as they clambered over one another and splashed it on the closest ones. Two to her left dropped to the floor and rolled, howling. It tripped up a couple of others, but not for long. They trampled over their fallen comrades, intent on the prize in the center of the room.

Elly pulled a rowan stake from her belt with her left hand and swung it to the side. Her arm slipped through the Creep directly in front of her, but connected with the one behind it. Both the real Creep and its illusion clutched at the spot where the stake went in and fell to their knees. She left the stake where it was; it wouldn't kill the Creep, but he'd be too pain wracked to do much more than crawl. She'd come back and finish him off later. Two more went down in sim ilar fashion as Elly shoved her way to the front of the pack, illusions peeling off as well and thinning out the throng.

Still, for every Creep that fell to her stakes, another took its place. In the brief glimpses she caught between Creeps, Elly could see them pouring in from everywhere now—not just through the broken bay window, but spilling down the stairs, shoving in through the hallway that led to the front door, and streaming in from the kitchen. *Cavale was in there.* Panic shot through her. She hadn't seen him since he'd backed those others through the doorway. With an effort, she forced herself to face forward again. She'd never be able to fight through the Creeps to get to him. *He can hold his own. Help Justin.*

From outside, there came startled, pain-filled yips. They started far away and got closer, fast, like someone had turned up the volume in another room. For a moment, she thought Cavale had made it outside, but then she saw the streak of red tearing its way through the Creeps. *Val.*

Elly didn't know what she'd been expecting, really. Seeing the succubi fight was like watching an exquisite dance. The vampire's movements were rhythmic, too, but hers were marked by a military precision: rake her claws through this Creep's spine, step to the right and drive a stake in the next's chest, step again and shear a third's head clear off its neck. She never stopped moving, just killed one and went on to the next. Some of her targets were illusions, but she course corrected easily when she encountered one.

The Creeps around Elly seemed to sense that death had entered the room. They started pushing back against her, trying to get away. Elly shoved forward, driving Silver and Pointy into the backs of these Creeps attempting to flee. As she got closer to where the one Chaz had dubbed Asshole had Justin, there was still a wall of Creeps two or three deep.

They hadn't quite realized there was a vampire wreaking havoc among their brothers and sisters.

She burst clear of the seething mass of them and found herself next to Val. Black blood was smeared across the woman's mouth; she must have bitten a few on her way in. Elly shuddered at the thought of anyone *willingly* swallowing Creeps' blood. Val nodded at her, then looked around and frowned. Elly followed her gaze.

The Creeps at the front were holding back, pawing at the air and drooling as they breathed in the scent of Justin's blood, but there was a good three yards between the front-runners and the place where Asshole held Justin. *He's keeping them away.* As if to prove it, one Creep edged forward from Asshole's left. It was a furtive movement, like the Creep thought she might be able to dart forward and make a snatch at Justin before his captor could react.

Asshole's head whipped toward her and he snarled. He wasn't in full, head-to-toe Creepskin, not yet, but his teeth were sharp, his claws out, his nose stretched into a snout. The woman whined and slunk back, her head bowed so low her chin touched her chest. If she'd had a tail, it would've been tucked between her legs.

Sunny emerged from the other side of the circle, taking up a position behind Asshole while Lia guarded her back. Black ichor coated the keris' blade. It streaked past the hilt and down over Sunny's wrist, winding like vines down her forearms. Her eyes flicked to Elly and Val, and Elly understood what she wanted. She circled a few steps to the right, passing through a phantom Creep to get a better angle of approach. Val stayed where she was. Asshole yanked Justin close against his chest, using him as a shield as he shuffled in a tight circle to watch them all.

"I can smell you back there, demon bitch," he said. "Take me down and they'll tear him apart."

"We won't let that happen." Val reached behind herself almost casually and caught a Creep by the scruff of its neck. Never breaking eye contact with Asshole, she dragged it forward. "Maybe you forgot: I was at Sacramento." She slid her palm under the Creep's chin, ignoring its sudden, panicked flailing, and wrenched its head sideways. The crunch of breaking vertebrae told Elly everything she needed to know.

Val took the dead Creep by the collar and tossed it at Asshole's feet. Its head lolled at an unnatural angle as it rolled to a stop. "You want me to count to three?"

He looked around the room and seemed to realize how much of it had cleared out since Val's entry. There was the circle around himself and Justin, and that was about it. The others had all slunk away. Cavale came in from the kitchen, a nasty-looking cut on his cheek and the sleeve of his jacket only hanging onto the shoulder by a few stubborn threads. He was marching a Creep along in front of him, holding a fork up to the scrawny man's neck: Twitch. From the four burnt-looking parallel scratches down the side of Twitch's face, Elly guessed Cavale had found Sunny and Lia's good silverware.

"The rest are running," said Cavale. "I'm guessing the woman's around here somewhere, but I haven't seen her yet."

"How about it, then?" Val stepped forward. Elly and Sunny did the same. "You going to let him go?"

Elly had to hand it to him—he hid his panic well. His snout grew even more canine; his incisors lengthened. You had to be close to see it, and she was a couple of feet closer than anyone else. Val could likely smell it on him. Her nostrils flared as she waited for his response.

Asshole turned a bit, shifting to put Justin more firmly between himself and Val. Elly could tell how he'd assessed the threats in the room: Val was the scariest, and she wouldn't argue that. But he'd twisted to keep an eye on Sunny and Lia, too. Which meant he'd forgotten what his alpha had told them about herself and Cavale.

He wasn't looking at her, so he didn't see the smile that quirked her lips. Val, did, though, and her slight nod was all the permission Elly needed.

Her boots pounded along, squelching in the blood of dead Creeps. She had to jump for it—Asshole was a good head and a half taller. He started to face her, realizing his fatal mistake far too late. Justin shrieked as he was yanked around again. Elly heard the *pop* as his shoulder came out of its socket.

Then she was there, barreling into Asshole. Her aim was true as ever: with one good stroke, the silver spike sank through his leather jacket and pierced his heart. Asshole gasped, sending a spray of ash from his already-turning insides out into the air.

Behind the others, Twitch let out an outraged howl. The other Creeps took an extra second or two to realize that the only thing keeping them from their wonderful feast was gone, but once they twigged onto it, they were clambering over one another to get to Justin.

Val, Sunny, and Lia were already on it, a whirlwind of blade and claw tearing through the first ones to move. Elly hauled Justin up from where he'd dropped into a crouch, intent on putting some extra distance between him and the slavering Creeps. He was muttering as he gained his feet, something she couldn't quite make out. "What was that?"

He looked up at her and she froze.

His eyes are yellow. She was certain they'd been brown earlier today.

A Creep broke out of the pack, just out of Val's reach. It loped forward, a rope of drool trailing from its mouth. Out of instinct, Elly let Justin's arm drop and readied Silver and Pointy, but she didn't get to use it. Justin pushed her aside with his good arm and stood waiting for the Creep. It pulled up short, scrabbling back a step when it got a look at his face.

Then Justin let out a string of syllables that made Elly's skin crawl. She'd heard it plenty of times before, but only from Creeps.

The one in front of him blinked, then whined low in its throat. It did what its packmate had done at Asshole's snarl earlier, ducking its head and backing away.

Then they *all* were backing away, slinking out of the house as quickly as they'd come. Twitch jerked himself out of Cavale's grasp and booked it out the window. Val, Sunny, and Lia ran down a few stragglers, but once the Creeps were outside, no one gave chase.

"Let them run," said Val. "They won't be back tonight."

Elly stood in the middle of the living room, surveying the damage. The place had been cozy and neat not an hour ago. Now, the carpets were saturated with blood, the end tables and coffee tables had been reduced to splinters, and the upholstery had been shredded by the Creeps' claws. The whole room reeked of blood and burnt flesh, and there were streaks of ash everywhere. Not to mention the Creeps' corpses strewn all around.

Justin was in the middle of them all, like the epicenter of an earthquake. He held his arm and looked at them all as, one by one, they turned to stare. "Elly?" he said, his yellow eyes locking onto her. He swayed dangerously off center and she reached out a hand to steady him.

What the hell did you do? she wanted to ask, but what came out instead was, "You're okay." The first-aid training Father Value had ingrained in her kicked in. She started running her post-fight triage checklist in her head: Justin's arm, Cavale's cheek, her own dripping jawline. As the adrenaline wore off, the pain rushed right on in to fill the void. She'd worry about herself after. Justin, his arm, and his newly yellow eyes were her priority. "We'll get that arm fixed for you. Can you walk to the couch with me?" She guided him to Sunny and Lia's torn-up sofa and helped him lower himself onto it.

He smiled weakly at her, then went slightly green. "I think I'm gonna throw up."

WHERE THE HELL is Chaz? He should have been there by now. Val surveyed the shambles that was Sunny and Lia's living room and found herself straining to hear the dull purr of the Mustang's motor coming down the street. All the times she'd given him shit for how loud it was, and now she'd welcome its peace-disturbing sound.

She dialed his cell again. Still no answer. *Five more minutes and I go looking for him.*

Cavale came to stand beside her. He had a wad of paper towels pressed to his cheek, blood seeping through slowly. Sunny and Lia had disappeared upstairs to change back into more mundane-looking skins and put on some clothes, saying something about "putting the ladies to bed." Elly sat on the couch beside Justin, murmuring softly to him. His arm hung off-kilter; they were going to have to pop it back into its socket soon.

"He'll turn up," said Cavale. "He might have pulled into the driveway and seen them all, realized there was no way in hell he could get past."

"I thought about that. But it doesn't explain why he's not picking up now. And I never heard the engine." She didn't know the specifics of the wards Sunny and Lia had laid, but she was fairly certain sound could get *in*, but not *out*.

"Val, we don't know how far the Creeps' illusion carried. Maybe they were doing something that made him think he couldn't get down the street."

"I'd have heard the car half a mile away."

"Okay. Well, he's a smart guy. He's probably going to roll in here with a perfectly good explanation in a few minutes." They didn't like one another, Chaz and Cavale, but Cavale could find a compliment for Chaz now and then. Where *was* he?

She shook it off and turned to the pair on the couch. "How's our man of the hour?"

Elly looked up. "We're out of puking danger for now."

Justin gave Val a weak smile as she crouched down in front of him. "My arm hurts."

"Yeah, it's going to." Val couldn't help but stare at the change in his eyes. Last night, they'd been dark brown. Now, they were the color of burnished amber, maybe a little darker than your average Jackal's, but not by much. She sniffed, trying to separate Justin's scent out from the rotten meat stench of the corpses in the room. To her relief, he was easy to find—not because he was sitting right there before her, but because to her nose he was still bright and human, smelling of sweat and blood and the same soap Cavale used.

"Why did they run?" He addressed the question to Val, but looked around at everyone. "I didn't think that last one was going to stop."

"I don't know." She smiled at him gently, at first confused as to why he looked so alarmed. *Fangs,* she realized. *And blood.* She swiped her sleeve across her mouth, but it wasn't going to do much more than smear the Jackals' ichor around. "Justin, do you remember what you said to them? What it was you yelled?"

"You were right there, didn't you hear?"

"Humor me."

He looked, if anything, a little embarrassed. "I told it not to touch me. And, um, to go away."

"No you didn't," said Elly softly. "At least, not in English."

Justin twisted to stare at her. "What are you . . . Oh. Oh, *shit.* Seriously?"

"You said earlier you were starting to understand some of the writing. Maybe you picked up a phrase from the book." The lie was obvious in the flatness of her voice and the way she ducked her head to look at her hands.

Cavale came to crouch beside Val. "I don't think he's buying it, El," he said, and passed a shard of a broken mirror to Justin. "Look at your eyes. I think it dug in further."

Justin took it and stared. And stared some more. "What the hell is this?" That yellow gaze swung wildly among them. "I'm still human, aren't I? I don't *feel* any different."

"You still smell human," said Val, pushing as much certainty into her tone as she could. "You're not one of them."

But she didn't miss the uneasy glance that passed between Elly and Cavale that said they weren't so sure.

Footsteps came clumping down the stairs as Sunny and Lia reappeared. They'd gone back to their preferred faces, and had donned paint-splattered sweatshirts and jeans. Lia carried a basin full of cleaning supplies; Sunny had an armload of rags.

Justin looked at them, then at the ash-smeared, blood-spattered disaster area that had been their living room. "Oh, no. Your things. Your *house*. I'm so sorry, you guys. I'll—"

"You'll nothing," said Lia. "You'll sit there and let Elly see to that arm."

"But there are bodies. What do we do with the bodies? You can't just, like, bury them in the backyard. The neighbors will know something's up, wards or no. It's an eleven o'clock news story waiting to happen."

Elly blinked. "Your arm's dislocated and we just got attacked by Creeps, and you're worried about what the neighbors will think?"

"He's polite," said Sunny. "And probably in a fair bit of shock. As for the corpses." She let the rags tumble from her hands and picked through the splinters that had been the coffee table. Her fingers closed over one of the rowan stakes. "There won't be any." She stepped over to the closest Jackal and toed it so it lay on its back. In one swift motion, she brought the stake down, into its heart. Ash began to spread from the spot. "It'll take a little longer since it's rowan, but it gets the job done." She grinned at Elly. "That spike of yours would make it go even faster, but I know some women don't like others touching their partners."

The spike sat to Elly's left. Her fingers twitched toward it, but she didn't snatch it up. After a moment, she smiled, chagrined, and pulled her hand away. "It's all right. I'll try not to be jealous."

"Good girl." Sunny took the stake with mock reverence. It lasted about ten seconds, until she turned to the small pile of Jackals she and Lia had taken care of in the fighting. She hauled them out one by one and set to staking.

Cavale glanced sidelong at Val. "I guess the meeting with the vampires didn't go so well?"

She shook her head. "Ivanov said we could handle it on our own. It was a test."

"What kind of a test?"

"He knows who you two are. Your Father Value's something of a legend. He wants to meet you, offer you some sort of jobs." Elly perked up a bit, but Val cut her off. "You don't want to take him up on it, Elly. Vampire turf wars never end well."

"I think I can decide that for myself," the girl said primly. "It's not like I have any other offers on the table."

Cavale grunted. "We'll talk about that later." He peered at Val. He knew her well enough to sense she'd left something out. "So he was testing us?"

". . . and me. He wants me to Hunt for him."

Cavale went still. The sounds of Sunny's staking and Lia's sweeping paused. Elly looked thoughtful.

Justin laughed into the silence. Hysteria tinged the edges of it, made it harsh. "Val's not a hunter. She's a *bookseller*. Booksellers are, like, peaceful, and . . ." He faltered and looked at Elly for help, but she was shaking her head.

"Are you kidding? You saw the way she took out those Creeps. Of *course* she's a Hunter." Her eyes shone as she said it, like a kid describing a cool scene in an action movie. Val half expected her to get up and start acting it out.

She couldn't deny it: fighting them had felt good. Like she'd never stopped. *No. Justin's right. I'm a bookseller. I am*. Only, she was more than that, too. She sighed. "I was a Hunter before I came out here, and Ivanov knows it."

"Why'd you stop?" She could see Justin reassessing his image of her, and it stung. She couldn't tell if he was disappointed that she'd stopped Hunting or if he was uneasy that she ever had in the first place. Those yellow eyes were too hard to read.

"There was a raid. Biggest nest we'd ever seen, probably a hundred Jackals squatting in an abandoned apartment building. Three stories aboveground, couple more below. We went in to wipe them out. We *did* wipe them out. But I was the only one who survived." If she closed her eyes, she'd see the carnage all over again. Bad enough that she could still hear Angelo's last labored, rasping breaths; she didn't need to see the light going out of his eyes, not right now. "I left. I gave it up and came here."

"Funny," said Elly, tapping on her knee. "You came here

to get away from Hunting. So did Professor Clearwater. Any particular reason you picked Edgewood?"

"Aside from it being on the other side of the country from Sacramento, no."

"And yet you both ended up here, and when Cavale left us, he settled down in the next town over." She cocked a thumb at the succubi. "From what I understand, Sunny and Lia came here to get away from things, too. Isn't that . . . a little bit much for coincidence?"

Before any of them could mull it over, Val's phone rang in her pocket, making her jump. She snatched it out, not bothering to look at the caller ID. "Chaz? Where the hell are you?"

There was a pause on the other end, then an older woman's voice spoke: "Valerie? It's Mrs. Hagerty from next door. I'm sorry if I'm interrupting you at the bookstore, but your friend's car is out in front of my house. It's running and the headlights are on, but I don't see anyone inside it."

Val's heart dropped into her stomach. "Thank you, Mrs. Hagerty. I'll come move it." She snapped the phone closed and stood, trying to keep the anger at bay.

"What is it?" asked Lia. "What's happened?"

"He never even left my street." Her hands balled into fists. The claws were back, digging deep into her palms. There was only one thing she could think of that could have stopped him from trying to get to Sunny and Lia's to help, and Val could see the sneering, foxlike face in her mind. "Katya took him."

24

THERE WAS NO conversation on the ride to Boston, even though Elly must have been bursting with questions. Val was glad she kept quiet, though. As well-intentioned as the girl's inquiries might have been, Val was only barely holding her rage in check. She didn't want to go snapping Cavalc's sister's head off after she'd spent the night protecting one of Val's own from the Jackals.

They parked on a side street in Southie. The Mustang was a bitch to parallel park; Val would make Chaz figure out how to wrangle it back out of the space if he was worried about his paint job. *Provided he's capable of driving at all.* The thought made her pick up the pace.

South Boston was predominantly Irish, which made Ivanov and his people the outsiders. Val had heard stories of mob activity, but the players were almost always human. She saw a few ogham marks scratched into brick walls, a clear indication that there was at least a coven or two of Irish bloodsuckers, but Ivanov's crew was in charge here as far as the supernatural set was concerned.

The *Stregoi* hung out at a bar on L Street, a tiny place

that had been built during the Depression. The sign by the door suggested its maximum capacity was fifty people, but any more than thirty would feel cramped.

Ogham marks gave way to Cyrillic lettering as Val, Cavale, and Elly got closer. She couldn't translate the words, but she knew Ivanov's sigil. It was everywhere here: chalked onto walls, spray painted onto street signs, carved into doorways. Every now and then, though, she saw something surprising. Some of the Cyrillic symbols had been slashed through, as though someone were trying to erase them. *No, those aren't scratches.* They were too uniform. They were Ogham runes. Ivanov's rival, looking to send a message.

A bouncer stood outside the bar, arms folded, an expression of boredom on his face. Ivanov's mark stood out on his arm in fresh, dark ink. It was so new, the tattoo was still smeared over with Vaseline. He held up a hand to stop them, maybe check their IDs, but Val growled, "Let us in," and pushed some Command into it. He stepped aside obediently, his eyes wide with outrage. It wasn't nice to order another vampire's minions around, but considering how Katya had *kidnapped* Val's, she couldn't really muster a shit about protocol or good manners.

Inside, the bar was wasn't quite at capacity, but it was damned close. Picking the vampires out of the crowd was easy: plenty of heads swivelled around as the three of them entered, but the humans quickly dismissed them. The four vamps kept staring, gaping at Val. A few sets of fangs slid out, but no one made a move. Elly and Cavale flanked her, just in case.

"Where's Katya?" she asked, catching the eye of the closest vampire.

He was tall and bulky, his tee shirt stretched tight over his muscled chest. Yet, when Val stepped up close to him, he looked distinctly uncomfortable. "I . . . I don't . . ."

"I'm right here, Valerie," came her silken voice from the rear of the bar. The crowd parted, revealing her standing beside a pool table. She'd shucked the suit and returned to her regular street-rat chic: a manufacturer-distressed tee shirt with the logo of an '80s hair band artfully flaking off, an equally fake-scuffed leather jacket, jeans that had been ripped on the assembly line, and a pair of Doc Martens that had possibly actually *earned* their scratches. "I didn't think we'd see you so—" she choked on the words. Val had been moving from the first syllable, crossing the room in the space of a breath and catching Katya by the throat.

Katya snarled. She planted her palms flat on Val's chest and *shoved*. It felt more like a kick. Val went flying, crashing back into a cluster of barflies and knocking them down like bowling pins. Cavale and Elly had started forward to help, but neither of them got very far before they were each restrained by a pair of regulars. One of the vampires made a grab for her, but Val was too fast, already back on her feet and lunging for Katya once more.

Her claws raked down Katya's face before the other woman could catch her wrist.

"I'll have your fangs for that," Katya hissed, squeezing until the bones ground beneath her fingers. Val swung her other arm up, but someone reached out and held it steady.

"Valerie. Katya. What is this about?" Ivanov had emerged from his office, still in his impeccable suit, and stood regarding the two vampires as though they were unruly siblings scuffling over a toy. *That's all Chaz is to them, really.*

"I came for my Renfield."

"He's missing?" Ivanov frowned. "He was with you when we left."

"And she was talking to him alone while you and I were in the house. Probably giving him Commands. I should never have—"

Katya let go of Val's wrist. "I did not."

"You did it once before. Why would I believe you now?"

Ivanov smiled. "Valerie. Katya wouldn't do that." He glanced at his second in command and corrected himself: ". . . again." He considered Val a moment. She'd managed to get the Jackals' blood off her face, but she hadn't taken the time to change her clothes. "I see your Hunt was successful." He gestured behind him and the men holding

Elly and Cavale released them. "And I also see you've brought me Value's children."

"She didn't bring us," said Cavale, brushing off the sleeve of his jacket. "We came on our own."

"To hear my proposal?"

He ignored Val's warning look. "If you'll agree to help Val with the Creeps, sure, we'll hear it."

The smile turned shrewd, one businessman recognizing another. "I believe we can work together. If you'd be so kind as to step into my office . . . ?"

Elly cleared her throat. "What about Chaz?"

Ivanov answered her, but it was Val he spoke to. "So quick to blame my Katya. I give you my word, she does not have him, and did not order him to make his way here. These Jackals you fought—is it safe to assume they know your boy has what they want?"

"They do."

"And they've seen you with Charles?"

Ice coursed through Val's veins as Ivanov's meaning sank in. ". . . yes."

"Then perhaps they've taken what is important to you, so you'll consider a trade."

"We never saw Bitch." Elly's voice was hushed. She looked at Cavale for confirmation. He nodded back grimly.

It made sense—more sense, even, than Katya trying to steal Chaz away again. The scent she'd caught outside of her house earlier hadn't been the Jackals descending on Sunny and Lia's. It had been Bitch, lying in wait. "I have to go," she said. There might still be a trail, if she could get home fast enough. She could have easily dismissed Bitch's scent as part of the Jackals' blood that covered them all. But if she went back to where the Mustang had been abandoned, got out of these clothes and retraced . . .

"I'm owed an apology," said Katya. "She can't come in here and *threaten* me, then just walk back out."

Val tensed. She could fight her way out, but not without endangering Elly and Cavale. She had no doubt that they were both good—she'd seen more than enough evidence of their skills in the last two hours—but the three of them against six vampires and a bar full of regulars weren't odds she wanted to play.

Ivanov spared her the decision. "Later, Katya. Let her tend to her own, hmm? If she can put her worries about Charles to rest, I believe her apology will be more heartfelt, don't you?"

Katya looked like she'd stuck her fangs into a lemon, but she relented. "Fine. Go. Give him my regards when you find him."

Cavale came forward and placed a hand on Val's shoulder. "You go on ahead. We'll come find you when we're done here."

She almost argued, but leaving Cavale and Elly here would kill two birds: the meeting would appease Ivanov, and Val could get to Edgewood much faster if she didn't have to drive. She handed the keys over to Cavale. "Be careful, okay?" It was almost exactly what she'd last said to Chaz, too. She fought down the pang of guilt. *No time for that.*

Cavale pocketed them and grinned. "If you find him before we're back with you, don't tell him I'm driving his baby." He gave her a little push. "Go," he said. "Before they change their minds."

With a deferential nod to Ivanov, Val got the hell out of the bar. She was halfway down the street before the bouncer on the door even realized someone had passed by.

ELLY WATCHED THE door swing closed behind Val. The vampires backed off, their expressions oddly relieved. What had Val done to set them all on edge like that? The only one who appeared sorry to see her go was Katya. She was old—Val had pegged her at around a hundred and fifty—but she looked like a grounded teenager, pouting at the door. She'd picked up a pool cue and was wringing it in her hands, probably imagining it was Val's neck. Elly could hear the wood cracking; she almost expected Katya to bite off a chunk of it.

"If you'll follow me," Ivanov said softly. Even he seemed reluctant to provoke Katya. The hush followed them down the short hallway, the murmur of conversation only starting up again as Ivanov closed the door.

The room was elegantly appointed. Where the front of the bar belied its age in its creaking floorboards and dated décor, Ivanov's office would have done equally well serving the head of a law firm. Leather-upholstered chairs sat on either side of the massive desk. A crystal decanter sat on a silver tray, though Elly was fairly certain the red liquid inside wasn't wine set to breathe. The framed paintings on the wall were probably originals, worth more money than she could ever imagine.

Cavale pulled out a chair for her. She could see him scanning the room for potential weapons. Aside from the door behind them, the only other way out was a tiny window about five feet off the ground. *You'd have to be a contortionist to get through that.* If there was trouble, it was a squeeze through the window or a dash through a bar filled with Ivanov's lackeys.

The back room of a tiny pub seemed like a strange place for someone like Ivanov to make the base of his operation. Father Value hadn't talked too much about the vampires' organization. Maybe being on his own away from the Brotherhood, he hadn't thought she or Cavale would need to deal with them. The best she could come up with was that the vampires tended to keep within their colonies, no more than ten or twenty per. In bigger cities, there might be ten major ones, usually less.

The rest of what she knew about vampires had to do with killing them.

"Would you like a drink?" Ivanov sat, glancing between the two of them with a satisfied smile.

"No, thank you," said Cavale. "We can't stay very long. Val needs us."

"Ah, Valerie." He said it with a sigh, as if she were a wayward child. "Quite the Hunter, isn't she?"

It was probably a rhetorical question, but Elly saw an opportunity. "She is. But I was told there weren't many

Creeps left up this way to fight. Why are you looking to bring her back to it now? And hire us, too?"

Ivanov smirked at her barrage of questions. "Even if their numbers are dwindling, it's still a job left unfinished, isn't it? And, since Valerie came to me needing help with a nest of them, I think you'd agree that they can cause much trouble even in their decline."

"Why us, then? The vampires out front looked tough enough. Why not appoint Hunters from your own ranks?"

At first, Elly thought he was gesturing between them. Then she realized he was motioning at her arm, where Silver and Pointy lay nestled against her skin beneath her sleeve. "Why use a rowan stake when you have silver to hand? It's the same principle. Use the best tools you have before choosing from the lesser."

She couldn't argue with that; the way Val had fought at Sunny and Lia's spoke to years of training. And she'd said she was rusty. "All right, then why us? Why not find the Brotherhood and bring them in on it? They have to know more than we do."

Ivanov shook his head. "But they don't, my dear. Not from what I understand."

Elly stole a sideways glance at Cavale. His posture was casual, almost bored, but below the desk's level—and out of Ivanov's line of sight—his index finger tapped rapidly against his thigh. *He's nervous.*

Ivanov didn't seem to have picked up on Cavale's agitation. "The man who raised you two was a font of knowledge *before* the Brotherhood threw him out. He trained recruits for decades, and his protégés were among the most successful. Then there was a falling-out. I've not been privy to the exact details, but let us say he wanted to try tactics more extreme than the Brotherhood had the stomach for.

"They turned their backs on him, but not before they tried taking his two wards away from him. He . . . refused."

One of her earliest memories was of being in their room, in the dark. She'd been curled up against Cavale, listening to raised voices on the other side of the door. One of them was Father Value's. She remembered their door opening, the light spilling in to reveal an unfamiliar silhouette. Then the darkness had bubbled up like ink and engulfed the figure.

She'd always thought the last part might have been a dream, but from Cavale's grimace, she now knew it wasn't. "He killed them, didn't he? The ones who came to take us?"

Cavale nodded. "He was chanting something. He'd lain wards to keep the Creeps away, but I think he activated them on the people who tried to come into our room. We did a lot of running, after that."

"He never stopped learning, did he?" said Ivanov. "I've somewhat of a fondness for rare books, myself, and there were more than a few times I caught wind of one, only to learn he'd found it a week or a day before I had. Once, it was by a handful of hours."

Elly had accompanied Father Value on the occasional book hunt, and knew at least a few of the hidey-holes where he'd stashed his precious tomes. Over the last few days, she'd toyed with the idea of retrieving and selling some of the less dangerous ones if she needed money. Perhaps she'd find a buyer in Ivanov.

"So what's your proposal?" asked Cavale.

"Merely that you make yourselves available to me, should the need arise. I'm willing to pay you a monthly retainer. You can do as you please most of the time, but if I call upon you, I will expect the job to get done promptly."

"I already have a job."

"Yes. You read tarot cards to gullible, tittering house-wives. How exciting."

Cavale let the insult pass. "That's what I do for pocket change. I meant my real job."

"You've done quite well for yourself, vanquishing the local beasties. I'm not asking you to stop, Mr. Evans. Merely to make me your priority client."

Cavale didn't respond. Ivanov turned to Elly. "And yourself?"

"I'll do it."

That got Cavale to sit up. "Elly—"

"I said I'll do it. Will you promise to send help when the Creeps come back for Justin? They're going to be plenty pissed about what we did tonight. If they don't come back and try again tomorrow, I'll have my spike melted down." She stuck out her hand to shake, her sleeve pulling back to reveal said spike's tip peeking out against her wrist. "We'll need the backup."

Ivanov didn't bother with a dramatic pause. He stood and shook. His stone-cold hand eclipsed hers. She could feel the power in his grip; if he wanted to crush her bones to dust, he could. But he didn't, smiling magnanimously as he settled back in his chair. "Good, good. You have my word, we'll come to your aid should you need it. Mr. Evans, I hope you'll consider the offer as well. Sleep on it, perhaps." He pulled a ledger and a pen from his drawer and set them aside. "Now, I have some figuring to do, and you've a missing person to find. Go, and tell Valerie I hope her Charles is safe."

CAVALE FUMED SILENTLY until they were on the highway. Elly watched Boston recede in the mirror, steeling herself for the argument. When it came, though, he didn't yell.

He sighed, which was so much worse.

"I know why you're taking his offer."

She sucked in a breath to answer, but he held up a hand. "Elly, you have a place to stay. I'm not . . . I'm not going to throw you out. You can crash with me as long as you want."

"I'm not going to leech off you."

"So do something closer to Crow's Neck."

"What, get a real job? Can you imagine me behind a desk? Cavale, I'd stab someone with a pen in the first week. Or even flipping burgers? I'd boil someone's head in french fry oil. Then you'd be bailing me out."

"So take cases with me. We can branch out, cover more of the state. Hell, you could write our shopping lists and I'd consider it rent well earned." He changed lanes, glancing at her as the streetlights splashed over her face. "You don't have to work for the vampires."

"No, I don't *have* to, but it's not a bad offer, either. Think about it—they find Creeps and point us right at them? It's what I want to do anyway. They're just doing the research for me."

"And what if it's not Creeps he points you at? What if he sends you after the other colonies? You heard Val; turf wars aren't something you want to be in the middle of."

She reached over and patted his arm. "I'll be okay. I promise. I'm a big girl now."

"Yeah, well. I'm still your big brother. I can't help worrying." He paused as if weighing whether to say more. She had to strain to hear him when he spoke again. "I never stopped worrying about you."

Tears pricked at her eyes. The chain of streetlights ended, and Elly was grateful for the darkness. She bit her lip to keep from sniffling.

Cavale's cell phone chirped in the center console, saving her from the burden of an awkward reply. Elly picked it up and read the name on the caller ID. "It's Val." She hit the speaker button and said hello.

The other woman sounded upset. "Bitch's trail went cold. I don't know where she took him."

Elly and Cavale exchanged a look. Creeps weren't known for taking hostages. Val had to know that, too, but better not to say it out loud.

"Sit tight," said Cavale. "We're on the way home. We'll do some scrying when we get there and we'll find him, okay?"

"Fuck," Val said, and, "Okay. *Fuck.*" Then she cut the call.

Cavale stepped on the gas. The Mustang roared toward home.

❦ 25 ❦

CHAZ WOKE UP feeling like he'd been kicked in the head. Come to think of it, maybe he had been. He remembered driving down Val's street, planning to roll through the stop sign then gun it onto the main road, when his headlights picked a person out of the early evening gloom. He'd jammed on the brakes, swearing. Then he'd seen the face peering in his window.

Bitch.

The last thing he could recall was her yanking him out of the car by his left arm. When he moved it now, the muscles twinged. *Now I know how taffy feels after it's been pulled.*

He sat up to squint at his surroundings. A bolt of pain shot through his skull as he did so, a headache settling in on its heels. *Do I have a concussion? Shit.* He peeled his eyes open again, trying not to look at the sunlight coming in around the raggedy, yellowed window shade.

The room was mostly bare. A bed with a lumpy, stained mattress took up one corner. Even with the crick in his neck and general achiness from spending the night on the floor, he was glad they hadn't deposited him on the bed. God only knew how many different kinds of bugs were living in it. Against the wall beside the door were the busted-up remnants of a dresser. He couldn't be certain that someone had been thrown into it—*no, through it*—but there was a rust-colored dent in the wall behind it at about head height.

Dust covered the floorboards. When Chaz brushed some away with the side of his hand, he uncovered an unpleasant-looking stain. Whether it was blood or Jackal ichor, he didn't know. Still, he didn't feel like sitting in a puddle of it anymore, no matter how old it was.

He got creakily to his feet, taking longer to stand up than an arthritic old man. The headache pulsed a warning at his being completely upright. He closed his eyes again and just stood there, taking slow, deep breaths until the pounding eased a bit. He could smell dust and old paint, stale bacon grease and body odor. There was the musty smell of a house that's been shut up for a while, and beneath it, something animal and rancid, like the rodents had moved in and made themselves at home while the owners were away.

Not rodents. Jackals.

Val might have been able to pick up their rotten meat smell a mile away, but Chaz had learned they exuded it when you were close to them, too. Rotten meat and pencil shavings, that was, and he could smell both.

This is their nest, then. I'll have a fuck of a time getting out. Unless. He shuffled over to the window, flinging an arm across his eyes as he lifted the shade. When he was relatively certain he could open his eyes without the brightness stabbing into his brain, he peeked.

Damn.

Crudely welded bars crisscrossed the window frame. From what he could see, even if he could pry them off, it was a hell of a drop to the ground. He was three stories up with no convenient trees or garage roofs for him to drop down onto.

But . . . it was *daylight*. It had to be nine, maybe ten o'clock. If there had been any Jackals standing guard last night, they were down for the count. He'd be like Sylvester in one of those old cartoons, tiptoeing past the sleeping, snoring bulldog.

Chaz grinned as he crossed the room to try the handle of the rickety-looking door. Even if they had him locked in, he could probably kick it open or see if it would give way with a few good shoulder blows. If they slept anything like Val did during the day, you could set a bomb off beside them and they wouldn't notice.

Still, better to be armed. He picked through the rubble that had been a dresser and found a good two-foot-long section he could use as a bat if need be. The end was pointed, but probably not sharp enough to use as a stake. Plus, it wasn't very likely the dresser had been made from rowan wood. Even if he could impale a Jackal with it, he'd probably only piss it off.

To his surprise, the doorknob turned easily. The hinges groaned as he opened the door enough to peek out into the hallway. Across from him was another closed door. To his left were more bedrooms. To the right he could see the newel post at the top of the stairs. *Right. Down and out, here we go.* One slow step at a time, he slipped out of the room, shifting his weight from one foot to the other only when he was sure the floor wouldn't creak beneath him. Halfway there, and no interruptions. Three-quarters and still safe.

Then, as he neared the stairs, a toilet flushed behind the door to his right. Chaz scuttled away, so his back was against the wall opposite. He didn't have time to run back to the bedroom, and if he broke for the stairs he risked being shoved down them. He held his makeshift stave up like Babe Ruth about to swing for the fences and waited for the door to open.

The kid came out, zipping his fly and adjusting his package. He was tall and scraggly looking, the kind of chunky where you couldn't tell if it was fat or muscle underneath until either you hit him or he hit you. His Slayer tee shirt and jeans had both been black, once upon a time, but now they were a dingy grey. His eyes were bright blue and wide with surprise.

They're not yellow. This dude's not a Jackal. He almost checked his swing until he realized, Jackal or not, Slayer here had been taking a piss three doors down from where Chaz had been shut up. Which meant he was in on it, somehow.

Fuck this guy.

The stave made a satisfying low *whoosh* as it arced at Slayer's head, but unfortunately for Chaz, the other man got his hand off his junk fast enough to bring his arm up and block the blow. His forearm took the impact, then he twisted his hand around and got a grip on it, wrenching the stave out of Chaz' grasp. He tossed it aside and sent it skittering down the hall. Then, bellowing, he charged forward.

Yeah, there was muscle under the flab.

Chaz hit the wall with a dull thud and felt the breath *whuff* out of his lungs. The headache flared again, reminding him that yes, it was still there, matter of fact, have some stars to go with that head crack. Getting oxygen back was a struggle, made all the harder by Slayer keeping him pinned in place with that thick forearm against his chest. Over his agonized air sucking, Chaz heard footsteps pounding up the stairs. Slayer was holding a shouted conversation with someone, but Chaz figured it was more important to devote his energy to staying conscious than anything else.

The stars receded, and by the time he was able to draw a shaky kind of breath, Slayer had been joined by two others: a skinny girl of seventeen or so, wearing a flannel shirt about six sizes too big, and an Irish-looking kid whose nose crooked to the right, probably the product of several bar fights. All three of them watched him, waiting for him to compose himself. The girl looked bored, picking at a loose thread on her shirt. The Irish kid kept his eyes on Chaz' hands, as if he expected him to pull a knife or a gun out of thin air. Slayer reminded Chaz of his junior high guidance counselor—the kind of person who could ask you a question and sit in unnerving silence waiting for an answer. And apparently the kind who wasn't afraid to slam kids into lockers when they got out of line.

Just like Mr. Baker.

Slayer spoke first, his voice surprisingly gentle for such a bruiser. "If I let you go, can you stand?"

Chaz bobbed his head, though he wasn't a hundred percent sure he could actually *stay* standing. His head throbbed like some kind of gremlin had been shoved inside and decided it wanted out.

"More importantly, if I let you go, will you promise not to try anything stupid?"

"Define stupid."

Slayer sighed. "If you're going to hit any of us, or try to run, you're gonna be in a world of hurt. I'd rather you be reasonable about this."

Reasonable? "Fuck you, buddy. Your people *kidnapped* me, and you're helping them keep me here. You want me to be reasonable? Suck my dick." He wished he could muster up the spit for a good bit of dramatic punctuation, but his mouth was dry. The last thing he could remember drinking had been a can of soda on the way to Val's last night.

"We can always tie you to the bed in there until sunset. Doesn't matter to me, really. You guys?" His companions shook their heads. "Or we can be nice about it. Beth can make some breakfast for you, and Sean and I will help you get down the stairs. How's that sound instead?"

Chaz thought about the stained mattress back in the other room. He could risk bedbugs or be cooperative and maybe get another chance at escaping. His stomach growled, making the decision for him. "Okay, fine. I'll behave." He wobbled a moment when Slayer eased him back to the ground, but he didn't keel over.

Beth headed down ahead of them. When she reached the first landing, Slayer and Sean each took one of Chaz' elbows and guided him along. He thought about trying to shrug them off and make a break for it, but now that he was moving at a normal clip, wooziness and nausea were setting in. He'd be lucky to make it to the kitchen without hurling.

That, and when Sean had moved forward to take hold of

him, Chaz had caught a glimpse of the gun tucked into his waistband. Useful to know for later, maybe, when he wasn't seeing double.

The good news was, he made it all the way downstairs without puking on anyone's shoes. Once they lowered him onto a chair, his stomach stopped flip-flopping and went back to growling. The kitchen wasn't any improvement on the rest of the place: paint peeled from the cabinets, water stains trailed down the walls, a film of grease covered everything in the room, and Chaz could smell the mold rotting out the floor beneath the sink.

"Breakfast" turned out to be toast and cereal. The bread was stale, the butter just shy of rancid. He choked that down, then turned to the Lucky Charms Beth had set in front of him. Good news: they were in one of those individual-serving cups, sealed away from the squalor in this place. Bad news: he didn't have the option of eating them dry. Beth had opened them for him and drowned them in reconstituted milk. It might not have been so bad if the tap water she'd used to mix it didn't taste like rust.

Still, it was food, and he'd probably—*probably*—eaten worse in his college days. He didn't know how long he'd be here if he didn't get a chance to attempt an escape, so it seemed prudent to eat now and build up some strength.

Slayer, whose name it turned out was Tom, produced a bottle of aspirin. "I'm sorry about knocking you against the wall up there, man," he said. "Just, you know. You were kind of trying to take my head off with a—what was that? A bed slat?"

"Part of a dresser." Chaz shook three pills out into his palm, thought about it, then added a fourth. He knocked them back with a swallow of rusty water from his glass. He tried finding a spot that didn't have grimy fingerprints on it, but had to settle for wiping the lip with his sleeve and praying no one had anything contagious. "So, uh." He looked around. Beth slouched against the counter. Her cigarette more interesting than her hostage. Sean had disappeared off into another part of the house as soon as he realized Chaz wasn't going to go all secret badass on them. "I guess this is the nest?"

Slayer—*Tom, gotta remember since I seem to be my own hostage negotiator*—nodded. "It is for now."

"It's awfully bright for . . . oh. There we go." He pointed to a door next to the one they'd brought him through. Someone had scrawled "Do Not Open" on the back of a flyer and tacked it up there. "I guess there's something nasty in the basement, huh?"

"A lot of something nasties."

He heard the threat behind it, but didn't react. A basement full of Jackals would only be a problem when night fell. He'd revisit it in six or seven hours if he was still here. For now, Tom, Beth, and Sean were his main concerns. "So what keeps you guys here?"

Tom frowned, puzzled. "How do you mean?"

"I mean, look around." Chaz waved his hand around the dirty kitchen. "This place is falling apart. I'm guessing you scrape together whatever you can to feed yourselves, or maybe you have to live off whatever's in their victims' wallets. How is this any kind of life?"

Up until now Beth had been staring off into space, so zoned out Chaz wondered what she was on. At his question she finally came alive. And she was pissed. She launched herself away from the counter to come stick a finger in his face. Dirt was caked under her nail; the edges of it were ragged, bitten. "They're going to make us what they are! We would've been like them two days ago, if it weren't for you and your people *stealing* it from us."

Chaz backed up, not wanting to get nicked by those filthy nails. "Why the hell would you want to be like them? Kiddo, from what I understand, they're bottom-feeders. You turn into one of them, and you're going to be *eating other people* for the rest of your life."

"Says the guy who fetches and carries for a vampire."

"Okay. Uh. Point. But all I mean is, you can do better than this. For yourselves." He didn't know *how*, exactly, and wasn't about to suggest they go throw themselves on the mercy of the Boston vampires. Ivanov and Katya might wear fancy clothes and arrive in fancy cars, but all that money and they were just as big a bunch of assholes as the Jackals.

"Do better? Fuck you. The world's been shitting on me—on all of us—for long enough. We're going to be part of something bigger. Stronger. A *family*."

"You don't . . . You don't have a family to go back to? A human one?"

Beth spat in his cereal. Bull's-eye. So much for breakfast. "Fuck them, too. These guys accept us for who we are. They *need* us, and we need them." Her voice took on the slightest singsong at this point, like something she'd learned by heart and recited often. The glaze crept back into her eyes.

It's like Val's Command. He glanced at Slayer-Tom, and saw the same look on his face. *They've got these kids convinced it'll actually get better for them. Those motherfuckers.*

Beth was still talking. "We'll live forever, and we can do anything we want. All we have to do is be patient a little longer. And be loyal. Like good packmates should be." She drew breath to say something else, but a moan from another room distracted her, snapped her out of it.

"Is someone hurt?" From the glare she threw his way, he thought maybe he'd done some damage on his way in last night, but he didn't feel like he'd been in a fight. Just like he'd been dragged behind a stampeding elephant.

Beth didn't answer him. She spun away and strode out of the room, swiping the aspirin bottle and a pair of spoons on her way.

Tom watched her go. He didn't resume the conversation, and Chaz got the sense that it would be bad form to keep prodding.

So the Jackals have promised to turn them, and Justin stymied that one when he read the book. Or Elly and Father Whatever fucked it up when they stole it. Either way, same thing. Val had said they were carrion creatures, picking off the low and weak, scavenging and stealing. This house, even, probably belonged to someone else. These kids and the Jackals had to be squatters. And no matter what the kids believed, they were still the Jackals' victims. It was just a different kind of preying going on here.

Tom's gaze kept cutting toward the door. The moaning grew louder, punctuated by weak, hitching cries.

Chaz kept his voice low, trying not to provoke the big man. "If you want to go check on whoever that is. I'll come with you and keep my mouth shut. I won't . . ." He sighed. "I won't try to run."

It was a stupid offer. He knew it. But Tom was a kid who was clearly worrying about his friend. Chaz sympathized with that. Out of all of them, in fact, Tom seemed the most normal, or at least not as fucked-up as the others. Chaz tucked that away, too. Maybe he could use it.

Tom took his measure for another minute. "Okay. Come on, hands where I can see them and all that."

"Yeah, I've watched cop shows, too. I know the drill."

They headed deeper into the house. Beyond the kitchen, a short hallway led to what might once have been the dining room. The table was missing, but the chairs remained. The last room was the family room. It had been converted into a cramped, filthy infirmary.

The smell hit Chaz like he'd walked face-first into a wall: burnt flesh, blood, ash. Four people lay on mattresses that had been dragged out of bedrooms. The fifth was sprawled out on a table, surrounded by candles. As Chaz got closer, he realized this was the missing dining room table. They'd painted sigils all over it, surrounding the girl who lay atop it. Her skin was an alarming shade of red.

Beth was tending to one of the figures on the floor. She sprang to her feet as Chaz and Tom entered, throwing herself between Chaz and the girl on the table. "Don't you touch her! Don't you touch *anything*."

Chaz held up his hands and backed off a step, but he couldn't stifle the question. "The fuck's going on in here?" He realized that, as bad as the girl on the table looked, the burnt-flesh smell wasn't coming from her.

That particular stench belonged to the four on the floor,

their faces marred like someone had splashed them with acid. The skin had boiled and bubbled; in places, the wounds were still weeping through the salve Beth had been applying.

Chaz struggled for something to say, but he could only repeat his first question: "The *fuck*?"

"Those ones are your friends' fault," said Beth. She hadn't moved away from the girl on the table. "They used holy water last night."

"I don't understand. These are humans, not Jackals. Holy water shouldn't hurt them." He left off the *And what the fuck were they doing attacking my friends, anyway?* This wasn't the time for a round of Serves You Right.

"They weren't *there*," she said, as if it were obvious. "They take on the wounds so the pack can keep fighting."

He gaped. "You're saying the Jackals get hit and these poor sons of bitches get their faces burnt off. Do I have that right?"

"They'll be okay," said Beth. "Marian will make them better."

"Who's Marian?"

"A friend. She fixes people." She gestured to the girl on the table. "It doesn't hurt us as bad as it hurts them. Caleb would burn up if he walked in the sun without a link to Ashley." A look passed between her and Tom, one Chaz couldn't decipher. Beth stepped to the side. "You can look," she said. "But if you try to touch the runes, I'll cut your fingers off." She pulled a jackknife from her pocket and folded out the blade. It was pockmarked with rust. If she *did* go to hacking at his fingers, it'd take several chops, and he'd probably get tetanus.

"Nooooot going to risk that, thanks." He peered at the runework from a good five feet away, well out of his reach. The markings were nothing like the circle Cavale had made for Justin yesterday, though Chaz thought he recognized the same style of eye-bending writing from the book. At last he stepped back, joining Tom back near the door. "So tell me something. You guys get the book back from my friends, let's say. That will let you guys become Jackals, too?"

Beth paused in the middle of crushing up aspirin between her spoons. "Yes?"

"What about these five? Do they get to be Jackals?"

"Everyone who's loyal does. They promised us."

"Hmm." Chaz scratched his chin. "So who will do the pain bearing for you guys? Or for the current pack?"

"What are you talking about?" She looked to Tom for help, but he was intent on Chaz, his expression troubled.

"I'm saying, if everyone in this house becomes a Jackal, there won't be any more humans to take on injuries when you fight. No more going outside during the day while someone else lies here looking like they fell asleep at the beach in the middle of July."

"There will be others. We'll find people willing to serve." She made it sound like it was a prestigious role.

"For what? What will you offer them? A lifetime supply of powdered milk? And who'd even pick this life? You'd have to have it pretty shitty to call this living . . . Oh." There went his tongue again, full steam ahead of his brain.

These kids looked hungry. Not just haven't-had-a-good-meal-in-a-month hungry, but broken down and weary, kicked in the teeth by life. Often. He thought about what Beth had said in the kitchen, about the world shitting on them. Maybe this *was* the good life, compared to whatever they'd been through before the Jackals found them. "Um," he said, backpedaling furiously. "Do I get to meet this Marian?"

Sean came in just in time to hear the question. He dumped an armload of tattered blankets near Beth before turning to Chaz. "Maybe. If we don't have to shoot you." He paused, considering, and a sly, eager grin broke out. "Actually, wait. Probably *definitely* if we have to shoot you. Want to make a run for it?"

26

OVER THE NEXT few hours, Chaz did everything he could to avoid getting shot by Sean. Mostly that involved keeping his mouth shut and his movements slow. He also had to leave the bathroom door open when he took a piss, but since it was either that or pee in the sink, he opted for the lesser indignity. His headache receded from migraine strength to mild-hangover bad, which was good. He was pretty sure he'd lucked out and didn't have a concussion.

Despite the glares she kept throwing in his direction, Beth let him help fix lunch. Mostly, Chaz wanted to be sure the plates he ate off weren't crawling with germs, but part of him hoped he could get on the kids' good sides in case the shit hit the fan later on.

Shortly after four, a key rattled in the front door lock. Tom planted himself between Chaz and the hallway, as though Chaz might be stupid enough to charge whoever was coming in. *I probably* should *make a go at it.* But the logical part of his brain suggested it was wiser to stay alive and learn what he could.

Bitch could have killed him last night, left him dead

behind the wheel on Val's street. She could have offed him on the way here, or tossed him down in the basement with the rest of the Jackals so they'd have a tasty breakfast when they woke up. Plenty of things she could have done, but instead she'd left him aboveground to be watched by the minions, and she must have given permission for him to be out and about. Otherwise Tom could have shoved him back in the bedroom and left him there. These were things he was meant to see, which meant she intended to give him back to Val when this was over.

Probably in exchange for Justin.

Well, fuck that. Val wouldn't make that kind of trade. Much as he'd appreciate it, they couldn't be given the power all willy-nilly to go around making new Jackals. So he'd wait and watch, and hope Val had some other plan in mind.

Two people came through the door: a mousy-looking woman in her midforties holding a tackle box to her chest like it had nuclear launch codes within, and a tall man wearing a sweatshirt with its hood pulled up. Chaz could smell the sunscreen on him and caught the glow of yellow eyes in his shadowed face. *This must be Caleb.*

The Jackal moved wearily, pushing Tom aside to come and look at Chaz. He was in human form, his face bland and forgettable except for the places where someone had drawn the same sigils Chaz had seen around the girl on the dining room table. Was that eyeliner they'd been applied with? Chaz kept his teeth clamped together so he couldn't be a smartass.

After a moment of silent scrutiny, Caleb grunted and turned back to Tom. "I'm going to bed. Tell Diane I delivered the message." He lumbered over to the cellar door and, ignoring the *Do Not Open* sign, cracked it open enough to slip downstairs.

That left Marian in the kitchen, eyeing Chaz. "He's not one of you," she said to Tom. She barely spoke above a whisper and flinched when she finished, as if she expected to be hit.

"No, ma'am."

"Am I treating him?"

Tom thought about it. "You probably should. Diane'll want to have him in good shape for the meeting."

She moved closer, but before she could set her tackle box down on the table, Chaz held up his hands. "I can wait," he said. "There's kids in the other room that are in a hell of a lot more pain than I am." He was starting to suspect that "Diane" was Bitch's real name; Val had said she was likely second in command.

He also wondered if Tom and his crew were being as hospitable as they were because Diane wanted to offer a good trade for Justin, or if *her* boss—her alpha—was afraid enough of Val that he didn't want to risk pissing her off by roughing up her Renfield. *When I get home, she's telling me what happened in Sacramento. No more hedging.* For years, she'd left it at "Things went bad, I left," and he'd not pushed for more. Whatever it was still hurt her enough, he didn't want to dredge up the old and the bad. The time for that was over now.

Marian glanced at Tom for confirmation. The big man's expression went from surprised to relieved to faintly grateful. "Yeah, okay. That'd be good." He led them into the parlor where Beth and Sean were tending to their friends. They backed away from the people on the mattresses and gave Marian space.

From her pocket, she produced a small pot of ointment and passed it to Beth. "For Ashley," she said. "A little goes a long way." Beth took it and moved over to begin smearing the sunburned girl with the stuff. Marian watched her for a few seconds, then nodded, satisfied, and turned to the other four.

As she set the tackle box down, Chaz realized he'd seen one like it before, at Cavale's. *So they both shop at Walmart. It doesn't mean anything.* Except, when she lifted the lid, he saw neat rows of hand-labeled vials and jars, just like Cavale's. Runes covered the inside of the lid, the style similar to what he'd seen scrawled on some of the walls at the house in Crow's Neck.

Marian selected a few jars and drew a small scalpel from the tackle box. She pricked the tip of her thumb with the blade and hovered over her first patient, a boy. She traced a bloody sigil on his forehead, murmuring as she did it.

Chaz watched, wondering if the burns would recede and the wounds would heal before his eyes the way Val's did. But the kid's face kept on looking like overcooked pizza cheese.

Marian set her scalpel aside and selected another from the box. She brought this one down through one of the raised, bubbly bits of skin. Chaz braced himself, certain the kid would bolt upright, screaming. Pus wept freely from the newly opened wound, but the kid on the mattress didn't even flinch. The sigil on his forehead glowed a dull red. Marian's murmurings took on a singsong quality. *Is she keeping him under? Like anesthesia?*

She worked efficiently, cleaning out the wounds and applying her salves. Gross as it was, Chaz couldn't look away. Blood and pus ran down the kid's face. The sigil pulsed every now and then, but Marian kept him asleep. Then, after inspecting her work, she dipped a finger in the fluids oozing out of the kid and started drawing even more sigils on him. *I'm never running Finger Painting Night at the store ever again.*

When she finished, she touched the mark on his forehead once more, changing it. Her chanting changed, too, into an intonation that sounded almost like Latin. She slapped her hand down on the floor near the kid's head. Chaz and Tom both jumped at the sharp, sudden noise.

The kid had apparently heard it, too. His whole body bowed, arcing until only the crown of his head and his heels still touched the mattress. His hands spasmed at his sides, and his mouth opened in a wordless scream. The sigils glowed brighter, then with liquid, sinuous movements, they slid over his skin and into one another, joining together in a twisted kind of web over his face.

Now the flesh knit back together, the dead, burned bits sloughing away to reveal fresh new skin beneath. After what seemed a long time, but must only have been a few seconds, the kid collapsed back onto the mattress, panting.

Marian sat back on her knees and wiped the sweat from her forehead. "Help him up," she said to Sean. "Let him go wash his face." She scooted back while Sean obeyed, then fished around in the tackle box for more supplies. She rubbed her hands and forearms down with alcohol wipes and poured iodine over the scalpels.

Then she repeated what she'd done with the first kid three more times. While she was working on the second, Beth finished smearing the girl on the table with the salve. She smudged one of the runes. Chaz noticed that it bore a resemblance to the one Marian had painted on the first kid's brow. The girl on the table, Ashley, sat up with a jaw-cracking yawn. Her skin was no longer lobster red, but had instead turned a deep tan, as if she'd spent the summer sprawled out on the beach. She stretched and peered around, frowning at Chaz and whispering to Beth.

"He's not staying long," Beth told her, raising her voice in reply. "Diane needs him."

Ashley gave him the hairy eyeball for a little longer, then hopped off the table and crouched beside Marian. "Thank you," she said. The older woman smiled tightly, but was too deep in her ritual to do more than nod.

Beth escorted Ashley out, their footsteps clumping on the stairs as they ascended. That left Chaz and Tom alone with Marian and her patients; Sean had yet to return.

Marian finished with her second patient, a slight Middle Eastern–looking girl who was maybe a hundred pounds soaking wet. Tom stuck his head out the door and hollered for Sean, who shouted back from the kitchen. When he ducked back in the room, he seemed to be weighing something. "I have to get her upstairs."

Ah. "It's fine, man. I'm not going anywhere. I haven't made a break for it yet, have I?"

"Sean's in the kitchen. He'll be back in here in a minute. His trigger finger's kind of itchy today, so, y'know. In case the thought crosses your mind . . ."

"Scout's honor," said Chaz, "I'm staying right here."

Tom stood there a moment longer, but when the girl on the mattress started chattering her teeth, he got moving. He scooped her up and left the room.

Chaz hadn't made any other attempts at escape today, but not for lack of wanting to. The opportunity simply hadn't presented itself. Now he had a handful of seconds to see how close he could get to freedom. If he could get outside, he'd see if Sean was any kind of a sharpshooter.

Marian had started in on the third kid, ignoring her own chance at escape.

He *should* run. But there was something he needed to know first: "You're Brotherhood, aren't you?"

She stiffened, but didn't turn to look at him. "I was."

"Seems like there's a lot of that going around."

That gave her pause. She snuck a glance in his direction. "What do you mean?"

"Just that I've met a couple of former members in the last few days." He folded his arms and leaned against the wall. "But those two *hate* the Jackals. So explain to me why it is that you're helping them."

"I'm healing these children," she said, a tiny, haughty thread sneaking into her voice. "Not them."

"Bullshit." Chaz stepped over to Ashley's recently vacated table. From there, he could see the floor around the mattresses. Carved into the wood were more runes and sigils. "Most of this is what a friend of mine calls Creepscrawl, but I don't have to be able to read it to know that some of this lettering's different. Matter of fact, the different stuff looks an awful lot like the writing inside your little doctor's bag there, doesn't it?"

She flinched. It was confirmation enough.

"You drew them. I don't know how you helped, what blanks you filled in, but you did it. So I'm asking you again: *why?*"

She took her hands off the injured kid and folded them in her lap. At first, Chaz thought she was being stubborn and refusing to answer him. Then he realized she was fidgeting with something on her left hand: a plain gold band.

Suddenly, it made a lot more sense: they were holding him here to get what they wanted from Val; they held the kids here with the promise of Jackal-hood so they could have lackeys. So how else to coerce a member of the Brotherhood to do their bidding? Chaz moved around the table slowly, like he was approaching a skittish cat. He knelt beside her and stared down at her wedding band. "They have someone you care about, don't they?"

Marian twisted around to look at him, her eyes brimming. "Yes. My husband."

"Fuck, I'm sorry." He risked a glance down the hall. Sean was just visible in the kitchen, hunched over the countertop and eating peanut butter straight from the jar. "Okay. Is he here? Do they have him upstairs? I bet we could take these kids, you and me. They don't have tricks up their sleeve like you do." *Just guns in their waistbands,* he thought, but that didn't seem too helpful. "And I'm, uh. Spry."

She shook her head. "He's not here. The alpha has him. To . . . 'guarantee my services.' " She sneered the last, though whether the disgust was directed at the Jackal or herself, Chaz couldn't tell.

It meant he needed a new tactic, then. No way she'd put her husband in danger for him. "Listen. I have friends who can help, okay? Got a vampire, couple of succubi, and like I said, two kids who used to be in the Brotherhood. Or were trained by a Brother, something like that. Help me out now and I swear to God, I'll make sure we come back for you and your husband. Please."

Footsteps started down the hall. "You two plotting in there?" Sean's voice was thick from talking with his mouth full.

Chaz ignored him. "Please. I'm trying to save a kid's life here, too. But I can't help either of you if they've got me over a barrel like this. Please."

She paused, watching him. Her shoulders lost some of their hunch. "I can't get you out, but I'll see what I can do before I leave."

Chaz sat back, adopting as casual a pose as he could before Sean entered the room. "Sorry," he said. "I was just asking her how she does all this. You've gotta admit, it's kind of unreal."

The Irish kid stared hard at them both; a smear of peanut butter clung to his bottom lip. He clearly wasn't buying it, but since Marian had gone back to chanting and slicing off bits of dead skin from her patient's face, he had no proof of shenanigans. He looked sort of disappointed.

IT WAS NEARLY sunset when Marian finished healing the last of the victims. Chaz wasn't left alone with her again; Sean made sure of that. Marian took her time cleaning up her tools and repacking her tackle box while Tom and Beth escorted the last kid out of the sick room. At last, she got stiffly to her feet and approached Chaz and Sean, who were loitering near the door. She darted a timid glance at Sean. "Caleb told me to look at him before I went home."

Sean huffed, but didn't argue. "Go on, then."

Marian took Chaz' hands in hers, like they were lovers reluctant to say good-bye. She pressed something small and smooth and hard into his left palm. *One of her little vials?* Marian's middle fingers rested on each of his wrists, her touch feather-like against the thin skin. Her fingertips were slick with oil; Chaz thought he smelled myrrh. She traced patterns there as she looked up into Chaz' eyes.

"He's all right," she said, after a moment. She let him go, and he felt warmth spread across his wrists as the sigil settled in. "No concussion." The headache ebbed a bit.

Luckily, Sean had been watching their faces, not their hands. Chaz pocketed the vial as carefully as he could and stepped back.

"Good. Diane'll be happy." Sean pulled a pair of crumpled twenties out of his pocket and passed them to Marian.

Chaz boggled. "That's it? Forty bucks? She healed the *shit* out of your people. She . . . fuck, she *undisfigured* them, and the most they left you to give her is *that*?"

Sean shrugged. "I just do what I'm told. You want to argue the point, they're waking up."

Marian shook her head in warning. "No, it's fine. It's enough. It's what's left over after room and board."

"Room and—" *Her husband.* The Jackal motherfuckers were keeping her husband hostage and *charging* her for it. *If I ever meet this alpha, I'm kicking him in the balls.* For now, though, Chaz bit his tongue. He didn't want to get Marian or her husband in trouble.

A female Jackal appeared in the doorway, looking sleep mussed but still dangerous. She sneered at Chaz before she addressed Marian. "Let's go."

"I'm ready," said Marian, retrieving the tackle box from where she'd set it down. She gave Chaz one last nod. "Good luck to you." She bustled past them both and scurried to the front door.

That was when Tom came down the hall, grimacing. "Diane's awake. She says it's time to go."

THE WHOLE PLACE reeked of rotten meat and refuse, of blood and ash, of myrrh and rosewater. The first two teams had cleared the way through the upper floors, but the majority of the nest had fallen back to the basement and barricaded themselves in. That's when the Councilmen had called in Val's team.

The six of them should have been enough: two vampires, Val and Clara, who after eighty years still kept her coal black hair in a flapper bob; Angelo and Charlotte, Renfields the women had chosen from the Brotherhood's ranks; and the twins, Kelly and Delilah, who had been full Sisters for over three decades. They were closer than most real families, had probably survived unscathed as much as they had because they were just that damned good together.

They descended in pairs, each checking that the way was clear and covering as the next two moved ahead. It was clean and textbook, just the way Angelo had learned it during his time with the LAPD SWAT team. The smell got worse with every landing; some of the blood spatters belonged to their friends. At least the previous teams had taken the bodies out with them when they'd retreated. They wouldn't leave their own behind for the Jackals to desecrate.

Or recruit.

The last door waited, marked Private and Keep Out, with a stomach-churning line of the Jackals' script scrawled beneath in red.

"It says 'Leeches go away.'" Clara smirked back at Val. "Looks like we'd better give up. They don't want our kind around here." She dipped a finger in the writing, and took a sniff. "No, wait. This is Davenport's blood. I liked him. Fuck these guys, let's kill them."

Charlotte needed no further prodding. She traced a sigil around the keyhole and took a step back. Then she brought her leg up and planted a solid kick just beneath. The door swung open, slamming dully against the wall inside. The room beyond was pitch-black, even to Val's preternatural vision.

"The hell?" said Clara, sniffing the air. "It's empty."

"Can't be." Kelly pushed past, the scent of myrrh trailing after her. Her hands, already glowing from the runes Delilah had painted on them with henna that morning, flared as she crossed the threshold.

Then the darkness took her.

VAL WOKE WITH their screams ringing in her ears. Ten years gone and it still felt like something had been ripped out of her, the wound left raw and ragged. It had been years since she'd dreamed of them—years since she'd dreamed at all. *The last time was the night I took Chaz as my Renfield.*

Because even though she knew she needed one, and even though Chaz was exactly *who* she needed, the idea of losing another had terrified her so much she'd had nightmares.

And now here she was again, on the cusp of losing not only Chaz, but Cavale and Elly and Justin, too. The Clearwaters had already died because she'd failed to protect them. What about her friends? What about Sunny and Lia and the lives they'd built here in Edgewood?

They can take care of themselves; they've been doing it for centuries. The others are still safe for now. Worry about Chaz first. The voice in her head chastising her wasn't her own, but Angelo's. He'd been their voice of reason.

He'd been *her* voice of reason.

"I wish you'd known him," she whispered, though she didn't know if she was talking to Angelo or Chaz. "You two would've liked each other."

Val heaved herself out of bed and headed downstairs, checking the messages on her cell phone as she went. The stone that had taken up residence in her stomach since Chaz' disappearance grew heavier as she listened to Cavale's report. They hadn't found him yet. They were still looking. The trail was as cold for them as it had been for her.

The mail was scattered across the foyer floor. Most days, Chaz stopped in during the afternoon and sorted through it for her, leaving the important bills on the hall table. Val scooped it up absently, more to move it out of her path than to see what was due. A familiar logo stopped her cold: the bookstore's owl with his wide-eyed gaze peeked out at her from behind the gas bill. It wasn't a flyer, but a bookmark.

On the back, where they'd left space for customers to jot notes to themselves, were two sentences:

What is yours for what is ours.
Ten o'clock.

27

ELLY PEERED THROUGH the window and into the darkened bookstore. Val had called them a couple hours ago, saying she was heading to the store and getting everyone the hell out, that they should sharpen their stakes and meet her there. She'd mentioned the note they'd left her: the nest was on its way, and they needed to be ready.

Even more unnerving: the whole damned street was deserted, the other businesses buttoned up tight. It was a perfect autumn night—clear skies, a bit of a chill in the air but nothing too bad—and yet no one was out for a stroll along this quaint stretch of road. Elly was fairly certain this wasn't the succubi's doing, but she couldn't feel other magic at play, either. She didn't trust it, but then again, if it kept the civilians out of their hair for the coming brawl, maybe she ought not to try too hard to see the teeth in this particular gift horse's mouth.

The bookstore's sign was flipped over to Closed. A typed note was taped below the sleepy owl: *Closed due to water main break. We'll reopen tomorrow.* The door was locked, but Justin had his keys with him. He led Elly and Cavale in, picking his way carefully around displays and furniture. Feeble light came in from the streetlamps, enough to keep them from tripping and breaking their necks, but not enough to see very well beyond that.

"What the hell is he doing here?"

Val's voice snapped from somewhere down back. Justin jerked away, colliding into Elly and trodding none too delicately on her foot.

Cavale set down his duffel bag full of stakes and holy water and addressed the direction her voice had come from. The lights were off back there, too, except for the pale fluorescent glow coming from beneath the office door. Everything was shrouded in gloom. "He insisted on coming."

"Insisted" was putting it mildly. There'd been an epic-scale shouting match, actually, which Justin had won. Elly had spent the last few hours teaching him how not to impale himself on a stake. Now they'd just have to hope that training stuck if a Creep got close enough.

There was a thud from off to the left, away from the back room door. Elly could make out the shape of another door back there, presumably the rare books room where Justin had taken his first peek at the Creeps' spell book. There wasn't much of anywhere to hide back there. *Was she clinging to the ceiling before we came in?*

Before Elly could get a gander at the ceiling tiles to see if there were claw marks, Val was stalking down the aisle toward them. Her stride said she was walking, but to Elly it looked like someone had sped up the film. "And *I* told you to leave him with Sunny and Lia."

"I'm right here." Justin's shoulders had lost their cringing slope as Val got closer. His voice trembled a bit, but it was an even bet whether it was from anger or fear of back talking a pissed-off vampire.

Elly thought about putting a hand on his arm and reining him in, but Cavale caught her eye and shook his head.

Justin stepped forward, past Cavale. "You can stop talking like I'm not in the room. I told them I was coming, and if they'd left me behind, I would've climbed out a window and walked over by myself."

Val kept coming at that eerie gait until she was nose to nose with Justin. To his credit, he stood his ground. "They were supposed to get you out of town," she said. "It's not going to be an exchange."

"Why not? They took Chaz, Val. They aren't fucking around."

"They weren't fucking around last night, either." She glowered down at him, nostrils flaring. "I thought you would have noticed that, what with all the fighting."

"So why let it escalate?" He turned to Elly, looking for help. "What was it you told me Father Value said to do when you were cornered?"

Elly winced. It had come out earlier today, when they were driving around looking for Chaz' trail. Justin had asked for a lesson in Creeps 101, and she'd gone over the basics. Including the rule both she and Father Value had been breaking since the night they'd yanked this book from beneath an altar: "If you're cornered," she recited, "give them what they want and get out of there."

"That. Exactly." He turned back to Val, ready to declare a triumph of logic, but Elly kept talking.

"It doesn't work like that. Not this time." She stepped around him, putting herself on Val's side both literally and figuratively. "They might not try drawing a circle around you and getting it out with a ritual like we did. They might just do it the easier way."

"There's an easier way?"

"Kill you and it will hop to one of them. An energy like that, its instinct is to reach its own kind. You were the closest thing around when you released it from the book, so it didn't have any choice. But if they release it from you when one of theirs is right there waiting to receive it, it'll make a beeline for the more compatible host."

". . . oh." He thought for a moment. "But what if it doesn't work? Then they don't have the knowledge either. What good is that?"

"If they don't want to risk losing it, they could always keep you until they figure it out. Chained up. Probably starving. Beaten, too, in case you try resisting them . . ."

Val pinched the bridge of her nose. "That's enough. You're here now, and it's quarter to ten. Too late to send you back." She glanced out the front window. Elly followed her gaze. Nothing moved outside. "I assume Sunny and Lia are coming, too, then?"

"They said they'd be here," Cavale said.

". . . it's like you summoned us." Sunny's voice came from everywhere and nowhere.

Elly whirled, trying to pinpoint it anyway, but the four of them were the only people in the store. *No, wait.* The shadows were deepest by the rare books room, probably why Val had been lurking back there, too. But now, instead of lying flat and uniform, like shadows ought to do, the darkness *writhed.* It licked up the walls like tongues of black flame, then subsided, leaving behind two feminine silhouettes.

Sunny and Lia sauntered forward, the shadows slipping away. Once they were away from that corner of the store, they became incredibly easy to spot. Both of them were wrapped in bright white bathrobes from neck to ankles. The hilts of their keris knives peeked out from the robes' deep pockets. They were in their demon forms again, beautiful and terrifying at the same time.

"We didn't know if anyone else would be here," Lia said. "Figured maybe it would be bad form to show up stark naked from the get-go."

"Kind of a dead giveaway that we're not, you know, normal," Sunny added, as if Lia's twilight-colored skin or her own seven-foot stature might go unnoticed. "Who else is joining the party?"

For a moment, Elly thought Val was going to chew out the succubi for not adhering to the plan. Then she seemed to recognize the futility of arguing about it now and simply sighed. *Maybe she was tucking the yelling away for later.*

"I don't know," said Val. "Ivanov hasn't returned my calls."

An awkward pause descended, as everyone avoided

saying what they were thinking. They'd nearly been overwhelmed last night. There was no way the Creeps wouldn't show up without an even stronger force tonight, and Night Owls wasn't warded against them the way Sunny and Lia's house had been.

The sound of the duffel bag unzipping made them all jump. Cavale tossed a piece of chalk to Elly, then gestured at the bag. "You guys go ahead and line up the stakes and holy water on the counter. We'll get at least a few wards in place." He nodded at Elly and set off toward the rear of the store. Elly headed for the front, wondering if Val had anything she could use to write on the plate glass window itself. One big rune to say *fuck you* to the Creeps.

She pulled up short three steps away from the window. "Uh, guys?"

Bitch stood on the other side, one hand around Chaz' throat, the other waving cheerily. Elly squinted. There was something wrong with the light. It took her a second to realize what it was: Bitch and Chaz should've been lit from above by the streetlights. Instead, the light splashed over them from the front, bright white instead of amber, more like someone had a car's high beams trained on them.

Then they disappeared.

Val was beside her. She'd been by the register an eye blink ago. She sniffed at the air, then strode over to the door, yanked it open, and stuck her head out. "They're not here yet," she said, pulling back in, "but they're close. I can smell them now." She stood there for a moment, staring out at the night. The confidence she'd had since Elly had met her had fled. Her shoulders hunched; her hands clasped and unclasped. Worry was written in every line of her body. When she spoke, Elly almost didn't hear. "Did he look all right?"

She thought about it. No use softening what she'd glimpsed in those few seconds. "Pissed off, mostly. But his nose was bleeding, and I think he has a black eye."

Val straightened up and lifted her chin. Anger replaced the worry in her stance, until that deceitfully lazy grace was back. "They'll pay for that."

Fury is an acceptable substitute for bravery. It had been one of Father Value's favorites. "They will." She resisted the urge to pat Val's arm—she'd never been so hot at the whole reassuring thing, anyway. Instead, she took up her chalk and got to work on setting the runes.

Five minutes later, as she was laying the last of the hastily drawn set, the first hulking shapes of the Creeps began slinking their way onto Main Street.

HE PROBABLY SHOULDN'T have opened with "Where's your other lackey?" when he saw Bitch and Twitch standing in the kitchen without Asshole. How could he have known Elly had stuck Asshole with that spike of hers and done him in? Lucky for him, Bitch—whose real name was indeed Diane—seemed to be under orders to leave him mostly unharmed.

Mostly.

His nose hadn't stopped leaking since she'd knocked him on his ass, and from the way she'd said "Behave" as they left the house, he knew she hoped he wouldn't, so she could make it bleed some more. They'd covered his face with a blanket that smelled of mold and dust, and shoved him into the backseat of a car whose shocks were completely shot. A couple of Jackals piled on top of him. He figured one had to be Bitch, from the elbow that dug none too gently into his ribs anytime they went over a bump. Every pothole brought a new flare of pain in his nose, in his aching shoulder. The headache had ramped back up, too. It sang in a chorus with his other injuries.

By the time they got to Edgewood, Chaz felt like an overused punching bag. He didn't bother playing it cool when they yanked him out of the backseat, gulping down mouthfuls of the crisp night air. He only got to enjoy it for a few seconds before Bitch came over and dragged him in front of the car. The brights blinded him, sending another jolt straight through his skull. She held him by the neck, and for a moment he wondered if she was about to throw him, like a stick tossed for a dog to chase. Only, in this case, the dog was a car.

I can run. If she throws me, I can run. He recognized the street they were on. The woods were to his right. If she threw him that way, he'd make a break for the trees. If she sent him sailing to the left, he'd see how far he could get toward campus.

But the throw never came. Through slit eyes, he saw her wave at the car. Then the driver killed the lights and the engine, and Bitch's grip moved to Chaz' arm. "What the hell was that?" he asked.

"Five-minute warning." Another pair of glorified rust buckets rattled their way up the hill and parked. More Jackals spilled out, and still more came loping out of the woods. *If she'd thrown me to the right, I wouldn't have made it far after all.*

Bitch handed him off to Twitch while she went to rally the troops. The kid seemed distracted, even more jittery than the last couple of times Chaz had seen him. He was a few inches shorter than Chaz, though they probably matched one another on the wiry scale. If it weren't for the whole Jackal thing giving the kid an unfair advantage, Chaz figured he could take him in a bar fight. Since scrapping wasn't an option, Chaz figured talking was worth a shot. The scrawny ones also tended to be the voices of reason. "You don't have to do this, you know," he said, keeping his voice low.

"Shut up."

"No, I mean it. You guys are kind of fucked right now. Look how badly last night ended—you lost one of your trio, and you *still* didn't get Justin. You think they're not ready for you now?"

Twitch's grip tightened, his fingers digging into Chaz' bicep. "Shut the fuck *up*. Josh was my friend."

Josh. That had to be Asshole. "Yeah, well, *your* friend was trying to kill *my* friend, so I have to chalk that one up to turnabout being fair play."

That was clearly the wrong thing to say. Twitch's already-feral face rippled. His nose and jaw darkened, sliding and lengthening into a snout. "No. Josh was trying to *save* your friend. I saw it. He was keeping everyone else off him, and that mousy little bitch stabbed him when he turned his back on her. So don't you fucking say another fucking word to me. Understood?" He was up in Chaz' face by then, his breath hot and rank as he ranted. Chaz could see a row of sharp teeth in that canine mouth.

"Okay," he said, holding his free hand up. "Okay, got it."

Twitch stared at him a bit longer before he stood down. Chaz had to rethink his bar fight theory—get this kid angry enough, and Twitch would kick his ass, scrawny or no.

Bitch wandered back over to them. "Let's go."

They headed down the hill, the majority of the Jackals melting into the shadows. Had anyone else been out and about, they'd have only seen Chaz, Bitch, and Twitch strolling along, but the street was eerily deserted. Chaz wondered if that was something the Jackals had done, or if Val had some kind of people-repelling ability she hadn't told him about. They passed the turnoff that would have led them to Sunny and Lia's and kept heading toward Main Street.

Chaz tried backpedaling as he realized where their final destination must be, but Bitch and Twitch dragged him inexorably onward. "You can't," he said. "There'll be people there."

"She had warning," said Bitch. "Any dead bystanders are on her conscience, not mine."

You say that like you have one at all.

No one was around on Main Street, either. Even the twins' coffee shop next door to Night Owls was closed. Chaz let out a sigh of relief, one that deepened as he saw the darkened front window of the bookstore. A shape moved within, too short to be anyone but Elly. Her hand came swooping up along the glass, completing a dark, smeary circle that began to glow a dark, warning red. Bitch swore when she saw it.

Elly saw them coming. She stepped back from the window into a pool of amber from the streetlights outside. She waited until they were all looking at her, then she waved, an echo of Bitch's greeting in the headlights, only her smile had a savage edge to it. Blood dripped from a gash on her palm.

They slowed to a stop in the middle of the street. Jackals swarmed around them, flowing out of the shadows, dropping from the rooftops like paint dripping from the edge of a canvas. *Too many,* he thought. *There's no way we had all these with us back there.*

A new shadow joined Elly in the window. Val.

Bitch stepped forward, leaving Chaz in Twitch's grasp. "Send out the kid," she said, her voice bouncing off the empty storefronts. "Yours for ours, like we said."

Val shook her head. "They're both mine."

Chaz registered Bitch's slight nod a second before Twitch spun him around and slammed a fist into his jaw. He saw stars. Blood coated his tongue and he leaned over to spit it out. He snuck a glance at the window on his way back up. Val stood there, fists clenched. He tried communicating *I'm okay* with a look, but he wasn't even sure his eyes were focusing correctly.

"Send the kid out," said Bitch. "Your friend's had a long enough day as it is."

"I can't do that." She was shouting through the glass, but Chaz could hear the regret in her tone. "Let Chaz go, and when we figure out how to get this thing back on the pages, we'll turn them over."

Another nod. This time Twitch hit lower, driving into Chaz' ribs. The air went out of him for the second time today, and this time, breathing it back in was agony. *Cracked ribs, nose possibly broken, might've knocked a tooth or two loose there. They're going to love me in the ER. If I get there.*

Inside, Val lurched a step toward the door before she stopped herself. Her claws were out. Chaz dug deep, past the pain, and stood straight. He shook his head no.

Bitch snorted and gestured at the seething crowd of Jackals lining the street. "Look around," she called. "It's, what, yourself, three kids, and a pair of slut demons in there? You might have been the shit in Sacramento, but that crew's all dead, from what I hear. Do you really want to be the last one standing again?"

Funny that he learned more about Sacramento from five seconds of Bitch mouthing off than he'd learned from Val in five years. But it made sense now—Val's separation from the Boston colonies, her occasional overprotectiveness. *She lost friends out there. Had she lost a Renfield, too?* He'd never asked, and she'd never offered up the information. She'd been a vampire for forty-something years, though. She must have had one in that time. *Before me.*

If he was honest with himself—and what better time to be honest, really, when a bunch of assholes were beating the shit out of you in front of your friends?—he hadn't asked because he was afraid the answer would make him jealous.

"Let him go," Val said again, and again Twitch got him in the gut. Chaz felt his knees sag, but the kid didn't let him fall over.

"We can start breaking bones next." She paused and tilted her head, examining Elly's bloody rune. "Or windows."

The rock came sailing from behind them. Chaz saw its shadow arc across the pavement as Val and Elly both dove backward. Then came the terrible crash of plate glass shattering, incredibly loud on the night air. The Jackals around them strained forward like hunting dogs awaiting their master's command.

"Last chance," said Bitch.

Someone moved behind the register—Cavale?—and a gallon-sized milk jug wobbled its way through the air, cap open, its contents pouring out as it tumbled. Howls went up beneath its low arc, and when it finally hit the ground off to Chaz' right, a clump of Jackals fell to their knees, scrabbling at their own skin.

"Get him out of here," Bitch ordered. She turned and chattered at the rest of them in that guttural tongue, and a wave of Jackals surged toward the store.

Chaz struggled against Twitch as the kid pulled him away. He saw two shapes slide out of the sides of the broken window: tall and sinuous, wielding what looked like daggers.

Sunny and Lia? More water bottles lobbed their way out, and Chaz was suddenly glad he'd slacked on bringing the recycling out for the last couple of weeks—Cavale must have taken them from the back room.

The store was receding. If Chaz couldn't get out of Twitch's grasp, he didn't know when—or if—they'd bring him back here again. They were at the corner of Hill O' Beans when Chaz remembered Marian's vial. He stopped fighting Twitch so he could reach into his pocket. Despite the Jackals using him as a seat cushion and the punches Twitch had thrown, the vial had survived intact.

Chaz squinted at it. His eyes took their time focusing, but finally he could read Marian's tiny handwritten label by the overnight lights coming out of the bakery's display window: Silver Nitrate.

"Fuck, dude." He doubled over, forcing Twitch to slow down. "Hang on, you broke my rib. I can't fucking breathe."

The kid finally stopped, loosening his hold on Chaz' arm, but not letting go. "You've got like ten seconds."

One shot at this. Chaz gulped a couple of breaths, the wheezing and snuffling only half faked. Twitch hovered over him, clearly wanting to keep moving. *Perfect.* Chaz lurched upright, bringing his right hand up with the vial cupped in his palm. It was a textbook movie-star slap. Twitch's whole head turned with the force of it. The vial shattered on his cheekbone, driving a sliver of glass deep into Chaz' palm.

There was a second in which he was sure it hadn't worked, that all he'd done was made his own situation worse.

Then Twitch's skin started to blacken and smoke, and Twitch began to scream. He let go of Chaz to clutch at his face, the side of it melting like thin plastic in a microwave. The lips peeled back from his snout; Chaz could see all the teeth on that side as they snapped and clacked with Twitch's barks of pain.

He didn't stick around to watch any more. When he turned back toward the store, he saw that the herd of Jackals advancing on Night Owls had thinned. What had seemed like a hundred of them lining the street had dropped way down—twenty or thirty of them, tops, and a few already down for the count. Shadows shaped like Jackals flickered in and out of existence, their solidity varying with the pitch of Twitch's screams. *So he's the illusionist, not Bitch.*

Was the illusionist, maybe. Chaz glanced back at the kid to make sure he wasn't going to come lurching after him like the villain in a slasher flick, but he was curled up on the sidewalk, fetal.

Chaz stumbled back toward the fray, sticking to the edges of the buildings. He could see Sunny and Lia now, their blades smoking as they danced through a knot of Jackals. It had been so long since he'd seen their true forms, he'd forgotten how captivatingly beautiful they were. He stood, mesmerized. Watching them fight was like watching a complex, brutal, marvelous dance. Then Cavale darted past him, intent on a target off to Chaz' left, and broke the spell. Chaz shook himself. He couldn't see Elly or Justin, but the woman trading blow for blow with Bitch was . . .

. . . was not Val.

He had time to think *Katya?* before a pair of hands shot out from the store's window and dragged him inside.

"I swear, when this is over I'm having you microchipped," said Val, as she pulled him into a hug.

✣ 28 ✣

ELLY DIDN'T TAKE her eyes off the front of the store. The number of Creeps had thinned, which meant the illusionist was dead or unconscious. It had made her job easier for a whole five seconds. Fewer targets meant she could toss holy water bombs more accurately. But before she could get a third gallon out the window, the vampires had arrived. At first she'd thought the illusionist was back in the game, since the ranks had swelled again. Then she realized the newcomers were *attacking* the Creeps, not fighting alongside them.

She caught a flash of fang, a glimpse of claw, and recognized a face from Ivanov's bar.

That nixed the holy water tossing for now. Too much risk of their new allies getting hit with the splash.

Val finished fussing over Chaz and brought him back to the bunker they'd made out of the register area. "He's going to need some looking after when this is done," she said.

It was the "when this is done" that mattered. It meant Val still had her priorities straight. "Welcome back. Stakes are to your left, if you're up for it."

He took one and looked out at the battle seething outside.

"I saw Katya out there. I thought they weren't coming to help."

"I made a deal," said Elly, prompting sharp looks from all three of her companions.

Justin winced. "Elly, you didn't have to—"

"Everyone keeps saying that. I didn't do it for any of you, okay? We'll talk about it later." It was mostly true. Ivanov's offer meshed with her own plans, meager and half-formed as they were. It let her earn her keep if she stayed with Cavale. But she'd seen the score last night and knew they couldn't hold out against that many Creeps. They'd survived the attack at Sunny and Lia's because of Justin, and who knew if he'd be able to do it again. So far tonight, he hadn't done anything intentionally Creep-like. His eyes were even yellower, but she didn't think that was voluntary.

Not even a week ago, she'd have ensured her safety and Cavale's, and let the rest of them fend for themselves. It was what Father Value had taught her from the start: *Take care of your own. Anyone else is expendable.* Part of her still insisted she should do just that: get out from behind the safety of this register, find Cavale in the street, and carve an escape route through the Creeps for both of them.

Except . . . Except this strange crew had grown on her. Even Val, who seemed to have about as much an idea of what to do with Elly as Elly had to do with her.

She couldn't leave them to die, no matter what Father Value had taught her.

Glass crunched at the front of the store. The Creeps who came barreling through let out agonized yips as they passed over Elly's chalk wards, but they didn't retreat. They split up, one to either side of the store, advancing even while their fur smoldered with magic. They dragged their claws across the rune lines, whimpering as their flesh burned. Elly hopped over the counter to intercept the Creep on her side. Val moved to meet the other. "Keep an eye on Justin," they both called back to Chaz.

"It's fucked-up when you do that in stereo," he said.

The Creep moved fast despite its injuries, knocking over

a stack of books as he lunged at her. Elly sidestepped and swung her spike. Its tip grazed his arm, the flesh withering along the cut. The Creep's momentum sent it flying past Elly and into a rack of comic books. Creep and rack tipped over together, comics fanning out across the floor. The glossy covers slid around as he tried regaining his feet, giving Elly time to get in closer. She shuffled along the floor, careful not to lose her own footing.

From the opposite side of the store came a crunch and a thud as Val dispatched her Creep.

Elly backed away from her, toward the register. Chaz placed himself between Justin and the Creep, both of their backs to the front of the store. Which meant neither of them saw the third one come bounding through the window.

Elly didn't bother with finesse: she danced in another step, drove the spike into her Creep's chest and kept going, leaping over him even as he collapsed into ash. She shouted, "Behind! *Behind!*" as she went, hoping Val had seen it and was already moving. But Val was up near the front, tangling with a fourth Creep who'd decided to stick her head inside and join the fun.

Chaz whirled and grabbed Justin, trying to yank him back out of the Creep's reach. *Too late,* thought Elly, even as she scrambled up behind them. The Creep drew its arm back to swipe at Justin. He was big, hulking even, taller than Asshole had been. Justin was about a second away from having his face ripped off.

Justin cringed back against Chaz, but then he pushed away—*toward* the Creep. He uttered a word in Creeptongue. It sounded something like *kazh,* only with an undertone that made gooseflesh break out on Elly's arms.

The Creep lowered its arm and thudded to the floor, looking up at Justin with its neck bared.

Elly shoved her way in front of the men. "What did you do?" She held out Silver and Pointy, which was still covered with the first Creep's blood. The one at her feet shrank back, but his eyes never left Justin.

"I, um. I told him to sit."

Val came vaulting over the register from the other side, her clawed hands covered in blood. She hauled the Creep up and held him there, one arm barring across his chest, the other wrapped around his head, her hand on his chin. One good twist and his neck would break.

Elly risked a glance back at Justin. It wasn't just his irises that were yellow anymore. Now it covered his whole eye, like a dog's.

There was a terrible, vertebrae-crunching *snap* as Val dispatched the Creep. "I'm not in the mood for hostages," she said, even though no one had objected. The Creep's body slumped to the ground.

Elly staked it, as much to get rid of the corpse as to be sure it wasn't faking somehow. *Never trust a Creep, not even a dead one.* She turned and peered at Justin. "How do you feel?"

"Fine," he said, then frowned. "I feel like . . . I don't know. Like my face is too short. And my teeth are too dull." He ran his tongue over them. "But they're the same teeth I've always had. Aren't they?" He bared them for Elly to see, a perfect row of white, even, *human* teeth. When she got close, he backed away, hands up as if to ward her off. "I, um. I kind of wanted to bite you just then. Sorry."

She moved out of chomping range. "It's dug in deeper. We need to get it out of him before he actually *can* change into a Creep."

Val took Justin's face in her hands, sniffing. "I can smell them on you," she said. She looked at Elly. "Do you think Cavale can try again?"

"There's no time for a ritual. We need to do it a different way. *Now.*" She wished Father Value were here. He'd have an answer, a good one. *Who am I kidding? He'd stake Justin and be done with it.*

"I'm open to suggestions."

Outside, the fighting was still going strong, but there were certainly fewer Creeps. Cavale seemed to have paired up with one of Ivanov's men; they moved through the throng with their backs together, letting the Creeps come to them.

Sunny and Lia had moved to guard the window now, keeping anyone from getting through. Their keris knives were held idly at their sides, the blades smoking.

Elly sighed. "You're not going to like the one I have."

"If it's all we've got, I'll deal with it. Go on."

"You have to turn him."

"I . . . *What?*" Val went even paler than normal. "Into a vampire?"

"Yes. Think about it. Creeps and vampires, when you turn someone, the important part's done within a matter of minutes. This has taken days, but it's still happening. If you do it now, maybe the vampirism can overtake the Creep taint." She was talking too fast, forced herself to slow down for the next bit. The important bit: "You don't have time to find out, Val. Too much longer and he'll be one of them."

Val's mouth opened and closed, but she couldn't seem to find a good argument.

Justin walked up to her, his sneakers stirring the dead Creep's ashes. "Do it."

She looked down at him. "You don't know what it's like. You haven't even had time to think about it."

"I've had time to think about the alternative. I've been thinking about that for three days."

"This is forever, Justin. No going back. What about all the things you haven't done? Hell, what's the last thing you ate?"

"We had McDonald's earlier."

"See? You want your last meal to be a Big Mac? It's blood from here on out."

"Val." He'd been timid and awkward these last few days. Now all of that was gone, replaced by a stubborn resolve. "If you don't help me, my last meal might be a *person*. Then Elly'll stake me and that'll be it."

"He's right. I'd stake him if he killed someone," she said.

"Big help," said Val. "Thanks."

Elly shrugged. "I'd do it nicely."

Justin wasn't finished. "Listen to me. These things killed Professor Clearwater. They killed Helen. *I don't want to be one of them*. And if that means becoming a vampire, fine. Don't make me be what they are. Please, Val." He clasped his hands in front of his chest, like a little boy begging to stay up past his bedtime. "Please."

She stared at him, long and hard. From outside came the sounds of Creeps dying—the hiss of silver burning their flesh, the tearing of limbs, the meaty ripping of vampire fangs in their throats. Katya's dark, tinkling laughter floated over it all.

Val glanced out there, then back at Justin. Her mouth set in a grim line. In that moment, her decision made, she looked old and tired, and more than anything, sad. Then she quirked the kind of grin Elly imagined you'd see on someone stepping up to the gallows.

"Your parents are going to kill me."

VAL LED THE procession to the back room, Justin behind her, Chaz lurching along after, one hand on his side. She could smell his worry. Elly stayed four steps behind Chaz, covering their retreat should a Jackal make it past Sunny and Lia. From the pile she'd seen at their feet, though, she didn't think it likely.

The fluorescent lights in the back were almost too bright after the darkness that had reigned at the front of the store. Val sat Justin in the chair and hunkered down in front of him. Those eyes were damned disconcerting, and hard to reconcile with the thought that this was *Justin* looking out from them. Elly was right; there wasn't much time.

"Last chance," she said anyway. "How are you going to finish your degree?"

"I'll take night classes. And see what they have for courses online."

"Got it all figured out, huh?"

"Enough of it."

College kids.

"All right, fine." She looked around. Elly was in the doorway, her back to them. She'd drawn a line of runes on the threshold, just in case. Chaz hovered nearby, his bruised face looking all the worse in the harsh light. When this was finished, she was going to have words with Bitch. Words and fists.

But first, she had a vampire to make. "Chaz, I need you to hold him steady."

Dutifully, he stepped behind Justin and held his shoulders, pulling him into the back of the swivel chair. But when he tried holding Justin's shoulders, the pain was clearly too much.

Elly glanced into the back room at Chaz' shout. "Hang on," she said, scuttling over to him. "I can help." She wiped the spike off on her jeans and tugged Chaz' shirt up before he could protest. Lightly, ever so carefully, she sketched a rune on his skin with the tip. She pricked her finger and chanted under her breath, smearing the blood over the scratches that had raised themselves up. After a moment, Chaz took a slow, deep breath.

"Hey, that's pretty good," he said.

"It's temporary. I took the pain away, but your rib's still broken. Go easy, okay? It's going to hurt like a bitch again in another ten, fifteen minutes." She was already heading back to guard the door before Chaz could nod.

Ready for another try, Chaz planted his hands on Justin's shoulders once more. He didn't question her; he didn't argue. It was clear from the look in his eyes that he didn't like the plan, but he followed her lead, anyway.

Hell, *Val* didn't like the plan. She didn't regret being what she was. After forty years of being a vampire, the novelty had yet to wear off.

That didn't mean she thought a kid who only last spring had been deemed old enough to legally buy booze was old enough to be a vampire. Justin still had a human life to live, things that drinking blood and sleeping during the day sort of ruled out. Give him another ten years and she might not have argued.

But he didn't have another ten years. He might not even have ten hours before the spell in his head made him a full

Jackal. Sometimes, life snatched your good choices away and left you with a set of new, shitty ones.

She'd have to explain herself to Ivanov later—new vampires normally weren't made without wading through the bloodsucker equivalent of a sea of red tape first—but Val set that aside, too. This wasn't the time to fret over politics.

"This is going to hurt," she said. "I'm sorry." She said it for Justin, but she meant it for Chaz, too. He nodded, once, and there was no use stalling any longer.

Val drove her claws into her chest. Her ribs and breastbone splintered beneath the force of the blow, and for a moment she thought she'd black out from the pain. She breathed in once, twice. The oxygen was utterly useless to her but the act itself was calming. Then she squeezed and felt her claws pierce the sac around her heart. The muscle spasmed wildly as she impaled herself. She held on, flinging her other hand forward to clutch onto Chaz' shoulder so she could stay upright. Justin sat sandwiched between them, his amber eyes wide as saucers.

After a moment, her body seemed to figure out that she was being struck with neither pine, nor cedar, nor dogwood, and her heartbeat settled to its normal rhythm beneath her claws. Val felt blood pooling in her palm, gave it another count of three, and withdrew her hand. Her chest made a sucking sound as the claws came free.

She stood swaying a moment, holding Chaz' gaze as the gaping wound in her chest closed. Skin first, bones later. She could feel them shifting around inside. When she was steady, she looked to Chaz. "Ready?" He'd gone ashen, but his jaw was set, his knees locked. His grip on Justin's shoulders tightened.

She dipped down low, coming up from Justin's solar plexus rather than smashing straight through his sternum. He grunted as she reached up through his chest. He might have tried to scream, but her fist was inside him, her knuckles brushing his lungs. Her clawed fingers found his heart. It fluttered and jerked as she closed her hand around it.

Justin's eyes had rolled up in his head. *Good. Better not to be awake for this.*

Val squeezed, her claws puncturing atria and ventricles. Justin bucked beneath her, but Chaz held him as still as he could. Val leaned on Justin's legs with her free arm, keeping him from thrashing off the chair. He groaned, long and low, his heart pulsing rapidly in Val's grip.

As her heartsblood mingled with his, Justin's struggles subsided. He took one last, shuddering breath, his eyes fluttering open once more. Clear, focused, awake.

Then he died.

Val pulled her hand from his ruined chest and sat back. With one of her clean claws, she opened a vein at her bloodied wrist and brought it up to Justin's mouth. He lay there, slack against the chair, as she dribbled blood over his tongue. He didn't move. She rubbed her wrist over his lips like a mother encouraging her baby to nurse.

"Is he . . . ?" Chaz asked, in the hushed tone you heard at wakes.

"Give him a minute," Val said. *I did it right, didn't I? Didn't I?*

Just as doubt was getting a solid hold, Justin's eyelids fluttered, then Val felt the twin stabs of his fangs sliding into her skin. She winced as the flesh tore even further, but she didn't pull back. Chaz let his shoulders go, and Justin surged up, clutching her wrist to his mouth and swallowing every few seconds. At last he stopped, pushing her wrist away. He panted, glancing down at the fist-sized hole in his stomach.

It was closing, but slowly, new flesh spreading like ice crystals along a pond's surface.

"You're new," Val said. "It'll take some time." She held up her wrist: the wound had already closed. She was bloody from the base of her hand to the tips of her fingers, and from the middle of her forearm to her elbow, but the spot Justin had been drinking from was completely clean. "I guess you were thirsty," she said.

"So that's it?" Justin stopped staring at his knitting flesh and looked around the room. "I'm a vampire now? I don't feel very different." He paused, then poked at his stomach again. ". . . okay, I guess that should hurt a lot more."

"You still have some changing to do, but for all intents and purposes, yes." She caught his chin. His eyes were no longer dog-like, but the irises had gone back to yellow instead of brown. Val sniffed, sorting past the scent of her own blood and the Jackals' scent clogging the air from outside. He definitely smelled like a vampire now; there was a heaviness that hadn't been there before. But there was more—not the putrid meat smell of the Jackals that had clung to him when he'd arrived with Cavale and Elly earlier, but something dry and hot that made her think of wide-open grasslands beneath a relentless sun.

"What is it?"

"I don't know. But I think you're okay. Do you still feel like your face is too short?"

He touched his nose, his lips, his chin. "No."

Chaz grinned. "Better question. Do you still want to bite Elly?"

Justin twisted around to look at her. She ducked her head into the room and eyed him, the silver spike held loosely in her grip. "Um. No."

"Good." Val pushed herself up out of her crouch and gave Justin a hand up. "Lean on me and we'll go have a word with our friends out front."

29

B Y THE TIME they got to the front of the store, there were only a handful of Jackals left outside. Chaz took over acting as Justin's crutch so Val could make a stop at the register. Elly's short-term remedy was just about up. As they limped down the aisle together, the pain returned. He felt like his chest was on fire. Still, the hole in Justin's middle trumped a few cracked ribs. Chaz gritted his teeth and kept going.

"Thanks," said Justin. He still had the fangs out, so it made his speech come out a little funny. Chaz got the sense he didn't know how to retract them yet. "Hey." He crinkled his nose, in what Chaz had learned over the years was his thinky-face. "Are we cool?"

It was a question Chaz had figured he'd deal with later, but now it was right there, in the open: Val had made someone else a vampire, and not him. Katya's offer had repulsed him, but when Val was turning Justin—even the part where she'd reached into his fucking chest—he'd felt jealousy wrapping its fingers around his throat. *Why, though? Because I secretly want to be a vampire? Or because now I have to share her?*

He looked at Justin. The kid hadn't asked for all this shit to happen in the first place. *Not his fault. Not Val's, either.* "Yeah, man. We're cool."

And he realized it was true.

"Hey." Val shouted over the din of the fighting outside. She was waving around a piece of white cloth that Chaz recognized as the dust rag they kept under the register. "We're ready to talk."

It took a bit more shouting before the battle crawled to a stop. Cavale trotted over to stand with them, Elly trying to be subtle about it as she inspected his injuries. Even after Ivanov's crew and the Jackals all stood down, Katya and Bitch kept trading blows. Neither of them seemed to be trying to land a killing blow, really. From their grins, they were *enjoying* beating the shit out of one another.

Finally, Lia stepped over beside Val and stuck her fingers in her mouth. She let out a shrill whistle that would've done a gym teacher proud. The women stopped smacking each other around and looked toward the store.

"Valerie?" Katya looked pouty. "I hope we're not surrendering."

"Not exactly." Val gestured to Chaz and Justin. They picked their way forward to her, glass grinding beneath their feet. "Circumstances have changed. Bring her over here."

"Gladly." Katya reached out, snake-like, and collared Bitch. The Jackal woman cried out in surprise. Chaz snickered. *She didn't know Katya was playing with her this whole time.*

When they got close, Bitch began sniffing. She was all Jackal-ed out, so she tilted her pointed snout into the air and snuffled. At a nod from Val, Katya released her hold. Bitch circled them warily, sniff-sniff-sniffing the whole way around. At one point, she sneezed and her whole body shook, like a dog with a noseful of pepper. She kept at it for almost a minute. Chaz half expected her to shove her face in Justin's butt in doggy-greeting.

Instead she stepped back, horrified. She didn't protest

when Katya clamped a hand on her arm once more. "What did you do to him?"

Val smiled, letting her fangs show. "He's mine now. He was before, too, but even more so now."

"The spell. Does he still have it?"

"Let's find out." In addition to the dust rag, Val had grabbed a pad of paper and a pen from beside the register. "Justin? Want to try writing for us?"

Chaz took the paper so Justin didn't have to unlatch. He held it up and watched as words crawled across the page:

JUSTIN KENNEDY. NOW LEAVE US THE FUCK ALONE.

He held it up for all of them to see. Bitch groaned. Sunny and Lia clapped and cheered. Chaz might've been tempted to appreciate the jiggling bits if it weren't for their knives leaving ominous smoke trails.

"Call them off," said Val. "We're done here."

Bitch turned around and gave an order in the Jackals' speech. At Chaz' side, Justin frowned, but didn't comment.

The Jackals wavered a moment, uncertain whether they should obey. Bitch barked another command at them— literally—and one by one, they slunk away into the night.

The vampires stood their ground, waiting on Katya. "Go home," she said, sounding bored. "Tell Ivanov I'm on my way." Unlike the Jackals, the vampires dispersed as soon as she was finished giving the order. Katya stood there, holding on to Bitch. "If you don't mind, Valerie, I think I'll bring her home as a present for Ivanov. I'll say you chipped in."

"I don't care what you do with her. Far as I'm concerned, it's over."

"It's a bad idea," said Bitch.

Katya shook her hard enough to make her teeth rattle. "Shut up. No one asked you."

"I'm just saying. My alpha's going to be upset enough as it is that we don't have the boy. If I don't come home, either, he'll take it out on the undeserving." She looked at Chaz as she said it, unblinking even after a cuff on the head from Katya.

"Wait," said Chaz. He looked at her for signs of a bluff, but he had no idea how to spot a lying Jackal. "The kids?"

"Mm-hm. Among other . . . associates."

Marian. Or her husband. Probably both. "We have to let her go."

"We should kill her," said Elly. She gripped the spike like she might just go ahead and do it. Though, at a warning look from Katya of all people, she lowered it to her side once more.

Katya rolled her eyes. "Charles. Look at what she did to you. Your poor face. You can't mean it."

Bitch watched the exchange, looking smug. She might have been lying. She probably *was*, but he couldn't take that chance. Those kids weren't bad, they were desperate. And he'd promised Marian he'd help her. What sort of help was it if he got her husband punished, or worse, killed? "I do. There are people there. Humans. They weren't hostages like me, but they don't deserve to be hurt, either."

Katya looked to Val. "Valerie, are you allowing this?"

Val tilted her head, trying to puzzle him out. *We really need to work out some sort of secret code.* "Yeah," she said at last. "I am."

Katya's pout deepened. She gave Bitch a shove to get her moving. "Go. If I can still see you in ten seconds, I'm coming after you." She started counting.

The woman smirked. "You've gone soft, Leech," she said to Val. "Not that I'm complaining." Then she flipped them all off and took off up Main Street at an easy lope. She blended into the shadows before Katya got to six.

"Well," Katya sighed, then unwound a long strand of black hair from around her fingers. She passed it to Cavale. "I assume you can use this to track her."

He took it and held it up to the light. "It'll do."

"Good." Katya sketched a bow. "Then I think I'll get home. Ivanov will be in touch." She looked at them all, her eyes lingering for a bit on Chaz and Justin before she showed

Val a mouthful of fangs. "With all of you." Then she was gone, heading off in the direction Bitch had run.

Justin let out a sigh that was more of a wheeze. "Holy crap. I think I've been holding my breath all this time."

"You have." Chaz hadn't felt him breathe since Val had handed him off. "You're kind of done needing as much air as you used to. Well, outside of using it to talk."

"Huh. Neat."

Elly came bustling over. If she was upset about letting Bitch go, she was saving the argument for now. She reached up to touch Chaz' face, her fingers cool and steady. "My kit's in with Cavale's stuff," she said, "I can help with the—oh, hello." She took his left hand and turned it over. Her palm was still leaking a bit, so she dipped her pinky in it and spread a line of blood on Chaz' wrist. The rune Marian had drawn with oil earlier flared. "Someone was protecting you."

"Really? Because I still feel like I got hit by a truck."

"It could have been worse. When Twitch was hitting you, I was sure he was going to puncture a lung." She said it absently, concentrating more on the sigil than on him. Then she looked up, and it hit him.

He knew why Marian had looked familiar.

"Elly? Uh. Do you have family? In the Brotherhood?"

Her face closed up; the tentative smile she'd been trying on fled. "No." Cavale cleared his throat and she relented. "Okay, maybe. I never knew my parents, but they were in it. Why?"

She was still cradling his hand. He turned it over carefully, giving her fingers a gentle squeeze. "I met a woman today who looked enough like you to be your mom. She's one of the people the Jackals have a hold over."

Elly squirmed away. "That's her problem," she said after a moment. "She hasn't given a shit about me for twenty years. If it's even her. Why should I go running off to the rescue?" Her voice was flat.

Chaz looked to the others for help, but no one seemed interested in talking sense to her—Sunny and Lia had disappeared; Val spread her hands, at a loss; Cavale shook his head and mouthed, "Let it drop."

So he did, for the time being. He had plenty of other things to worry about. There'd been enough fighting for one night, and Elly looked like she wasn't sure she was done with the stabby-stabby just yet.

Justin looked around, self-consciously. "I want to learn how to Hunt," he blurted. He seemed to be getting some of his strength back, was no longer leaning on Chaz quite as heavily. When everyone turned to look at him, he flinched. "They killed the Clearwaters. I can't just let that go." He turned a shy smile on Elly. "I sort of hoped you'd be willing to teach me."

Elly stared at him, agape, then looked to Val and Cavale. They were about as helpful to her as they'd been to Chaz a moment ago.

"It's up to you two," said Val. "I'm done with Hunting. I meant that."

Cavale grinned. "All you, kid."

She stared out at the empty street, considering. Chaz got ready to haul Justin backward in case she decided the proper response to this was an attempted staking. At last, she turned back to Justin. "Fine. Now can I do my job?" She stalked off into the store, ducking down behind the register to retrieve her kit.

Justin unhooked his arm from around Chaz, testing his ability to stand on his own. He was a little wobbly, but otherwise fine. A thought struck him, and he leaned in, keeping his voice low. "Think she'd be my Renfield?"

Chaz clapped him on the shoulder. "Don't push it."

"Yeah. Okay."

Sunny came shuffling out from the back of the store. She'd donned a fluffy white bathrobe and her bunny slippers. Her face had reverted back to her everyday look. The curved knives were gone, too. In their place, she held push brooms and mops. "We've got a lot of cleaning up to do," she said, handing one of the brooms to Cavale.

The store lights flicked on, row by row. Lia must have found the breakers. The front half of the store was in utter chaos. Val groaned and held her hand out for one of the other brooms just as the first splashes of blue and red flashed across the storefront. Whatever had been holding Edgewood's finest away from Main Street had finally worn off.

Chaz headed over to Val, catching her before she could go and meet the officer climbing out of his car. "You're covered in blood," he said. "I'll handle this."

"You look like shit."

"Yeah, but I don't look like someone punched a hole in my chest."

She grimaced but had to concede the point. "Fine. I'll get Justin to come out back, too."

He caught her arm as she turned to go. "Hey. We need to talk."

She covered his hand with hers. "I know."

THEY GOT BACK to Val's house an hour before sunrise. Chaz had, through some combination of smooth talking and bull-shitting, managed to convince the officers that the damage had been done as part of a drunken drive-by, no idea who the culprits might be. He'd needed help from Sunny and Lia—a "tiny bit of a mind-whammy," as he'd put it to Val—to get the officer to overlook his battered face and the pile of Jackal corpses lining the sidewalk.

They'd swept up the glass and ash and washed away as much of the blood as they could for one night. Chaz would be meeting with the window people in the afternoon about replacing the plate glass.

Justin had crashed out almost as soon as Val got him settled in her bed. He still had changing to do, and tonight she'd have to teach him how to find blood, but for now, he needed sleep more than anything. Elly and Cavale had gone back to Crow's Neck, dropping Sunny and Lia off at home on their way.

Now Val sat in her living room, alone with Chaz. He'd found a bottle of scotch in her liquor cabinet and poured himself a double. The bottle was beside him in case he needed any more. His fingers tapped out a rhythm against the glass while he thought. Val couldn't read him, not completely. He smelled hurt more than anything, but his face gave none of it away. Finally, he sighed and set the glass down.

"You never told me about Sacramento," he said.

Val wished she had a glass of her own to fidget with, but all she had was leftover lamb's blood from Ivanov's visit. It wasn't quite the same as a real drink, even if she mixed some whiskey in. "It was another life."

"One that's coming back to you now, like it or not." He sat forward, on the edge of the armchair. Elly had wrapped him in an Ace bandage and drawn runes all over it. He was walking straighter, which was good to see, and when he breathed, nothing grated in his chest.

Val was curled up on the corner of the couch, feeling the unnerving sensation of her bones shifting as they finished knitting themselves back together. Every now and then, one of them gave an alarming crackle as it settled into place. "It's done. I meant that."

"Ivanov's not the type to let that go. He's got Elly working for him. He'll try to drag you in, too. But that's not the point right now."

"Then what *is* the point?"

"You never told me. That's all. I think I deserve to know."

"You're right. You do." *No more hedging.* She straightened up. "I was a Hunter. There was a huge nest that we were called in to take out and it went badly. I lost my whole team. We killed the Jackals, but I'm the only one who made it out." She closed her eyes, hearing Delilah's screams echoing through the dark. "I decided it wasn't worth it anymore."

"Who was on your team?"

"Another vampire. Her name was Clara. Four members of the Brotherhood. Kelly and Delilah were both sisters and Sisters." He nodded, hearing the capital when she said it. "Two fighters, more like what Cavale does."

"What were their names?"

"Charlotte and Angelo." It was hard to say his name. She couldn't remember the last time she'd spoken it aloud.

Chaz sat back, reaching for the scotch. "There it is."

"What?"

"The last one. Angelo. He meant something to you, didn't he?" There was no accusation in his tone, simply resignation, like he'd received long-anticipated bad news.

"They all meant something to me. They were my family."

"But him most of all. Was he your Renfield?"

Oh. Val smiled. "Don't you dare," she said, but her voice was soft. "Come here." She patted the cushion beside her. At first, she didn't think Chaz was going to come sit with her, but at last he relinquished the armchair. Val scooted closer to him and laid her head on his shoulder. He put his arm around her and leaned back. They sat like that for a few minutes, not speaking. Val sought out his free hand and laced her fingers through his. "He was my Renfield, yes. And I miss him. I didn't want to take another after he died. I didn't think I ever would." She sighed with the memory of his loss. "It hurt so goddamned much, you know?"

Chaz didn't answer, but she felt him nodding. He rubbed her shoulder, too, comforting her when he was the one who actually needed to be comforted.

She lifted her head up and kissed his cheek. His skin got warm beneath her lips as he blushed. "But I'm glad I did. I found you, and you've been amazing, right from the start. When they took you, I was afraid it was all happening again. I spent the last day and a half scared shitless."

"Yeah, me, too."

"I'm sorry. I shouldn't have taken my eyes off you for a second."

"You shouldn't have to worry about that," he said. His grip on her hand tightened. "This . . . Angelo. He obviously could have held his own with them. I couldn't. I can, what, pour blood into a tea set and do your taxes. That's one fuck of a downgrade."

"Chaz." Val sat up and turned his chin so he was looking her in the eye. "I don't compare you to him, so don't you do it, either. You're who I need. That's my call. Okay?"

He blinked, surprised. The hurt smell went away, even though some of the sadness remained. "Okay."

"Really okay?"

"Swear to God." He let go of her hand and crossed his heart. His crooked grin was back, too.

She could do more convincing later, if need be, when the sun's weight wasn't bearing down on her eyelids. "I have to get up to bed," she said, pulling Chaz in for one last hug. She was careful not to hurt his ribs. "You take it slow today, okay?"

"I will."

Val walked him to the door, waiting while he got in the Mustang and pulled out of the driveway. She didn't go back inside until he turned the corner and the roar of the engine faded away.

ELLY KICKED OFF her boots and collapsed onto the bed in Cavale's guest room. She was tired and sore, but all in all, the night had been a success. She'd wanted to start the search for Bitch and the rest of her nest right away, but Cavale had convinced her they both needed a few hours to sleep and recharge. He had the lock of hair Katya had given him. They'd be able to find her with that when they were ready.

She listened to the sounds of Cavale checking the locks downstairs: back door, front door, windows, cellar. The stairs creaked as he ascended them, and she could follow his progress down the hallway. He paused outside her door and knocked softly.

"I'm awake."

He came in and sat on the bed beside her. "Good job tonight."

"You, too." She reached up and touched his cheek, where she'd applied butterfly stitches to a couple of nasty scratches from the Creeps' claws. "How are those holding up?"

"They itch a little, but they're fine." He smiled. "I had a good doctor."

Elly rolled her eyes, but she was grinning, pleased at the praise. "We're going to have to hit the drugstore later. I used up most of the supplies on Chaz."

"I'll get a shopping list started."

"Like hell you will. I'll do it." Suddenly shy, she pushed up to her elbows so she could look out the window. "I mean, if you want me to."

"Hey." Cavale took her hand and waited until she was looking at him again. "My house is your house, Elly." He squeezed her fingers. "I figure, if you're going to be teaching Justin, you might as well stay close by. If Ivanov needs you in Boston, you can take my car. Unless you'd rather live in the city. It might be easier to find your mother that way, if you change your mind about it. Better resources. It's your call." Now it was his turn to look shy. "But I'd like it if you stayed."

She paused, looking away as she tried to find the words. "I know you all want me to find this woman. I just . . . don't care. If we find the nest and the alpha, and that frees her, great. But she's not my family."

She looked Cavale in the eye. It was easier this time. "You are."

EPILOGUE

One month later

Justin poked his head into the back room. "Val? Chaz? I think you guys had better come see this."

Chaz took his feet off the supervisor's desk, where he'd been working out the next week's schedule. With both Justin *and* Val restricted to postsunset hours, he'd had to do some finagling with the rest of the crew. It was a huge pain in the ass, but at least now that fall was in full swing and the days were getting shorter, both of them were available earlier in the evening. "What's up?"

Val surfaced from further in the back, where she'd been unpacking a shipment. Justin shifted from foot to foot. He'd gained some confidence along with his vampirism, and Elly's Hunting lessons had helped him shed some of the shyness, but learning the ropes also meant relearning his limits, and it made him self-conscious. There were times Val had to remind him that normal people *couldn't* lift six boxes of books at once, or while it was nice to get the shelving done quickly, he really needed to keep the speed down to human level.

"It's, uh. I think you just need to come see."

"Oh God, did you dent my car?" He'd sent Justin out to pick up some books from an elderly couple on the other side of town who wanted to sell their collection. Val was planning to look them over tonight and see what she wanted to buy.

"No! No, but, um. Just come see?"

Val sighed and followed him. Chaz scrambled along after them, tallying up the things he'd do to Justin if there were so much as a scratch on the Mustang.

But when they got to the car, everything seemed fine. "In the trunk," said Justin. He put the key in the lock and opened it up.

Chaz peered inside. "Oh. Huh. Couldn't fit their stuff, huh?" The trunk was filled with swag from the last few trade shows he'd attended: book bags with publisher logos, tee shirts with the covers of new books or catchy slogans for popular series, buttons and key chains and posters galore, and, most importantly, tons and tons of books. He probably had three years' worth of advance reading copies sitting in there. "You could've put the boxes in the backseat."

Justin looked at him like he'd lost his mind. "You don't see it?"

Chaz took another gander, squinting around in case there was some big ugly bug clinging to one of the books. "Uh. No? What am I missing? Val?"

Val was staring into the trunk, too, her brow furrowed in consternation. She glanced at him. "Oh. Wait. Here." She extended her fangs and pricked the pad of her thumb with one. She smeared a drop of blood over each of Chaz' eyes. "Now look."

He turned back to the trunk and jumped about a mile. "GAH! What . . . what the fuck . . . No. *Who* the fuck is that?"

There was a dead man curled up atop the swag. At least, he *looked* dead, his skin all grey and saggy. A bit of bone shone through on his forehead. He looked up from a promo copy of the newest James Patterson thriller and grinned at them with yellowed teeth. "Hiya."

"Justin?" said Val, offering the dead man a weak-fingered wave.

"Yeah?"

"I think you'd better go call Cavale and Elly and get them to come by. I don't have the slightest idea what to do with a wraith."

"A wraith that's living in my trunk," Chaz corrected.

As if that clarified anything.